# HUGO'S GRAVEYARD

by

Edward Lewis

# CONTENTS

# WHO IS HUGO MARCUS SELENSKI?

No one cared when Hugo Marcus Selenski robbed a bank on June 10, 1994. News of the robbery and subsequent prosecution by the United States Attorney's Office for the Middle District of Pennsylvania got little attention by the local media. All that changed in June 2003, when the bodies of two missing people and the charred remains of three others were discovered at a Kingston Township, Pennsylvania, home Hugo shared with his then girlfriend, Christina Strom.

Hugo became a household name overnight. Whenever someone mentioned "Hugo," it referred to Selenski. He gave reporters one-on-one jailhouse interviews or communicated with them by mail, and was known to give a quick comment or two as he smirked for television cameras and photographers on his way to and out of court proceedings inside the historic Luzerne County Courthouse. Women were attracted to his bad-boy and charming image as Hugo claimed to have received marriage proposals and women's underwear in the mail. A few female employees at the courthouse had his picture posted in their cubicles.

Spend some time with Hugo and one can detect his controlling influence of winning people over with his charm. Luzerne County's chief prosecutor in 2009, District Attorney Jacqueline Musto Carroll, described Hugo as a serial killer. Confident and bold, Hugo graduated high school second to last in his class and yet, has the legal mind to follow every move of his complex criminal cases. When his lawyer argued for a jury from another county to decide his fate on double homicide charges, Hugo Marcus Selenski boldly stood up in court and loudly demanded a jury from Luzerne County. Hugo got his wish and won – if only for a few minutes.

Hugo is naive. A few months before a judge scheduled his second trial on double homicide charges, Hugo demanded to go it alone, to represent himself by ousting his three court appointed attorneys claiming they were filing petitions and motions without his knowledge. He won as a judge permitted him to represent himself placing one of the three attorneys on stand-by.

Hugo Marcus Selenski was born in Sioux City, Iowa, to Ruth Ann and Robert M. Friend Jr. on August 1, 1973. The couple had two daughters before Ruth divorced Robert five years later, and married Ronald Selenski, a federal bank examiner who adopted Ruth's three children. The large family resided in a modest, ranch style home on Westminister Road in Dallas Township, an area called the Back Mountain of Luzerne County in Northeastern Pennsylvania, about 125 miles north of Philadelphia.

Hugo attended elementary school at Gate of Heaven, a parochial school under the Scranton Catholic Diocese. As a boy, he played mini-football and Little League baseball. He attended junior and senior high school in the Dallas School District where he played quarterback in junior high before being thrown off the team in 10th grade for missing too many practices. Hugo graduated Dallas High School in 1991 with a 1.5 grade point average, earning a placement of 152 out of 153 graduating students that year. His classmates voted Hugo as the senior "most likely in detention," the 1991 Dallas school yearbook says. Prior to graduation, Hugo's troubled life had already begun with a series of multiple arrests for vehicle thefts, drunken driving and driving with a suspended license. He had already fathered a girl by the time he graduated and fathered a second daughter in January 1994. He also had a third child born out-of-wedlock.

While still in high school, Hugo signed up for the delayed entry program with the U.S. Marine Corps. He was discharged in August 1991 when he failed to attend boot camp due to injuries he suffered in a motorcycle crash. He re-enlisted in the Marine Corps in October 1991 and was sent to Parris Island, South Carolina, for basic training. Military authorities discovered he owed more than $3,000 to Luzerne County Juvenile Court for restitution regarding his prior criminal convictions and was promptly discharged for fraudulent enlistment after 12 weeks of boot camp.

At age 19 in February 1993, Hugo was charged with drunken driving and underage drinking. Three months later in May 1993, he was charged with a second drunken driving offense and underage drinking. By this time in his life, Hugo had become addicted to alcohol, marijuana and cocaine. He spent some time in rehabilitation but failed to complete the program.

Then on June 10, 1994, Hugo, 20-years-old at this time, and his roommate Earl Nagle, 32, devised a scheme to rob a branch of Mellon Bank on North River Street in Plains Township, Pennsylvania, not far from Wilkes-Barre.

Federal court records say Hugo and Nagle stole a Chevrolet Citation from a pharmacy in Kingston and drove to the bank in which they entered wearing ski masks and armed with a 9mm semi-automatic handgun. Once inside, Hugo "racked the action," a move necessary to chamber a live round of ammunition before firing. Nagle approached a window threatening a teller as the two men fled the bank with approximately $4,100 in a duffel bag. As they sped away in the stolen car – Hugo was driving – a dye pack exploded in the bag staining bundles of cash. Nagle held the duffel bag out the passenger side car window to escape the alarming smoke. The two men abandoned the stolen car on West Carey Street in Plains Township where they had left Hugo's Toyota pick-up truck.

Agents with the Federal Bureau of Investigation received an anonymous tip that the two men who robbed the Mellon Bank were Hugo and Nagle. They shared an apartment on East Fourth Street in Wyoming Borough, not far from the bank, the tipster said. Armed with search warrants, federal agents searched the apartment and Hugo's parents' house on Westminister Road in Dallas Township where they found dye residue in the washing machine agitator, indicating Hugo tried to "launder " the stained cash. After the robbery, Hugo burned some of the ink-stained money and his clothes in the backyard of the Westminister Road home. He briefly left the area buying an airline ticket to Las Vegas, Nevada, to see his biological father and also discarded the 9mm handgun in the Colorado River. Hugo surrendered to federal authorities in Scranton when he returned to Pennsylvania on June 28, 1994. Nagle was captured in Wilkes-Barre, the same day Hugo returned from Las Vegas.

Hugo and Nagle pleaded guilty to federal charges of bank robbery and firearms used during a violent crime in September 1994. For his cooperation in the investigation, Hugo avoided a lengthy prison sentence being sent away for seven years and Nagle was sentenced to a little less than six years. Hugo was released from the Lewisburg federal prison on Jan. 19, 2001. Nagle died from natural causes on June 22, 1999.

A few months into his freedom, Hugo began dating Christina Strom, whom he met when he was a teen, in September 2001. Shortly after their relationship began, Hugo moved in with Strom at her grandmother's house on Miller Street in the tiny borough of Luzerne. Strom would later have mixed emotions when she allowed Hugo's jailhouse pal, Paul Raymond Weakley, to stay at the house.

Strom described her relationship with Hugo as being "great" and "wonderful" when it was only the two of them. After Weakley moved in, Strom grew to dislike Weakley because she felt Hugo was spending more time with his jailhouse best friend. "Once Paul moved in, they were always together. We didn't seem to be together as much as we were before. Our relationship started going downhill, it seemed after Paul got out. It seemed all Hugo wanted to do was be with Paul," Strom testified at a court proceeding in June 2006.

In happier times, Strom helped Weakley find an apartment on Pulaski Street in Kingston. "I was friendly with him. I helped him pick out a car when he first got out (federal prison). Chose his first apartment with him. I was just trying to help him get on with his life," Strom testified.

If Strom hoped to resume her life with Hugo now that Weakley was out of the Miller Street home, she was mistaken. Hugo continued to be with Weakley and soon, the two men would be hanging around with Patrick Raymond Russin, Hugo's childhood friend.

Strom disliked Russin. After she purchased a home on Mount Olivet Road in Kingston Township, Russin moved in. "I only let (Russin) stay because he had nowhere to go. (Russin) was living out of a garbage bag and Hugo asked me if he could stay there with us because he didn't have anywhere to go. We had a falling out years before in the early, in the early

1990s," Strom said in her testimony. "(Russin) owed me money. And I just didn't want him anywhere around me."

# PAUL WEAKLEY OPENS CASE

Luzerne County Detective Lieutenant R. Gary Capitano was investigating a robbery at a home in Kingston Township on March 25, 2003, when Ellen M. Smaka was confronted by two men. Capitano immediately set his sights on Weakley, a convicted criminal who served a decade in federal prison on charges of manufacturing explosive devices in Battle Creek, Michigan, in 1992. Weakley served his time behind bars at the United States Penitentiary in Lewisburg, Pennsylvania, about a 90 minute drive from Luzerne County. With no place to go when released from captivity on March 14, 2002, he reunited with Hugo, his jailhouse pal, first staying at the Miller Street house with Strom until he found an apartment on Pulaski Street in Kingston.

During Capitano's investigation of the Smaka robbery, he questioned Weakley on June 3, 2003. Weakley implicated Hugo and Russin in the robbery, saying they came to his Kingston apartment with Smaka's high school diploma. Weakley had more information he shared with Capitano – much more information.

What Weakley explained ended a 13 month mystery and began a complex investigation into multiple murders, missing persons, burning bodies, robberies, burglaries, drug trafficking and money laundering. It involved an aggressive media hungry for information only to be heightened by a daring nighttime prison escape that led to a three day manhunt ending with a conditional surrender and political repercussions in the aftermath. The case as it unfolded included tense and turbulent court proceedings pitting the district attorney against a very demanding judge, a former district attorney himself.

The investigation would be like no other in the history of Luzerne County, the largest populated county in Northeastern Pennsylvania with more than 313,000 residents. Federal authorities, which assisted local and state law enforcement agencies with a number of grand jury indictments and search warrants, identified Hugo and his friends as "The Enterprise." The investigation stretched into neighboring Monroe County where a jewelry store owner was held hostage at gunpoint in his own home while a plan to ransack his business quickly imploded.

Prosecutors decided to take different approaches through the legal system with Hugo and his friends. Charges were strategically filed and plea deals were made as sentencing hearings were delayed for years to guarantee the cooperation from those willing to testify against Hugo.

Weakley's so-called confession to Capitano came at a time when he faced burglary charges filed by Pennsylvania State Police Trooper Gerald Sachney. Weakley was accused of stealing water filters, computers, computer accessories and customers' information from his employer, Hi-Tech Water Group, a residential water purification business. Weakley was hired by Hi-Tech in April 2002, and stole the items two months later in June. He was arrested on Oct. 1, 2002, on charges of burglary, theft, receiving stolen property and deceptive business practices. Sachney would file additional counts of receiving stolen property when he was caught with more than $4,000 of Hi-Tech equipment in April 2003.

Weakley was in a bad situation. He was serving three years of federal supervised release, or probation, for his bomb making in Michigan when he was arrested by Sachney for burglarizing Hi-Tech. His probation was transferred to Pennsylvania from Michigan in January 2003. A federal judge during a February 2003 court hearing ordered Weakley to home confinement with electronic monitoring for six months. That meant he had to wear an electronic bracelet locked around his ankle that alerted authorities to his location 24 hours a day. He was only permitted to leave his apartment for work, religious services and medical appointments. Weakley wanted to cut a deal to avoid more prison time, telling Capitano that missing pharmacist Michael Jason Kerkowski and Kerkowski's girlfriend, Tammy Lynn Fassett, were dead, and he knew where the bodies were buried.

Weakley's burglary case would have to wait. He signed a court document on June 3, 2003, waiving his right to a speedy trial.

Capitano certainly wanted to hear more and, along with Sachney, they interviewed Weakley more in depth on June 4, 2003. The convicted felon reiterated his theory that Hugo and Russin killed Kerkowski and Fassett, and he only "assisted" Hugo in reburying the bodies. Weakley claimed Kerkowski and Fassett were killed at Kerkowski's home in Hunlock Township in early May 2002, and initially buried in a wooded area behind the Dallas high school football stadium in Dallas Township.

It made sense to the two seasoned investigators. Hugo graduated from Dallas High School in 1991 and he knew the area having grown up nearby on Westminister Road. Investigators would learn Kerkowski and Fassett were killed on May 3, 2002.

Weakley attempted to earn credibility by describing Hugo as a monster, telling Capitano and Sachney he was talking to them because "Selenski was out of control and needed to be stopped." After the interview, just before 5:30 p.m. on June 4, 2003, Weakley was escorted by investigators in an unmarked state police 2001 Chevrolet cargo van. They drove past 479 Mount Olivet Road in Kingston Township where Hugo lived with Strom several times with Weakley pointing out that the bodies were buried near a concrete pad, which was the well that provided water to the home and a trailer on the property. They arrived on Fairground Road, a dirt road behind the football stadium at about 5:53 p.m. Weakley led investigators in the woods looking for the initial burial hole, but more than a year later and not originally from the area – having been released from federal prison less than two months before Kerkowski and Fassett were killed – Weakley was unable to find the first gravesite.

As it turned out, there was no burial site near the football field, and Russin had nothing to do with the murders of Kerkowski and Fassett. Weakley wanted to insulate himself from his role in the murders by blaming Russin as investigators would later learn Russin had a solid alibi on May 3, 2002.

Weakley violated his federal probation by testing positive for marijuana on May 20, May 22 and June 3, 2003. Faced with the Hi-Tech burglary charges and revocation of his federal probation, the criminal justice system was about to give up rehabilitating Weakley. He decided to tell all, in his own version, to Capitano and Sachney on June 3 and June 4. His information was hard to digest and, at first, Capitano and Sachney were speculative, sometimes mystified. The two investigators had their work cut out for them. They took a chance and believed what Weakley, a convicted criminal, had told them.

Capitano and Sachney surely have seen many homicides and heard crazy stories in their careers but this one, as explained by Weakley, would take them down a path they have never encountered before. Weakley was a double edge sword and a known liar on top of a convicted felon. His lies would be exposed and come back to haunt him by skilled defense lawyers.

# SEARCH OF MOUNT OLIVET

At the time of Michael Jason Kerkowski's disappearance in May 2002, many believed, including Wyoming County District Attorney George Skumanick, he fled to avoid sentencing on convictions he sold prescription medications illegally.

Kerkowski, 37-years-old when he was killed, owned and operated The Medicine Shoppe pharmacy in a tiny strip mall on state Route 29 in Eaton Township, Wyoming County. Kerkowski's life began to unravel in 2000 when he was suspected of selling controlled substances without prescriptions and committing insurance fraud from his pharmacy. His wife, Kimberly, filed for divorce on April 30, 2001, around the time when Kerkowski began dating Tammy Lynn Fassett.

Kerkowski was arrested four times between April 2001 and January 2002 on various charges, including involuntary manslaughter as investigators alleged his illegal dispensing of prescription medications caused the overdose death of Joseph James Mekuta on Oct. 10, 2000, court records say.

Mekuta was 38-years-old and suffered reflex sympathetic dystrophy, a chronic and painful condition that usually affects arms, legs and the immune system. Mekuta was being treated by three physicians and had all his prescriptions filled at Kerkowski's pharmacy. When Mekuta died, authorities wrote in arrest records they recovered approximately 50 different prescribed medications containing thousands of pills from his bedroom. An autopsy by forensic pathologist Dr. Gary Ross determined Mekuta died from amitriptyline poisoning. Amitriptyline is in a group of drugs called tricyclic antidepressants used to treat symptoms of depression, and is sometimes used to treat chronic pain, eating disorders and certain skin problems.

Kerkowski was put on trial and convicted by a Wyoming County jury on Feb. 28, 2002, of three counts of delivery or dispensing a controlled substance by a practitioner in bad faith. Two months after the verdict and before another jury was about to be seated for a second trial in connection to Mekuta's death, Kerkowski opted to plead guilty on April 25, 2002, to recklessly endangering another person as prosecutors in Wyoming County withdrew the involuntary manslaughter charge under a negotiated plea deal. When Kerkowski pleaded guilty, Hugo was the lone spectator in the courtroom, seated behind Kerkowski. Hugo's presence in the Wyoming County courtroom would be revisited during his second trial at the Luzerne County Courthouse 13 years later.

Kerkowski could have faced more than 40 years in state prison. His sentencing hearing was scheduled on May 14, 2002, at the Wyoming County Courthouse. He failed to appear and many, including Skumanick, believed he fled to avoid being sent to prison. The families of Kerkowski

and Fassett thought otherwise, separately filing missing persons reports with the Pennsylvania State Police in the first week of May 2002.

Despite the missing persons investigations, Pennsylvania Crime Stoppers featured Kerkowski as the Fugitive of the Week for June 10, 2002.

As it turned out, Weakley became the key to ending the mystery of what happened to Kerkowski and Fassett.

After Capitano and Sachney interviewed Weakley on June 4, 2003, it was time to draft a search warrant for the Mount Olivet Road property. After spending the night going over their notes, they wrote the warrant that totaled nine pages, with Sachney signing first followed by Capitano. Early in the morning on June 5, nearly a dozen state troopers, several Luzerne County detectives and Kingston Township police officers gathered at the Pennsylvania State Police barracks in Wyoming Borough to review what was about to take place. Three troopers would conduct foot surveillance in the rear of the 6.1 acre property while another trooper repeatedly drove past the property in an unmarked vehicle.

Shortly before 11 a.m., authorities met at Francis Slocum State Park, less than a half-mile away from the target, while Capitano and Sachney presented the search warrant and affidavit to Luzerne County Judge Patrick J. Toole Jr. in Wilkes-Barre. Authorities waiting nearby would execute the search warrant once they received confirmation that Toole had signed it.

All that changed when Hugo's dogs – a Rottweiler, a Pit Bull and a German Shepherd – began barking at the three troopers near the rear of the property. The command to converge onto the property was made by Pennsylvania State Police Lieutenant Richard Krawatz as a parade of marked and unmarked police cruisers drove up the gravel driveway. Hugo was outside setting up a tent in the large open yard.

"Subsequent to my arrival at the Selenski/Strom residence, I had informed Selenski of the purpose for the Pennsylvania State Police presence on the property, that begin, the search of the property for human remains following the approval of the search warrant, which was in the process of being approved," Krawetz's homicide investigation action report says. "When I informed Selenski of this, he related that Pennsylvania State Police did not need a search warrant, he would, and did give his permission for Pennsylvania State Police to search, as we would not find anything. Selenski went further to state that he would even help Pennsylvania State Police dig, as once again he reiterated that we would not find anything. I informed Selenski that although he gave Pennsylvania State Police permission to search, (we) would wait for the search warrant to be signed before (we) began searching. Additionally, I informed Selenski that it would not be necessary for him to assist (us) in searching for human remains, as (we) would handle that task. It should also be noted that during the time period that (state police) was waiting for word that the search warrant had been approved and signed, Selenski exhibited nervousness."

"When approval was granted, and I had been notified via telephone, the search of the area in question commenced," Krawetz continued in his report. "At this time, Selenski became fixated on the area in question, constantly observing the digging process. When Hugo's copy of the search warrant application was subsequently provided to him, he commented that the contents of the search application was ridiculous."

Hugo may not have known it then, but it was the last day he was a free man – minus three days when he escaped from jail in October 2003.

Krawetz and the army of troopers were on the property for about five minutes before Judge Toole authorized the search warrant. A cadaver dog named Jake, trained in detecting human decomposition, the only state police dog to do such a task at the time, was released from a police cruiser and quickly began sniffing the property. At 12:15 p.m., Jake settled on the area behind the concrete pad for the home's water well. The chemistry of the soil was different in this area, and showed evidence it was disturbed at some time.

While authorities expanded and intensified their search of the property, Hugo was asked to accompany Corporal Gary Vogue to the Wyoming barracks for questioning. He was not in custody, Krawetz said, but authorities wanted to know more about him. Hugo sat in the rear seat of an unmarked cruiser as he was driven to the state police barracks, less than a 10 minute ride from the Mount Olivet Road home. He arrived at about 1 p.m. and was kept in a room normally used for patrol troopers to complete daily reports. Meanwhile, authorities carefully began removing soil where Jake, the cadaver dog, had a hit. Shortly before 2 p.m., confirmation was made that a body had been found.

Hugo met Sachney at the barracks but he refused to answer any questions without a lawyer, despite not being in custody. He was free to leave at any time as authorities could not legally hold him. Trooper Vogue was instructed to give Hugo a ride back to his house. While en route, Vogue received word via radio to return Hugo to the barracks. Driving around a rear garage behind the barracks, Hugo noticed Weakley walking in a rear door. "He said, 'What's my buddy Paul doing here?'" Vogue said.

Hugo was removed from the cruiser and arrested on charges he fired a shot from a .32-caliber handgun during a robbery of Kerkowski's father, Michael Stanley Kerkowski, in October 2002. Hugo's defense lawyer, Demetrius Fannick, would argue a year later that Hugo was not read his constitutional Miranda warnings when taken into custody on June 5, 2003. That important fact led to a judge's dismissal of an alleged incriminating statement about the bodies, and initiated what would be the first of many lengthy appeals in state appellate courts delaying future court proceedings for years to come.

Troopers John Yencha and William Spagnola took turns watching Hugo, who by this time, was handcuffed and chained to an eye bolt fastened into the floor. Yencha was unaware of the search at the Mount Olivet Road property, having been called in early to start his shift. Hugo initiated a conversation with Yencha, talking about his federal incarceration and asking how long he was going to be there. "He kept asking, 'What's going on?' He asked where Trooper Sachney was, he kept asking me," Yencha testified at a court proceeding. "Finally I said, 'You know more than me, you tell me what's going on?'" Hugo tossed the cover sheet of the search warrant at Yencha. "I said, 'It looks pretty serious, are they going to find any bodies?' He said, 'Yeah, five of them.' I thought he was being sarcastic."

It was that statement by Hugo, "Yeah, five of them" that prosecutors were forbidden from using against Hugo. Fannick, his lawyer, had successfully argued before Luzerne County Judge Peter Paul Olszewski Jr. at a suppression court hearing that Hugo was not read his Miranda warnings when he was arrested for the alleged robbery of Kerkowski's father.

Spagnola relieved Yencha, and again, Hugo initiated conversations with him, talking about who he had seen while in federal prison. He also indicated he would be able to free himself from the handcuffs and chain. While Hugo was being watched by Yencha and Spagnola, Sachney and Capitano were meeting with Hugo's girlfriend, Christina Storm, who had arrived at the barracks before Vogue was ordered to return Hugo to the barracks. When Sachney and Capitano finally did meet with Hugo, they told him a body had been found. Hugo smirked and said it was a joke. Authorities digging in the hole near the concrete pad stopped what they were doing when they came upon the body later identified as Tammy Lynn Fassett. Her hands were bound behind her back by plastic flex ties. As the digging slowly resumed, investigators noticed plastic flex ties wrapped around her ankles and neck. When her body was removed, investigators uncovered the body of Michael Jason Kerkowski. Plastic flex ties were found around Kerkowski's neck and hands that were bound behind his back. Duct tape was around his wrists and across his eyes and mouth.

A team of specialists consisting of a forensic archeologist and an anthropologist removed the bodies from the hole on June 6, 2003. Fassett and Kerkowski were buried about three feet below the surface mixed with coal and soil purchased at a local store. The bodies were transported in separate vehicles by Luzerne County deputy coroners Tom Moran and Dan Hughes to Wilkes-Barre General Hospital in Wilkes-Barre for autopsies.

The autopsies were performed on Sunday, June 8 by forensic pathologists Luzerne County Coroner Dr. George E. Hudock, now deceased, and Dr. Michael Baden, a former chief medical examiner for the New York State Police. Results of the autopsies revealed Fassett and Kerkowski died from strangulation. Forensic odontologist Dr. Lowell Levin assisted in the identification of the bodies through dental records.

Back on June 5, when state police troopers converged onto the property on Mount Olivet Road, reporters and photographers began gathering across the street, about 100 yards from where the digging was taking place. Trooper Martin Connors walked down the gravel driveway and confirmed two bodies had been found and Luzerne County District Attorney David W. Lupas would be making a statement. Television reporters were busy preparing for their 5 p.m. newscasts and had trouble getting a live signal due to the hilly terrain. At about the same time, Trooper Leo Hannon and another trooper were leaving the barracks to transport Hugo to Magisterial District Judge James E. Tupper on Carverton Road in Kingston Township to be arraigned on charges he robbed and fired a gun at Kerkowski's father, Michael Stanley Kerkowski, in October 2002.

Nobody from the media knew Hugo or what had happened on the property earlier in the day. As reporters huddled on the side of Mount Olivet Road staring at the activity of investigators and prosecutors, a reporter received a tip, "The guy who lives there" would be at Tupper's office in a few minutes.

"The guy who lives there" was handcuffed and sitting in the district courtroom with a trooper while Hannon was inside a private office with Tupper reviewing the charging documents. "The guy who lives there" appeared upbeat despite being in custody. He turned around and asked the only reporter in the courtroom, "Is this going to be in the paper tomorrow?" Without waiting for an answer, he asked the reporter, "Have you been up on the hill? I don't know why they're there?"

Tupper walked out of his office wearing a long black robe sitting down behind the bench fixed atop a stage. Tupper looked down at "the man who lives there" reading the charges of robbery, aggravated assault, terroristic threats and recklessly endangering another person. Tupper set bail at $300,000 straight. Unable to post bail, "the man who lives there" was jailed at the Luzerne County Correctional Facility.

The criminal complaint and affidavit introduced Hugo Marcus Selenski to the media. Once his name was learned, his lifestyle became open season in the coming months and years. Hugo was charged for the alleged robbery of Michael Stanley Kerkowski, who claimed Selenski fired a shot above his head in the basement of his home on Vine Street in Lehman Township.

The charging documents told a story that Kerkowski, the pharmacist, had introduced Hugo to his father, describing Hugo as his "best friend" who helped him through his legal troubles in Wyoming County. Kerkowski told his father he trusted Hugo more than his lawyers. The information in the affidavit of probable cause quickly answered why Skumanick, the Wyoming County District Attorney, was at the Mount Olivet Road property earlier in the day on June 5, 2003.

After Hugo was jailed, Lupas and other investigators walked down the gravel driveway to speak with reporters just before 6 p.m.

"We do have confirmation that there are located on this property the human remains of two individuals. Because of the sensitive nature of the investigation, we cannot release many more details other than that, other than to tell you that this is a very intensive and ongoing investigation and ongoing as we speak right now," Lupas exclaimed without identifying Hugo or mentioning his arrest until he was asked about it by a reporter. "The affidavit speaks for itself," Lupas promptly replied.

A reporter asked Hudock, the Luzerne County Coroner, a question that made Lupas cringe. Hudock responded by saying he believed the bodies were in the ground in excess of six months, saying, "The characteristics of the ground helps preserve bodies so it's very difficult without an anthropologist to give us a specific answer." While Hudock was speaking, Lupas leaned and whispered in the ear of Luzerne County Assistant

District Attorney Joseph Giovannini who, in turn, walked behind the group and pulled Hudock by the arm removing him from the posse of reporters and photographers. Lupas feared Hudock was saying too much to the media.

"We're involved with an intensive, sensitive investigation," Lupas said, adding "With the integrity of the investigation, we can't answer your questions right now."

# MEDIA CIRCUS

The investigation at the Mount Olivet Road property did not stop when the bodies of Tammy Lynn Fassett and Michael Jason Kerkowski were removed from the hole. Capitano, Sachney and other investigators were talking to Patrick Raymond Russin. Weakley had implicated Hugo and Russin for the homicides of Fassett and Kerkowski as Weakley claimed he only assisted Hugo in moving the bodies from near the Dallas football field because Hugo did not trust Russin. That is the story, one of many false stories, Weakley told.

Although circumstantial, cell phone records obtained by search warrants indicated Hugo and Weakley were calling one another multiple times the day Fassett and Kerkowski were killed. Russin certainly was not in the clear. He was eventually charged with two other homicides and, along with Weakley and others, accused in a residential burglary where a number of firearms were stolen from a Dallas Township house in January 2003 and a burglary at a clothing store in Plymouth on May 24, 2003.

On Friday, June 6, 2003, authorities obtained a second and third search warrant for the Mount Olivet Road property and Strom's 1999 Honda Accord that Hugo primarily drove. The warrants were signed by the same judge, Toole, and as he did for the first and all others that followed, the affidavits of probable cause that accompanied the warrants were sealed, preventing the public and media from reading them.

The second and third warrant expanded the search to collect any forensic and trace evidence to the homicides of Fassett and Kerkowski. They also included evidence to the homicides of two black males with street names "Rudy" and "Redman," any firearms, telephonic equipment and written documents. A piece of paper with a telephone number and the words "Rudeey and Redman" was found inside a kitchen drawer inside the house on June 5.

Authorities continued to search the property in concentrated groups. One group carefully searched along a line of trees while another group continued to focus in the area where the bodies were unearthed. Jake, the state police cadaver dog, sniffed the property for a second day, and a back-hoe removed soil and debris near an in-ground pool adjacent to the house. A large pile of wood Hugo had thrown together in the field in front of the house for a bonfire was dismantled. There were more investigators walking around the property and more vehicles coming and going than the day before. There was too much going on to believe two bodies were only found. The media did not know then, but investigators uncovered charred human remains in a pit and garbage bags near the house. Trooper Martin Connors told the media on June 5, "There were no other signs of buried bodies." Technically, Connors was correct, no other bodies were unearthed.

When Weakley provided information about how he helped Hugo rebury the bodies of Fassett and Kerkowski, he also implicated Hugo and Russin killed two male drug dealers known to him as "Rudy" and "Redman," and their bodies were burned in a pit on the property. The pit was behind the in-ground pool where investigators dressed in white coveralls were carefully shifting earth looking for bone fragments, jewelry and other evidence. Thousands of bone fragments were recovered in the three garbage bags next to the house.

Russin was interviewed multiple times by state police Corporal Mark E. Filarsky and Luzerne County Detective Tim Judge. What investigators learned was Russin was a lifelong acquaintance of Hugo's and moved into the Mount Olivet Road house in March 2003. Through his association with Hugo, Russin became friends with Weakley. Phone records from the house and Strom's cell phone she used for her job as a vehicle insurance adjuster were traced to cell phones used by Frank James, known as Rudy. Multiple phone calls were placed from the house to James, and from James to the house, beginning April 29, about a month after Russin moved into the house.

Russin told investigators that in March 2003, Hugo, Weakley and himself discussed various ways to rob drug dealers for money and drugs.

He called it the "Connecticut Plan" and had targeted another man known as Rudy, Isaac Garfield and his friend Sherman "Moses" Bobb, according to court documents. Hugo said the only way for the plan to work was to kill Garfield and Bobb because both knew and sold drugs to Russin who, in turn, had information both men kept a large sum of money and illegal drugs at New York's Finest, a clothing store in Plymouth Borough. Their plan was delayed when Weakley was arrested by Sachney on May 5 for selling stolen water filters. He was jailed at the Luzerne County Correctional Facility and bailed out the next day by Hugo's girlfriend, Strom. Shortly afterwards, they resumed their talk of the "Connecticut Plan " that ended in the shotgun slayings of two men and their bodies being burned in a pit outside the house.

Of course, all this became known by investigators in the coming days. The media had no idea what happened at the Mount Olivet Road property. Information trickled to reporters that charred remains were found in garbage bags, forcing Lupas to reluctantly confirm the discovery during a news conference on June 9, 2003. "At this site, we uncovered evidence of other possible human remains which had been, some of which have been received and currently undergoing forensic analysis at this time," Lupas said.

Reporters found out that two informants – Weakley and Russin – were cooperating with investigators. During the news conference, Lupas repeated his position that the investigation is ongoing but refused to admit and confirm information asked by reporters. He did say investigators were relying upon others for information. "There's information that we are receiving from individuals, there's information that we are receiving from processing the scene. To reveal specific details at this point could jeopardize the investigation," the district attorney said bluntly.

Search warrants were obtained for Weakley's apartment on Pulaski Street in Kingston, a storage unit leased by Weakley on Union Street in Luzerne, Weakley's 1993 Ford Aerostar, and another storage unit leased by Kerkowski's wife, Kimberly, on Lower Demunds Road in Dallas. All the search warrants were issued by Judge Toole and sealed from public view.

Newspapers on June 10, 2003, reported charred human remains were found on the property forcing the district attorney's office to issue a news release acknowledging that fact. Lupas held another news conference where he released results of the autopsies for Fassett and Kerkowski, and personally confirmed the remains of three people were found at the Mount Olivet Road property. "I can now officially confirm for you that in addition to the positive identification for Michael Kerkowski as well as Tammy Fassett, as I had indicated to you, we can now confirm to you the forensic analysis has revealed the human remains of three individuals, bringing the total to five," Lupas noted, adding that the investigation will take its own course. Lupas did not say where or how the human remains were found, telling reporters, "…the area where the remains were discovered is being examined and analyzed for further evidence."

Addressing leaks to reporters, Lupas said he instructed the many law enforcement agencies involved in the case that he and only he will release information. "I realize and I'm receiving calls and I understand there are a lot of rumors circulating and a lot of other information being reported about this case. What you are hearing today is from the source and this is confirmed information. Other information that I've been reading and hearing did not come from the Luzerne County District Attorney's Office. I want that to be crystal clear to every member of the media. The only information that I've released is what I released yesterday (June 9) and what I'm releasing at this (June 10) press conference. The way I'm going to handle the media in this matter is going to be fair so that what I give out will be given out at one time to all members of the media at the same time in settings such as this."

The next day, June 11, 2003, a dramatic scene unfolded at the Mount Olivet Road property. It was raining but activity did not stop. Shortly after 1 p.m., a state police cruiser drove up the gravel driveway and strategically parked in front of the detached garage. There, a trooper removed a man from the rear seat using an umbrella to shield him from photographers 100 yards away. The mystery man was escorted up the hillside and hidden by dense woods. They were out of sight for about 20 minutes before the man was hurried back from the cruiser. As the cruiser drove down the driveway, photographers rushed across Mount Olivet Road to take pictures. Upon seeing the photographers, the trooper turned driving across the field onto another gravel driveway and pulled onto Mount Olivet Road away from photographers, nearly colliding with a passing vehicle. As it turned out, investigators led two mystery men into the woods that day – Weakley and Russin.

Law enforcement agencies that were called to assist the Luzerne County District Attorney's Office, Pennsylvania State Police and Kingston Township police were the Lackawanna County District Attorney's Office, Pennsylvania Attorney General's Office, U.S. Attorney's Office, the Federal Bureau of Alcohol, Tobacco, Firearms and Explosives, the Federal Bureau of Investigation and Wilkes-Barre City Police Department. Not to mention forensic pathologist Dr. Michael Baden, forensic odontologists doctors Lowell Levine and John Hosage, and Anthony Falsetti, an associate professor of anthropology at the University of Florida. Levine, Hosage and Falsetti were called upon to analyze the bodies and bone fragments.

"All resources necessary to handle this situation are being utilized and I am extremely encouraged by the level of cooperation among the different law enforcement agencies which have been brought together in this investigation," Lupas stated in a news release on June 13, 2003. "It is at the highest level possible and I intend to keep it that way."

Lupas again addressed at length leaks to reporters.

"There's a lot of information and rumors floating about in the public and with the media. I will not comment on rumors. I deal with facts and evidence and information which can be confirmed. Obviously, there's a great deal of information known to investigators which cannot be publicly revealed at this time to ensure the integrity of the investigation. And the last thing anyone wants is to jeopardize this information. Just like a poker game, you don't show the cards that you are holding in your hand to your opponent."

Lupas continued his criticism of the media by reporting stories that gave attribution to unnamed sources. "I know certain media outlets are reporting certain information citing sources close to the investigation, or unnamed police sources. Rest assured, any of that information did not and is not coming from me. When I release information on this case, it will be in a form such as this, you can quote me and I will stand up like a man. You can quote me by name. I think it is very important to everyone involved and to the public that we be careful of speculation and rumors. Investigators are hearing much of the same things you are hearing," Lupas directly told reporters at the news conference.

Lupas simply said, "No comment" when asked about the two men investigators had escorted at the Mount Olivet Road property on June 11.

In a June 19 news release, Lupas reiterated his position he would not respond to "rumors, speculation and tips," asking reporters to understand that information known by investigators "cannot be publicly revealed…as not to impede or jeopardize the investigation."

The district attorney stated forensic analysis on the bones was continuing and assistance and cooperation "among the various law enforcement agencies involved remains at an unprecedented level and all necessary resources continue to be utilized to maintain a firm grasp on the situation."

In the immediate days after the bodies were found, reporters knew that a drug user had given information to investigators. At the time, reporters did not know Russin was cooperating with investigators and therefore, focused on Hugo's former girlfriend Carey Ann Bartoo, the mother of one of Hugo's children.

Involvement by Bartoo into the murders was non-existent. She did, however, involve herself with Weakley, Russin and others. Bartoo adamantly denied she snitched to investigators about the bodies or that she knew about the deadly shootings. Her involvement with Hugo was easily pieced together by arrest records.

Dallas Township police said Bartoo, Greg Pockevich, Weakley and Russin conspired to burglarize a house during the morning on Jan. 6, 2003, stealing 19 firearms, ammunition, jewelry, Harley Davidson motorcycle parts, clothing, electronics, a bed comforter, money and personal documents. During the investigation of the break-in, Hugo ironically implicated Russin, Weakley and Pockevich to the crime. Township police got a break in their investigation on May 23, 2003, when police in another part of Luzerne County sent out a county-wide broadcast for all police departments to be on the lookout for a copper colored Jeep Cherokee that was involved in a threat to a person outside a store with a firearm.

Kingston Township police spotted the Jeep parked outside Bartoo's apartment on Meadowcrest Drive later that day. Police kept an eye on the Jeep and watched Bartoo leave the apartment driving away before stopping her. Bartoo denied being involved in any type of threat and denied anyone was left behind in her apartment. Police did not believe her, surrounding the Meadowcrest Drive apartment watching window shades move in a second floor window.

Bartoo subsequently consented to allow police to search her apartment. Inside, police detained two males and a female, and found items stolen during the burglary of a Dallas Township house on Jan. 6. A large amount of heroin, marijuana, syringes, spoons and pipes were found throughout the apartment, according to court records.

Weakley and Russin were never prosecuted for the burglary. As it turned out, Bartoo and Pockevich took the fall and eventually agreed to a negotiated plea deal with prosecutors. Bartoo pled guilty to receiving stolen property, criminal conspiracy, possession of drug paraphernalia and hindering apprehension, and was sentenced on Feb. 4, 2004, to three to 12 months in jail. She was given credit for time served allowing her release from confinement. Pockevich pled guilty to criminal conspiracy, receiving stolen property, possession of drug paraphernalia and hindering apprehension on March 11, 2005, and was sentenced to 39 months probation.

Bartoo's freedom was short-lived. The federal Bureau of Alcohol, Tobacco, Firearms and Explosives charged Bartoo with conspiracy to possess firearms in relation to drug trafficking, a felony, for her role in the theft of the firearms from the Dallas Township home. In the complaint, Bartoo was accused of being the lookout as Russin and Weakley entered the house and stole the 19 firearms and other items. After the burglary, Pockevich told investigators that he and Bartoo traveled with Russin and Weakley to a house on Barney Street in Wilkes-Barre to trade a bag of handguns for cocaine and money. Russin later claimed they received $1,000 cash and $1,000 worth of cocaine for six or seven semi-automatic handguns from his drug dealers on Barney Street. After the trade, Russin told investigators that he went with Weakley to a house on Blackman Street in Wilkes-Barre to get rid of other firearms, according to the federal complaint.

As she did in Luzerne County Court, Bartoo pleaded guilty in federal court to possessing stolen firearms. She was sentenced May 30, 2006, to 15 months in federal prison followed by three years of supervised release.

# MOUNT OLIVET PURCHASE

Before Strom purchased the Mount Olivet Road property at the end of April 2002, she lived with Hugo at her grandmother's house on Miller Street in Luzerne. Fassett and Kerkowski were still alive.

When Weakley was released from federal prison, Strom let him stay at the Miller Street residence because he had no place to go. It was in late March 2002, when Hugo summoned Strom to a second floor bedroom in the Miller Street house where he showed her a large amount of money scattered across a bed. Strom did not know the source of the money or where it came from having been told different explanations by Hugo and Weakley. Hugo claimed he had a patent on weight lifting gloves and the sale of a baseball card collection as the source of the cash. Strom thought otherwise, believing the money came from Kerkowski. She directly asked Weakley about the source of the money. Weakley refused to say.

In early 2002, Strom began talking about purchasing her own house or buying land to build a log cabin. Hugo noticed the Mount Olivet Road property for sale and told Strom about it. Without a job or a source of income, he negotiated a sale price of $160,000 with Robert Steiner, the seller of the Mount Olivet Road property. Steiner initially asked for $190,000 for the property that included a detached garage on six acres of land that was mostly wooded. A house trailer was located in a field in front of the Mount Olivet Road house.

Ernest Culp, a landscaper, owned the house trailer but paid rent to live on the property.

Before the closing on the property on April 30, 2002, authorities alleged Hugo gave Steiner a series of "under the table" payments that totaled more than $10,000 toward the purchase price in addition to a $9,000 down payment on behalf of Strom on March 29. In order to explain the source of funds to purchase the property, Strom issued a written statement to her mortgage lender that she saved $325 a month for more than three years. When she purchased the property, Strom was employed as a vehicle claims adjuster with Geico Insurance earning approximately $50,000 a year. She had a company car, a company credit card to purchase gasoline and a company cell phone she used for personal calls.

Although Hugo negotiated the purchase of the property with Steiner, the deed would be in Strom's name only. At the closing, Strom issued a check in the amount of $10,079.50 to her attorney, Joseph Blazosek, to close the deal with Steiner.

Immediately, there was a problem. Strom knew she did not have the money in her checking account to cover the check, having only $600. Strom needed to issue the check to Steiner because the interest rate she received from her mortgage lender was about to expire. Hugo knew the check would not clear. A few days later on May 4, 2002, a Saturday, Hugo called Strom with good news that he deposited $9,900 in cash in Strom's account to cover the check for $10,079.50 Strom issued on April 30.

A day before, May 3, 2002, investigators say Fassett and Kerkowski were killed.

Robert Steiner, who sold the Mount Olivet Road property to Strom, did not move out until May 15, 2002. Strom and Hugo continued to reside at Strom's grandmother's house on Miller Street allowing Steiner to stay at the Kingston Township house until he was ready to move to Florida. A few days after the closing in early May 2002, Hugo pulled onto the gravel driveway and drove up to the house where he met Steiner outside. Hugo asked Steiner if he could leave because he wanted to look around.

Weakley told investigators after Steiner left, he walked around with Hugo looking for a place to bury the bodies of Fassett and Kerkowski. They settled on a depression in the ground but realized they did not have enough dirt to bury the bodies and Weakley made several trips to a local agriculture store to purchase bags of soil.

Ernest Culp, the man living in the house trailer on the property for nearly 20 years, looked out his window and saw a man walking around the detached garage. Culp wanted to introduce himself and say hello to his new landlord. He walked through the field and saw Hugo holding a shovel and Weakley pacing. The shovel worried Culp, especially in the area where he saw soil turned over next to the well, the source of water for the house and Culp's trailer. "I was concerned. I thought maybe there was a problem with the waterline, so I asked him why they were up there with a shovel," Culp testified during a June 2006 court proceeding. "(Selenski) initially said they were going to put a gas tank under the ground in this area so they can store gasoline for their quads. I had concerns about putting a gas tank there so close to the waterline."

Culp told Hugo he was worried about gasoline contaminating the water source for the house and trailer. "Well, (Selenski) basically agreed it was a stupid idea to put a gas tank up there," Culp said. Culp later learned Hugo wanted to install some type of underground greenhouse near the well to grow marijuana.

Once the hole was deep enough, Weakley watched Hugo remove the bodies from the trunk of Weakley's vehicle. The bodies were wrapped in comforters taken from Kerkowski's house where investigators say Fassett and Kerkowski were killed. Kerkowski's body was placed in the hole first, then Fassett's body. When the job was done, Hugo instructed Weakley to get rid of the comforters. Weakley drove to a carwash in Kingston where he threw the comforters in a dumpster.

DAY OF DISAPPEARANCE

Tammy Fassett planned to stay the weekend of May 3 to May 5, 2002, at Kerkowski's house in Hunlock Township. They were having a birthday party on Saturday, May 4, for Kerkowski's youngest son, Connor, who was turning three. Kerkowski was outside in the afternoon on May 3 cutting grass on a lawn tractor as Fassett was using a weed wacker to prep the lawn in preparation for the party. As Kerkowski and Fassett were doing yard work, Hugo and Weakley pulled into the driveway.

They all entered Kerkowski's house and sat in the kitchen talking when the telephone rang and answered by Fassett with Kerkowski's mother, Geraldine Kerkowski, on the other line.

Geraldine Kerkowski called to invite her son and Fassett to stop by their house on Vine Street in Lehman Township to see a new television she and her husband, Michael Stanley, had purchased.

"I was calling to ask if they were going to come down to the house, to my house. Tammy said, 'Not right now, we have company,'" Geraldine Kerkowski said, believing the phone conversation took place between 2:30 and 4 in the afternoon on May 3, 2002. Kerkowski and Fassett had to pick up his two sons, Tyler, 6, and Connor at a daycare center in Kingston around 5:30 p.m. and depending on the time when their "company" left, they were either going to stop by to visit his parents before or after picking up the children. When Fassett and Kerkowski failed to show, Geraldine and her husband thought they had either forgotten or were busy.

"We just assumed that they weren't coming and we decided to go to dinner," Michael Stanley Kerkowski said. Michael Stanley and his wife went to a restaurant near their house that evening and later took a long ride on state Route 118 coming close to the Lycoming (County) Mall, about a 60 mile drive. They returned to their Lehman Township house around 10 or 10:30 that night. After walking in the house from the garage, they noticed two messages on an answering machine.

"The first message was from the daycare center stating that my son had not picked up the children. And they had to be picked up by 6 o'clock. The second message was from his (son's) wife, Kimberly. She cursed us up and down and Michael for leaving the kids and not picking them up," Michael Stanley said.

A sense of fear immediately fell upon Geraldine and her husband. They traveled to their son's house finding it in the dark. No lights were turned on. Their son's truck, a 1999 Toyota 4Runner and a lawn tractor were parked in an unusual way inside a garage and Fassett's car was parked in the driveway. "My son always backed the car into the garage. Always backed it in. This time it was pulled in forward, and it was more in the middle of the garage where it usually is to one side so you could have more room," Michael Stanley explained.

Michael Stanley and his wife cautiously entered the house and the garage and immediately suspected something was wrong. "The first thing we noticed was that the screen door to the house was propped open with a chair. Like someone was moving furniture out and they didn't want the door to hit them," Michael Stanley said. After entering the house, they noticed items out of place. A vacuum cleaner was left out, a baker's rolling pin that normally hung on a kitchen wall was found under a couch in the basement, and a surveillance recording system mounted under the kitchen counter was turned off.

"He had a video security system that photographed cars coming up the driveway. That was turned off. And he always had five or six extra tapes right next to it. They were missing. And there was no tape in the machine," Michael Stanley said.

Fassett's overnight bag containing personal items was on a bed in a bedroom. A comforter was missing from a bed in another room. Michael Stanley eventually found his son's wallet with $100, his son's watches and Fassett's bracelet on a night stand. Underneath shoes in an armoire, Geraldine Kerkowski found $40,000 wrapped in rubber bands inside a zippered bag. For the next few days, Michael Stanley and his wife called everyone they knew, including Hugo, asking if they had seen their son. "(Selenski) claimed he had no idea where he would go."

Michael Stanley and his wife filed a missing persons report with the Pennsylvania State Police on Monday, May 6, 2002. Fassett's older sister, Lisa Sands, whom she lived with in Meshoppen in neighboring Wyoming County, also filed a missing persons report the same day.

The two separate reports were filed with the Pennsylvania State Police at different barracks. The Kerkowskis filed their report at the Shickshinny barracks of the state police while Sands filed her report with the Tunkhannock barracks.

Lisa Sands recalled speaking with her younger sister on the phone as they always did several times a day.

"She called me that Friday (May 3) at 11:30 in the morning and we talked until noon," Sands said. "She said she was coming home at 4 o'clock to pick up Jonathan (Fassett's son) to go down for a birthday party. And, she never showed up at 4. And, um, the later it got, the more worried I got. And Jonathan kept saying, 'Maybe she'll come Saturday morning.' Sometimes she lost track of time but I kind of knew a little better. I called down and left a message, all I got was the machine, all I got was the machine.

"I didn't think anything about her not showing up on time because she's done that before," Sands explained about Fassett's habits. "On the same night, on that Friday, Mr. Kerkowski's father called my house at night around 9:30 or 10 p.m., and asked me if Tammy was home or if she picked up Jonathan. This is what I thought was strange, he (Michael Stanley Kerkowski) called our house looking for Tammy."

Lisa Sands said she worried a little while she laid in bed but was able to fall to sleep. The next morning, Lisa believed her sister would arrive at the house to pick up Jonathan.

"I got up around 7 or 8 that morning (May 4) and assumed Tammy would come pulling in around 9 or so. Jonathan got up and I fixed him some breakfast and he asked me to call his mother, which I did around 9:30. All I got was an answering machine again and so I left another message. As the day went on, I called at least two or three more times, maybe more during the day. By the time I knew it, it was time for bed and Jonathan asked me to call one more time and I did and still no answer," Lisa Sands recalled.

When Lisa did not hear from her sister in 36 hours, her worry became overbearing. She looked up the phone number for Michael Stanley and Geraldine Kerkowski and frantically called them.

"I asked them if they had heard anything and that's when they told me they went to Mike's house and they found that the screen door was propped open and Mike's surveillance system was missing. The tapes were gone," Lisa said.

Lisa and Tammy's eldest son, Dustin, traveled to Kerkowski's Hunlock Township house on Monday, May 6, 2002, meeting Michael

Stanley and Geraldine. "I looked inside her car, her car seemed fine, her coat was in the back seat, her red jacket. There was her mail on the passenger side seat but her keys were missing, her purse was missing. I went in the house with the Kerkowskis and they showed me how things were. That was the first thing I noticed on the counter, the TV and the tapes and the surveillance system were missing."

Lisa then noticed a hook on the wall in the kitchen where the rolling pin was missing and the vacuum sweeper in the middle of the room plugged into an electrical outlet.

"I knew something was wrong. I said to Dustin, 'Pull your sleeves over your hands, that was the first thing I did too. I don't know why we did that and I don't know why it came to me to do that but it was automatic. I pulled my sleeves over my hands. I didn't want to touch anything," Sands said.

Later that day, state police troopers searched Kerkowski's Hunlock Township house finding that the household appeared to be in order, including all of Kerkowski's clothes in the closet and dresser drawers. The discovery of Kerkowski's clothes still hanging in the closet and neatly folded in drawers was an important clue for investigators. It meant Kerkowski did not pack luggage and flee the area as Skumanick, the Wyoming County district attorney, believed. Geraldine Kerkowski provided important details to troopers, recalling her telephone conversation with Fassett: "We have company."

The statement told troopers that someone was inside the Hunlock Township home with Fassett and Kerkowski. A next door neighbor on Pritchards Road told investigators she heard a loud vehicle leaving the Kerkowski driveway sometime late afternoon on May 3, 2002.

Kerkowski did not appear for his sentencing in Wyoming County on May 14, 2002. Many believed he fled to avoid being sent to prison. An arrest warrant was issued for his capture. Skumanick wanted to sentence Kerkowski "In Absentia," meaning without the defendant being present. Kerkowski's attorneys, Mark Bufalino, Malcolm Limongelli and Adam Limongelli, believed Kerkowski's absence was "involuntary or at least undetermined as evidence by the Pennsylvania State Police investigation into Mr. Kerkowski's disappearance," court records say. Skumanick moved to forfeit bail in the amount of $145,000 be paid on Kerkowski's behalf.

Wyoming County President Judge Brendan J. Vanston in a court order dated July 30, 2002, denied Skumanick's request to sentence Kerkowski without Kerkowski being physically in the courtroom. "Mr. Kerkowski did not flee the courtroom, he just did not appear as required," Vanston wrote in a two page opinion. "(Kerkowski's) counsel asserts that he may be dead or is being held against his will. Facing a substantial sentence,

Kerkowski had an obvious motive to flee. On the other hand, his absence is equally consistent with being deceased. Consequently, this court has determined that it is incumbent upon the district attorney to establish that the defendant voluntarily absented himself. Simply put, all that needs to be done is to offer credible evidence that Kerkowski lives…"

Skumanick on May 20, 2002, filed a petition in Wyoming County Court requiring credit bureau agencies to provide state police with copies of all Kerkowski's credit card usage in an attempt to locate Kerkowski. If Kerkowski had indeed fled and used a credit card to rent a motel room or purchase items, a record of the transaction would be kept at credit bureaus. Pennsylvania Crime Stoppers, an organization that seeks the public's help in locating fugitives, named Kerkowski "Fugitive of the Week" on June 10, 2002. A reward of up to $2,000 was offered that led to Kerkowski's capture.

When state police unearthed the bodies of Fassett and Kerkowski on June 3, 2003, Skumanick drove the 25 miles from the Wyoming County Courthouse in Tunkhannock to the Mount Olivet Road property in Luzerne County parking his GMC Yukon on the side of the gravel driveway. He got out, walked up the driveway and met briefly with Luzerne County District Attorney David Lupas and state police troopers before approaching the hole where the bodies were found. Skumanick stayed for less than 30 minutes and left without making a comment. Two months after Kerkowski's body was discovered, Skumanick's office in Wyoming County had the criminal charges against Kerkowski dismissed due to his death.

# BEST FRIEND

It was during Michael Jason Kerkowski's legal troubles in Wyoming County when he introduced Hugo "as his best friend" to his parents, saying they could trust him more than his lawyers. Kerkowski had contracted Hugo's "services" because Hugo had been through the criminal justice system himself after robbing a bank in 1994.

Kerkowski had marital problems with his wife, Kimberly, who filed for divorce in April 2001. Kerkowski moved out of their Hunlock Township home staying with his parents in Lehman Township, but eventually returned to his home when Kimberly moved out. During their separation, Kerkowski gave his father $60,000 to hide. "When his wife…when they were getting…when they separated the first time, he came to stay with us for a couple weeks and he brought with him his safe, which had his papers and stuff. And also, $60,000 that he had saved that he did not want to leave at the house because (Kimberly) would spend it if she found it," Michael Stanley Kerkowski said.

Michael Stanley hid the money in a heating air duct that was not being used in the basement of his Lehman Township home. Only three people knew where the money was hidden: Michael Stanley, his wife Geraldine and their son. After their son disappeared, Michael Stanley and his wife drove to their son's house finding items out of place and $40,000 in an armoire in a bedroom. With the $60,000 Kerkowski had given his parents and the additional $40,000, Michael Stanley had $100,000 of his son's money. As Michael Stanley frantically called anyone he could, asking if they knew the whereabouts of his son, Hugo told him he had no idea where Kerkowski would go.

A year before investigators found the bodies of Fassett and Kerkowski buried outside the Mount Olivet Road house, Hugo was interviewed by state police at the Shickshinny barracks on June 5, 2002, in connection to the disappearances. Hugo told investigators he was a close friend to Kerkowski and had been helping him with legal problems in Wyoming County. Hugo claimed he had no idea where Kerkowski had gone and the last time he saw Kerkowski was in April 2002. Nearly seven months later in January 2003, Hugo was interviewed again, this time inside the Dallas Township Police Department, claiming Kerkowski was hiding in Belize, South America.

On June 11, 2002, more than a month after Fassett and Kerkowski were last heard from, Kerkowski's estranged wife, Kimberly, reported a burglary at the Pritchard Road house. State police found that the house had, indeed, been ransacked. A front window was forced open, ceiling tile blocks and insulation in the basement were thrown about, closets were opened and the garage door leading into the house was open. Weakley admitted to Capitano and Sachney that he participated with Hugo in the burglary at the house on May 11, 2002. Weakley told investigators that he and Hugo forced open a gun safe inside the house finding no money.

Michael Stanley and his wife knew something horrible had happened to their son. There was no way, they said, their son would get up and leave, especially a day before their grandson's birthday party. The signs were obvious to them. Kerkowski's vehicle was at the Hunlock Township house, his clothes were neatly folded in dresser drawers and a large amount of money was found in an armoire. If their son had fled to avoid sentencing, wouldn't Kerkowski at least take some clothes and the cash? Michael Stanley and his wife were mentally exhausted. They were fearing the worst and hoping for the best. They were vulnerable hoping for any information and Hugo took advantage.

Hugo knew about the $100,000 Michael Stanley had hidden in his house. He would patiently play upon the heartache and mental anguish of Michael Stanley and his wife to get the money by any means necessary. In the ensuing months, Hugo would succeed in getting the money.

Michael Stanley and his wife would report they received mysterious phone calls at their home in June and July 2002 from people claiming they were in contact with their son. One of the callers identified himself as "Eric" who requested to meet at a local coffee and donut store on Memorial Highway in Dallas Township, not far from their home. "He said, 'I want to meet with you because I'm in contact with your son and I'd like to talk to you. So we met in the parking lot at the donut shop in Dallas (Township)," Michael Stanley explained.

Michael Stanley may not have known it at the time, but he was meeting Weakley in the parking lot. Eric was a fictitious name.

Michael Stanley pulled into the parking lot, noticed a man waving at him and parked next to the vehicle. He got out and sat in Weakley's car. "When I got in the car, he informed me that he was a computer expert and he needed $10,000 to upgrade his computer so that my son could be in touch with him. I told him that, you know, I don't know who you are. I'm not giving you any $10,000. And I suggested that I go home and talk it over with my wife," Michael Stanley said. He left in a hurry and traveled the short distance to his house and told his wife about the encounter. Geraldine accompanied her husband returning to the parking lot near the donut store. Together, they sat in Weakley's car.

"I told him that I'm not giving anybody any money unless my son contacts me and tells me to do it. And my wife and I got out of the car and left. And that was the first and last time I ever saw him," Michael Stanley said about Weakley.

A few days later, Michael Stanley contacted Hugo and told him about the meeting with "Eric" in the parking lot. "I finally got through to him on the telephone and told him what happened. And he informed me, 'Don't give anybody any money until you check with me.'"

Soon after the mysterious meeting in the parking lot took place, Hugo contacted Michael Stanley saying he was going to stop at their house. "The first time was more or less a social visit…we sat on the back porch…he asked 'How we were doing, did we need anything.' You know, to keep in touch with him," Michael Stanley said.

It was the first of several visits to the house of Michael Stanley and Geraldine by Hugo, whose motive was to "feel them out." Hugo sensed an opportunity to exploit their weakness.

Hugo would visit Michael Stanley a few more times in the summer and fall in 2002, telling Michael Stanley what he wanted to hear, which was that his son was alive and needed money. "We were on the back deck and he told me my son didn't run. He told us that Michael was putting together a new trial, and he needed money for the trial. (Hugo) explained my son was going to name doctors, he had proof of jury tampering and that Michael needed $30,000 to start his case. (Hugo) wanted $30,000 to start and I told him I didn't have any money. (Hugo) said, 'I know you do and I know where it is.' (Hugo) told me it was hidden in an air duct over the furnace. And like I said before, there were only three people that knew where it was," Michael Stanley said.

Michael Stanley prodded Hugo to tell him where his son and Fassett were, or at least put him in phone contact with them. Hugo said he was unable to accommodate any communication with Kerkowski "for security reasons." Only three people in the Kerkowski family knew where the money was hidden, in the unused vent behind insulation in the basement. Believing Hugo was telling the truth, Michael Stanley reluctantly gave Hugo $30,000. Michael Stanley did not report to the state police of his meeting with Hugo or what Hugo had told him. Kerkowski was believed to be a fugitive by investigators.

Two months passed before Hugo again made contact with Michael Stanley in August 2002, saying his son needed more cash. During this strange encounter, Michael Stanley asked Hugo if he could talk to his son. "I'll see what I could do," Hugo replied, walking away with another $30,000.

The $60,000 Kerkowski had given his father in a security box to hide in April 2001, had been given to Hugo within three months. Michael Stanley was not only in turmoil, but his emotions were being played upon by Hugo. His son had disappeared and unknowingly, he had become the victim of a cruel scheme to rob him of money without any violence. Hugo was a desperate man and knew Michael Stanley had more of his son's money. Michael Stanley was realizing he was never going to talk to his son despite promises by Hugo.

On another visit at the elder Kerkowski house, Hugo told the grieving father what he wanted to hear. "Today is the day you're going to talk to you son," Michael Stanley said what Hugo told him. "(Hugo) was out in the backyard and he just kept walking up and down the yard with his cell phone." Hugo left the house and later sent Patrick Russin to get money from the parents. Michael Stanley was getting tired of this cat and mouse game with Hugo. They wanted proof that their son was alive and came up with their own plan. "My wife made up five questions that only my son would know the answers to…and I gave them to (Patrick) Russin," Michael Stanley said.

Russin left the house with only the list of five questions. Hugo later made contact with Michael Stanley. "I kept bugging Hugo Selenski to let me know when I'm going to get my answers…he called me one day and said, '(Answers) are going to be mailed to somebody in Swoyersville.' And I said who. He said, 'Well, I have to find out right now.' So one day I was on the side of the garage and he and Pat Russin pulled into the driveway. They both got out of the car and he walked over to me and said, 'The answers are going to be mailed to somebody called Nona.' That's my wife's mother and I said, okay. And then he and Pat Russin both got in the car and drove off. That day, I went down to get my wife's mom and I told her if she gets anything in the mail to just save it for me. But we never received anything."

Hugo was persistent. He continued to play on the broken hearts and minds of Michael Stanley and his wife. In September or October, a date

Michael Stanley couldn't recall, Hugo arrived once again at their house bringing a six-pack of beer.

"We started out on the deck. And we sat there for a couple of hours while he walked up and down the yard again, with the cell phone saying, 'They're trying to get in touch with your son. They'll eventually get him.' We sat on the deck until it got dark and I said to him, 'I think we should move inside.' So we went down to the basement. While we were in the basement, he began to drink. He had two beers and they were in my refrigerator. And then I had a six pack of beer alongside the refrigerator and he asked if he could start drinking that. And I said, 'Those beers aren't cold' and he didn't care."

The topic of conversation in the basement continued along with the charades Hugo was doing with a cell phone. Hugo was sitting on a couch and Michael Stanley was in a chair against a wall. Hugo abruptly asked for $40,000, presumably the money he found inside an armoire in his son's house.

"He pulled out a gun and I told him I had no more cash. I just didn't want to give him any more money," Michael Stanley said. "Because I was starting to feel, you know, I was never going to talk to my son. He pulled a gun on me…I looked at him, and the next thing I knew, the gun went off. He said, 'It's either your fucking life or the money.'"

Hugo again asked for $40,000 knowing Michael Stanley had that exact amount hidden inside the house. Michael Stanley testified at the preliminary hearing in June 2006, that the gun fired with the round passing inches above his head.

Terrified, Michael Stanley stood up and walked upstairs with Hugo behind him still holding the gun. "The money was upstairs hidden in one of the roofing joists," Michael Stanley said. "After I gave him the $40,000, we proceeded downstairs again. And at that time, I didn't think anything of it, but he said I'll take the bottles and get rid of them for you. He took all the beer bottles with him and we both walked up the steps and at the time my wife was just coming home from shopping. And she came in the house and we went out the door, he got in his car and left."

Michael Stanley never told his wife about the shooting nor did he immediately report the near death experience to state police. He covered up the bullet hole in the basement wall with shoe polish. After the last meeting with Hugo in the parking lot of a fast food restaurant, Michael Stanley had enough and reported Hugo's scam to the Pennsylvania State Police.

Sitting inside a pickup truck on Dec. 17, 2002, Hugo told Michael Stanley he had been "in touch" with his son and needed more cash, the same excuse Hugo had been telling the grieving father throughout the summer and fall. "I have no more money, I knew I was not going to ever talk to my son. And I said to him, 'That's it, I'm done with you.' And he said, 'Well, you know, there's about five or six cars outside with guys in them just waiting to kill you when you walk out. Probably at this present time, your house is on fire. You know how your son disappeared, your other son can disappear like that. Your wife can disappear like that.'"

Michael Stanley was livid and scared. "I said to him, 'Well, you do what you have to do but I'm getting out of this truck. And I did…nothing happened." He raced to his mother-in-law's house in Swoyersville to pick up his wife.

When Hugo made the threat, his buddy Timothy Reese was inside the restaurant eating food. After he finished eating, Reese waited outside while Hugo and Michael Stanley were talking inside the truck. Reese would later say Hugo wanted him to be some type of tough guy.

When Michael Stanley got home, he called the Pennsylvania State Police to report the shooting and being scammed by Hugo.

The case was assigned to Trooper Leo Hannon who, along with Trooper Edward Urban, a member of the Pennsylvania State Police Forensic Services Unit, processed Michael Stanley's Vine Street home, recovering a spent .32 caliber round in the basement wall.

Remaining desperate for money, Hugo tried one last time to scam Michael Stanley. On May 3, 2003, exactly one year since he last heard from his son, Michael Stanley spotted Hugo standing on the rear deck of his home ringing the doorbell. Michael Stanley looked out the window and refused to open the door for Hugo.

Hugo left and called the house phone. "He said, 'I'm just calling to tell you that the boy is in, he wants to talk to you, if you don't want to talk to him, do whatever you want. I told him there is no way I'm going to get in contact with you again," as explained by Michael Stanley.

Thirty-three days later on June 5, 2003 investigators unearthed the bodies of Michael Jason Kerkowski and Tammy Lynn Fassett from outside the Mount Olivet Road house where Hugo was residing.

Law enforcement held possession of the Mount Olivet Road 6.1 acre property for 34 days. Digging was more common in those early days considering the bodies of Tammy Fassett and Michael Jason Kerkowski and the charred bones of three individuals from a burn pit and garbage bags were discovered. Investigators conducted grid searches on the property, walking in straight lines crossing each other's paths. Equipment from the Pennsylvania Department of Transportation was used to scan the ground. No more human remains were found.

Investigators were engaged elsewhere away from the house, interviewing those connected and associated with Hugo, Weakley and Russin.

Hugo's court-appointed attorney, Demetrius (Tim) Fannick, was busy during this time. Fannick, an all-conference basketball player at Dallas High School in the late 1960s and early 1970s, and a graduate of Gonzaga University School of Law in Spokane, Wash., would stand by Hugo for the next three years, working without pay, defending Hugo's constitutional rights. Three weeks after the discovery of the bodies, and before the charred remains were positively identified, Fannick filed motions in Luzerne County Court seeking to compel the district attorney's office to release a list of items seized from the property. It was a bold move by

Fannick, considering Judge Pat Toole on June 5 and June 6 sealed the search warrants for 60 days and the property remained under the control of law enforcement. Fannick wanted to know what items were taken from the property. At least it would give him a start with how to proceed with his defense.

As it turned out, according to inventory receipts that were returned and attached to search warrants, investigators had listed "two human corpses" as the first items seized. Dirt, coal, hair, clothes, plastic flex cuffs, insects, shovels, copper wire, rope, shotgun pellets, black plastic garbage bags filled with debris found near the house, black plastic garbage bags filled with debris near the roadway for pick up, pornography magazines, sex toys, video tapes and photographs were taken.

Also taken were mortgage documents, an identification card, a gun cleaning kit, a bow saw, a chainsaw, burlap, paper with names and phone numbers, bags of potting soil, two black sweatshirts, a black jacket with the logo FBI Narcotics, two black ski masks, a gasoline container, metal handcuffs, duct tape, two pair of New Balance sneakers and a baseball bat.

Fannick would lay the foundation of a lengthy appeal in appellate court years later about the items seized from the property that investigators alleged were used by Hugo and Weakley in the violent home invasion and robbery of Monroe County jewelry store owner Samuel Goosay.

Fannick had another trick up his sleeve. He believed all items seized from the property should be thrown out because investigators converged onto the property on June 5, 2003, before Judge Pat Toole authorized the search warrant. Pennsylvania State Police Lieutenant Richard Krawetz had given the command to go onto the property when Hugo's dogs began barking at three troopers conducting surveillance from a neighbor's yard. Fannick further challenged that information Weakley provided to investigators on June 3 and June 4 was "13 months old and was stale," referring to the May 3, 2002, deaths of Fassett and Kerkowski.

Weakley initially told investigators the bodies of Fassett and Kerkowski were buried in woods near the Dallas football field. A day before the search warrant was executed at the Mount Olivet Road property, investigators had escorted Weakley to the woods in search of the first burial site. No such gravesite was located as investigators later learned Weakley provided false information.

Fannick argued that the search warrant, based on Weakley's information, was misleading and not credible.

After a lengthy court hearing on June 11, 2004, Luzerne County Judge Peter Paul Olszewski Jr. determined that items seized from the Mount Olivet Road property were legally taken. In response to Fannick's arguments, Olszewski determined that Weakley's information was the backbone for the search warrant was not stale, and any omissions from the affidavit of probable cause did not render the search warrant defective.

At the same hearing in June 2004, Fannick was successful in having Hugo's unsolicited statement, "Yeah, five of them," which answered a question by Trooper John Yencha if any bodies would be found, prohibited from being used by prosecutors against Hugo.

Olszewski opined that Hugo was not given his Miranda warnings, as required, when he was arrested by state police troopers on June 5, 2003, for the robbery of Michael Stanley Kerkowski in 2002. Yencha was assigned to watch Hugo, and the two men engaged in a conversation inside the state police Wyoming barracks. Yencha was unaware of what was happening at the Mount Olivet Road property and asked Hugo "You know more than me, you tell me what is going on?"

In response, Hugo gave Yencha the cover sheet to the search warrant that explained investigators were looking for the bodies of Fassett and Kerkowski, and a green handle shovel.

Yencha unknowingly asked Hugo if any bodies would be found. "Yeah, five of them," Hugo replied. It turned out, Hugo was read his Miranda warnings *after* he made the self-incriminating statement.

Olszewski's ruling was a blow to prosecutors in which they could not produce the statement to jurors.

"The conversation between (Selenski) and Trooper Yencha was clearly initiated by (Selenski) and was not (a) typical interrogation as is customarily engaged in between law enforcement officers and criminal defendants. Trooper Yencha read the search warrant cover sheet provided by (Selenski) and advised (Selenski) this was a serious matter. The trooper then specifically posed a question which went to the very substance of the investigation, whether law enforcement would find bodies buried on (Selenski's) property. While there is absolutely nothing to suggest that Trooper Yencha was acting in bad faith, his motivation is not determinative of its legal effect or consequence," Olszewski wrote in his opinion.

A year before Olszewski issued his precedential rulings for Hugo's trial, Fannick in another bold move filed a motion that basically challenged Hugo's arrest. On Aug. 21, 2003, at the time when Hugo was only charged for robbing Michael Stanley Kerkowski, Fannick claimed prosecutors were "intentionally delaying the filing of the information…in order to shorten the time within which (Selenski) would have an opportunity to prepare for trial and thus place (Selenski) in a severe disadvantage in defending his case at trial."

A preliminary hearing on the robbery charges involving Michael Stanley Kerkowski was held July 3, 2003, before Magisterial District Judge James Tupper who, in turn, ruled prosecutors established a case against Hugo, sending the case to Luzerne County Court. After a preliminary hearing, the district attorney's office – by rules of criminal procedure – file what is called an information that lists the charges filed against a defendant. A formal arraignment is scheduled where a defendant can enter a plea of guilty or not guilty, and the case is placed on the court's calendar for trial.

By Fannick's account, Hugo's formal arraignment and the filing of the information on the robbery charges was being intentionally delayed by the district attorney's office.

"(Selenski) believes that the Commonwealth will delay his arraignment until the fifth month of his incarceration, schedule his trial for the sixth month, and thus allow him only 30 days within which to file his request for discovery, obtain discovery, file any pretrial motions, and otherwise prepare for trial," Fannick stated in a petition he filed with the court.

When a person is arrested and held for trial, the district attorney's office must release all evidence – called discovery – to the defendant's lawyer. Fannick was seeking a "level playing field" that would allow him sufficient time to obtain discoverable materials to prepare his defense on the robbery charges.

Luzerne County Judge Michael Conahan on Sept. 2, 2003, denied Fannick's attempt to reduce Hugo's straight bail of $300,000. At the time,

Hugo had not been charged with homicide but he was clearly a suspect. Fannick again argued, in his attempt to reduce Hugo's bail, that the district attorney's office intended to keep Hugo incarcerated on the robbery charges while conducting an unrelated criminal homicide investigation. Simply put, Fannick claimed the district attorney's office wanted Hugo in jail until investigators were ready to charge him with homicide.

Another Luzerne County judge, Hugh Mundy, on Sept. 10, denied Fannick's request to force the district attorney's office and state police to turn over evidence because the formal arraignment had not taken place in the robbery case. Clearly, the district attorney's office was using the court calendar to their advantage to keep Hugo in jail.

Fannick wanted records from the state police and the Wyoming County District Attorney's Office by way of issuing a subpoena on Aug. 6, in regards to the missing persons investigation and/or fugitive investigation regarding Kerkowski. Hugo had been questioned at least twice about Kerkowski's disappearance. Fannick wanted to know what his client told investigators.

In denying Fannick's request for investigative records pertaining to Kerkowski's disappearance, Mundy said that the request is a discovery issue, the process Fannick had earlier asked a judge to compel the district attorney's office to begin by way of scheduling a formal arraignment on the robbery charges involving Michael Stanley Kerkowski.

A few days earlier on Sept. 4, Judge Pat Toole, who authorized and sealed the search warrants for the Mount Olivet Road property in June, agreed to a compromise between the district attorney's office and Fannick.

Under the compromise, Fannick was permitted to obtain copies of the search warrant affidavits. Toole warned, however, that the search warrants were to remain sealed and not released to the public. Fannick had been provided redacted search warrant affidavits on Aug. 8, 2003.

After the compromise was reached with the search warrant affidavits, Luzerne County Assistant District Attorney Joseph Giovannini said prosecutors had not sought an extension to keep the search warrants under seal. That meant the seal on the affidavits would expire on Oct. 5, 2003, a Sunday when court offices are closed.

The next day, Monday, Oct. 6, was filled with anticipation. Since prosecutors did not seek to keep the search warrant affidavits sealed, it was a sign investigators were ready to make an arrest for the homicides of Fassett and Kerkowski.

That morning, District Attorney David Lupas held a news conference regarding the investigation at the Mount Olivet Road property. He began by thanking and commending the investigators for their hard work.

"Particularly, I want to recognize two individuals, one is Detective Lieutenant Gary Capitano, whose persistence and dedication to his job basically uncovered this whole situation, along with Trooper Gerald

Sachney of the Pennsylvania State Police. Both of whom have been leading the way tirelessly in this case. I want to secondly recognize (Pennsylvania State Police) Lieutenant Frank Hacken, who put in countless hours into this investigation, coordinating matters, (he) truly displayed a real pattern in his work to see that justice is done in this matter."

Lupas also thanked state police Commander Carmen Altavilla and Kingston Township Police Chief James Balavage and his department before making it known that Giovannini, a part time assistant district attorney, was assigned as lead prosecutor.

By appointing Giovannini to prosecute Hugo, Lupas ignited a fuse of complexity resulting in a major blunder haunting the case at the trial stage. Prosecution of a case such as what the investigation revealed required a full-time assistant district attorney if not the district attorney himself. As it turned out, Giovannini would not see the case to the end, having resigned from the district attorney's office in December 2004, citing, "His need to devote sufficient time to attend to the demands of his private law practice."

Giovannini admitted to a newspaper reporter that the case required "a full-time position." Four months earlier in July 2004, Assistant District Attorney Ingrid Cronin – who had been assisting Giovannini – resigned from the same district attorney's office for private practice. Cronin was replaced by Assistant District Attorney James McMonagle, who became the lead prosecutor when Giovannini left.

By everyone's surprise during Lupas' news conference on Oct. 6, the district attorney announced that Hugo and Russin were being charged for the criminal homicides of Frank James, of New York City, and Adeiye Keiler, a legal alien from Guyana, South America, and not for the homicides of Fassett and Kerkowski.

"Today's arrests are the result of a very intensive and methodical investigation that brought together a cooperative effort by a multitude of law enforcement agencies who utilized a significant amount of resources," Lupas said. "The investigation into the homicides of Michael Kerkowski and Tammy Fassett, whose bodies were discovered buried underground on June 5, 2003, at 479 Mount Olivet Road, Kingston Township, is continuing to make significant progress and remains a top priority of my office and all the investigators."

"It started out as a result of a search warrant that we served on the property owned by Selenski and his girlfriend, Christina Strom," Altavilla said. "Through this initial search warrant, we developed information which led us not to the original two subjects that we were looking for, that being Tammy Fassett and Michael Kekowski, but to the initial bodies to which we are charging today, James and Keiler. This was a long investigation. It was a total and complete investigation and I can honestly say no element was more important than the other. We had terrific cooperation, fantastic cooperation from the Kingston Township Police Department, from the Luzerne County detectives, from the (federal) Bureau of Alcohol, Tobacco and Firearms and the district attorney's office. The question that probably arises is why did it take so long. It's a complex investigation; it's a continuing investigation."

As he did in the early days of the investigation after the bodies were found, Lupas took a shot at the media for reporting. "As I told you from day one, I wasn't going to respond to rumors and speculation. We deal in evidence and fact. That is what we are presenting today. I told you three or four months ago, this is the type of investigation we have never seen in this county with resources that were brought in with the expertise, forensic anthropologist and the like. Again, we're going to be guided not by rumors or speculation but where the facts and evidence lead us. And today, (that) led us to the arrest of the two individuals for two counts of criminal homicide and other charges."

Lupas said the jaw bones of three individuals were found in garbage bags outside the Mount Olivet Road house. He noted investigators were at a "comfort level" to file the criminal homicide charges against Hugo and Russin at that particular time.

Hugo and Russin were arraigned by Magisterial District Judge James Tupper, the same district judge that had arraigned Hugo on June 5, 2003, for the robbery charges involving Michael Stanley Kerkowski. The two men were also charged with two counts of robbery, two counts of abuse of corpse and a single count of criminal conspiracy. Hugo remained jailed at the Luzerne County Correctional Facility while Russin was sent to the State Correctional Institution at Retreat, a state prison in Newport Township, about 10 miles from Wilkes-Barre and the county courthouse.

After the arraignment, Fannick spoke to reporters outside Tupper's office.

"(Selenski) denies all of the allegations," Fannick began saying, "Mr. Selenski looks forward to defending this case in court which we intend to do vigorously. He denies the allegations, that's all they are, allegations. The state police, and the district attorney's office and myself, we don't get a vote in this. His guilt or innocence will be decided by a jury, those are the people who will be voting ultimately in this case.

"From day one, I've been looking forward to information regarding the allegations. I filed motions, they've been denied. I'm still looking for that information. It's been said these (charges) are slam dunk cases. If they are, then they should give the information now."

Fannick's reference to "Slam Dunk Cases" came from a headline in a newspaper that reported a story quoting anonymous sources about the forthcoming arrests.

Fannick went on the offensive to attack the credibility of the district attorney's two primary witnesses, Weakley and Russin. By coining the phrase "Pat the Rat," in reference to Russin, Fannick would continue to challenge the two men throughout the case and trial.

"(They are) totally unbelievable and totally not credible," Fannick said. "If you look in this affidavit alone, you will see the state police interviewed Russin four, five, six times. I'm curious to see the tapes of those interviews to see which one, which version this (case) was developed. I believe if you look at this affidavit and compare it to the first affidavit that was filed, you'll find a totally different version of the events as portrayed by Mr. Russin. He's not believable. This is clearly a case at the end of the day, the judge will instruct the jury that Weakley and Russin are to be considered corrupt courses. It's our position from day one that Russin and Weakley are not credible people."

Fannick said he interviewed numerous people that investigators had not questioned. Earlier in the day, state police Commander Carmen Altavilla said more than 600 interviews with potential witnesses had been conducted before Hugo and Russin were charged with criminal homicide.

"I'm surprised by a lot of things that have happened in this case," the famed defense attorney said. "I'm surprised that Selenski has been charged. I conducted my own investigation. Quite frankly, I've spoken to numerous people that state police have not even interviewed, which I believe provided relevant information to the case. I'm anxious to see who (investigators) interviewed and what they have to say and who they have not interviewed."

Before ending his time with the media, Fannick lofted one more challenge at the district attorney's office. "If you have such a good case, let's see what it is."

# RUDY AND REDMAN

Hugo was all fired up when his girlfriend, Christina Strom, posted bail permitting Paul Weakley to be released from the Luzerne County Correctional Facility on May 6, 2003. Weakley had been charged by Trooper Sachney for the attempt to sell stolen water filters and computer equipment from his former employer, Hi-Tech Water Group, to a competing business.

With Weakley out of jail and Russin by his side, Hugo continued to talk about their scheme to rob drug dealers. They put their plan in motion on May 13, 2003.

Russin got the plan moving by redirecting efforts from contacting Isaac "Rudy" Garfield and Sherman "Moses" Bobb and instead called Frank James, known on the street as Rudy.

James was at Wilkes-Barre General Hospital in Wilkes-Barre, visiting his girlfriend when he was contacted by Russin on May 13, 2003. James, a native of Brooklyn, New York City, was associated with the Bloods street gang and had been living with his girlfriend for nine months becoming friends with Adeiye Ossasis Keiler, who was known as "Redman."

Keiler was born in Guyana, South American, and relocated to Brooklyn in August 2000, spending some of his time at an apartment on Mercer Avenue in Kingston.

James' girlfriend was discharged from the hospital on May 9 but was readmitted the next day due to complications from giving birth. James visited her and stayed the night of May 12 into May 13, 2003. On the morning of May 13, James left the hospital after he was contacted by Russin.

A few hours after James left the hospital to meet Russin, he returned with Hugo driving Strom's Honda Accord that had a smashed driver's side window. Hugo gave James, his girlfriend and their newborn son a ride, telling her, "If I knew you were bringing home the baby, I would have brought the better car."

James sat in the rear seat with his baby boy while his girlfriend sat in the front passenger seat. Hugo drove them to a pharmacy on Amber Lane in Wilkes-Barre where James' girlfriend picked up a prescription before driving them to an apartment in the Sherman Hills apartment complex in Wilkes-Barre, arriving between 4 and 5 p.m. on May 13, 2003. Keiler was inside the apartment as James stayed outside with Hugo. Despite being a short distance away, James called Keiler on his cellular phone instructing Keiler to bring out his sneakers and leave out a rear door. Nobody knew it at the time, but it would be the last time their girlfriends would see them alive.

James and Keiler were under the impression they were going to make a drug deal with Hugo, something that could have taken place inside

Hugo's car. Instead, the plan to lure drug dealers to the Mount Olivet Road property was working.

Hugo drove James and Keiler to the Mount Olivet Road house hanging out in the detached garage. Russin believed Hugo wanted to "feel out Rudy and Redman" to see how much money and drugs they had on them. Russin said Hugo had him order and pick up a pizza for James and Keiler. They sat around talking about the Mount Olivet Road property and Hugo's plan to "start a crack house and make some money and do some business." After the pizza was eaten, Russin said Hugo drove off with James and Keiler returning to the house only to leave once again. It was getting dark when Hugo returned to the house with James and Keiler a third time. At about 7:30 that night, James called his girlfriend and told her he was in Kingston Township and would be coming home with food. It was the last conversation his girlfriend had with the father of her child. As the sun was setting, Strom returned to the house and noticed Hugo coming out of the detached garage. Strom suspected Hugo was under the influence of narcotics having witnessed him using cocaine in the past.

Russin claimed he did not see Strom the rest of the night and fell asleep on a couch with a television turned on. Russin awakened around 1 a.m. on May 14, when Selenski entered the house "all fired up."

Hugo was getting impatient and asked Russin which guy had the money and drugs. Russin reiterated that James was not the original target despite using the same street name as Isaac Garfield. Russin said he witnessed Hugo load a Remington 16 gauge shotgun before he was told to have James and Keiler go into the detached garage. "Before I went down…to the bottom of the driveway, he went to the kitchen and he grabbed the shotgun. I had seen him in the process of loading the shotgun," Russin testified during a preliminary hearing on Dec. 18, 2003. "Then I went down to the car and then I took them out to the detached garage then I, then I walked back to the house and he was coming out of the house with the shotgun. I told the guys, 'come out, come on out.' I just yelled it through the door. So I start walking, I get a little head start of them. They started coming out. I started walking back to the house and while I'm walking back towards the house, I hear a gunshot, which I know to be a gunshot now. I turned and I looked to my left and I could see a silhouette of a man, and he goes down like Jell-O. He looked like Jell-O. He lifted off the air, and he went down like Jell-O. He fell to the ground," Russin testified.

James was instantly killed. Seeing his friend fall to the ground and fearing for his own life, Keiler ran around the detached garage with Hugo chasing him. Not knowing the area or the surroundings, Keiler ran back into the garage through the personal door entry and attempted to close it. Hugo managed to push it open and knocked Keiler to the floor. Hugo had Russin handcuffed Keiler's hands behind his back and bound his legs together with duct tape. Keiler became Hugo's hostage. Russin was instructed by Hugo to search Keiler, finding three bags of crack and $40. Hugo gave Russin the shotgun and went outside under the cover of darkness to wrap James' body in a tarp. The body was dragged to the side of the detached garage furthest away from the house.

Hugo's three dogs, a Rottweiler, a German Shepard, and a Pit Bull, did not bark in response to the shotgun blast. Strom had told investigators the dogs would bark at almost anything including the moon but would not act up if Hugo was at the house. Strom claimed she did not hear a shotgun blast that morning.

Ernest Culp, the self-employed landscaper living in the house trailer on the property, did hear the shotgun blast. He would ask Weakley later on May 14 about the blast in which Weakley replied he had no idea what he was talking about. Weakley had shown up at Culp's trailer just after sunrise to help the landscaper build a retaining wall for a customer in Lake Winola in Wyoming County.

After James was killed and his body dragged away from the house, Russin – now armed with the shotgun – kept Keiler prisoner inside the detached garage. Russin said he heard Hugo whispering, believing he was talking to Strom outside the house.

Russin said he and Hugo smoked crack and talked to Keiler about Sherman Moses. Hugo and Russin escorted Keiler at gunpoint into the house hiding him in a second floor bedroom for several hours. At one point, Keiler was allowed to use the bathroom while Russin stood guard holding the shotgun. After Keiler was taken back to the bedroom, Hugo told Russin to go outside and search James' body for crack and money. Russin claimed he was unable to find anything.

Hugo and Russin were laying on a couch on the first floor inside the house when Strom awakened around 7 a.m. She exited her bedroom and entered her home office to check her business appointments on a computer. While Strom was in the office and being distracted by Hugo, Russin went to the second floor and sneaked Keiler to the basement where he was kept in a closet. Russin stayed in a basement bedroom while Strom took a shower and retrieved clothing from the basement laundry room.

"I sat there and (Keiler) was asking me if everything was going to be all right. I just said, 'Listen to what he says and you'll probably be alright,'" Russin testified during a court proceeding in 2006. Russin continued to sit with Keiler as Hugo hurried Strom to leave the house. She left around 8:30 that morning to inspect vehicles that were damaged in Shickshinny and Scranton. Strom said she did not see any blood when she got into her car that was parked next to the detached garage.

Keiler was taken to the kitchen on the first floor and sat at a table. Russin sat next to Keiler as Hugo kept getting up from a chair. The two men and their prisoner talked about Sherman Moses and Moses' clothing store in Plymouth, New York Finest. Keiler told his captors that he believed Moses sold clothing from the store and narcotics from the second floor of the building. Keiler offered to help Hugo and Russin in their plan to rob Moses. Immediately after Keiler's offer to help, Selenski smiled telling Russin, "I'm starting to like this guy."

Any hope at pardoning Keiler was short lived. Hugo got up and walked behind Keiler making a trigger sign with his hands indicating he was going to kill him.

"We got up from the table and we started walking out to the outside. I'm walking out first. (Keiler) is walking out second, and Hugo is walking out third. I go off to the left. Then Hugo comes off. I veer off quick because I knew something is probably going to happen. I veered off quick to the left. (Keiler) comes out with his handcuffs on, and Hugo is right behind him. For some reason, when (Keiler) is walking, he sort of turns around. At that point, Hugo grabbed the shotgun, which I believe, I don't know if it was on the outside of the door or on the inside of the door. He grabs the shotgun, turns the shotgun and fires a shot into (Keiler)," Russin testified.

Keiler immediately stumbles and falls to the ground. Hugo orders Russin to grab Keiler's feet and drag him closer to the detached garage. Russin sees Keiler turning his head to look at him at the same time Keiler is trying to get up. Russin yells at Hugo that Keiler is "still alive." Hugo fires a second shot, killing Keiler in the driveway between the house and the detached garage.

The two men worked quickly. Listening to orders from Hugo, Russin tossed a few tires in a pit behind an in-ground swimming pool. Hugo and Russin dragged James' corpse to the pit and were walking to Keiler's body at the same time Weakley pulled into the driveway to pick up Culp.

Weakley first goes to see Hugo and Russin and is shown the bodies. Russin in the meantime tossed more tires into the pit along with a few tree stumps. Gasoline was poured on the bodies and tires before Hugo ignited the inferno. As the fire erupted in the pit, Hugo's uncle, Robert Higdon, turned into the driveway. In response to seeing Higdon, Hugo runs and hides.

"(Selenski) got all nervous and started running into the house. (Higdon) was still in his SUV, I do believe, at this time. He was asking me where Hugo was. I told him he wasn't home but (Higdon) said he seen him back here," Russin said.

Higdon was on his way to a construction project building a boat house on Harveys Lake when he passed the Mount Olivet Road property and saw smoke and fire. Hugo owed Higdon money and Higdon stopped to collect.

Higdon got out of his truck and began walking toward the burning pit. He stopped when Russin yelled that Hugo was not home. When confronted by Higdon that he spotted Hugo running, Russin yelled to

Hugo to come out. Hugo emerged and spoke to his uncle for about 10 minutes before Higdon left. It was a close call for Hugo and Russin as Higdon probably would have seen the two corpses burning in the pit. After Higdon left the property, Hugo told Russin to keep the fire going as he left to attend a court hearing at the Luzerne County Courthouse regarding child support.

Russin said the fire was huge, describing it as a "big, massive fire" but under control. Cinders burned for days as Hugo and Russin used shovels and a steel rake to break up the charred bones that were later shoveled into garbage bags.

A week after burning the bodies of James and Keiler, Russin said that he, Hugo and Weakley drove to New York Finest in Plymouth and smashed an already broken window in the rear of the building. Russin claimed Weakley stayed in the vehicle, a mini-van, acting as a look-out when he and Hugo entered the building searching for money and narcotics. Finding neither, Russin said they stole a chandelier, a scale, a video camera and a stereo.

Hugo changed his appearance after James and Keiler were killed by shaving the hair on his head and growing a goatee. Russin claimed he was standing with Hugo outside the Mount Olivet Road house preparing for a college graduation party for Hugo's sister when state troopers drove up the gravel driveway on June 5, 2003. A tent-rental company was arriving at the house the same time state police converged onto the property.

Upon seeing the state troopers, Hugo turned to Russin saying, "Did you say anything?"

"I believe my response was 'No, but I was talking to Paul (Weakley) yesterday (June 4) and he was up in Scranton.' (Weakley) would be up in Scranton because he was on federal probation," Russin said he told Hugo in response.

The claim by Russin that he stood next to Hugo when state police came onto the property would be challenged a decade later in court.

Russin agreed to answer questions by investigators, later admitting he fabricated the story on how James and Keiler were killed, initially telling investigators that the two men were executed at the same time. He said he never called the police or 911 because he did not want to get in trouble.

Russin said he finally told the truth to investigators in a follow up interview on June 10, 2003. "I just had, I had enough. I don't know why I just finally felt comfortable to come out with it. It was done. It was over. It was over for me. I felt if I told the truth, it was done."

Hugo and Russin were charged Oct. 6, 2003, for the criminal homicides of James and Keiler and abusing the bodies in the fire pit. Exactly a month later under a negotiated plea deal, and without the benefit of a preliminary hearing, Russin pled guilty to two counts of third degree murder, robbery and abuse of corpse, and a single count of criminal conspiracy. He agreed, according to the plea deal, to testify against his lifelong friend, Hugo. Russin's sentencing hearing was continued many times due to Hugo's trial being postponed.

Four days after being charged with the homicides of James and Keiler, Hugo escaped from the Luzerne County Correctional Facility on Oct. 10, 2003.

# ESCAPE

*"I knew from the beginning I was gonna go. I didn't want to escape until they charged me with murder. I knew the escape was going to cause publicity but not as much as I'd seen."* – Hugo Selenski, June 2, 2004.

Cell 9 on the maximum security level at the Luzerne County Correctional Facility was widely known as "The Cell."

The 18-inch-by-18-inch window opening with one-quarter inch steel mesh and a three-quarter inch metal bar was not repaired properly after being damaged during an escape by inmate Cecil Weldon Robbins on July 30, 1989. Robbins ended up in a small yard in the compound trapped by a razor wire fence, triggering alarms that alerted correctional officers.

Thirteen years later with the Robbins breakout all but forgotten, another escape occurred with different results. What followed was the unbelievable image of a bed sheet rope hanging from Cell 9 and a mattress hanging over the razor wire fence. Scott Bolton, who along with Hugo climbed out the opening, was found critically injured on the roof of another building 70 feet below the opening on the seventh floor. Hugo successfully escaped initiating a three day manhunt until his conditional surrender from the Mount Olivet Road house.

A window, broken in two pieces, was held in place by caulk and its weak metal frame was attached to the brick mortar using what appeared to be rivet pins. The flawed cell window was on the seventh floor of the prison, some 70 feet above the roof of another building and a small yard. An escape was considered impossible. What inmate would risk their life by climbing down 70 feet? Any inmate who made it would be faced with the razor wire fence encircling the yard of the castle-like facility.

At 8 p.m. on Oct. 10, 2003, correctional officers completed a headcount and found all 35 inmates locked in their cells on the maximum security level. Hugo and Bolton were permitted to be cell mates at the request of Hugo. Both were accounted for but less than two hours later, they were missing.

Shortly after 8 p.m., cell doors were opened for inmates to enjoy recreation time in the day room on the level. Hugo was observed using a telephone and Bolton walked undetected by correctional officers into Cell 9, located in the far corner of the cell block and partially hidden from the officers' block post. Inmates were not permitted to go into any other cell but their own, a policy that was not strictly enforced.

Bolton reached up to see how weak the cell window was when a piece of broken glass fell to the pavement in the yard below. When Bolton told Hugo what he did and what happened, the decision to escape was made right then.

Just four days earlier on Oct. 6, Hugo and Patrick Russin were charged in the homicides of Frank James and Adeiye Ossasis Keiler. Hugo was also a suspect in the homicides of Tammy Fassett and Michael Jason Kerkowski, whose bodies were found buried outside Hugo's house. Russin was jailed at a state prison 10 miles away.

Around 9:30 the night of Oct. 10, the overnight supervisor Lieutenant John Barry arrived for work at the prison. Barry was concerned about assignments and meeting minimal staffing requirements considering it was a Friday night. Some 70 feet above Barry on the maximum security level, Hugo and Bolton were preparing to escape. Sometime between 9:40 and 9:45 p.m., the two men used a bed sheet and a broom handle to pull in the flawed cell window frame. They did not need any makeshift chisels to break the window frame from the concrete wall. A mattress was tossed out the opening and a rope of 15 tied-together bedsheets was tied to a metal bunk and thrown out reaching the roof of a lower building where Barry was standing in the shift commander's office. Barry heard a thump above his head, later learning the noise was Bolton landing on the roof above him.

Hugo climbed down the bed sheet rope and was seen through a window by a correctional officer on the second floor. The escape was detected and others were alerted about the attempted get-away. By the time correctional officers positioned themselves outside the perimeter of the facility, Hugo was on the other side of the razor wire fence hidden by the cover of darkness. Hugo ran across Water Street and a small parking lot and down an embankment to the shore of the Susquehanna River, using heavy brush and trees to conceal himself from correctional officers. He hurriedly ran north along the river bank until he came upon railroad tracks near the North Cross Valley Expressway and North River Street in Plains Township. Later that night after Hugo passed the heavily traveled intersection, firefighters and police set up a roadblock using high-wattage lights.

Radio traffic about the escape and search heated up scanners shortly before 10 p.m. Wilkes-Barre police officers pulled up to the jail located in a neighborhood mixed with houses and county-owned buildings about four blocks from center city. By 10:10 p.m., a few reporters arrived in front of the jail standing in the same parking lot where Hugo ran across less than 30 minutes earlier. At the time, reporters knew an escape occurred but were not aware of "who" or how many inmates escaped.

Correctional and police officers holding small hand-held flashlights initially concentrated their searches around the jail. Some walked off and shined their flashlights into parked vehicles and up into trees. The brightest flashlight that night was carried by tow truck driver Robert

Kadluboski, whose company City Wide Towing, had the towing contract for the City of Wilkes-Barre. Wearing a hat with FBI letters, Kadluboski walked around freely mingling with correctional and police officers before saying to one reporter that the escapees were Hugo Selenski and Scott Bolton.

Police summoned the Wilkes-Barre Fire Department for its ladder truck to access the roof. Ladders were placed against the building as armed police officers climbed to the roof balancing along the edge.

There were conflicting reports that both men were still on the roof while other information suggested one inmate made it out. The roof had many dark areas that made it easy for an inmate to hide. Armed officers crawled their way along the roof's edge eventually finding Bolton critically injured at the end of the bed sheet rope.

Police set up battle lines pushing reporters and photographers further away and placing "Do Not Cross" tape in front of the jail. Dim yellow lights casting shadows on the jail's walls highlighted the bed sheets that remained hanging from the cell window. It was a stark image.

Bolton was placed on a stretcher and wheeled out of the jail's front entrance by Wilkes-Barre emergency medical technicians. Before he lost consciousness on the roof, he told a police officer, a correctional officer and a paramedic that Hugo pushed him out the window. Bolton was transported to Community Medical Center in Scranton and later flown by helicopter to the Milton S. Hershey Medical Center, about 90 miles away in Hershey, Pennsylvania.

A few minutes before 10:30 p.m. patrol units from the Pennsylvania State Police at Wyoming and Shickshinny arrived at the jail. State police were not immediately called by jail officials or Luzerne County 911 to respond. Troopers later said they heard "chatter" on their radios about the escape and responded on their own.

Hearing about the escape, Kingston Township Police Chief James Balavage immediately drove to the home of Luzerne County Detective Lieutenant Gary Capitano, one of the two lead investigators on Hugo's case. Unbeknown to Balavage, Capitano was on a hunting trip that weekend.

Shortly before midnight, Luzerne County District Attorney David Lupas arrived at the jail, giving a short impromptu news conference that was broadcasted live on local television stations interrupting night talk shows.

"All available manpower and resources have been called out," Lupas said, adding, "What I really want to do is put the public on guard, particularly for anyone living in the immediate area of the prison. To be on the lookout and be on guard. Obviously, this man is considered dangerous."

*Did Hugo have help from the outside?* a reporter asked.

"I don't have, I'm not in possession of any information of that nature. Investigators are trying to ascertain anything of that nature," Lupas responded. "Obviously, prison officials are being spoken to and interviewed. The warden and prison officials are going to have to offer some explanation as to how this could have occurred. Investigators want to get any information we can from them. I'm very shocked and alarmed and very concerned right now as I think everyone should be. We're going to do everything in our power to see that he's apprehended. If the public sees him or anyone fitting his description, or believe they have any information whatsoever, please be cautious and please notify the authorities immediately."

Lupas quickly ended the brief news conference. About 15 minutes later, a possible Hugo sighting came across police radios. It gave a location at a residence on South River Street in Wilkes-Barre, about two miles south from the jail.

State police troopers and city police officers, including Lupas, hurried to their vehicles racing down North and South River streets passing through red traffic signals with sirens and lights. When they arrived at the double-block house, police learned the sighting was a false report – a man showed up at his house intoxicated and got into an argument with a woman. The drunk man found himself at the wrong end of armed troopers and officers aiming their weapons at him.

For the next several hours, tips about Hugo's whereabouts continued to light up police radios. A report had Hugo getting into a taxi cab and being dropped off on North Washington Street in Wilkes-Barre, while another report had Hugo driving a red pickup truck that crashed on a dirt road in Luzerne, where he previously lived with his girlfriend Christina Strom on Miller Street. A red pickup truck was found in the area but was not linked to Hugo.

Personnel in several boats searched up and down the Susquehanna River aiming bright lights along the shoreline. The river search was called off at 3:45 a.m. due to heavy fog that made the scene even more dramatic. Canine units from the Luzerne County Sheriff's Department and the nearby Department of Veterans Affairs Medical Hospital were brought in to help in the search. Jail officials retrieved some of Hugo's personal belongings from his cell the canines used in an attempt to pick up his scent.

False sightings continued to harass those searching for Hugo. He was reportedly spotted walking across the Veterans Memorial Bridge, located next to the Luzerne County Courthouse that spans the Susquehanna River linking Wilkes-Barre and Kingston. Another bogus sighting had Hugo hiding behind the jail's work release building a block away.

Police and firefighters set up checkpoints along major roadways and heavily traveled intersections within a five mile radius of the jail.

At 4:30 a.m., Lupas held another news conference inside the Luzerne County Emergency Management Building, about 200 yards from the jail.

The EMA building turned into a command post in those early hours of the search. Reporters and photographers were kept in a cramp hallway as Lupas and police officers mingled in the much larger conference room.

Lupas was joined by Pennsylvania State Police Lieutenant Frank Hacken and prison Warden Gene Fischi at the news conference. They stood behind a podium to address the media.

"A massive manhunt is continuing for the capture of Hugo Selenski. There have been a multitude of law enforcement agencies out. Right now, law enforcement is following up on leads. He still remains at large and still considered dangerous. As far as I'm concerned, this is going to be a 24 hour operation," Lupas announced, noting Hugo was wearing gray sweatpants and a white tee-shirt when he escaped. When inmates are taken to court proceedings, they wear jail issued clothing of green, orange or yellow with the jail's LCCF logo on the back. When inmates are locked inside, they are permitted to wear sweatpants, shirts and sweatshirts.

"I'm shocked, upset and disturbed by this happening," Lupas continued. "Obviously, our main concern is finding Selenski and putting him back where he belongs and calling out any and all available resources. Once the fog lifts and they get clearance, we'll have helicopters out. Everything possible that can be done is being done. Local bridges are lit up, fire personnel and EMA personnel throughout the county are assisting us with their equipment in lighting up areas along the river. A number of agencies provided boats and hovercrafts. The close proximity of the prison is an area where they're concentrating their efforts in searching."

"Hugo Selenski has many associates, friends and family in the area. We want to send out a strong message, anyone who aids him, we will aggressively prosecute them," Hacken said, noting interviews were being conducted and the search perimeter was expanding based on intelligence.

Warden Fischi provided some information about events leading up to the escape, including how Hugo and Bolton acquired the bed sheets they devised to climb down the outside wall. "Correctional officers made rounds. Inmates are locked down until 8 p.m. Head counts and rounds were made at 8 p.m. Inmates were let out from 8 to 10 p.m. There were four guards working the floor, one in control (booth)," Fischi explained. "They mingle with the inmates in the day room area. One reported that Selenski was on the telephone at approximately 8 or 8:05 p.m. On that block alone, we have approximately 18 cells that were double bunked. We have about 35 inmates on that block. We're going through, counting sheets to see if they were in fact storing themselves or if anyone gave them their sheets."

Fischi said a jail lieutenant was outside the facility and heard a noise at about 9:40 p.m. At about the same time, a correctional officer on the second floor ran to the command post where Barry was stationed after seeing Hugo outside a window climbing down the bedsheet rope.

"Guards were sent outside the perimeter. That's when we found Scott was still laying up on the roof. He was hurt but there were no signs of Hugo," Fischi said.

Lupas said the investigation, going into its seventh hour, was looking into the possibility that Hugo and Bolton had help on the outside. Investigators were certain to learn how long the two men planned their escape. Lupas warned anyone who assisted and aided Hugo would be "pursued and prosecuted."

Lupas said Hugo's girlfriend Strom, and Michael Stanley Kerkowski and his wife, Geraldine, were aware of what was happening. The Kerkowskis were away on a bus trip when Hugo escaped.

There had been reports of vehicle windows near the jail being smashed shortly after the escape occurred. Hacken did not dismiss a possible connection but reassured every call was being investigated.

A reporter asked, *"Within how many hours do odds of catching Selenski diminish?"*

"It's always nice to catch someone quickly," Hacken responded, "We're confident in our investigation, our intelligence is better so a day or two. We'll catch him and he will be prosecuted for the homicides he committed."

Despite a mattress being seen over the barbed wire fence, Hacken said he could not confirm if a mattress had been used in the escape. Fischi said the height of Cell 9 where Hugo and Bolton escaped is 70 feet above the roof of a lower building where Barry had been standing inside.

Lupas ended the news conference saying the command post would be moved to the state police barracks in Wyoming, about seven miles north of the jail and on the west side of the Susquehanna River.

Undetected and hidden by the cover of darkness, Hugo followed the railroad tracks along the river and walked under a bridge for the North Cross Valley Expressway. He kept walking until the tracks veered to the right across River Street in Jenkins Township, about four miles north of the jail and about 200 yards south from the Eighth Street Bridge. Sometime in the early morning hours on Oct. 11, Hugo knocked on the door of his aunt, Catherine Falzone, on Stark Street in Pittston. Falzone knew Hugo had escaped, allowing him to enter her home.

Hugo was kept in a second floor bedroom given food, a change of clothes and permitted to use the telephone. Sometime in the late evening hours on Oct. 12 or early morning on Oct. 13, state police Trooper Leo Hannon Jr. received information Hugo was at the Stark Street residence. At 3:30 a.m. on Oct. 13, Hannon knocked on the door and spoke with Falzone and her 17-year-old son. The two were transported to the Wyoming barracks and separately questioned giving identical statements.

Falzone said at about 7:30 p.m. on Saturday, Oct. 11, she gave Hugo a change of clothes, $14, a bottle of water and a ride to a wooded area on "Orange Road" in the Back Mountain where Hugo claimed he had a car waiting for him. Orange Road does not appear on any municipal map in the Back Mountain.

Prior to Hugo's whereabouts becoming known at the Stark Street house, the search continued on Saturday and Sunday. A house on Blackman Street in Wilkes-Barre, the same house that Russin claimed stolen handguns were traded for crack in January, and a house in the Breslau section of Hanover Township, were searched based on false tips. Strom's house on Mount Olivet Road in Kingston Township was visited several times by state police. Eventually, Strom's house was placed under 24 hour surveillance.

Lupas briefed the media again at 5 p.m. Saturday, Oct. 11, in the parking lot at the state police barracks in Wyoming. By this time, the forensic services unit of the state police processed Cell 9 and recovered the bed sheet rope, a broomstick and bed sheet used to pull in the flawed cell window frame, and the mattress. With no knowledge of Hugo's whereabouts, Lupas was more critical of the jail and county officials. The only new information involved the filing of escape charges against Hugo.

"My job as a prosecutor is to prosecute criminals," Lupas began, "Selenski was incarcerated after thousands of man hours that have been put in this investigation. As to how he escaped, other people are going to have to answer to the public for that and answer those questions, being prison officials and county officials. Some of the common sense questions the public has, are the same common sense questions that I have which is very simple, 'How can something like this occur in this day and age in the year 2003 when an inmate can simply pop a window out of the prison, climb out and run away.' That's very alarming and very discouraging and very concerning to me. Investigators have been receiving a number of leads and tips throughout the day. They are following up on each and everyone of them. We hope to make some progress."

A reporter asked, *Did Selenski or Bolton have help from the inside?*

"That's a question and a concern of how they got out," Lupas responded, "The fact of the matter is he did get out. Selenski is out. The number one priority is his capture. How it happened, obviously, it will be looked at. I intend to notify the Department of Corrections of the state that they should probably take a look at this entire situation. There are common sense questions from the public and there are common sense questions that I have. How did these two individuals come in possession of 12 or more bed sheets? I'm extremely concerned with the escape for someone who we consider a very dangerous subject."

Lupas did not respond to a question whether investigators knew the person Hugo had been talking to on the jail telephone before he escaped.

The district attorney told reporters he did not know if Hugo had changed his clothes, or if there was any evidence if Hugo injured himself when he climbed over the barbed wire fence. When asked again about Kerkowski's parents, Michael Stanley and his wife Geraldine, Lupas responded: "Obviously, they've been notified. I don't want to say they're under protective custody but they've been advised and are taking appropriate measures."

"I'm very upset and very concerned with what happened," Lupas continued in his criticism of the jail and county officials. "I'm focusing and investigators are focusing all their energies right now in apprehending Selenski. A study or review of the prison would be a question that needs to be answered after these priorities are settled first. An escape of this nature is inexcusable and unacceptable. That's plain and simple."

Wyoming Valley residents remained on edge considering what they read about Hugo in the two local newspapers: The Times Leader and the Citizens' Voice. Hugo escaped four days after he was criminally charged with two counts of criminal homicide, robbery, abuse of corpse and a single count of criminal conspiracy. He was charged the same day when several search warrant affidavits were unsealed describing a series of horrors in which Weakley described Hugo killing 18 people, and the reported abduction of a female college student from Penn State University in State College, Pa., on Halloween in 2001. Weakley further claimed he saw bones and jaw fragments under the porch at the Mount Olivet Road house, one of Hugo's dogs carrying a human arm and a body floating in the well, the water source for the house. Information in the search warrant affidavits painted a picture of a mad man.

Saturday, Oct. 11 ended with no confirmed sighting of Hugo. The next day, Sunday, Lupas and state police Trooper Tom Kelly briefed the media in the parking lot at the state police barracks. It was coming up on 48 hours after Hugo escaped.

"From my standpoint, I just want everyone to know that thousands of man hours were put into an investigation and incarceration of Hugo Selenski and to have this occur, to me, is quite unbelievable. Personally, I'm angry, frustrated and disgusted by this chain of events and prison officials, I think, have a lot of explaining to do and a lot of questions to answer."

Lupas questioned how Hugo and Bolton, who twice escaped while out on the prison's work release program, were permitted to become cell mates. "I'm not anyone who runs the prison but my common sense leads me to believe that that person (Bolton) is a high escape risk. And I'm concerned about the fact that he was teamed up with Mr. Selenski as a cellmate."

Monday morning, Oct. 13, Luzerne County First Assistant District Attorney Joseph Carmody, who would later become an elected magisterial district judge, and Hugo's lawyer, Demetrius Fannick, appeared on NBC's *Today* morning show while Lupas went on CBS's *The Morning Show.* Carmody and Lupas were linked by satellite from inside the Luzerne County Courthouse while Fannick was inside the studio of *Today* in New York City. Both segments featured Hugo's escape and showed videos of the bed sheets hanging from the cell window at the jail.

Lupas and Carmody appeared on the national televised Monday morning news shows but did not disclose Hannon's visit to the Falzone house in Pittston late Sunday night into Monday morning.

Later in the afternoon, the Luzerne County Prison Board consisting of the three county commissioners, Thomas Pizano, Thomas Makowski and Stephen Urban, and two appointed lay persons, Dr. Thomas Kowalski and Constance Wynn, joined Warden Fischi, deputy wardens Benjamin Grevera and Roland Roberts, and county solicitor James Blaum, at a news conference inside the courthouse. Not only was the local media covering the dramatic story, reporters from the Associated Press, CNN and FOX News began showing up in the Wyoming Valley. Before the prison board and county officials began their news conference, they agreed to only allow Fischi address the media. No other person, including the elected commissioners, talked or provided information on how Hugo escaped. Throughout the hour-long conference, Makowski routinely whispered in

Blaum's ear who, in turn, whispered in Fischi's ear when he felt a question should be avoided. Makowski was the former commissioner chairman, a post that was held by Pizano, who were both Democrats, while Urban was the lone Republican commissioner.

Beginning from a prepared statement, Fischi assured the public that the jail was safe.

"Since the discovery of the escape, steps were immediately taken to ensure against any type of copycat attempt. At this time, I want to ensure the community and general public that the Luzerne County Correctional Facility is a secure institution. A thorough review of the main facility, including the cell tower has been completed and we have determined that all cells, doors and windows are secure. Since I became warden in 1994, this is the first escape of an inmate from the main facility to the exterior of the prison walls. We, the Luzerne County Prison Board and the prison administration accept full responsibility," Fischi said in the prepared statement.

Fischi announced that steps had been taken to review the policies, procedures and personnel performance of prison employees, including an inspection of the main facility. He said county Engineer Jim Brozena had been instructed to seek experts in prison construction to review its operations. Seven years earlier, Fischi made county officials aware the jail was "busting at the seams" and the design of the structure would pose a problem with overcrowding. After he finished reading the prepared statement, Fischi offered to "take limited questions" from reporters.

First question: *"Should you resign?"*

"No, I don't believe I should resign. I feel we took every effort we can. We did everything we could. At this point and time, it's under investigation."

A reporter asked, *"Are there motion detectors in this place, on the outside and if so, were they functioning?"*

"The only motion detectors we have on the outside of the building are in…" Fischi began saying until Blaum offered an answer: "I'm going to interrupt there, I believe that's a security issue, the warden can speak generally; I don't want him to say where any motion detectors might be located."

Fischi was asked a second time about motion detectors in which he replied, "Again, that could be a security issue. I really can't answer that."

Fischi claimed 911 was called from the jail after Barry heard a thump on the roof above him and a correctional officer saying there was an escape. "He immediately hit the siren for the escape and contacted 911 for assistance."

Addressing a concern Lupas had earlier expressed, Fischi confirmed Bolton had twice escaped while on work release, a special program granted by judges that allows inmates to leave the jail for employment. "What happened was, (Bolton) never returned to the facility."

Fischi then described to reporters the layout of the maximum security level, saying the fifth and fourth floors – the seventh floor when standing outside looking at the cell tower – are tiers.

"On the fifth floor, we have 18 cells. With those cells, we have approximately 35 inmates. And they might mingle only on that floor. Even when they go to yard (exercise), they have the yard up on the roof of the facility. The only way you would come down is if they're going to court or to see a doctor or something."

A reporter asked if inmates are permitted in other cells other than their assigned cell?

"There has never been a practice that prisoners can go in anybody else's cell. If they happen to go in a cell, they are written up with a misconduct, and they go in front of a board which determines whether they are guilty and then a misconduct is issued and they are locked up for a length of time." Fischi explained.

Reporters continued to grill Fischi about motion detectors and surveillance cameras. Built in 1865, the castle-like structure was designed to house 90 inmates. An $11 million construction project in the mid-1980s included a seven story prison tower – the one Hugo escaped from – that raised the inmate capacity to 250 inmates in single cells. Since the opening of the prison tower in 1987, 229 cells were changed to double-occupancy without the approval from the Pennsylvania Department of Labor and Industry. Six day rooms in the prison tower were converted to living space with each capable of holding 12 inmates. During a routine inspection by the Department of Labor and Industry, the converted day rooms were found not to be acceptable housing areas. Prison officials had to dismantle the bunks that were used for 12 inmates in each day room or face hefty punishments and fines.

Fischi said there were 520 inmates housed at the jail the night of Hugo's escape.

Responding to another question about motion detectors and surveillance cameras, Blaum said the prison tower was erected in 1983 subject to policies and procedures at that time.

"We have never been found to be non-compliant with regard to the windows or any other part of the structure of the facility since the tower was erected in 1983 and opened in 1987," Blaum said, adding that the strength and security of the cell windows were intact. "As we stated in our statement, our engineer is going to bring in consultants to review that issue. As the warden stated, a review of all windows in the facility have been made and it has been determined that none have been tampered with and we're confident in their security."

"We had at least three major checks, we called in extra staff, we went through that place at least three different times and the reports I received were there was no other tampering," Fischi said about inspecting the cell windows since the escape.

A reporter asked Fischi if any cells were missing bed sheets. Blaum immediately answered saying, "That is still subject of an investigation. There has been no determination made as yet whether or not other cells in that block were used or part of this escape plan."

Blaum said each cell has two beds and each bed has two sheets. He refused to answer in which cell the mattress was taken from.

Regarding Hugo's clothing, Fischi said inmates wear their own clothes. "They have their own clothing, in other words, they purchase their own sweat (pants), of course, that's what they sleep in also. If they ever leave that floor for any reason, they must be in uniform. But when they're on the floor, they are basically lounging like you would be in your own home. The cell is their home and basically, they lounge in their sweatpants and T-shirts."

Fischi, Blaum and the prison board ended the one-hour news conference saying if Hugo was captured, he'll likely be housed on the same floor in which he escaped.

Not to be outdone by the prison board, Lupas – whose office is across a foyer from where the prison board's news conference was held in the commissioner's meeting room – held his own, his fourth in four days. Local reporters who were used to Lupas' demeanor noticed a difference in his tone and body language. He repeated many of his previous statements criticizing the jail and its officials.

"In advance, I can tell you there isn't a whole lot of news to report," Lupas began, "other than what I've been briefing you on and telling you all along, obviously, there's been a number of leads, leads continue to come in to investigators, and they're following up on each and every lead they receive. This is a massive manhunt, numerous resources have been brought in, numerous law enforcement agencies have been brought in to assist with the search. As I stated previously, law enforcement officers have been working non stop since this incident occurred Friday evening and they will continue to work non stop until Hugo Selenski is captured and reincarcerated in prison where he belongs."

Lupas did not release information that Hugo stayed at the Pittston house of his aunt, Catherine Falzone, or that Falzone and her son were questioned by investigators at the state police barracks.

"I don't want to comment because that would reveal some information pertaining to the investigation," Lupas said in response to a question if investigators were closer to capturing Hugo. "Obviously, we're not stating or confirming any actual sightings of Mr. Selenski or anything of that nature. There are a number of leads, again, every lead that comes in is pursued and followed up and state police continue to do that."

The district attorney continued to criticize the prison and its operations, intentionally side-stepping questions about this "massive search" for Hugo.

"We, and I are not in charge in the running of the prison. I know some of your questions and many of your questions revolve around that issue. Our job, as law enforcement, is to investigate and prosecute crime. When we place someone in the prison, it is the prison's responsibility and prison officials responsibility to ensure their security of that facility and of the public. As I stated previously, there are numerous questions that arise that pop into everyone's head. Those questions need to be addressed by prison officials. They've got a lot of explaining to do and a lot of questions to answer," Lupas said.

Asked by a reporter how many people or agencies are involved in the search for Hugo, Lupas replied: "There are numerous law enforcement agencies ranging from the state police who brought in a substantial amount of manpower, county detectives from the district attorney's office, Wilkes-Barre police and local police. A briefing was held Saturday with local police departments in all the neighboring municipalities. There are probably hundreds of law enforcement personnel who are on the lookout in some way shape or form working on this case. In addition, there was a nationwide alert for Mr. Selenski."

What Lupas left out was the involvement of four New York City police officers trained in apprehending fugitives. The four NYPD kept a watchful eye on Hugo's Kingston Township house. Members of the U.S. Marshal's Fugitive Task Force and the Luzerne County Sheriff's Department were also involved in the manhunt.

State police Trooper Tom Kelly said the FOX show *America's Most Wanted* planned to do a segment about Hugo's escape but Major League Baseball playoffs preempted the show.

A reporter asked, *"Selenski's family doesn't think he may be a danger to the community. What are your thoughts on that?"*

"I think he made a daring escape, he took a lot of chances to escape from prison. That leads me to believe he may be willing to take a lot of chances in eluding police so that's why I believe the public should be aware very cautiously," Lupas responded.

Lupas' news conference ended just before 5 p.m. Television reporters and photographers ran over each other leaving the commissioners' meeting room to get to their satellite trucks parked outside the courthouse to prepare for their upcoming broadcast.

Prior to Lupas' news conference, Assistant District Attorney Tim Doherty told a reporter that authorities had no idea where Hugo was hiding. A great fear among investigators, Doherty said, involved Hugo acquiring a vehicle.

Shortly after 9 p.m. Monday, Oct. 13, state police informed the media Hugo had been captured. It was quickly learned Hugo was already at the state police barracks in Wyoming awaiting to be transported to Magisterial District Judge John Hopkins in Edwardsville to be arraigned on the escape charges. A news conference about Hugo's capture was scheduled for 10 p.m. at the barracks.

The parking lot was filled with local and national reporters, photographers and law enforcement personnel. Local television networks interrupted regular scheduled programming and CNN aired the news conference live. Before what probably was the largest gathering of reporters and photographers Lupas ever encountered, he stood behind a podium with a row of law enforcement officers behind him.

"I'm very pleased and happy to report that at 8:47 p.m., Hugo Selenski was back in custody of law enforcement," Lupas said. "Members of the Pennsylvania State Police had him in custody after he turned himself in at that time. I want to say that I believe it was the non-stop, persistence and hard work and the pressure put out in the public by all members of law enforcement which caused Mr. Selenski to turn himself in. Again, as I stated earlier, we had a very unfortunate incident occur last Friday, but I'm proud and happy to report to you as I predicted earlier when I stated that it was a matter of time whether it took a day, a week or a month that law enforcement would not stop until Mr. Selenski was back in custody and back behind bars where he belongs."

Lupas never used the word "capture," when he provided a few details to how Hugo was apprehended. As it turned out, Hugo orchestrated his own surrender from the Mount Olivet Road house where the bodies of Tammy Fassett and Michael Jason Kerkowski, and the charred remains of Frank James, Adeiye Keiler and an unidentified person were found months earlier.

While Lupas said Hugo would be lodged "in a prison at an undisclosed location," the media quickly learned he would be incarcerated at the State Correctional Institution at Dallas, about 10 miles away in Jackson Township.

"As far as where he was over the past 72 hours, the investigation is continuing," Lupas said. "Investigators are continuing to try to trace back his whereabouts, where he was, who he came in contact with and whether anyone aided, abetted or assisted him or harbored him while he was considered a fugitive. That investigation is not stopping and is continuing."

Hugo called his court appointed lawyer, Demetrius Fannick, to arrange his surrender, specifically requesting two law enforcement officers: State Police Lieutenant Richard Krawatz and Kingston Township Police Officer

Charles Rauschkolb. Hugo wanted Fannick to be present and not to alert the media until he was in custody.

Lupas said at the Monday evening news conference that "There were no deals or anything of that nature given the terms of his surrender. I'm not going to comment on how the contact came about other than law enforcement was contacted and he voluntarily turned himself in."

State Police Captain Carmen Altavilla, commander at the state police barracks in Wyoming, said authorities were at the Kingston Township house every day since Hugo's escape. Altavilla dodged questions about the house being kept under 24 hour surveillance.

Sometime between 4 and 5 p.m. on Oct. 13, state police troopers visited the house and asked Christina Strom, Hugo's girlfriend, if she was willing to consent to a search of her property. She refused, Altavilla said.

While Lupas said it was unknown how long Hugo was at the house, several law enforcement officials said they believed he was inside the house for more than a day.

Hugo was transported to District Judge Hopkins' courtroom where he was arraigned on charges of escape and weapons for escape. He was wearing fatigue pants and a purple T-shirt, different clothing than the sweatpants he wore when he escaped. Strom would later say she was eating at a restaurant when Hugo went to the house. Hugo left a note for her saying he "loved her."

The discovery of the bodies and charred human remains and Hugo's escape made him known nationally.

Not only did Lupas, Carmody and Fannick appear on the national morning news shows, Fannick provided his own account of what led up to Hugo's surrender in media interviews.

A few hours before Hugo turned himself in, his father, Ronald Selenski, was featured on one of the local television networks pleading for his son to surrender. After that broadcast, Hugo phoned his father and said he hated how the media was treating his family.

At 7:45 p.m., Hugo called Fannick from the Mount Olivet Road house.

"He had made some requests and asked if I could negotiate those requests," Fannick said. "I contacted the state police and informed them I needed to speak with Krawetz. He called me back and I told Krawetz that Selenski had contacted me and was ready to surrender." Fannick said Krawetz had to check with his superiors regarding Hugo's requests.

"There were minor things going back and forth about whether I would be allowed. My client requested me to be there. I didn't want anything to be messed up," Fannick said.

State police agreed to Hugo's terms. Krawetz and Rauschkolb met Fannick at the end of the gravel driveway to the Mount Olivet Road property at 8:45 p.m. As they drove toward the house, Fannick noticed the outside flood lights were turned on.

"As we got closer to the house, Mr. Selenski walked out with his hands in the air. Krawetz, Officer Rauschkolb and I got out of the cars. They asked Mr. Selenski to step off the porch into the driveway and asked him to kneel down and to put his hands behind his head. He immediately complied without incident. I don't think there were any weapons drawn," Fannick recalled.

Fannick said Strom was not inside the house when Hugo called him at 7:45 p.m., and she was not inside when Hugo surrendered 62 minutes later.

A month after Hugo surrendered, the Pennsylvania Department of Corrections on Nov. 13, 2003, issued a report of their security review of the Luzerne County Correctional Facility. Eleven days later on Nov. 24, a report by Robert Kimball & Associates, an architectural and engineering firm hired to study the jail, was released. Both reports contained heavily redacted findings and recommendations.

The DOC report was most damaging. It claimed "Staff complacency and inattentiveness to duty characterized by reading newspapers and watching television while on duty appeared to be the norm at the Luzerne County Correctional Facility. This, along with the absence of fundamental security practices including tool control, key control, search procedures, inmate accountability, places the facility at considerable risk for further undesirable events to occur."

The report by Robert Kimball & Associates was less critical, identifying the jail as an outdated indirect surveillance facility. "While staff is in many cases the last line of defense in preventing escapes, the existing prison is severely overcrowded and the design is outdated. These two factors complicate matters to a large degree when it comes to preventing escapes and maintaining security," the Kimball report stated.

The Kimball report found cells designed for one inmate housed two inmates and with the doubling of each cell at the Luzerne County Correctional Facility increases many "accidents waiting to happen."

During an interview on Feb. 17, 2004, Fischi said he was surprised by the DOC report, saying he never witnessed any correctional officers reading newspapers or watching television while on duty. Fischi again explained that Hugo and Bolton were cellmates among 35 inmates on the maximum-security level on the fifth floor that was designed to hold 18 inmates. Prison officials were forced to place two inmates per cell due to overcrowding, Fischi said, noting each inmate is provided two bed sheets that are washed once a week.

"You have 72 sheets on that block because you have 35 or 36 inmates. Their cell alone had four sheets and four sheets from the cell they went out of," Fischi said about the escape. "If he (Selenski) went up to any of the weaker inmates up there and says, 'I want four of your sheets or I want those sheets out of there,' they're going to give it up and not say anything about it."

Fischi suggested Hugo and Bolton, who both had muscular physiques, likely intimidated other inmates for their bed sheets. Hugo and Bolton manufactured a 'shank' from an electrical cover and had a plate full of pepper acquired from little packets delivered with meals.

"What I found basically, a pan of pepper which would blind an individual and a receptacle taken off the wall that might have been sharpened to maybe use as a weapon," Fischi said.

Fischi then talked about the notorious window in Cell 9.

"The last time the window was broken was in 1989. I was the business manager at the time and not in tune to what was going on. I believe there was a court case against the window manufacturer," Fischi recalled. "We did know there was a problem with the welded bars on the window. It's every window, it's the same way. The DOC will tell you that no prison can guarantee you that they'll never have an escape. This same team will go up and recommend changes to their own facilities.

"My heart just fell," Fischi said about the night of Hugo's daring escape. "I couldn't believe it. I didn't think anyone would have the guts to go out that way. My main concern at that point was to find out if anyone was missing. We were running around the perimeter, checking the roofs, checking these offices, checking anywhere where they could possibly go. I always have concerns.

"Can I sit here and say I guarantee no one can escape this prison? That's a hard pill to swallow. I don't think anyone can tell you that. I will be much more relieved once I get the outside perimeter fence. I do have concerns about the windows in this place. And I'm not just talking about the window, that window. That cell is closed and is locked and will stay that way."

It took more than a year before the window in Cell 9 was repaired and the cell itself reopened.

During a jailhouse interview from the State Correctional Facility at Dallas on June 2, 2004, Hugo admitted he was going to escape soon after he was imprisoned at the county prison on June 5, 2003.

"I knew from the beginning I was going to go. I didn't want to escape until they charged me with murder. I knew the escape was going to cause publicity but not as much as I'd seen," Hugo said.

Hugo claimed Bolton approached him with the idea to escape in September 2003, soon after Bolton was captured after being on the run for more than two years. Bolton failed to return to the prison while on work release, a program where inmates can go to a job and return to the prison at the end of their shifts.

"The man is a moron," Hugo said of Bolton. "When he got there, he came right up to me and asked if I wanted to escape. I told him he was in no physical shape to go. I told him to do push ups, lose weight. I could have escaped out of any cell."

Hugo denied he pushed Bolton out the cell window, a claim Bolton has made.

In a letter dated Aug. 12, 2004, addressed to the Luzerne County Clerk of Court's office requesting a new public defender, Bolton stated: "…try real hard to understand that I'm just a lot confused because of gaps in my memory – all connected to me being pushed/thrown out a window of 80 to 100 feet by a nut case multi-murderer Mr. Selenski where in I died and was brought back and put into a medically induced coma while doctors, and surgeon, great ones I'd say put me (Humpty Dumpty) back together again."

"Bolton went around saying I pushed him. He was too big. I told him not to go because he wasn't in shape. He lost his grip and fell in front of me," Hugo said.

Hugo claimed he was the first to climb down the bed sheets and waited for Bolton to force himself out the cell window. That appears unlikely considering Fischi said a correctional officer saw him through a second floor window and alerted others to the escape. Hugo was not going to wait around on the roof for Bolton to climb down the bed sheets while correctional officers were alerted to the escape and running outside the facility.

Hugo said he walked north along railroad tracks and heard the boats searching the Susquehanna River. From that statement, Hugo most likely stayed along the river at least until 3:45 a.m. on Oct. 11, 2003, when the river search was called off due to heavy fog that had settled. While on his way to his aunt's residence on Stark Street in Pittston, Hugo said he walked past a police officer.

"I walked right by a police officer; I think it was in Pittston and he looked me straight in the face. I asked him how he was doing," Hugo claimed.

Hugo said he regretted getting his aunt, Catherine Falzone, involved by going to her residence where he hid for a day. He also denied seeing his girlfriend, Christina Strom, during his flight of freedom.

State police charged Falzone on Feb. 4, 2004, with hindering apprehension or prosecution and obstructing administration of law for her alleged role in permitting Hugo to stay at her house. The criminal complaint that charged Falzone was written by Trooper Leo Hannon Jr., who also filed the escape charge against Hugo.

The criminal complaint says Hannon knocked on the front door at Falzone's residence at about 3:30 a.m. on Oct. 13, 2003. Falzone and her

17-year-old son agreed to be questioned about Hugo, and were provided a ride to the state police barracks in Wyoming.

There, Falzone told investigators she heard a knock on her front door in the early morning hours of Oct. 11. As she opened the door, she saw her nephew, Hugo, and invited him inside. Falzone told investigators she was aware Hugo escaped having seen media reports the night before. Hugo stayed at Falzone's house until the evening hours of Oct. 11, when Falzone provided Hugo a ride to Orange Road in Kingston Township. Falzone claimed Hugo told her he had a car waiting for him. Falzone added she "wanted to call (police) and was planning to call" but had not done so, according to the criminal complaint.

Falzone's case would linger through the court system for years. Under a negotiated plea deal filed on Oct. 5, 2006, Falzone pled guilty to obstructing administration of law. Prosecutors withdrew the hindering charge against Falzone. She agreed to testify against Hugo at trial.

A technicality also caused Hugo's escape case to drag on through the court system for years as District Attorney David W. Lupas and Judge Peter Paul Olszewski Jr. battled the merits of the case.

Lupas and his team of prosecutors believed the escape case merged with the homicide case for the preliminary hearing.

When a criminal case is filed in the Luzerne County Clerk of Courts office, a docket number is assigned to that particular case for identification purposes. A criminal case is filed with the clerk of court only after the preliminary hearing. Hugo had yet to have a preliminary hearing on the homicide charges when he escaped from prison.

After Hugo's apprehension and the filing of escape charges, prosecutors filed a petition on Oct. 17, 2003, to transfer the escape case to Magisterial District Judge James Tupper, who would preside over the preliminary hearing on the homicide charges.

Luzerne County President Judge Michael T. Conahan authorized the transfer of the escape case to Tupper for the preliminary hearing, which was held Dec. 18, 2003.

Tupper determined prosecutors established a case against Hugo, sending the homicide charges for the shotgun killings of Frank James and Adeiye Keiler to county court. Hugo, through his attorney, Demetrius Fannick, waived the escape case to county court, neglecting to hear any witness testimony about the escape.

When the two separate cases were filed in the clerk of courts office, the homicide case was tagged 3966-2003 and the escape case was given 3967-2003.

Throughout pre-trial court proceedings, those two docket numbers appeared on disposition sheets, petitions and motions. It was not until Jan. 26, 2006, when Fannick filed a motion seeking to have the escape charges dismissed claiming prosecutors "never filed a written notice" to consolidate the escape case with the homicide case.

Fannick further argued prosecutors failed to bring Hugo to trial for the escape in a timely manner under the speedy trial rule, known in Pennsylvania as Rule 600. Hugo was arraigned for the escape on Oct. 13, 2003, and should have been brought to trial within one year, or 365 days. When Fannick sought to have a judge dismiss the escape charges on Jan. 26, 2006, 839 days had passed.

Prosecutors immediately responded by filing their own motion in court seeking to have Fannick's request rejected to have the escape charges tossed out. Prosecutors claimed disposition sheets contained the two docket numbers pertaining to both the homicide and escape cases. "There have been numerous status conferences, discovery hearings, suppression hearings ordered and held by the court, all of which are docketed and pertain to both 3966 and 3967 of 2003," according to a motion prosecutors filed in response to Fannick's request to dismiss the escape case. Prosecutors further claimed that the trial management order written and filed by Judge Olszewski on Jan. 16, 2004, included the homicide and escape docket numbers.

In a one page order dated Feb. 15, 2006, Olszewski granted Fannick's motion dismissing the escape charges against Hugo, which infuriated

Lupas. Attached to the order was an opinion written by Olszewski explaining his reason why he dismissed the escape charges.

Referring to the prosecutors' argument that Conahan permitted the transfer of the homicide and escape charges to a magisterial district judge for a preliminary hearing, Olszewski said the authorization by Conahan did not fulfill the consolidation legal requirement.

"The commonwealth's petition requested to transfer venue and jurisdiction of the escape charges to the district (judge) having venue and jurisdiction over the homicide charges. Neither the commonwealth's petition, nor Judge Conahan's order mentions joinder of cases for trial," Olszewski opined. "It is even more obvious that Judge Conahan was neither requested nor did he independently contemplate whether the mandatory criteria (of consolidation) were present."

Olszewski continued to criticize the district attorney's office in his opinion, ruling that prosecutors failed to let known the cases were consolidated, and only moved to consolidate the escape and homicide cases after Fannick had requested the escape charges be dismissed. Olszewski said prosecutors failed to establish that Rule 582, the Pennsylvania statute that consolidates separate criminal cases for trial, was authorized by Conahan. After Olszewski issued his ruling on dismissing the escape charge, a clearly angry and upset Lupas held a brief news conference with reporters in the courthouse rotunda, two floors below Olszewski's chambers.

"We completely and wholeheartedly disagree with the court's decision to dismiss the escape related charges," Lupas said while biting his lower lip. "We believe the court had ignored the complete record of the case where in the court itself, had continually treated and recognized the charges as being consolidated in its management and scheduling (order) of the case. If not, why didn't the court hold the trial on the escape charges when they were originally listed and scheduled. Review the docket, the court orders treated them as one and continued and rescheduled them as one case. Quite frankly, I'm taken back by the court's decision. Our prosecution team remains focused and ready to forge ahead in this case. But a decision such as this may warrant an appellate review by a higher court."

Olszewski issued his ruling to dismiss the escape charges against Hugo two weeks before Hugo's trial for the killings of Frank James and Adeiye Keiler would begin. Prosecutors immediately filed an appeal of Olszewski's dismissal of the escape charges to the Pennsylvania Superior Court.

The appellate court on Feb. 6, 2007, reinstated the escape charges against Hugo.

When prosecutors filed a petition to transfer the escape case for a preliminary hearing with the homicide case before District Judge James Tupper, the appellate court ruled that action in itself, "Most certainly gave notice to both Selenski and the trial court of the Commonwealth's intention to pursue the charges together. This conclusion is borne out of Judge Olszewski's trial management order of Jan. 16, 2004, which included the docket number of (escape)…"

Hugo's trial for the killings of James and Keiler ended in March 2006. The Pennsylvania Superior Court reinstated the escape charges on Feb. 6, 2007. As time went on, Hugo would face the escape charges with other attorneys.

After the homicide trial for the victims James and Keiler ended, Fannick withdrew from representing Hugo, saying he could no longer work for free as he did for nearly three years. Attorney Michael Senape was appointed by a county judge to represent Hugo on the escape case. When Senape resigned from being a conflict lawyer in February 2010, Attorney David Lampman II was appointed June 17, 2010, to represent Hugo on the escape case.

Lampman filed a motion on Sept. 9, 2010, to continue the escape trial claiming he needed more time to review thousands of pages of discovery material provided to him by the district attorney's office, and to inquire about the 20 people investigators had interviewed about the escape.

Luzerne County Judge Chester Muroski, who would eventually preside over Hugo's cases for a time, denied Lampman's request to continue the escape trial.

Nearly seven years after he climbed down a rope of bed sheets from the seventh floor at the county prison, Hugo pleaded guilty to escape and weapons or implements for escape during a court hearing on Sept. 16, 2010. In exchange for the guilty plea, the district attorney's office withdrew the case against Falzone.

# PAT RUSSIN'S PLEA AGREEMENT

After being charged along with Hugo for the murders and burning the bodies of Frank James and Adeiye Keiler, Patrick Raymond Russin was jailed at the Pike County Prison, about a 60 mile drive from the Luzerne County Courthouse. Following his conditional surrender on Oct. 10, 2003, Hugo was jailed at the State Correctional Institution at Dallas in Jackson Township, about 10 miles from the courthouse.

On Nov. 3, 2003, then Luzerne County President Judge Michael T. Conahan signed an order allowing Russin to be released into the custody of state police for the purpose of transporting him to the state police barracks in Wyoming and afterwards, the Luzerne County Courthouse on Nov. 6, 2003.

Late in the afternoon, Russin appeared with his attorney, William Joseph Ruzzo, before Conahan where a plea agreement was to be presented. Assistant district attorneys Joseph P. Giovannini and Ingrid S. Cronin were representatives from the district attorney's office.

Without the benefit of a preliminary hearing, Russin agreed to plead guilty to two counts of third degree murder, two counts of robbery, two counts of abuse of corpse and one count of criminal conspiracy to commit robbery. As customary in the court of common pleas, Conahan questioned Russin with questions to analyze his mental well-being and if he understood the plea agreement. Russin said he understood.

Giovannini advised Conahan that sentencing guidelines called for a sentence of 20 to 40 years in state prison.

"You understand fully what's going on here today?" the judge asked, to which, Russin replied, "Yes, I do."

Giovannini reviewed the plea agreement in open court indicating the agreement would require Russin to cooperate with investigators, testify against Hugo and Russin's sentencing hearing will be held after the completion of Hugo's trial for the murders of Frank James and Adeiye Keiler.

Conahan accepted the plea agreement as the court proceeding ended at 4:45 p.m. on Nov. 6, 2003.

Hugo's attorney, Demetrius "Tim" Fannick, said he was not surprised by the plea agreement but questioned the timing and also questioned Russin's credibility as Russin provided misleading information several times to investigators.

A day after Russin pled guilty, District Attorney Lupas withdrew the robbery case against Hugo involving the swindling of cash from Kerkowski's father, Michael Stanley Kerkowski, during visits to the elder Kerkowski's home in 2002. Lupas told reporters he withdrew the robbery case against Hugo due to the ongoing investigation of the homicides. It was the robbery charges filed against Hugo on June 5, 2003, the day the

Mount Olivet Road property was searched, which kept him in jail on high bail. Now that Hugo was charged with criminal homicide, which is a non-bailable offense in Pennsylvania, he was not going anywhere. The withdrawal of the robbery case allowed investigators, detectives and prosecutors to focus their time and energy on the homicide cases.

With Russin's murder case all wrapped up with a plea agreement, prosecutors had to present evidence to establish a case against Hugo at the preliminary hearing before Magisterial District Judge James Tupper, the same district judge that arraigned him on several previous cases, including the criminal homicide case on Oct. 6, 2003.

The preliminary hearing was held Dec. 18, 2003. As agreed upon, Russin testified against his former friend. And as expected, District Judge Tupper sent Hugo's criminal homicide charges to Luzerne County Court to be settled.

Enter Luzerne County Judge Peter Paul Olszewski Jr.

Hugo's criminal case was assigned to Judge Olszewski, a former district attorney himself before being elected to the judicial bench in the 1999 election. Lupas was an assistant district attorney during Olszewski's entire tenure as district attorney and successfully campaigned to win the seat during the same election year.

Despite having a five year age difference between the two legal professionals, they seemed not to get along from the many courtroom squabbles and difference of opinions. Their turbulent relationship dates back years and showed its ugly head during the homicide case of Henry Stubbs III, who stood trial for the horrific killings of a woman and her 6-year-old daughter in Wilkes-Barre on Dec. 7, 2001. During a pre-trial hearing of Stubbs on Dec. 7, 2002, Judge Olszewski blasted Lupas saying the district attorney was "unprofessional and unprepared." Lupas personally prosecuted Stubbs, who was convicted in the two murders and sentenced to life in prison without parole.

The legal community and certainly those reporters who covered the courthouse were aware Olszewski and Lupas did not get along, personally and professionally. It was only a matter of time before their tensions erupted. Only this time, Lupas was not the first chair prosecutor for Hugo, having assigned Giovannini and Cronin, two part-time assistant district attorneys, to prosecute.

After District Judge Tupper sent Hugo's case to county court, Hugo was scheduled for a formal arraignment on a criminal information listing charges of criminal homicide charges, abuse of corpse, criminal conspiracy and robbery. It is by this time prosecutors must file their notice of seeking the death penalty. In Hugo's case, they had by filing a Notice of Aggravating Circumstances with the court on Feb. 6, 2004.

Hugo was removed from the State Correctional Institution at Dallas and taken to the Luzerne County Courthouse for his formal arraignment before Judge Olszewski Jr. on Feb. 9, 2004. Hugo was advised that prosecutors intended to seek the death penalty if he was convicted on one or both first degree murder charges. Inside the courtroom, Hugo, through his attorney, Fannick, pleaded not guilty. Olszewski scheduled the trial to begin Sept. 7, 2004, although Hugo's trial date would be continued multiple times.

As sheriff deputies led Hugo out of the courthouse and back to state prison following the day's proceeding, he blurted out to reporters in a hallway that he wished "Lupas was prosecuting." In response, Lupus refused to engage in "outside-the-courtroom banter" while noting the strong facts and evidence prosecutors had against Hugo.

Fannick had much work to do and work he did. The esteemed defense attorney fought for records from the district attorney's office and challenged the June 5, 2003, search warrants for the Mount Olivet Road property, claiming state police used "stale" information supplied by Paul Weakley.

When prosecutors sought a hand writing sample from Hugo, Fannick wanted the sample restricted to the homicide case of Frank James and Adeiye Keiler and not be used in any other state or federal investigations.

In response, Fannick sought a hand writing sample of Patrick Russin, including Russin's mental health records.

The hand writing sample was important as a handwritten note containing the word "Rudeey" and two phone numbers was found inside a kitchen drawer at the Mount Olivet Road home. Rudy was the nickname of Frank James.

Olszewski on June 29, 2004, issued a two page ruling stating Hugo and Fannick were entitled to learn about plea agreement deals with witnesses or other defendants, but stopped short of ordering any similar deals with federal prosecutors.

Pre-trial hearings continued throughout the summer as Olszewski permitted Russin's mental health records to be reviewed by Fannick.

One such legal fight that was a blow to prosecutors was Olszewski's ruling that prohibited an alleged incriminating statement by Hugo made on June 5, 2003.

When Hugo was arrested for robbing and firing a shot above the head of Kerkowski's father, Michael Stanley Kerkowski, he was secured by wrist restraints attached to an eye-bolt fastened into the floor inside the state police barracks in Wyoming. As Trooper John Yencha was watching Hugo, he tossed the cover sheet of the search warrant at Yencha. Yencha read the cover sheet and then told Hugo, "It looked serious." Then Yencha asked if any bodies would be found, in which Hugo replied, "Yeah, five of them."

Fannick argued the incriminating statement was made before Hugo was read Miranda rights to remain silent.

Olszewski agreed as he prohibited the use of the incriminating statement by Hugo along with other rulings in a decision issued July 7, 2004. "Defendant's motion to suppress the defendant's statement given to Trooper John Yencha wherein Trooper Yencha asked the defendant whether the police would find any bodies at the defendant's property and the defendant responded, "yeah, five of them," is hereby granted and said statement by the defendant is hereby SUPPRESSED," Olszewski wrote in his ruling.

As expected, the district attorney's office appealed Olszewski's decision to prohibit the incriminating statement with the Pennsylvania Superior Court. The appeal, filed July 23, 2004, delayed the Sept. 7 trial date, the first of many postponements of the trial.

On March 28, 2005, the appellate court upheld the ruling by Olszewski, delivering a blow to what probably was the best self-incriminating piece of evidence prosecutors had against Hugo. Prosecutors requested the Superior Court to reconsider, which was denied. Prosecutors then sought the Pennsylvania Supreme Court to review the appeal. That request was also denied, ending any hope for a jury to hear the self-incriminating statement. Hugo's incriminating statement was out.

While the incriminating statement issue dragged on for months, Olszewski ruled on other key issues, including threatening sanctions against the district attorney's office for missing court imposed deadlines of turning over evidence, called discovery.

Fannick wanted prosecutors to surrender laboratory reports from a garage door panel seized by state police as the panel contained suspected brain tissue of Frank James. Prosecutors had a deadline of June 1, 2004, which was extended another month to July 1, 2004, to surrender the scientific report of the garage door panel and lab reports from the prosecution's expert, forensic pathologist Dr. Michael Baden, to Fannick.

Prosecutors missed the deadline and Fannick quickly filed a motion for sanctions, seeking to prohibit prosecutors from using any evidence found on the garage door panel. Following a brief court hearing on the issue, Olszewski ordered prosecutors to make the garage door panel available as well as any tissue or blood samples removed from the panel for inspection by Fannick's expert by July 30, 2004, and Dr. Baden's reports by Aug. 9, 2004. Prosecutors missed the latter deadline saying they simply did not have Dr. Baden's report to give to Fannick, nor did they have a report from their own handwriting sample.

Regarding the handwriting sample study by the prosecution's expert, Giovannini said the report was being finalized. On the missing Dr. Baden's reports of his analysis of the garage door panel, Giovannini said he had turned over autopsy reports of Kerkowski and Fassett, but Fannick and Olszewski said those autopsy reports were not relevant to Hugo's case in the killings of Frank James and Adeiye Keiler.

Giovannini was taken to task by Olszewski during a Sept. 1, 2004, hearing on Fannick's request for sanctions. Fannick told the judge in the days leading up to the hearing, he faxed two letters to the district attorney's office seeking an update on Dr. Baden's reports. No response was returned. Olszewski asked and then demanded that "courtesies" be displayed between the two opposing parties.

"Let me make it real clear so there's no misunderstanding. I would expect both counsel to extend common courtesy to each other and if you don't, that's unfortunate and unprofessional," Olszewski said. Giovannini said it seemed the "courtesies seem to be going one way here, Judge. Why is it my responsibility to do research for him? We gave him 15,000 pages of documents, if he can't find those two reports in there, that's not my fault. That's his."

Again, Olszewski said the two reports given to Fannick, the autopsies of Kerkowski and Fassett, had no relevance to Hugo's current case. At one point during the hearing, Olszewski told Giovannini to sit down. "We don't have the dam reports," Giovannini bolstered.

With the trial indefinitely on hold due to the appeal filed by prosecutors with the Pennsylvania Superior Court regarding the incriminating statement, Olszewski permitted prosecutors until Nov. 30, 2004, to provide Dr. Baden's reports of his analysis of the human tissue on the garage door panels to Fannick.

Months after the tense hearing, Giovannni in November 2004, submitted his resignation saying the part-time position of an assistant district attorney became more like a full-time job and he needed to spend more time with his private practice. Cronin left months earlier when she accepted a private practice position. Shortly after Cronin left, Assistant District Attorney James L. McMonagle Jr. was assigned by Lupas to assist Giovannini. With Giovannini's departure, McMonagle became the first chair prosecuting Hugo. McMonagle would be assisted by assistant district attorneys Samuel Sanguedolce and Christopher O'Donnell till the end of Hugo's first trial.

Pre-trial hearings continued as one, and then a second proceeding was unexpected.

Olszewski on Aug. 15, 2005, scheduled a hearing for Aug. 17, "to determine the exact circumstances surrounding the opening of any and all

Sealed Orders by this Court." Fannick saw the opening of sealed orders related to Hugo's case without authorization as bordering a mistrial.

Blame was placed on a safe that measured 2 ½ feet wide and 2 feet tall that was stuffed with sealed court orders and search warrants with many that were old and stale.

But Olszewski didn't buy that excuse.

Robert Reilly, who headed the Luzerne County Clerk of Courts office, where criminal records are filed, had the safe in his tiny second floor office at the courthouse. Reilly assigned an intern to draft a list of sealed search warrants that had expired. The 10 page list was then given to the district attorney's office on Aug. 8, 2005. Shortly thereafter, First Assistant District Attorney Jacqueline Musto Carroll assigned a young assistant district attorney and a county detective, who happened to be Detective Lieutenant Capitano, to review the list and stack of what they were told were expired sealed search warrants. To speed up the process, the young assistant district attorney opened many of the sealed envelopes only to learn that some of the contents were not search warrants but judges' orders. When Capitano spotted Fannick's name on one of the orders, they immediately stopped opening sealed envelopes and notified Musto Carroll, who then went to find and notify Olszewski. Olszewski was not in the courthouse and neither were other judges, so the files were returned to the Clerk of Courts Office and the judge was notified the next day.

Two documents related to payment of two experts for Hugo were opened but not read by the young assistant district attorney and Capitano.

Following the Aug. 17, 2005, hearing, Olszewski scheduled a second hearing for Aug. 25 after being advised by Reilly, the clerk of courts, on Aug. 21 that the 10-page list given to the district attorney's office had case numbers highlighted and a notation, "Do not unseal Hugo." In response, Lupas filed a motion requesting to reschedule the Aug. 25 hearing as he and most of his staff were attending a planned police chiefs conference that day. Olszewski denied the request and held the hearing.

As the first hearing was an inquiry to determine how sealed envelopes were open, the second hearing had a different and charged-up flare. Olszewski lashed out at the young assistant district attorney saying, "Let me make it abundantly clear. He had no authority to open any of these envelopes. It can't be sugar coated."

After the hearing, an irritated Lupas called Olszewski's second hearing a "witch hunt" and a "fishing expedition." Lupas for the first time directly blamed Reilly and suggested Olszewski and Fannick were making the issue bigger than what it was. "All this boils down to is a simple case of someone in the clerk's office put documents on a pile that they shouldn't have been placed on. Mr. Fannick or whoever wants to make more out of this than there is, they're simply on a fishing expedition and there's no fish to catch. That's all of this," Lupas said.

Fannick later said he found Lupas' remark "inappropriate."

Fannick went on the offensive and filed another motion for sanctions against the district attorney's office, this time seeking to preclude the death penalty, which was ultimately denied.

As the combative hearings subsided, Lupas in June 2006, after Hugo's first trial for the killings of Frank James and Adeiye Keiler, ignited another firestorm by seeking the removal of Judge Olszewski from presiding over any and all of Hugo's proceedings in the future.

# VERDICT CONFUSION

Pre-trial hearings continued in Luzerne County Court during 2005 and early 2006 as many of Hugo's associates, including Christina Strom and Paul Weakley faced their own legal troubles in federal court.

Hugo's trial for the killings of Frank James and Adeiye Keiler began March 1, 2006. With many of Hugo's associates entering into plea agreements with federal prosecutors, they were required to testify against Hugo.

Before the jury was brought into the courtroom, Olszewski held an on-the-record meeting in his chambers with assistant district attorneys James McMonagle, Christopher O'Donnell and Samuel Sanguedolce, and Hugo's lawyers, Fannick and attorneys John Pike and Stephen Menn to discuss thousands of bone fragments. Experts by prosecutors indicated the sufficient number of bone fragments recovered from the burn pit and garbage bags at the Mount Olivet Road property constitute between three and 10 individuals. Fannick wanted to preclude or limit testimony before the jury regarding the "three to 10 individuals" findings. Olszewski denied the motion but advised prosecutors to have their experts "mold" their testimony about the thousands of bone fragments to two people. Despite the cautionary warning, the bones would be shown to the jury.

In his opening statement to the jury, McMonagle explained the timeline of events as best as investigators learned, from picking up James at Wilkes-Barre General Hospital where his girlfriend gave birth to a boy, to the actual shotgun killings of James and Keiler and the burning of their bodies. There was no mention of Kerkowski and Fassett by McMonagle.

Fannick, in his opening statement, congratulated Hugo for patiently waiting 33 months since he was arrested June 5, 2003, until the start of his trial. The defense attorney asked the jury to question the credibility of two key prosecution witnesses, Patrick Russin and the plea agreement he entered with prosecutors, and Paul Weakley.

Prosecutors called 36 witnesses to include Russin and Weakley while Hugo's defense team called 12 witnesses. After Fannick rested, prosecutors called two rebuttal witnesses before finally ending their presentation of evidence and witnesses. The trial commenced March 1 and ended March 11, 2006, which was a Friday. Prosecutors and Hugo's defense team had the weekend to catch up on rest and plan their closing arguments set to take place Monday, March 13, 2006. In Pennsylvania, the rules of criminal procedure dictates the defense team goes first in their closing argument followed by prosecutors, so first up was Fannick. And Fannick did not disappoint.

It's customary for defense attorneys and prosecutors when they give closing arguments to review the entire trial, evidence and witnesses. In Fannick's case, he took it one step further.

Fannick reminded the jury that the Mount Olivet Road property was under the control of state police for 34 days and thoroughly searched by nearly 500 law enforcement personnel. Reviewing the shotgun blasts that supposedly killed Frank James and Adeiye Keiler, Fannick said there are 275 to 300 pellets in each shotgun shell.

Standing in front of the jury, Fannick emptied three shotgun shells pouring the pellets into a coffee can intending to show the jury the 825 to 900 pellets that would be discharged from the three shotgun blasts Hugo fired. Fannick rattled the can and then flung the pellets across the courtroom floor. "We have people getting shot in front of garage doors with pellets. We have pellets. We have 900 pellets," Fannick said while rattling the coffee can and pouring them onto the floor in front of the jury near the end of his three hour closing argument.

Olszewski gave the jury a 30 minute break before returning to the courtroom to hear McMonagle's closing argument.

McMonagle began reviewing testimony from witnesses, including Russin and Weakley, and laid a foundation leading up to the shotgun pellets. "There's no pellets on the garage door because they're all in

Rudeey's (James) head. He's shot from the left and slightly behind. The pellets are all in Rudeey's head."

McMonagle reminded the jury that the body of Frank James was pulled around the garage and covered with a tarp as Adeiye Keiler was handcuffed and duct taped. Keiler was then taken into the house and kept away from Strom who was getting ready for work. After Strom leaves, McMonagle tells the jury, Hugo kills Keiler with the shotgun as they walk outside down stairs toward the garage.

"When you look at Pat Russin's testimony and see what kind of a person he is, he would not be smart enough to create this piece of art of framing (Hugo) for these murders. The Commonwealth submits to you that it's proven its case beyond a reasonable doubt and that after you go and deliberate, you should come back with a verdict of guilty on all counts. Thank you," McMonagle ended.

Following the charge by Olszewski instructing the jury about reasonable doubt, how to measure the credibility of witnesses and the definition of each criminal charge Hugo faced, the jury began deliberating at 2:20 p.m. on March 13, 2006. Nearly three hours into deliberations, the jury foreman sent a question to the judge, "Two people present, can someone be found guilty of murder (any degree) if you know they were present but the evidence cannot prove they actually caused the victim's death by pulling the trigger of the firearm that caused the victim's death."

Olszewski reviewed the question with Hugo's attorneys and prosecutors in his chambers. The judge advised that he was going to re-read a provision of the instructions given during the charge that includes, "under the Commonwealth's theory of the case, the Defendant cannot be found guilty of any degree of murder unless they believed Mr. Selenski pulled the trigger of the firearm that caused the deaths."

The jury returned to the courtroom at 5:05 p.m. when Olszewski re-read the provision of the instructions given during the charge. Olszewski had the jury return to the deliberation room.

At 7 p.m., the jury had another question: "Can we hear the ruling or rules on accomplice testimony as it pertains to this case?" Olszewski proposed he would re-read an instruction regarding accomplice testimony, which was done in open court beginning at 7:06 p.m. while describing the term accomplice.

"A person is an accomplice of another person in the commission of a crime, if he has the intent of promoting or facilitating the commission of the crime and, number one, solicits the other person to commit it; or two, aids or agrees or attempts to aid such other person in planning or committing the crime. Put simply, an accomplice is a person who knowingly and voluntarily cooperates with or aids another person in committing an offense," Olszewski explained to the jury.

Before the jury returned to the deliberation room, Olszewski expressed the time was approaching the 8 p.m. hour and the jury had been in the courthouse for 12 hours. The judge allowed the jury to have dinner from 8 p.m. until 8:30 p.m. before asking Hugo's lawyers or prosecutors if they wanted to introduce a motion for sequestration.

"Judge, unfortunately, I would have to move for sequestration under the circumstances. We're in the middle of deliberations and I would move for sequestration," Fannick asked.

"Commonwealth agrees, judge," McMonagle replied.

Olszewski came short of apologizing to the jury but explained to the jury that sequestration would be necessary as they were engaged in deliberations. The judge said he previously did not sequester the jury during the trial as he believed jurors were listening to his daily instructions not to listen or read local and national news, not to discuss the case with other jurors or their families.

Preparations had been made ahead of time to sequester the jury at a hotel where televisions were removed from each hotel room. The jury deliberated until 8:35 p.m. when Olszewski released them for the night. Deputy sheriffs accompanied the jury to a hotel in downtown Wilkes-Barre, about three blocks from the courthouse. Deputy sheriffs also stayed at the hotel where the jury had an entire floor to themselves.

The next morning, March 14, after the jury returned to the courthouse under guard, they sent three additional questions to Olszewski at 10:14 a.m. "Redefine third-degree murder. Is it the same in pertaining to all cases when third degree murder is applied? Question two: "If a witness in this case pleads guilty to third-degree murder in this particular case, does that mean we are to infer that the defendant in this trial did not murder the victims? Question three: "May we have the plea agreement for Pat Russin?"

Olszewski said he had difficulty interpreting the second question, suggesting to Hugo's lawyers and prosecutors that he would instruct the jury, "to find the defendant guilty, you must find that he is the shooter."

Regarding Russin's plea agreement, Fannick and McMonagle suggested not providing it to the jury, which Olszewski agreed.

The jury returned to the courtroom at 10:35 a.m. to hear the answers to their three questions. At 11:55 a.m., the jury sent additional questions: "Did Pat Russin plead guilty to murder in the third degree to Frank James (Rudy) or Adeiye Keiler (Redman)? Second question: "If not, whom did he plead guilty to in the third degree?" Third question: "Can two individuals be charged with the same murder?" Fourth question was a request for a chalkboard and chalk.

As Fannick and McMonagle did not want Pat Russin's written plea agreement with the jury during their deliberations due to the plea agreement requiring Russin to testify against Hugo in other crimes, Olszewski proposed he would read the plea agreement and omit Russin's continued cooperation.

In answering the third question, Olszewski told the jury, "To find the defendant guilty of any degree of murder for either Frank James and/or Adeiye Keiler, you must find that Hugo Selenski, and no one else, shot and killed either or both individuals." The judge acknowledged that a chalkboard will be provided in the deliberation room.

The jury returned to the deliberation room at 12:02 p.m.

At 4:32 p.m., the jury foreman sent a note to Olszewski indicating, "We, the jury, are deadlocked on Counts 1 and 2. We need direction/instruction," and requested, "Can we please have re-explanation on reasonable doubt."

Surely, the questions made Fannick, Pike and Menn hopeful and prosecutors gravely concerned.

Olszewski at 4:39 p.m. advised the jury that Count 1 - criminal homicide - related to Frank James and Count 2 - criminal homicide - related to Adeiye Keiler, and re-read the definition of reasonable doubt. The jury returned to the deliberation room at 4:55 p.m.

At 7 p.m., Olszewski had the jury return to the courtroom.

"Ladies and gentlemen…You've been deliberating now for some 10 hours today and I'm very candidly concerned about your ability to be productive after so many hours and under the circumstances that you have. So I'm making the decision that you're going to go back to the hotel and you'll have dinner there," Olszewski advised the jury, noting that jurors would be permitted to contact their families and arrange to have clothing delivered at the hotel.

The third day of deliberations, March 15, began at 9:15 a.m. At 11:30 a.m., Olszewski received a note from the jury foreman: "We, the jury, have exhausted all possible conclusions in the decision of Count 1. Is it apparent to us all that we can no longer discuss this matter and come up with a unanimous verdict. Please be advised that all other counts are final with this panel."

Olszewski reviewed the note in his chambers with Hugo, his lawyers and prosecutors. The judge said he would instruct the jury on the definition of a hung jury.

Following the in chambers meeting, the jury entered the courtroom at 11:35 a.m., announcing they reached verdicts on Courts 2 through 7. Olszewski advised the jury that considerable expenses were made to bring Hugo to trial and many including families were anxiously waiting or hoping the jury would reach a unanimous verdict on all counts.

With that said, the jury returned to the deliberation room at 11:44 a.m. only to be brought back into the courtroom for the final time at 1:55 p.m. where it was announced the jury could not reach a unanimous decision on

Court 1 first-degree murder but was unanimous on Court 1 second-degree murder and Count 1 third-degree murder. Verdicts were reached for Counts 2 through seven.

As the verdicts were announced, Hugo was found not guilty for the killing of Adeiye Keiler, two counts of robbery and a single count of criminal conspiracy. The jury found Hugo guilty on two counts of abuse of corpse for burning the bodies of Frank James and Adeiye Keiler.

Soon after the jury foreman read the verdicts in open court, Fannick requested a sidebar conference with Olszewski and prosecutors.

"Does anyone understand what they meant by saying that they were unable to reach a unanimous verdict on Count 1, first degree murder, but they were unanimous on second and third? What does that mean?" Fannick asked.

"That's what I asked about in chambers. I didn't understand the question but I'll inquire," the judge replied.

"I mean, I don't understand. I mean, they said they're hung but they said they were unanimous," Fannick said.

The jury had three options for criminal homicide: first degree murder, second degree murder and third degree murder.

Olszewski asked the jury foreman to explain the confusion as it appeared the entire jury had difficulty in understanding an open count of criminal homicide.

"I asked if the jury was unanimous with regard to murder of the first degree and you told me, no, that all 12 did not agree guilty and all 12 did not agree not guilty; is that correct?" Olszewski asked.

"Correct," the jury foreman said.

"Okay, the confusing part is when I asked you about second degree and third degree, I believe you misspoke?"

"Yes, yes," the jury foreman replied.

"Okay, the question that I have then, in regard to murder of the second degree for Count 1, did all 12 agree guilty? I assume they did not; is that correct?"

"Correct," the jury foreman said.

"And I assume that all 12 did not agree not guilty on second-degree murder?

"Correct," the jury foreman said.

"And that with regard number…" Olszewski began when another juror spoke up saying, "That's not correct. We all agreed not guilty."

"I'm sorry Your Honor, did you just say not guilty?" the jury foreman asked.

"On second-degree murder, all 12 agreed not guilty?" the judge asked.

"We agreed not guilty, yes."

To clarify the mass confusion in the courtroom, the jury was polled requiring each juror to separately say their individual verdict for Count 1 second-degree murder and again for third-degree murder. The jury had already announced they could not reach a unanimous verdict for first-degree murder resulting in Olszewski announcing a mistrial for the killing of Frank James.

The jury left the courtroom at 2:15 p.m. March 15, 2006.

Hugo played the odds and won a huge victory being found not guilty in the murder of Adeiye Keiler and was fortunate that a mistrial was declared for the Frank James killing. As he sat at the table inside the courtroom, his family cried behind him.

As the jury deliberated on the final day until the time they announced their verdicts, and the time it took to clarify the confusion, Detective Lieutenant Gary Capitano was in his office in the courthouse to pick up an arrest warrant for Hugo, charging him with the murders of Michael Jason Kerkowski and Tammy Lynn Fassett. Capitano did this of his own accord having not been advised to do so by Lupas as the arrest warrant was drafted as the first trial was coming to an end.

After the jury left the courtroom and Capitano returned with the arrest warrant and criminal complaint for the murders of Kerkowski and Fassett, Hugo along with his lawyers stood before Olszewski.

"Mr. Selenski, you've been found not guilty of Counts 1, 2, 3, 4 – well, not Count 1. Not guilty of Counts 2, 3, 4 and 5. There's a mistrial that's been declared with regard to Count 1. You have, however, been convicted of two counts of abuse of corpse. Abuse of corpse in the Commonwealth of Pennsylvania is a misdemeanor of the second degree. It's the equivalent of a DUI charge, grading wise, has a statutory maximum of two to four years per count," Olszewski said while scheduling Hugo's sentencing date for May 1.

About this time, Fannick contemplated asking for bail but opted not to do so, realizing what was about to take place.

"We understand that there may be other issues separate than this case and I would prefer to have my client where he is. So I don't want a bail issue coming up, so I'm not making any motion for bail at this point," Fannick said.

Then Hugo spoke.

"Judge, there's obviously other issues coming out here in a few minutes. And I just wanted to be very clear to you that every time I'm in the custody of the state police, they constantly attempt to interview me when my attorney is not there. I do not want to be interviewed. I do not want to be spoken to. If they have to transport me, that's fine. But I do not even want to be spoken to by the state police, especially without Attorney Fannick. I just want that on the record. I don't want another Mr. Yencha issue that is…I mean, I don't know. I just want it on the record. I want to let you know. They attempt to interview me every time when he's not there," Hugo said before Fannick turned to him and said, "Keep your mouth closed."

"If there's going to be…if there is any action going to be taken by law enforcement authorities, Mr. Fannick is here and I assume that Mr. Fannick would be consulted. Is that correct?" Olszewski asked.

Capitano replied, "Yes, Your honor."

At 3 p.m., Hugo was arrested for the murders of Kerkowski and Fassett. At 4:30 p.m., he was before Magisterial District Judge James Tupper in Kingston Township to be arraigned and, once again, jailed without bail. Listed in the affidavit of probable cause supporting the charges includes Weakley's statement that Hugo and Pat Russin murdered Kerkowski and Fassett, and Weakley helped Hugo bury the bodies behind the Dallas High School football field, and later re-bury the bodies at the Mount Olivet Road property. As Russin was called a liar and "Pat the Rat " during Hugo's first trial, Weakley would take his place for round two.

Following the trial, several jurors criticized how prosecutors presented the case they felt was filled with unanswered questions with the investigation and testimony from admitted liars. Based on the theory presented by prosecutors, Hugo could not be convicted as an accomplice, only as the trigger man. Lupas explained the investigation, as presented during the trial, had Hugo solely responsible for the killings of Frank James and Adeiye Keiler. Simply put, Hugo did not help or assist in killing the two men. Jurors apparently had trouble grasping the theory presented by prosecutors.

As turbulent as Hugo's first case was, having to wait 33 months through rounds of appeals, dramatic pre-trial hearings and a prison escape, the events during Hugo's next phase was short of a fictional fantasy. What would come as no one expected was more and longer appeal delays, the never ending battle between the district attorney and judge forced into a corner, a carousel of appointed judges to oversee the case with a judge being charged with domestic abuse, an inmate being charged in a murder plot to kill Paul Weakley, lawyers coming and going, election campaigns changing the tide, an attorney and private investigator being charged with witness tampering, Hugo defending himself without counsel and a robbery and kidnapping trial in neighboring Monroe County.

The murdered victims changed but the main cast of characters remained the same: Hugo, Pat Russin and Paul Weakley. Gone would be Hugo's lead defense attorney, Demeterius Fannick, and eventually the two co-defense attorneys, John B. Pike and Stephen Menn. Also to leave would be Lupas who won a seat on the Luzerne County Court of Common Pleas during the 2007 election in a landslide victory.

Shortly after Hugo was charged for the murders of Michael Jason Kerkowski and Tammy Lynn Fassett, Lupas appointed himself as first chair to prosecute. If the loss in the first case did anything, Lupas became more direct and confrontational.

The Times Leader newspaper based in Wilkes-Barre, Pa., had invited Al Flora, a well-respected defense attorney, to write a column titled, "Ask the Lawyer" reflecting his thoughts during Hugo's first trial. In a question and answer format published March 17, 2006, Flora described Fannick as an "excellent criminal trial lawyer," probably earned $1 per hour defending Hugo on a capital murder case, and in securing Hugo's acquittal on murder charges would raise his reputation in the legal community.

As for Lupas, Flora noted the district attorney would receive criticism for the way the Hugo case was handled mainly due to "lack of experience."

Two days after Flora's "Ask the Lawyer" column was published, Lupas countered with his own in a letter to the editor published in The Times Leader March 19, 2006. "To begin with, anyone who knows Al Flora knows that his ego is so big that it can barely fit within the boundaries of Luzerne County."

Lupas' letter to the editor continued to say Flora did not like him and Flora had not gotten over his loss when Lupas personally convicted Henry Stubbs for the killings of a mother and her 6-year-old daughter following a two-week trial in May 2003 that was held before Olszewski. Flora and Attorney Shelley L. Centini defended Stubbs, who was sentenced to two consecutive life terms in prison.

"While Mr. Flora and I have clearly been adversaries in the courtroom and while being on opposite sides of cases, I have never resorted to the type of degrading, untrue and pathetic cheap shots that he has resorted to. It is very unfortunate that a man who is supposed to be a professional would conduct himself in this manner," Lupas ended his letter to the editor.

While Lupas and his office were the targets of criticism from legal professionals and newspapers, he continued to stay the course being supported by Lisa Sands, sister of Tammy Fassett and Kerkowski's parents, Michael Stanley Kerkowski and his wife, Geraldine.

"Our faith has to be strong. The only salvation, the only way we'll feel good is when (Hugo) is convicted of our son's murder and Tammy's murder. That, to me, would be the day of closure," Michael Stanley Kerkowski said in an interview on March 20, 2006.

"I have a lot of faith in District Attorney David Lupas and his team that he got together to do the case. And I pray every night that things go the way they're supposed to go. I want this done the right way. I want this guy to get what he deserves. I want him to know what he did to our son and feel that kind of pain," Gerry Kerkowski said during the same interview.

Hugo would go with attorneys John B. Pike and Stephen Menn to defend against the murder charges related to the killings of Kerkowski and Fassett as Fannick bowed out, citing he could no longer work for free. Fannick officially left Hugo's side on April 12, 2006, in a court order signed by Olszewski.

Hugo addressed the separate cases and Fannick in a lengthy six page letter to a newspaper reporter dated April 2, 2006. In Hugo's letter, he claimed the constant "stalling" leading up to his first trial was the fault of the district attorney's office. "All the media knows that once trial started, I became relatively quiet and subdued compared to my typical outspoken way. All I ever wanted was to get to trial. My quips and comics leading up to trial were all merely gimmicks of the truth toward the DA's office for the constant stalling of my case. I'm not normally disrespectful toward law enforcement and some people probably took offense to my antagonizing ways but all the 'behind the scene' actions of law enforcement involved in my case and constant lies on behalf of the DA's office at the beginning was so blatant that I felt it to be more personal than simple investigative techniques," Hugo wrote in his April 2, 2006, letter.

Directing his thoughts about Fannick, Hugo wrote he disagreed with the defense lawyer about not calling more witnesses but Fannick made him "see what I couldn't and realized the importance of saving certain defense issues for the future case of Kerkowski - Fassett."

"Furthermore, Attorney Fannick not only successfully defended me, he set the entire stage for my future case in an invisible fashion that was nothing short of genius. Whether I have Fannick or not in the next case, he's already done half the work for it with his ability to see that 'forest (sic) for the trees' that went right over my head," Hugo wrote.

Soon after Pike and Menn, who would soon be joined by Attorney Michael Senape, took control of Hugo's defense, they wanted Hugo moved from the State Correctional Institution at Dallas in Jackson Township, Luzerne County, back to the county correctional facility. Pike and Menn needed access to Hugo and it was easier to visit Hugo at the county correctional facility than a state prison. Hugo's place of prison had been an issue throughout his two cases as his lawyers complained they had trouble gaining access to him when he was housed at a state prison. To better circumvent, Olszewski in February 2006 ordered the county correctional facility to remove handcuffs from Hugo whenever he met with his lawyers to "freely review and exchange documents" during their attorney-client meetings.

While Fannick was permitted to end his time representing Hugo, he did attend as Hugo's lawyer when Hugo was sentenced on the two counts the jury convicted him on, abuse of corpse. Security was heightened outside and inside the courthouse by Sheriff Barry Stankus on May 1, 2006, when Hugo was brought before Olszewski for his sentencing hearing. Olszewski sentenced Hugo to two-to-four years in prison on the two abuse of corpse counts. Hugo was also given credit for 1,061 days served in jail since his arrest June 5, 2003.

"This was more than just the burning of a body or making it difficult for police or victims to recognize, Judge," McMonagle said during the sentencing hearing. "The defendant took great pains, in the Commonwealth's view, to completely obliterate two people from the face of the earth and quite frankly, Judge, he was successful in doing that because he was only convicted of two counts instead of the remaining charges."

If there were concerns from Hugo's lawyers about where Hugo was going to be jailed, Olszewski ordered Hugo to state prison as the sentence imposed was a state sentence anyway. As an official matter, Olszewski denied a request by Pike and Menn to keep Hugo at the county correctional facility.

Lupas, First Assistant District Attorney Jaqueline Musto Carroll and Assistant District Attorney C. David Pedri, held a news conference

May 19, 2006, to announce Hugo and Paul Weakley were being charged for the murders of Kerkowski and Fassett. The criminal complaint filed against Hugo on March 15, 2006, was withdrawn. And, much different to the many search warrants that were executed in June and July 2003, the theory of the investigation had Hugo and Weakley killing Kerkowski and Fassett. The search warrants in June and July 2003, contained fabricated tales from Weakley but the fabrications and lies he told were uncovered by investigators. Weakley's lies would come back to haunt him years later.

And once again, Hugo along with Weakley appeared before Magisterial District Judge James Tupper in Kingston Township to be arraigned on two counts of criminal homicide, two counts of robbery, three counts of criminal conspiracy and one count of theft.

As in Hugo's first case when prosecutors wrapped up a plea agreement with Pat Russin in November 2006, which required Russin's cooperation and testimony against Hugo, a plea agreement would also be filed involving Weakley, but this time, it would be in the U.S. District Court for the Middle District of Pennsylvania on Jan. 25, 2008.

Leading up to the preliminary hearing held before Tupper on June 14, 2006, members of Hugo's family had T-shirts designed with the phrase, "Lupas vs Hugo Round #2" that were worn and displayed.

During the hearing itself as the prosecution was directed by Lupas, the district attorney and Hugo engaged in several outbursts. The first occurred when Detective Lieutenant Gary Capitano was on the witness stand and showed a picture of Fassett's body after the body had been removed from the shallow grave outside the Mount Olivet Road home. Flex ties were around Fassett's ankles. "Judge, I'd ask that you advise the defendant not to make any comments. This is a serious matter, this is a court of law, and I think he should recognize appropriate decorum," Lupas said.

"You're making a mockery out of your courtroom," Hugo shot back. "No, you are," Lupas responded. "You're making a mockery out of this…" Hugo was saying until Tupper chimed in, "All right, gentlemen, gentlemen."

Their next testy exchange occurred about one hour later as Lupas was introducing store receipts for bags of soil Weakley purchased at the Back Mountain Feed and Seed, which was used to bury Kerkowski and Fassett. "No, you can't say anything to me," Lupas said to Hugo. "I'm not talking to you, I didn't say a damn thing to you. Leave me alone. I didn't say anything to him."

"Everytime I come over here, he has to make smart remarks," Lupas said in court.

"I didn't say anything to him," Hugo said, as Tupper noted, "He (Lupas) was talking to Attorney Menn at the time."

"I didn't say nothing," Hugo said, with Lupas saying, "Just sit there and keep your mouth shut."

Menn jumped in saying if Hugo needed to talk to him, he could talk to him. "Keep smiling, keep smiling," Lupas said to Hugo.

One key issue that would result in long delays of Hugo's second trial would be the preliminary hearing testimony of Michael Stanley Kerkowski. The elder Kerkowski testified at length about how he was introduced to Hugo through his son and after his son's disappearance on May 2, 2002, Hugo kept telling the elder Kerkowski that his son was alive and needed cash for a new trial in Wyoming County. The elder Kerkowski further testified about Hugo threatening to burn his home and harm his family.

Michael Stanley Kerkowski died at his Dallas Township home Sept. 19, 2006. Prosecutors would seek to use the elder Kerkowski's testimony at the preliminary hearing during Hugo's trial, which ultimately was appealed several times to the Pennsylvania Superior Court.

As expected, Tupper forwarded all charges against Hugo and Weakley to Luzerne County Court. And as expected, the cases would be assigned by then Luzerne County President Judge Michael T. Conahan on July 13, 2006, to Olszewski to oversee Hugo's and Weakley's cases. With Olszewski presiding over Hugo again, Lupas went on the attack.

As the district attorney's office filed an appeal with the Pennsylvania Superior Court on Feb. 16, 2006, challenging Olszewski's ruling of Feb. 15, 2006, that dismissed escape charges against Hugo, Lupas blamed

Olszewski for intentionally causing a delay in sending the escape record to the appellate court. Olszewski was legally bound to turn over Hugo's escape record to the Superior Court by April 10, 2006, but according to the district attorney's office, the judge had not sent the escape record. Lupas on June 21, 2006, filed a motion with the Superior Court to compel Olszewski to forward the escape record to the appellate court. In a statement issued the same day, June 21, 2006, Lupas said, "Upon checking the status of the appeal, I discovered that the higher court's review of this matter is being unnecessarily delayed because the records should have been sent to them at least 10 weeks ago."

On another front and behind the scenes, the parents of Kerkowski and Fassett's sister, Lisa Sands, at first quietly objected and complained about Olszewski presiding over Hugo's second trial for the murders of their loved ones. Michael Stanley Kerkowski and his wife, Geraldine, spoke with a reporter from the kitchen of their home on Sunday, July 16, 2006, ultimately deciding to write a letter, dated July 17, 2006, expressing their concerns to President Judge Michael Conahan. The Kerkowskis were going to give Conahan five days to respond or they would go public. Lisa Sands also wrote a letter to Conahan, dated July 20, 2006, begging for another judge besides Olszewski.

After the fourth day and finding out Lisa Sands shared the same concerns, the Kerkowskis publicly expressed they wanted a different judge to preside over Hugo's second murder trial including Weakley's trial. Prior to coming out, the Kerkowskis and Lisa Sands had a private meeting with Lupas and his staff on Thursday, July 20, 2006. After the emotional private meeting, Lupas said, "both families expressed a lot of concern about the judge appointed to the case. They made it known that they aren't happy. I'm reviewing it to legally see what we can do about it."

Lupas first step was a letter dated July 24, 2006, to President Judge Conahan and Court Administrator William T. Sharkey, requesting the cases of Hugo and Weakley be assigned to a different judge.

Hugo and Weakley were scheduled to be formally arraigned on the criminal information charging them with two counts of criminal homicide, two counts of criminal conspiracy to commit homicide, criminal solicitation to commit homicide, two counts of robbery, two counts of criminal conspiracy to commit robbery and one count of theft on July 27, 2006. Olszewski presided over the formal arraignments held via video conference and scheduled their combined trial to begin Jan. 22, 2007.

A day before, July 26, 2006, Lupas and his office filed a notice of aggravating circumstances officially notifying the court they intended to seek the death penalty for Hugo and Weakley, if convicted of first-degree murder.

Also on the same day, Lupas filed a motion for "recusal of Judge Peter Paul Olszewski Jr.," citing an "appearance of impropriety should Judge

Olszewski continue in this case and/or his continued involvement would tend to undermine public confidence in the judiciary in these matters…" Included in the motion by Lupas were the affidavits by the families of Kerkowski and Fassett, and included Olszewski's law clerk, Daniel Pillets, who was said to have provided "strategic trial preparation advice" to Fannick, suggesting Pillets "bragged" to numerous witnesses that the dumping of shotgun pellets during Fannick's closing arguments in Hugo's first trial was his idea.

Lupas also included Olszewski's intentional delay in sending the escape record to the Pennsylvania Superior Court and mentioned a radio talk show host boasting he spoke with Olszewski about Hugo.

On Aug. 1, 2006, at 11:20 a.m., Olszewski scheduled a hearing on the district attorney's recusal motion for Aug. 4, 2006. Hours later, at 4:15 p.m., the district attorney's office filed a motion for the appointment of a "Neutral Jurist" to rule on the recusal motion citing the same reasons as was listed in the recusal motion with new details describing how prosecutors planned to proceed.

In seeking a neutral jurist, Lupas stated Olszewski declined to be interviewed by detectives from the district attorney's office in preparation for the Aug. 4 recusal hearing, and prosecutors intended to issue a subpoena to Olszewski and call him as a witness where he would be open to testify about disputed facts, referencing the delay in sending the escape record to the Pennsylvania Superior Court. And once again, Pillets was listed in the neutral jurist request for his "strategic advice" to Fannick.

A day after Lupas filed the neutral jurist motion, Olszewski on Aug. 2, 2006, filed an order delaying the Aug. 4 recusal hearing. On Aug. 9, 2006, Olszewski filed an order recusing himself from further proceedings of Hugo and Weakley, issuing a 27 page Memorandum addressing each allegation Lupas raised against him.

"The Commonwealth adopts the positions of the Kerkowski and Fassett families and questions this Court's 'impartiality and neutrality.' The Commonwealth alleges in Selenski I, this Court did not 'play by the rules,' 'leaned heavily towards Selenski,' and 'doesn't seem to care about justice.' The Commonwealth fails to cite a single example or circumstance wherein this Court failed to comply with any rule of procedure or rule of evidence," Olszewski wrote, noting it appeared Lupas was "judge shopping."

Olszewski listed 20 of his rulings that denied Hugo's request to preclude certain statements and evidence. "The record is replete with instances where this Court displayed sensitivity and exercised substantial effort to insure the Commonwealth received a fair trial," the judge wrote.

Olszewski included the district attorney's appeal to the Pennsylvania Superior Court over his ruling that stricken Hugo's incriminating statement was ultimately upheld.

"It is obvious judges are often called upon to make critical decisions resulting in significant impact on the lives of litigants and sometimes the community. The vast majority of these decisions are routine. Evidence is presented, the relevant law applied and the result usually clear. They are for the most part unemotionally made in a neutral, impartial and unbiased manner. Judges wish to harm no one. Trial judges desire to be correct but at the same time, acknowledge their fallibility, hopefully learn from mistakes and aspire to be better," Olszewski noted.

As for Pillets giving "strategic advice" to Fannick, Olszewski wrote he often conferred with Pillets on legal issues and Fannick was given free reign to conduct the demonstration of pouring shotgun pellets into a coffee can and dumping them on the courtroom floor.

"This Court is also aware of the circumstances under which Mr. Pillets met with the investigators shortly after closing arguments. He denies employing the same exact words which appear in the brief, but certainly acknowledges expressing the sentiment that he assumed the idea originated with him because he believes Mr. Fannick was present in chambers when it was said," Olszewski explained in his Memorandum.

"With reluctance, I have concluded that the greater good, in this instance, requires the focus to remain on the trial of these Defendants and nothing else. I know with absolute certainty and can express with unequivocal confidence that I harbor no bias or prejudice towards the

Commonwealth and could in fact preside impartially. Given the unique circumstances presented, this sentiment must yield to ensuring public confidence in the Courts and the administration of justice," Olszewski wrote in recusing himself.

With Olszewski removing himself from presiding over Hugo's second case, long term family court judge, Chester B. Muroski, a former district attorney, was assigned on Aug. 9, 2006, to the Hugo and Weakley cases. Muroski's first order adopted Olszewski's trial management order maintaining the trial date of Jan. 22, 2007.

Olszewski's mention of "public confidence" would be shattered years later in an unrelated juvenile justice scandal that saw Conahan, who retired in 2007 and became a senior judge, and Luzerne County President Judge Mark Ciavarella, then the county's juvenile judge, indicted by a federal grand jury in 2009. Olszewski was not involved in the juvenile scandal. Muroski would replace Ciavarella as president judge in Luzerne County.

Two weeks after Muroski was assigned to oversee the cases of Hugo and Weakley in Luzerne County, Pennsylvania State Police at Hazleton charged the pair with kidnapping and robbery in Monroe County.

# GOOSAY ROBBERY AND TRIAL

While Hugo's murder case for the killings of Michael Jason Kerkowski and Tammy Fassett slowly proceeded with pre-trial motions in Luzerne County and delays due to appeals filed in Pennsylvania Superior Court, Hugo's trial for the kidnapping and robbery of Samuel Goosay took place in Monroe County in July 2009.

Goosay, a jewelry store owner, finished eating hot dogs and beans for dinner inside the kitchen of his home in Chestnuthill Township, Monroe County, when he heard a crash at the rear door just after 6 p.m. on Jan. 17, 2003. Goosay quickly turned and was confronted by two men wearing ski masks. One of the men threatened him with a handgun.

The two masked men shoved Goosay to the floor pulling his arms behind his back securing his wrists with metal handcuffs. He was blinded by duct tape across his eyes before he was pushed into his master bedroom, sitting on the edge of the bed. For the next 20 minutes, the two men interrogated Goosay, demanding the keys and the combination code to his jewelry store, Finishing Touches. If he didn't give what they wanted, Goosay was going to be killed. The two men kept asking where in the house he kept cash. His wallet containing $800 was taken from his pants pocket. It was a perfectly planned robbery by the two men whom investigators identified as Hugo Selenski and Paul Weakley. Or so they thought.

The robbery at the Goosay residence was not random. Hugo and Weakley stalked Goosay by visiting his jewelry store in the shopping plaza on state Route 611 in nearby Tannersville, Monroe County. They were getting to know the store's layout, where diamonds were kept in safes at night, the security key pad, and the rear exit. On this particular day, Hugo and Weakley were ready to pounce. They followed Goosay home and waited in the rear yard, realizing he was alone. Goosay's wife, Ellen, of 37 years at the time of the violent home invasion was at a jewelry show in New York City.

Goosay did not know the two men who were holding him hostage inside his own home. They threatened to kill him unless he cooperated by providing the keys and combination code to his jewelry store. Goosay gave his abductors the code knowing there were several steps to properly deactivate the alarm. Believing their plan was working, Weakley left the home driving Goosay's car to the jewelry store while Hugo rummaged through the house looking for money and jewelry.

Lifting the duct tape above his eyes, Goosay felt he had an opportunity to overtake Hugo, who was on his knees and had his back turned while searching a night stand alongside the bed. Hugo had taken off the ski mask and placed the handgun on a dresser.

"I stood up, picked up the gun off the dresser and pointed it at the guy's head who was at that point on his knees on the floor looking through my wife's bottom drawer. I told him, I told him to get out of our house. Get the fuck out of the house. He at that point realized I wouldn't be able to shoot anybody, and so he stood up and grabbed the gun. He and I fought. We ended up in the hallway of the house fighting for the gun," Goosay testified in Monroe County Court on July 8, 2009.

A much younger and stronger Hugo managed to get the gun away from Goosay. Hugo was on top punching Goosay in the head and stomach. After the struggle, Goosay was lifted off the floor and pushed back onto the bed where Hugo fastened his ankles with a set of plastic flex ties. Hugo was not overwhelmingly concerned that Goosay saw his face. "I'm not from the area anyway. You'll never recognize me. You'll never know who I am," Hugo told Goosay.

Hugo used a washcloth in an attempt to clean up blood on a carpet, a task Goosay saw when he courageously lifted the duct tape above his eyes again.

For the next 90 minutes, Hugo talked to Goosay about, of all things, the stock market and investments. Hugo continued to rummage through the house not knowing he dropped a glove in another bedroom. At one point during their chatty conversation about the Dow Jones, Hugo politely asked Goosay for a cigarette, removing a pack from the hostage's shirt pocket. Hugo got an ashtray and lit Goosay's cigarette as the two sat on the bed and smoked.

"I'm not stupid enough to leave this cigarette here," Hugo told Goosay, flushing the butt down the toilet. Hugo removed a pillow from its pillow case that he used to fill it with jewelry. He then placed it in a large bag containing new bed sheets Goosay's wife had recently purchased. Realizing he was missing a glove, Hugo threatened to burn the house down if he did not find it.

During Hugo's quest for jewelry and money, the telephone rang inside Goosay's house. Hugo picked up the portable headset and placed it against Goosay's ear to listen. The caller was the alarm company reporting to Goosay that the burglar alarm was activated at Finishing Touches and police had been dispatched to the business. An angry Hugo whacked Goosay in the back of the head with the gun and fled Goosay's house with the pillow case containing jewelry valued at $50,000 and new bed sheets.

Goosay hobbled to the kitchen and cut the flex ties from his ankles with a knife. Unable to cut the flex ties around his wrists, Goosay called 911 to report the home invasion.

In leading up to Hugo fleeing Goosay's house, Weakley parked Goosay's car in front of Finishing Touches. Wearing a dark hooded sweatshirt, Weakley approached the front door unlocking it with keys stolen from Goosay's house. Weakley entered the jewelry store as a witness, Kimberly Smith, was sitting in her car that was parked nearby. Smith was employed at Personal Touch Cleaners in the shopping center. The two businesses were close to each other as Smith knew Goosay and his wife, Ellen.

Smith closed Personal Touch Cleaners around 7:30 that night. She had trouble starting her car and called her husband, waiting for him in the parking lot when she spotted Goosay's vehicle near Finishing Touches. Believing it was Goosay, Smith got out of her car to say hello quickly realizing it was not her friend. Smith flagged down a security officer at the shopping plaza and soon heard the alarm sound from inside Goosay's business. It was 7:27 p.m.

Smith did not see the man run out the front door, the same door he entered. She did notice a white vehicle speed away from the rear of Finishing Touches.

Weakley used a cell phone to call the Goosay residence at 7:27 p.m., the same time the alarm sounded. He also called Hugo's cell phone at 7:35 p.m. and 7:49 p.m. to find out where to pick him up along the highway.

Pennsylvania State Police Corporal Shawn Noonan arrived at Goosay's house and used a knife to cut the flex tie from his wrists. The flex ties that bound Goosay's hands and ankles, and the duct tape that covered his eyes were collected as evidence by the State Police Forensic Services Unit. It was not the only evidence found at the Goosay property.

State Police Corporal Jody T. Radziewicz, a member of the Forensic Services Unit, a specially trained unit that processes major crime scenes, noticed shoe prints in snow on the property beginning at the driveway where it connects to Old State Route 115 shortly after he arrived at the house at 9:20 p.m. While standing at the beginning of the long driveway getting briefed by Noonan, Radziewicz detected the shoe prints in the snow came from two different shoes.

Radziewicz also noticed a distinct pattern in the snow, a checkerboard type pattern presumably from a bag that was set down. The unique pattern measured 16 inches in length and 7 ½ inches in width.

Radziewicz followed the shoe prints to the Goosay house finding numerous shoe tracks around the actual home going in all directions. Radziewicz identified one of the shoe tracks came from a pair of New Balance sneakers because the heel in the shoe print had an "N." The other shoe print in the snow came from a boot, possibly a work boot, Radziewicz calculated.

Radziewicz was unsuccessful in his attempt to make a hardened cast of the different sets of shoe prints in the snow.

Taking numerous pictures including of the injuries on Goosay's face and wrists, he had suffered a broken nose and bruises, Radziewicz continued his efforts at collecting evidence. A plastic flex tie that Noonan had cut away from Goosay was found on the kitchen floor, and another plastic tie was found on the living room floor. When Radziewicz entered the master bedroom, he noticed dresser drawers and papers cluttered on the bed. A ski glove was found in another bedroom, a blood stained towel on top of the stove in the kitchen and an ashtray were all collected.

Goosay's car that was left outside Finishing Touches was towed to the state police barracks in West Hazleton where it was processed by Radziewicz. A bag found inside the car had the same unique pattern as that in the snow in front of Goosay's house. Inside the bag, Radziewicz found two towels stained with blood, two latex gloves and a receipt from a CVS Pharmacy on state Route 611 in Tannersville.

A black leather glove was recovered from Goosay's car that was on the driver's side floor.

When investigators searched Hugo's property in Kingston Township in June 2003, Trooper Joseph Cocco, a member of the state police Forensic Services Unit, found a pellet gun and duct tape inside a white Honda Accord that was parked inside the detached garage. The pellet gun was located in a pouch behind the front passenger seat, and the duct tape was on the rear floor of the Honda. Trooper Edward Urban, also a member of the Forensic Services Unit, discovered New Balance sneakers in a plastic bin inside the detached garage, along with two black ski masks in a clothes basket. Urban found duct tape, plastic flex ties, a plastic flex tie, a pack of Camel cigarettes and metal handcuffs inside the detached garage.

The New Balance sneakers seized from the detached garage corresponded in tread design and size of the shoe prints left in the snow outside Goosay's house. Forensic testing of the blood stained towels from inside the bag of Goosay's car was traced to Weakley.

Investigators learned Weakley sold jewelry and coins stolen from Goosay's house at DeWitt Antique Jewelry and Coin Company in Dewitt, N.Y., receiving $3,400 for the jewelry and $500 for the coins. Weakley provided his identification and completed a sales agreement using his real name.

When Weakley provided Luzerne County Detective Lieutenant Gary Capitano and State Police Trooper Gerard Sachney information about the whereabouts of missing pharmacist Michael Kerkowski and his girlfriend Tammy Fassett, he also gave details about the Goosay home invasion.

Hugo and Weakley were charged by state police on Aug. 16, 2006, for the robbery, kidnapping and assault at the Goosay house on Jan. 27, 2003. The home invasion happened approximately eight months after the homicides of Kerkowski and Fassett, and three weeks after Weakley, Patrick Russin, Carey Bartoo and Greg Pockevich burglarized a Dallas Township house stealing firearms.

178

Prosecutors in Monroe County withdrew the case against Weakley on June 17, 2008, when he was charged by federal authorities that covered a wide range of crimes in Luzerne and Monroe counties, including the homicides of Kerkowski and Fassett and the Goosay robbery.

As for Hugo, he opted for a jury trial that was held before Monroe County Judge Margherita Patti Worthington. Attorney Wieslaw T. Niemoczynski represented Hugo as Monroe County Assistant District Attorney Colleen M. Mancuso prosecuted.

The trial began July 8, 2009, with Mancuso in her opening statement telling jurors what to expect from the evidence that was going to be shown against Hugo, including references to the homicides of Kerkowski and Fassett in neighboring Luzerne County that involved flex ties and duct tape. Mancuso told the jury items seized from the Kingston Township home where Hugo lived were identical to the items used to take Goosay hostage, including an identical pair of New Balance sneakers that matched the shoe prints in snow outside Goosay's residence.

"This case is all about identity, that's what this case boils down to," Mancuso said to jurors.

"What the (assistant) district attorney didn't tell you is that Mr. Goosay was presented with photo arrays to try to pick out whoever did it, and he failed to pick out Mr. Hugo Selenski. He failed to pick out Mr. Selenski. There's another fellow not mentioned by the (assistant) district attorney but certainly mentioned in the homicide case that the district attorney alluded to by the name of Paul Weakley who has in fact pleaded guilty to offenses related to Mr. Goosay and also the homicides," Niemoczynski told jurors.

Niemoczynski said there was no scientific evidence linking Hugo to the robbery and assault upon Goosay.

Mancuso called Goosay as the first witness to testify. Goosay explained he arrived home, made himself hot dogs and beans for dinner, and was confronted by two men wearing ski masks who forced themselves into his house through a rear door. One of the men was carrying a firearm as the other man was carrying a bag, Goosay testified.

Goosay explained he was handcuffed behind his back and blinded by duct tape across his eyes. He was guided to his bedroom where he was questioned about money hidden in the house, and the combination code and keys to his jewelry store. Goosay said one of the men left in his car about 15 minutes later.

Mancuso asked Goosay if he could identify the man who stayed behind and assaulted him in the hallway of his house. "Can you point him out?" Mancuso asked. "Yes, it's the fellow sitting with the blue shirt and the blue tie," Goosay said pointing to Hugo sitting next to Niemoczynski in the courtroom.

Goosay said he could not positively identify which man handcuffed him behind his back and could not say which man demanded $20,000.

Within a week after being assaulted and robbed, Goosay said he provided a description to state police investigators of the man who stayed behind in the house. He further testified state police first presented a photo array of possible suspects to him about four to six months after the home invasion, and a second time about nine months later.

Trooper Shawn Noonan said Goosay was unable to pick Hugo from the photo arrays that were shown to him both times.

Goosay testified he was shown another photo array of possible suspects by Scott Endy, a special agent with the federal Bureau of Alcohol, Tobacco, Firearms and Explosives.

Endy testified he obtained a photograph of Hugo that was taken four months after the Goosay home invasion, and presented the Hugo photo with eight other photographs of men to Goosay on Jan. 13, 2005, nearly two years after the home invasion. The picture of Hugo was taken sometime in May 2003. Endy testified Goosay picked and initialed the Hugo picture.

Trooper Gerard Sachney, having been called as a witness by Niemoczynski, testified blood found in the clasps of a flex wire tie was not consistent with Hugo's blood. There was no forensic evidence found on the ski masks seized from the detached garage in Kingston Township, Luzerne County, and the ski glove found in Goosay's house, Sachney said when answering questions from Niemoczynski.

DNA evidence found inside the glove excluded Hugo, Niemoczynski claimed.

Forensic testing of blood found on the carpet in the hallway of Goosay's house where Goosay fought with Hugo, testing on the blood soaked towel found on the stove, and blood on a towel taken from the bag inside Goosay's car also excluded Hugo. On cross-examination by Mancuso, Sachney said blood on the towel in the bag was consistent with Weakley, and the blood soaked towel on the stove was consistent with Goosay.

Niemoczynski informed Judge Worthington that Hugo would not be testifying in his own defense. The advisement caused Worthington to colloque Hugo about his right to remain silent.

While Worthington was questioning Hugo, the defendant was polite, telling the judge that he conferred with Niemoczynski and it was in his best interest not to testify.

Niemoczynski began calling Hugo's family to testify, younger sister Ruth Ann Pollard and brother Ronald Selenski. The siblings testified Hugo often shaved his head bald and normally would sport a goatee. Pollard and Ronald Selenski further testified their older brother was not a smoker, disputing earlier testimony from Goosay that Hugo shared a cigarette with him when he was held captive inside his house.

After two days of testimony, Mancuso and Niemoczynski gave their closing arguments.

"Do you remember when we opened this case, I told you that this is a case about identity, the identity of the person who actually did the things that Mr. Goosay so vividly described for you in this court? Because identity is one of the absolutely most significant issues you have to deal with," Niemoczynski told jurors. "In other words, did the things happen as described? The accused person sitting here in court, right there, Hugo Selenski, is the accused person, the person who actually did it? Is the evidence strong enough? Does the evidence have the quality to constitute proof beyond a reasonable doubt?"

Niemoczynski reminded jurors of the testimony of Sachney who, upon questioning, said blood evidence excluded Hugo. Several times during his closing, Niemoczynski pointed out Hugo's appearance, noting the blue shirt and eye glasses he was wearing. The defense attorney also pointed out hair on Hugo's head, using Hugo's appearance to distance the defendant from the photographs in the two photo arrays shown to Goosay. Niemoczynski claimed in his closing argument that the flex ties and duct tape can be purchased at any department store and likely are found in most home garages. "If these guys went to my garage today, okay, and on the basis of wire ties and duct tape, I could be standing trial here because you can get them anywhere."

About the New Balance sneakers that Radziewicz, the state police trooper who processed Goosay's house, identified as shoe prints in the snow, Niemoczynski said that brand is "so common," noting that two brands of New Balance sneakers were seized from Hugo's house but jurors were not shown a picture of Hugo wearing those particular sneakers.

It was now Mancuso's turn to address the jury. Like pieces to a jigsaw puzzle, Mancuso described a scenario that Hugo must be the man responsible who attacked Goosay.

Evidence such as the duct tape, handcuffs, ski masks and the white Honda Accord, all of which were found at the Mount Olivet Road house four months after the home invasion, were identified by Goosay and witnesses, Mancuso said.

Mancuso said the duct tape that had Goosay's eyebrow hairs still attached was forensically tested and shown to be similar to the roll of duct tape in Selenski's house.

"Duct tape, where else do we know where duct tape comes into play? Duct tape is found on the remains of Michael Kerkowski junior's body when he's pulled out of (Selenski's) backyard, duct tape on his face," Mancuso said, noting to jurors that flex ties used to bound the hands and ankles of Goosay were similar to the flex ties found on the bodies of Kerkowski and Fassett.

Mancuso said the New Balance sneakers seized from inside a closet at the Mount Olivet Road house in June 2003, "Have the same wear markings as the pair that were in the snow at Mr. Goosay's home four months earlier."

Illustrating Hugo's effort at taking beer bottles he emptied at the home of Michael Stanley Kerkowski, Mancuso said, Hugo did something similar by flushing a cigarette butt down the toilet.

"It shows who he is, his identity. He's not going to leave any evidence behind. He took the beer bottles out of the house where he was drinking after he fired a round toward Mr. Kerkowski, Senior. It's his personality. It's who he is," Mancuso told the jury.

Worthington sent the jurors home for the night. The next morning, July 10, 2009, the judge gave instructions to the jury reminding the panel the burden of proof is upon the prosecutor. During the course of the trial, jurors heard testimony about the homicide case in Luzerne County prompting the judge to tell the panel that Hugo was not on trial in Monroe County for the murders, but any testimony and evidence related to the killings was presented to "show proof of identity, plan, motive and opportunity."

Worthington instructed jurors on each of the 13 charges Hugo was on trial for, describing elements needed above reasonable doubt to find him guilty.

It did not take long for jurors to deliberate. Two hours after they began, the panel returned with 13 guilty verdicts. Hugo was unphased when the jury foreman read the verdicts. "It is what it is. I'll deal with it from here," Hugo was quoted in The Times Leader newspaper on July 11, 2009.

At his sentencing held Sept. 21, 2009, Hugo had a change of behavior. Worthington asked Hugo if he had anything to say before she imposed his punishment. "No ma'am," Hugo replied.

Mancuso reviewed the presentence investigative report, an outline of Hugo's life, which is used for sentencing purposes. Mancuso said Hugo has led a life of crime since 1990, and has violated parole numerous times, receiving misconducts while imprisoned in different correctional institutions. The assistant district attorney claimed Hugo had shown no remorse and likely sent considerable time planning the home invasion with Weakley.

"The planning of this, finding where Mr. Goosay lives. I've been to Mr. Goosay's house. And when he describes how to get there, it's still difficult to find it, much less someone finding his home out in the middle of the woods," Mancuso said. "The best thing, I think, that we can do for society is to warehouse Mr. Selenski. I think he is a danger to this society. He's a danger to the people of Monroe County and to the Commonwealth of Pennsylvania."

Reviewing the presentence investigative report, Worthington noted Hugo's 16 arrests as an adult with nine convictions and two revoked paroles while mentioning the effort Hugo and Weakley undertook to plan the robbery of Goosay.

"One of the things that struck me and that I recall is that Mr. Goosay wasn't even asked for directions to his store, meaning that Mr. Selenski and his cohort knew how to get there…this was so planned, so sophisticated, so heinous. And it's certainly something, Mr. Selenski, that I will never tolerate in this community, what you did here, never," Worthington said to Hugo.

As Worthington continued to read the report, noting the numerous convictions and pending criminal charges in Luzerne County, Hugo yelled out for the judge to hurry, initiating a short verbal exchange of words between the two.

"Get to the sentencing," Hugo bloated out. "First of all, please be quiet," Worthington replied. "I mean, you're wrong in half the stuff," Hugo said. "Please be quiet, Mr. Selenski, or I'll have you removed."

"With all due respect," Hugo began saying until Worthington told him for a third to keep his mouth shut. "Go to the maximum," Hugo yelled out.

"Please shut your mouth; Be quiet," the judge said.

Immediately after the exchange, Worthington sentenced Hugo to no less than 32 ½ years to no more than 65 years in state prison.

The Pennsylvania Superior Court upheld Hugo's conviction and sentence on appeal in an 11 page opinion filed on April 20, 2011.

## 'EVERY DAY OF MY LIFE, I REGRET MY ACTIONS'

While the flex ties, duct tape and the preliminary hearing testimony of deceased Michael Stanley Kerkowski would cause delays in Hugo's Luzerne County trial, the first delay came Nov. 20, 2006, when Judge Muroski granted a request by Hugo's lawyers, John B. Pike, Stephen Menn, and Michael B. Senape for more time to file pre-trial motions.

What also became an issue again was the location of Hugo's incarceration. By this time in late 2006, Hugo was housed at the State Correctional Institution at Frackville, about a one hour drive from the Luzerne County Courthouse. Muroski had issued an order in early December 2006 calling for Hugo to be transferred from the state prison to the Luzerne County Correctional Facility indefinitely so he could meet with his defense team. Muroski issued the ruling as Pike, Menn and Senape claimed the state prison prohibited face-to-face contact and only permitted attorney-client meetings through glass while talking on a phone.

Lupas and his team of prosecutors, First Assistant District Attorney Jaqueline Musto Carroll, Assistant District Attorney C. David Pedri and now Assistant District Attorney Jarrett Ferentino, moved to return Hugo back to state prison. Muroski later tweaked his motion allowing Hugo to meet with his lawyers at the Luzerne County Correctional Facility but needed to be returned to the state prison in Frackville after their meetings.

A few days after Hugo was sent back to Frackville, Hugo sent a letter to The Times Leader newspaper congratulating Lupas about his prison home. Hugo claimed he was at first "angry," but "then I had to laugh. You consistently walk into trials grossly unprepared and it would only seem fitting of you to try and prevent your opponent from proper preparation. Your actions make much more sense now, and I must congratulate you on a job well done," Selenski wrote to The Times Leader.

Surprisingly, Lupas responded that Hugo enjoyed creating press for himself. About a month after Hugo's letter was published in the newspaper, Lupas and his office received good news on Feb. 6, 2007, from the Pennsylvania Superior Court that reinstated escape charges, which were dismissed by Olszewski. The reinstatement of the escape case electrified Lupas' campaign for judge, which he announced three weeks earlier on Jan. 12, 2007. First Assistant District Attorney Jacqueline Musto Carroll also announced her campaign to replace Lupas as district attorney. At the conclusion of the 2007 campaign, Lupas would be moving from the first floor to the third floor of the courthouse wearing a black robe and Musto Carroll would be getting the bigger office as district attorney.

Leading up to May 2007, attorneys for Hugo and Weakley would file pretrial motions seeking separate trials, dismissal of the cases, suppression of evidence and statements and the suppression of evidence from Hugo's trial in Monroe County.

Muroski on May 17, 2007, issued his opinion on multiple issues, including severing the trials of Hugo and Weakley and allowing prosecutors to use the preliminary hearing testimony of deceased Michael Stanley Kerkowski. One such Muroski ruling prohibited prosecutors from using evidence of the Monroe County kidnapping and robbery of jeweler Samuel Goosay. When Muroski came down with his ruling, Hugo had not gone to trial yet in Monroe County.

Lupas and his prosecutorial team had a difference of opinion and filed an appeal with the Pennsylvania Superior Court on June 12, 2007, challenging Muroski's ruling that prohibited the Monroe County evidence to be used against Hugo and Weakley during their Luzerne County trial. The appeal ultimately placed Hugo's trial on hold and ended Lupas prosecuting the case at trial as he would be successful in his campaign for judge for the court of common pleas in the November 2007 General Election. With Musto Carroll also successful in her campaign for district attorney, she would take over as first chair prosecuting Hugo and Weakley, assigning Assistant District Attorney Michael S. Melnick to the Hugo prosecution team already consisting of assistant district attorneys C. David Pedri and Jarrett J. Ferentino. Melnick, a highly experienced trial lawyer, was fresh off the successful prosecution of Harlow Cuadra and Joseph Kerekes, who were convicted of killing their pornographic movie rival in Dallas Township in 2007.

The appeal filed by prosecutors sought the evidence in Monroe County would be useful in the Luzerne County trial to show Hugo's motive, intent to commit other crimes that were common in the planning, design and execution of such crimes listing 12 similarities that flex ties and duct tape were used in the murders of Kerkowski and Fassett, used in the kidnapping and robbery of Goosay, and flex ties and duct tape were found at the Mount Olivet Road property where Hugo lived and where the bodies of Kerkowski and Fassett were found.

It would be nearly two years later, April 17, 2009, when a panel of the Superior Court in a 2-1 decision reversed Muroski's ruling of May 17, 2007, allowing prosecutors to use the Monroe County evidence against Hugo. Pennsylvania Superior Court Judge Correale Stevens, himself a former district attorney and judge in Luzerne County, noted in the appellate court's opinion, "These similarities are striking. They reveal a highly identifiable method of selecting, overtaking, restraining and robbing a victim that, when viewed in its entirety, places the same signature on the two crimes at issue."

Hugo's attorneys would later appeal the Superior Court's ruling to the Pennsylvania Supreme Court, which they rejected in a one page order Dec. 17, 2009.

During Hugo's two year trial hiatus while the appeal lingered in the Pennsylvania Superior Court, Paul Raymond Weakley was charged by the

U.S. Attorney's Office for the Middle District of Pennsylvania on Jan. 25, 2008, with criminal conspiracy relating to Racketeer Influenced and Corrupt Organizations, commonly known as the RICO Act. The federal charge filed by an information incorporated most of Weakley's crimes associated with Hugo, including the Goosay kidnapping and robbery and the murders of Kerkowski and Fassett. Hugo was identified as an "unindicted co-conspirator" in Weakley's federal charges. Also filed in federal court on Jan. 25, 2008, was a plea agreement for Weakley to plead guilty to the RICO conspiracy charge and agreed to cooperate with investigators and testify against Hugo. The plea agreement called for a life sentence for Weakley.

With Weakley's plea agreement in federal court, his murder case in Luzerne County was withdrawn, giving prosecutors the time to solely focus their sights on Hugo.

During Weakley's sentencing hearing held June 13, 2008, before U.S. District Court Judge Thomas I. Vanaskie inside the federal courthouse in Scranton, Pa., Gerardine Kerkowski and Lisa Sands spoke.

"I wish that all could see inside my body and see what a broken, demolished heart really looks like. You will never in a million years know the pain, the heartache, the stress and the anguish you have caused my family. Michael was my first born and he was everything to me and my husband making us very proud of all of his accomplishments," Geraldine Kerkowski tearfully said.

"Mr. Weakley, I want you to look at these pictures and look closely at the loving young woman, mother, daughter, sister and friend to everyone who came in contact with her. Not only that she was my best friend, as well, not just my sister. What you and Mr. Selenski did to her was totally uncalled for. She didn't deserve to be murdered like that nor did Mr. Kerkowski. If our family had our way, you and Hugo wouldn't be safe anywhere. You animals don't deserve to live on earth anywhere as far as I'm alive," Sands told Weakley.

Then it was Weakley's turn to address the court.

"I have something I would like to read to the families. I would like to apologize to you, the family and dear friends of (sic) Tammy Fassett and Michael Kerkowski for the horrendous crime I committed against your loved ones. I understand no words I can say can undo what I have done or even attempt to justify my actions in so brutally ripping from so many people, a daughter, a son, a mother, a father, a sister, a brother and an aunt and a friend to so many people.

"Every day of my life I regret my actions on that May afternoon almost six years ago, though, not for the punishment I'm about to rightfully receive but for sacrificing a piece of my humanity and for causing so much anguish and suffering in so many good people. I'm not asking for forgiveness, as I'm not sure that if I was in the same position I would be ready to give it myself, I just simply want you, the family and friends, to understand that I'm truly sorry for what I have done," Weakley ended.

After reviewing Weakley's criminal history dating back to when he was 11-years-old, Vanaskie imposed a life sentence. Under the terms of the plea agreement, Weakley agreed to cooperate and testify against Hugo. Weakley would be housed in several federal penitentiaries, including one in Tucson, Arizona, where he was stabbed multiple times by other inmates for being a "snitch." Fortunately, Weakley survived the attacks he received in federal prison and after causing a scare saying publicly he would not testify against Hugo, he eventually re-considered.

While Pat Russin was considered the best witness for prosecutors during Hugo's first trial, when his credibility was questioned and given the moniker "Pat the Rat," Weakley would take his place for Hugo's second trial.

Behind the scenes, Hugo was not getting along with his attorneys, John P. Pike, Stephen Menn and Michael B. Senape. With a limited number of attorneys in Luzerne County qualified to defend capital cases, the pool of eligible lawyers was shallow. Pike and Menn on Nov. 3, 2008, filed a motion seeking to withdraw as Hugo's lawyers as "there is an irreconcilable conflict and difference of opinion" with Hugo on how to proceed with their defense. At the end of 2008, Menn resigned his position as a conflict counsel, a pool of attorneys who are appointed to represent defendants when there is a conflict of interest by the Luzerne County Public Defender's Office.

Prosecutors moved to prevent Pike and Menn from leaving Hugo's side arguing defendants have a right to counsel but are not entitled to the counsel of their choice. Prosecutors further argued that the request by Pike and Menn, two well-respected and seasoned litigators, to withdraw was a deliberate attempt to delay Hugo's trial.

Judge Muroski held an "in camera" hearing on Dec. 16, 2008, to inquire into the irreconcilable differences between Hugo, Pike, Menn and Senape. Hugo had not requested new lawyers to defend him but did not object to the withdrawal of Pike and Menn.

Muroski on Jan. 28, 2009, allowed Menn to leave but ordered Pike and Senape to continue to represent Hugo. Menn was allowed to end his work with Hugo since he resigned as a conflict attorney and was not earning a county salary anymore. Muroski appointed Attorney Robert Buttner to Hugo's defense team in August 2009.

Hugo's merry go-round of attorneys would continue for years including a several month period when Hugo represented himself. Judges presiding over Hugo's case would also frequently change.

Judge Muroski, who was retiring to become a senior judge, on Dec. 23, 2009, assigned Hugo's case to senior Judge C. Joseph Rehkamp, who recently relocated to Luzerne County from Perry County, Pa. Rehkamp would have Hugo's case for less than one month as he was charged by Pennsylvania State Police on allegations of domestic assault on Jan. 16, 2010. The domestic charges against Rehkamp were dismissed Feb. 16, 2010, but his time serving as a senior judge for the Luzerne County Court of Common Pleas came to an abrupt end.

When Rehkam was relieved of his duties by now President Judge Thomas F. Burke, Hugo's case on Jan. 27, 2010, was assigned to Judge William Amesbury who was elected to the court of common pleas in the 2009 General Election after serving as a magisterial district judge in Wilkes-Barre. In one of his first filed rulings on Hugo, Amesbury said the trial would start as early as April 26, 2010. But, Burke reassigned Hugo's case back to Muroski on March 11, 2010, who by this time was a senior judge. Muroski would have Hugo's case through the end of 2011.

Hugo's defense team would continue to change and evolve as Senape was permitted to leave when he resigned as a conflict lawyer and was replaced with the appointment of Attorney Thomas M. Marsilio, also from the county's conflict office, on June 3, 2010.

Marsilio would then file a motion indicating he had a conflict as he represented Kerkowski's wife, Kimberly Kerkowski. Marsilio was relieved by Muroski on June 17, 2010. With Marsilio's exit, Muroski appointed Attorney David V. Lampman II.

With prosecutors and Hugo's lawyers all set, Muroski on July 29, 2010, scheduled Hugo's trial to begin Nov. 15, 2010. But the scheduled trial date was wishful thinking as the turnstile of prosecutors and Hugo's lawyers would continue.

# ANOTHER TRIAL DELAY

An item listed in a pretrial motion filed by Hugo's attorneys on Jan. 26, 2007, would be reargued in 2010 and resulted in another lengthy appeal with the Pennsylvania Superior Court. The item was to prohibit prosecutors from using the June 14, 2006, preliminary hearing testimony of Michael Stanley Kerkowski during Hugo's trial. Michael Stanley Kerkowski died of natural causes on Sept. 19, 2006.

Muroski denied the request May 17, 2007, allowing prosecutors to use the testimony. Nearly three years after they were denied, Hugo's lawyers on March 29, 2010, filed a motion to "Reconsider/revisit suppression of Kerkowski testimony." Hugo's lawyers argued they were limited in asking questions at the preliminary hearing level and were not able to properly impeach Michael Stanley Kerkowski as if it was a trial in the court of common pleas. Since Muroski's May 7, 2007, ruling, Hugo's lawyers said they obtained information they did not know when the preliminary hearing was held June 14, 2006, such as a firearm found in a shed behind the home of Michael Stanley Kerkowski, several cellular phones were found after the elder Kerkowski died, monetary transactions between the elder Kerkowski and Hugo and a recorded phone conversation involving the elder Kerkowski and Hugo on May 2, 2003.

With the newly discovered information, Hugo's lawyers argued they were not able to properly impeach Michael Stanley Kerkowski at the preliminary hearing, a proceeding where defense attorneys are limited in asking questions.

District Attorney Jacqueline Musto Carroll and assistant district attorneys C. David Pedri, Jarrett J. Ferentino and Michael S. Melnick opposed the idea to reconsider/revisit the preliminary hearing testimony of Michael Stanley Kerkowski. Prosecutors argued appellate courts have consistently held that a deceased witness's preliminary hearing testimony is admissible in trial before the Court of Common Pleas where the defendant was provided with a full and fair opportunity for cross-examination.

Muroski heard arguments from the opposing sides during a tempered hearing May 18, 2010, where Hugo yelled out he was having issues with his lawyers. "We got big problems here, big problems," Hugo blurted out, noting they were disagreeing with him and they haven't agreed in years. Hugo made the outburst over Pike's argument that Hugo received money from Michael Stanley Kerkowski. Muroski gave Hugo 15 minutes to talk with his lawyers but the recess was more of an argument between them. Muroski ultimately decided to allow Hugo's lawyers and prosecutors time to file respective legal briefs that delayed the June 3, 2010, trial indefinitely.

It took Muroski 64 days to issue his ruling, filed July 21, 2010, allowing prosecutors to use the preliminary hearing testimony of Michael Stanley Kerkowski. Based on Muroski's ruling, Hugo's attorneys filed an appeal with the Pennsylvania Superior Court delaying the trial yet again. By everyone's surprise, the Superior Court in an unusually speedy decision denied the appeal on Nov. 4, 2010. Hugo's lawyers then asked the Pennsylvania Supreme Court to review the appeal that was denied by Pennsylvania's highest appellate court on March 9, 2011. With the appeal now dead, prosecutors on March 11, 2011, requested Muroski to schedule Hugo's trial date, which was set to begin with jury selection June 27, 2011.

But the June 27, 2011, trial start date was too good to be true. Three weeks earlier, June 3, Hugo's lawyers filed a motion seeking a continuance indicating their "mitigation expert" was unavailable through the end of 2011 due to other state and federal capital trial commitments.

Without the mitigation expert attending Hugo's trial, his lawyers believed Hugo would be "substantially prejudiced" if the proceeding went to the penalty phase. President Judge Thomas F. Burke Jr. signed the order on Senior Judge Muroski's behalf, continuing Hugo's trial indefinitely.

Meanwhile, Deputy Court Administrator John P. Mulroy filed an order reassigning Hugo's case to Judge William Amesbury on June 28, 2011. This order made it the fifth time Hugo's case had been reassigned. Judge

Olszewski was the first jurist, then after his recusal, the case was with Judge Muroski. When Muroski retired to become a senior judge at the end of 2009, the case was given to Judge Rehkamp. After Rehkamp was charged with domestic violence charges, which were later dismissed, Hugo's case was given to Judge Amesbury before being reassigned back to Judge Muroski in March 2010.

With Hugo's case back before Judge Amesbury, the second year judge on July 1, 2011, scheduled a pre-trial conference for Aug. 31, 2011, to hear a motion filed by Hugo to defend himself and to waive mitigating evidence in the penalty phase if such a phase should prove necessary. Only Judge Amesbury would recuse himself from presiding over Hugo's case on July 29, 2011, claiming a member of his legal staff had a long-standing personal relationship with a "key witness" and some members of that witness' family. Amesbury was out for the second time.

Hugo must not have known the hot potato shuffling of judges handling his case as on June 29, 2011, he filed a hand written motion seeking to proceed "ProSe," meaning he wanted to defend himself.

Hugo's letter, dated June 17, 2011, begins, "Dear Judge Muroski, Enclosed please find what I believe to be a properly prepared motion requesting I be granted allowance to continue pro-se," before continuing to ask for a "timely hearing" to better understand how to circumvent court filings. He ended his letter stating, "I, in no way agreed to this mitigation postponement and never would have agreed to it. Att. Pike knows that. You absolutely know I never would have agreed." Hugo claimed without providing a reason why he believed his trial was continued again due to political reasons and the upcoming General Election in November 2011.

Several days after Hugo filed his motion to defend himself, he filed a motion July 6, 2011, seeking to have human skeletal remains recovered from the burn pit and garbage bags tossed out as he thought the fragments were "highly prejudicial" and not relevant to the murder charges he faced involving Kerkowski and Fassett. If the bone fragments were to be introduced during the trial, Hugo said his defense strategy "will have to change course." Hugo further wanted to stay at the state prison he was currently housed, which was the State Correctional Institution at Retreat, noting it was hopeless to restore any revival of a working relationship with his lead defense lawyer. For years, Hugo's lawyers had fought to get Hugo returned to the county correctional facility only to receive little consideration from judges and strict opposition from prosecutors.

Enter Joseph J. Van Jura.

John P. Mulroy, district court administrator, filed an order on Aug. 24, 2011, assigning Hugo's case to Judge Joseph J. Van Jura.

Van Jura, a solicitor for several school districts in Luzerne County, was one of three attorneys nominated by then Pennsylvania Governor Ed Rendell in January 2010, to fill vacant positions on the Luzerne County Court of Common Pleas created when judges Conahan and Ciavarella were indicted by a federal grand jury in a juvenile justice scandal, and Judge Michael Toole was federally charged with honest services fraud for improperly influencing a court case. Van Jura was confirmed by the Pennsylvania Senate to take the judge seat of Toole in March 2010.

When Van Jura was given Hugo's case, he was faced with Hugo's efforts at representing himself without counsel. The newly assigned judge scheduled a pre-trial conference for Aug. 31, 2011, sending his order to Hugo's lawyers demanding to know when their mitigation expert would be available.

When the proceeding began as Judge Van Jura reviewed Hugo's handwritten motion to go-it-alone, he called it "crazy."

For nearly two hours, Hugo requested to defend himself telling the judge he had been kept in the dark and has been disagreeing with his attorneys for years, pointing out the latest friction was the request to continue the trial due to their mitigation expert, Melissa Lang, not being available. Hugo said he had no knowledge such a request was made to delay his trial.

"Mr. Selenski, why do you wish to proceed pro se in this matter?" Van Jura asked, receiving a lengthy response from Hugo. "Because everytime I come into a status conference, everybody goes into those chambers and they decide what's going to happen and they don't even say anything to me. And then when I balk…when I balk, nobody listens to it.

"Quite frankly, I'm irritated with it. I'm sick of motions that I don't know about that go in. The mitigation issues that went in, as far as I'm concerned, I'm 100 percent against it. There is no reason to postpone this case. I mean, I could go on and on with a litany of issues. I'm just irritated with it, Judge," Hugo said.

"Let me assure you, not just today, but prior to today, the era of transparency has begun for everyone," Van Jura said.

"It's never happened. That has never happened once. Not one judge as ever denied anybody here in this room to sit in chambers and speak without me," Hugo said. "I'm irritated about what went in without being discussed with me or without me having anything to decide upon it.

"I mean, I'm not trying to be obstinate to the court or anybody else. I agree with what you said, what the DA said, 100 percent. The fact remains, everything that goes on back there (chambers), I don't know about and I'm not informed about until the judge comes out here, decides, hits the gavel and I'm stuck there. I can't balk and it's disrespectful to the court," Hugo added.

After hearing Hugo's complaints about decisions being made without his knowledge, Van Jura spent a considerable amount of time reviewing Hugo's rights to counsel and if he understood the seriousness of his case. Hugo said he understood.

Van Jura's "crazy" remark at the beginning of the proceeding was not forgotten. District Attorney Musto Carroll suggested if Judge Van Jura felt it was necessary for Hugo to undergo a mental health evaluation, she reminded everyone in the courtroom that prosecutors were prohibited from obtaining Hugo's evaluation report. Hugo quickly snapped.

"I absolutely object. If there's a problem, all (Judge Van Jura) has to do is unseal the mitigation expert examination we have so far; let him read it and use that. There has been a whole psychological evaluation done, psychological, psychiatry. I mean, I don't see why he couldn't just use that," Hugo said, not realizing he let it be known by prosecutors that a psychiatric evaluation was performed on him. Those psychological reports are sealed and remain sealed until it is decided the report will be used during the trial. In Hugo's case, a mitigation report was completed and sealed, ready to be used if his case went to the penalty phase.

After Hugo let the cat out of the bag that a mitigation report on him was sealed, Musto Carroll reminded Van Jura that she has a motion for Hugo to undergo an examination by the prosecutor's psychiatric expert.

Musto Carroll said their expert's report would be unread and sealed and only used during the penalty phase if the proceedings reach that far.

Van Jura said everyone was "getting off the subject," and asked Hugo why if he would allow him to represent himself, would it cause an inconvenience, delay or disruption.

"Judge, if you're going to base your opinion on that, I mean I can't sit here and tell you it's not going to be an inconvenience. I mean, it's asinine to think that it's not. You and I both know it's going to be an inconvenience. I mean, I will do everything I can to make it as less of an inconvenience as possible. I'm ready. I have been ready. I will be ready," Hugo said.

"Can we also agree that it would cause a temporal disruption in the flow of the trial of you doing it as opposed to having…" Van Jura was asking before Hugo jumped in, "I won't lose my temper if that's what you're worried about."

Van Jura expressed concerns that the progress of the trial would be delayed, disrupted and slowed down if he allowed Hugo to represent himself. Hugo disagreed.

Musto Carroll raised a concern about one of Hugo's handwritten motions seeking discovery, or evidence in his case. The district attorney said the simple request Hugo made for discovery filed in the Clerk of Court's Office on July 6, 2011, shows Hugo was not familiar with his own case as there were, at that point, more than 30,000 pages consisting of search warrants, investigative reports, witness statements and evidence.

"I think the concern that is being raised is…my question to you is, if you do not have that and if you do not have access to it, what kind of time frame are we looking at for you to familiarize yourself with it?" Van Jura asked.

"I'm ready for September," Hugo said in response.

In discussing the vast amount of discovery materials, Hugo said he had not received any new discovery documents since 2009, then he said he had received some documents. Pike said the exchange of evidence with prosecutors had been ongoing but Hugo was only permitted to have two boxes inside his state prison cell.

Pike said there were maybe 500 to 1,000 pages of discovery Hugo may not have seen since 2009.

"What you're representing to me is you have already read and are familiar with 2009 backward?" Van Jura asked. "Yes, the vast majority of the case," Hugo said.

"Not vast majority. Are you familiar with all of it?" the judge asked. "Yes, yes, judge."

"Judge, with all due respect, his answers are changing as they become convenient. This man's life is at stake. Somebody has to protect this record and understand what he is saying to make sure that him taking this case by himself is obviously a very serious matter and we want to make sure he has everything he needs in the event that you find that this is knowing, intelligent and voluntary," Musto Carroll said.

Hugo said he would indemnify himself that he would not appeal any post conviction issues. "I will do whatever you need," Hugo said.

Following additional arguments about defense experts, mitigation experts and a paralegal assigned to assist Pike, Buttner and Lampman, Van Jura ended the proceeding without making a decision but ordered everyone to return to the courtroom the following morning at 10 a.m.

When the hearing resumed Sept. 1, 2011, Van Jura again reviewed Hugo's rights to counsel and if he wanted to defend himself. "Mr. Selenski, I am granting your petition to proceed pro se," Van Jura said. "Thank you, Judge," a smiling Hugo responded.

Van Jura appointed Pike, Buttner and Lampman as Hugo's stand-by counsel and scheduled Hugo's trial to begin Sept. 19, 2011.

"Mr. Selenski, will you be ready to proceed to trial on that date," Van Jura asked Hugo.

"I asked for the (court) order that I could have everything at (State Correctional Institution) Dallas, or excuse me, (State Correctional Institution) Retreat. All Retreat asked for is an order from you that I must have all of my legal work there and they will grant it. There's a two box limit without an order from you, Judge," Hugo replied.

Hugo assisted Van Jura with issuing the court order that Hugo needed at the Retreat state prison.

"It is hereby ordered that Mr. Selenski, while housed at the State Correctional Institution at Retreat, be given reasonable but full and complete access to that information," Van Jura noted.

"The reasonable is going to cause me problems, Judge," Hugo said.

"Strike reasonable. To be given full and complete access," Van Jura corrected his order. "They will give it to me as long as you said he needs it," Hugo replied.

"That he be given complete, continuous and full access to that information," Van Jura ended his order. "Thank you, Judge," Hugo quipped.

The discussion quickly shifted to Hugo's mitigation and psychiatric evaluations and reports with Musto Carroll asking Van Jura to have the prosecution's hired expert psychiatrist to conduct their own evaluation. Since Hugo had firmly stated with no uncertain terms that he was not going to raise or introduce his mental status or an infirmary defense, but his reports do exist, Musto Carroll said prosecutors needed to be prepared in the event such reports are used by Hugo during the penalty phase. Prosecutors would not be able to read their expert report as it would be sealed and only unsealed if Hugo introduces his psychiatric report as a mitigation issue. As Van Jura denied prosecutors from having Hugo be evaluated by a psychiatrist, the issue would snowball more than a year later in 2013 by allegations that prosecutors secretly obtained Hugo's psychiatric evaluations from prison.

With the trial approaching Sept. 19, 2011, Van Jura denied a request by Pike, Buttner and Lampman to completely leave Hugo's side and ordered them to remain as Hugo's "stand-by counsel." As a previous judge granted a request by prosecutors for the jury to be taken and view the Mount Olivet Road property for themselves, Van Jura denied that request, thus releasing the county sheriff's department from having to provide a "high level of security."

Another pre-trial conference was held Sept. 15, 2011, to settle any outstanding issues in preparation of the start of trial scheduled to start in four days. And to no one's surprise, Van Jura honored a request from Hugo to continue the trial as he claimed he was unprepared and needed more time.

Hugo in a handwritten letter dated Sept. 29, 2011, to Van Jura stated he had not received "needed material" from Pike and any and all communication with the attorney had been turned off. One issue Hugo raised in his letter related to a subpoena issued by prosecutors and delivered to the Pennsylvania Department of Corrections for everyone who visited Hugo in state prison. The list of visitors was included in discovery evidence prosecutors turned over to Hugo. In reviewing the visitors list, Hugo noted to Van Jura that Pike is listed as visiting him three times in five years. Hugo added that he has been "cautious" in letting his true feelings be known and simply wanted all of his materials delivered to him. Any chance of a reconciliation between Hugo and his lawyers, especially Pike, had been destroyed. Van Jura ordered Buttner to provide Hugo with the requested documents by Oct. 7, 2011. Van Jura scheduled another status conference for Oct. 12, 2011, to finalize plans to begin selecting a jury Nov. 14, 2011. But then another issue came to the forefront…Christmas.

Van Jura's term as judge was to expire Jan. 2, 2012, having been nominated by Pennsylvania Gov. Ed Rendell and confirmed by the Pennsylvania Senate in 2010 to fill the unexpired term of former judge Michael Toole, who was forced to resign when charged in a corruption probe in 2009. There were doubts Hugo's trial, if it were to begin Nov. 14, would not be finished by the time Van Jura's judgeship expired. Jury selection was expected to take up to two weeks with Thanksgiving and the day after as days off. The trial in chief, as it is known, was anticipated to take two weeks but with Hugo representing himself, the time frame took it closer to Christmas. It was anyone's guess how long the jury would take to deliberate each charge. Furthermore, if Hugo was convicted on one or both first-degree murder charges, then next would be the penalty phase where prosecutors argue their aggravating circumstances seeking the death penalty and in response Hugo would provide mitigation evidence in an effort to convince the jury not to impose death. Once arguments are completed in the death penalty phase, the jury deliberates a second time but for how long, it was anyone's guess. These were the concerns made at the Oct. 12, 2011, status conference wondering if the trial and potential penalty phase could wrap up by Dec. 30, 2011.

Any anxiety about finishing Hugo's trial before Van Jura was set to hang up his black robe were settled Nov. 9 when the trial was indefinitely continued due to Hugo's request for attorneys. Once the boxes containing 30,000 pages of discovery were delivered to Hugo, he felt overwhelmed and in response, he filed a petition on Nov. 8 seeking the appointment of substitute counsel. Van Jura on Nov. 9 officially discharged Pike and Buttner and ordered Lampman to continue to represent Hugo with the pledge a second attorney qualified in defending death penalty cases will be assigned. Hugo's trial was postponed once again. And, once again changes would be forthcoming for Hugo as there would be a new judge, a new top prosecutor and new attorneys. One thing that remained constant, Hugo's trial would continue to be continued.

Before the end of the year, one character returned to the Luzerne County Courthouse. After nearly a dozen postponements, Patrick Russin's sentencing hearing was held Dec. 22, 2011, before Senior Judge Muroski who gave him 10 to 20 years in state prison for his role in the killings of Frank James and Adeiye Keiler and burning their bodies. Muroski would amend the minimum sentence to nine years, and seven months in response to a petition filed by Russin's attorney, William Ruzzo, who claimed Russin should have been given additional credit for time served.

# PROSECUTION AND DEFENSE TEAMS EVOLVE

Jaqueline Musto Carroll was seeking her second term as district attorney in 2011, an election year for several county offices. She was first-chair prosecuting Hugo along with assistant district attorneys C. David Pedri, Michael Melnick and Jarrett Ferentino. As a prosecutor for most of her career, Musto Carroll had name recognition and was well-respected inside and outside the courthouse.

Faced without a Republican challenger, a young attorney, Stefanie Salavantis, successfully won a write-in campaign in the Primary Election held May 17, 2011, to be the Republican candidate for district attorney in the General Election.

The juvenile justice scandal that began in 2009 continued with corrupt judges, lawyers, school board officials, county elected officials, county employees and businessmen and women having been either indicted by a federal grand jury, federally charged by the U.S. Attorney's Office or had been sentenced or about to be sentenced in federal court. There certainly was a public misperception that anyone associated with the Luzerne County Courthouse was corrupt. It was deemed by political analysts as "The Perfect Storm" for new elected blood and a change in the style of county government from a three-commissioner body to a home rule charter guided by a council of 11 elected officials.

Historically, Democrats had been elected to the major county offices and ruled the majority of the three elected commissioners for years in Luzerne County. The last Republican to be elected as district attorney was Correale Stevens who served from 1988 to 1991 before becoming a judge in Luzerne County and eventually being elected statewide to the Pennsylvania Superior Court.

The corruption cloud lingered over the Luzerne County Courthouse like a stalled hurricane impacting the 2011 election season.

Salavantis, who obtained her license to practice law two years earlier and with no prosecutorial experience, narrowly defeated Musto Carroll in the General Election held Nov. 8, 2011. The official vote tally was Salavantis 31,801 and Musto Carroll 30,839, a margin of 962 votes.

With Salavantis' coming out on top replacing Musto Carroll, some changes occurred to Hugo's prosecutorial team. Out was assistant district attorney C. David Pedri, who would later become the solicitor for Luzerne County and eventually, the county manager. Melnick would be relieved from prosecuting Hugo in 2013. Ferentino remained and was joined by Attorney Samuel Sanguedolce, who was one of the three assistant district attorneys who prosecuted Hugo in the first trial in 2006. Sanguedolce would be named by Salavantis as first assistant district attorney and, by all intent and purposes, would run the district attorney's office. Assistant

District Attorney Mamie Phillips would be the third prosecutor assigned to the Hugo prosecutorial team.

Another highlight from the 2011 election would be Fred A. Pierantoni III, a magisterial district judge for 20 years serving the greater Pittston area of Luzerne County, being elected to the Luzerne County Court of Common Pleas when six judicial seats were open. Pierantoni came in second for judgeship receiving a total of 39,912 official votes.

Swearing-in ceremonies took place in the rotunda of the Luzerne County Courthouse on Dec. 30, 2011, when Salavantis and Pierantoni began their new elected careers. Days later, President Judge Thomas Burke assigned Hugo's case to Pierantoni, who would remain presiding over Hugo's case until the end. A familiar name was also assigned by Burke, Attorney Daniel J. Pillets, was appointed as special law clerk to Pierantoni. Pillets was the one who suggested to Fannick to empty shotgun shells into a coffee can and dump the pellets onto the courtroom floor during closing arguments in Hugo's first trial.

One of Pierantoni's first directives, Jan. 6, 2012, was to appoint Attorney Shelley L. Centini as a special conflict counsel to represent Hugo at a rate of $85 per hour without benefits with a cap of $40,000 subject to change at the discretion of the judge. Centini was young, experienced, highly energetic, well-respected and mostly feared by lawyers opposing her. A no-nonsense type of litigator, Centini was known for her tenacious legal mind and a staunch opponent of the death penalty.

Centini immediately got to work receiving approximately 15 boxes of discovery consisting of 30,000 plus pages of documents, search warrants, witness interview statements and forensic analysis reports from experts. Centini held the certification requirements to defend capital cases while Lampman was in the process of being certified. A second certified capital defense attorney was needed.

Attorney Edward J. Rymsza from Williamsport, Lycoming County, Pa, was hired Jan. 24, 2012, at a rate of $85 per hour not to exceed $10,000 without further order of the court.

As Centini and Rymsza were taking on the monumental task of familiarizing themselves with Hugo's case and most importantly, gaining Hugo's trust, prosecutors Sanguedolce, Ferentino and Melnick had filed motions to record the testimony of three witnesses due to declining health and frail age. Their video tape testimony would, if needed, be played to the jury during Hugo's trial.

Following a status conference Feb. 3, 2012, Pierantoni continued Hugo's trial to allow Hugo's newest lawyers to get better prepared and allowed prosecutors to record the testimony of two aging witnesses. A request to record the testimony of a third witness was withdrawn.

Pierantoni scheduled Hugo's trial to begin Sept. 10, 2012. All sealed motions filed by Hugo's previous attorneys mostly related to defense funding were ordered to be unsealed, inspected by Hugo's new defense team and immediately resealed.

In what was probably a shock for prosecutors, they learned Hugo's new defense team did their due diligence in learning about the complex case by filing on May 7, 2012, a 54 page legal brief, called a supplemental omnibus pretrial motion as an addition to the omnibus motion filed by attorneys Pike and Menn on Jan. 26, 2007.

Centini, Rymsza and Lampman were seeking to eliminate the death penalty, prohibit prosecutors from introducing aggravating circumstances if the trial proceeds to the penalty phase, total dismissal of the case citing double jeopardy, prohibit the introduction of color photographs of the bodies of Kerkowski and Fassett, requested a specialized jury questionnaire rather than the normal questionnaire jurors fill out, prohibit the use of human skeletal remains that were recovered from the Mount Olivet Road property, prohibit the introduction of Hugo's past drug use and distribution of drugs, disallow any information about Hugo's prior incarcerations, prohibit any mention of the Ellen Smaka robbery investigation as Hugo was questioned by detectives and to preclude evidence seized during the search of Janna DeSanto's home. DeSanto was said to be working as a paralegal for Hugo who wrote to him in prison following his Oct. 10, 2003, escape from the Luzerne County Correctional Facility. As they spoke during the years, Hugo asked DeSanto to keep some of his materials related to his case at her home. Eventually, DeSanto would have 13 boxes of Hugo's materials including Hugo's defense strategy, letters from witnesses including Weakley, confidential correspondence between Hugo and his attorneys, and papers from Hugo's legal affairs in Monroe County for the Samuel Goosay robbery and kidnapping case.

Prosecutors filed their response to each issue Hugo's lawyers wanted to address while objecting to many, agreeing to some and acknowledged they did not intend to introduce certain witnesses or solicit specific testimony from witnesses. As for Hugo's history of incarceration, prosecutors strongly wanted to use his years behind bars where he met Paul Weakley, who was serving a federal sentence for manufacturing explosive devices in Michigan.

As Hugo's lawyers and prosecutors battled with filing motions, petitions and legal arguments at pre-trial hearings, the Pennsylvania State Police announced they uncovered a plot to have Weakley killed.

# PLOT TO KILL WEAKLEY

Michael Joseph Scerbo was arrested by Pike County detectives on forgery and identity theft offenses on Aug. 10, 2005, one of his many arrests dating back to 2001 when he was charged with impersonating a public servant and unlawful restraint. Scerbo's connection to Hugo was easy to make. Scerbo was jailed at the same time with Weakley at the Pike County Correctional Facility in 2008, and later Scerbo and Hugo were cell neighbors when they were both housed in the Restrictive Housing Unit at the State Correctional Institution at Retreat from June 13 to July 6, 2011, and again Aug. 19 to Nov. 17, 2011. Scerbo was at the Retreat state prison serving the full sentence of two years for his forgery conviction in Pike County. On the day of his release, April 27, 2012, Scerbo walked into the arms of State Police Trooper Stephen P. Polishan and Luzerne County Detective Lieutenant Gary Capitano.

Several months before Scerbo was to be released, the security office at Retreat contacted state police to report Scerbo was attempting to solicit the murder of Weakley. Court records filed against Scerbo say he contacted an inmate who he believed had strong ties to a known criminal gang based in Philadelphia, Pa., with the belief many gang associates are incarcerated at numerous federal prisons throughout the United States, including a federal prison in Arizona where Weakley was housed. Scerbo was eventually told he would be meeting with a gang associate in the Retreat prison's visitation room.

At the time in early 2012, Hugo's trial was scheduled to begin in September 2012. Unbeknown to Scerbo, he met with an undercover state trooper pretending to be a gang associate from Philadelphia on March 29, 2012. Scerbo indicated numerous times throughout the conversation he wanted Weakley killed as Weakley was to testify against Hugo.

Scerbo called Weakley a "rat," and needed to be murdered two months before Hugo's trial was to begin and was willing to pay $1,000 for the hit. When Scerbo was arrested by Trooper Polishan and Detective Lieutenant Capitano, he agreed to be interviewed, waiving his rights to remain silent or have an attorney with him.

During the interview, Scerbo explained he was jailed with Weakley at the Pike County Correctional Facility in 2008. Weakley told Scerbo he cut a deal with prosecutors to serve a 30 to 60 year sentence for the killings of Kerkowski and Fassett instead of a life sentence in exchange for his testimony against Hugo. After Weakley pled guilty to a federal RICO charge that incorporated the Kerkowski and Fassett killings and the Samuel Goosay robbery and kidnapping, he was eventually sentenced to life in a federal prison and sent to a facility in Arizona. Meanwhile, Scerbo was transferred to the Retreat state prison where he met Hugo in 2011.

Scerbo said he devised his murder plot when he solicited another inmate to find a hit man who would kill Weakley.

Scerbo was charged with criminal solicitation to commit homicide. Following a court proceeding in the case, First Assistant District Attorney Samuel Sanguedolce spoke with reporters. "When we learned of Mr. Scerbo's plan, we did in lieu of an actual hitman obviously, we sent in an undercover trooper from Philadelphia and he was able to audio record the admissions of (Scerbo)."

Had the Retreat security office not learned of the plot, Sanguedolce said Weakley would have been in danger. "The word that we understood at the time, he was designed to meet with someone who had inmates at that very prison. Luckily, that information was intercepted before it got to its destination and we were able to send a trooper in to get this information from (Scerbo)," Sanguedolce noted.

Scerbo pled guilty to the charge, criminal solicitation to commit homicide, before Luzerne County Judge Michael T. Vough on Jan. 14, 2013, and was sentenced on May 16, 2014, to 15 to 30 years in state prison.

Weakley did not stay quiet as he filed a civil lawsuit against the federal Bureau of Prisons alleging his concerns about being an informant went ignored. After being sentenced to life in prison on June 13, 2008, Weakley officially entered the federal prison system on Sept. 26, 2008, and was

sent to the U.S. Penitentiary Coleman in Florida where he claimed he was
beaten by two inmates wielding metal pipes three weeks after he arrived.
Weakley then alleged in his lawsuit he was transferred to the U.S.
Penitentiary Big Sandy in Kentucky on Dec. 29, 2008, and was stabbed
"no fewer than 26 times and left for dead" by two inmates on Jan. 1, 2010.
Three days after being transferred to the U.S. Penitentiary Lee in Virginia
on July 7, 2010, Weakley alleged in his lawsuit he was stabbed four times
in the neck by two inmates. A federal judge in Arizona dismissed
Weakley's lawsuit on June 28, 2012.

# HUGO'S LAWYERS GO ON OFFENSIVE

Hugo's lawyers did not rest, seeking sanctions against the Luzerne County district attorney's office for serving a search warrant at the home of Janna DeSanto on July 7, 2010, and seizing 13 boxes of what they called mostly confidential materials protected by attorney-client privilege. During a court hearing on the issue on June 12, 2012, DeSanto said she was not hired as a paralegal and was just helping as Hugo's friend. She described how she indexed each box and was aware of what each box contained.

Prosecutors in Luzerne County placed the seized boxes in their evidence room where they remained for several months. A "taint team" consisting of independent individuals, detectives and/or lawyers not involved in Hugo's criminal investigation was established. For this "taint team," an attorney from neighboring Lackawanna County was put in charge of searching the boxes since DeSanto lived in Moosic, Lackawanna County. The attorney got to decide what was attorney-client privilege and what prosecutors could keep.

Hugo's lawyers said the process was a disaster as DeSanto and Hugo never received an inventory of items seized from the boxes and had no knowledge of what legal materials, indicating Hugo's mental evaluation, attorney-client communications and defense strategy could be in the possession of prosecutors. Hugo's lawyers, at minimum, wanted the Luzerne County district attorney's office disqualified from prosecuting Hugo.

As Centini and Rymsza were actively going after sanctions and perhaps disqualifying the Luzerne County district attorney's office, they would lose their third wheel, Lampman, who was considered the brains of the case.

One of the last acts by Lampman was a motion to have Hugo wear civilian clothes whenever he appeared for pre-trial hearings. Normally, inmates wear custom prison jumpsuits consisting of labeled shirts, pants and slippers and inmates are shackled at the ankles and wrists when scheduled to go before a judge. The only time inmates wear civilian clothes is when they appear before a jury to prevent any type of influence simply by wearing prison garb. In addition, shackles are removed from inmates before the jury is brought into the courtroom to avoid a preponderance of guilt. Lampman and attorneys Centini and Rymsza in their request rightfully argued that Hugo's case "has touched off an avalanche of pretrial publicity" and the appearance of Hugo in prison clothing would generate unfavorable prejudice toward Hugo "in the eyes of the public."

Some would say Hugo's lawyers were asking Hugo to be treated differently than any other inmate brought to court for a pre-trial hearing.

No matter how one would review the request, Judge Pierantoni granted the motion without any response from prosecutors.

Lampman's departure was the result of an increasing caseload of defendants. Hugo's lawyers simply wanted to focus on Hugo and review the enormous amount of records in anticipation of the September 2012 trial. To ease his burden, Lampman filed a motion on June 20, 2012, to reassign his caseload and withhold additional conflict counsel appointments until the conclusion of Hugo's trial. Simply, Lampman wanted no new court-appointed clients and wanted his existing court cases defending clients reassigned. Lampman had been assigned to Hugo's defense team in his capacity as a conflict counsel earning $27,983 annually on June 17, 2010, and while working on Hugo's complex case, he also handled many other defendants participating in two other homicide trials while being assigned additional cases including appeals filed in appellate courts. In an unprecedented response, President Judge Thomas F. Burke Jr. and Judge Pierantoni reviewed and denied Lampman's request.

While Lampman requested a several month hiatus from his role as conflict attorney, he was advised he would be receiving additional cases to ease a growing backlog of criminal cases. Lampman was forced to resign his position as a conflict counsel on July 3, 2012, similar to the way Attorney Menn was permitted to leave Hugo's defense team.

Centini and Rymsza relied heavily on Lampman's knowledge about Hugo's case as he represented Hugo for many years. With Lampman now gone, Centini and Rymsza moved to continue Hugo's trial as they believed they were still learning about Hugo's complex case in addition to finding and searching for more case files scattered in many locations. Centini reengaged her effort at sanctions or, at best disqualify, prosecutors due to the seizure of 13 boxes of Hugo's materials from DeSanto's home. Centini wrote she has accumulated 26 banker size boxes, three smaller boxes, five binders and three cabinet drawers and loose materials including computer discs with thousands of pages of documents, photographs and videos. In the six to seven months Centini and Rymsza had been preparing their defense, they had not been able to review, sort and organize the entire massive file. They informed Pierantoni they had only scratched the surface, estimating they reviewed less than a quarter of the documents. Hugo's lawyers also complained about funding for Hugo's defense, saying they continued to work despite not being paid or receiving delayed payment and experts had not been paid by the court.

Centini wrote prosecutors had nine years to prepare while she and Rymsza were given only nine months to get ready. With Lampman gone, many tasks he handled such as funding, finding experts and organizing the enormous file without the benefit of a paralegal or volunteer now fell on Centini and Rymsza.

They continued to say they made professional and personal sacrifices for the seven months since they were appointed but their sacrifices created a situation that could not continue for much longer. Prosecutors opposed the request to continue the September 2012 trial but Centini and Rymsza felt they needed more time to provide effective assistance to Hugo. During a pre-trial hearing July 19, 2012, Centini pleaded with Pierantoni for more than one hour saying she could not be "effective" in defending Hugo if the September trial was not continued. Pierantoni rejected the request, keeping the September trial date. On his way out of the courthouse, Hugo said, "I'll be ready," noting Centini was not happy but, "ready than all the other attorneys I've had put together. She's ready to go."

In response to Hugo's lawyers request to dismiss the case citing double jeopardy and violation of Pennsylvania's speedy trial rule, eliminate the death penalty, limit prosecutors from introducing evidence and certain photographs and prohibit any mention of "future dangerousness" during the penalty phase, Pierantoni issued his rulings Aug. 3, 2012, accompanied by a 65 page memorandum. As expected, the judge refused to dismiss the case and the death penalty, but prohibited prosecutors from introducing any role Hugo may have had in the Ellen Smaka robbery and the use of human skeletal remains recovered from the burn pit and garbage bags at the Mount Olivet Road property. Prosecutors were also prevented from showing the jury Hugo's mugshot. Despite the Ellen Smaka robbery reference, prosecutors had already noted they intended to keep that from the jury as well as the skeletal remains.

Four days after Pierantoni issued his rulings, Hugo's lawyers on Aug. 7, 2012, filed an appeal with the Pennsylvania Superior Court placing the September trial in doubt. Prosecutors immediately responded the next day, Aug. 8, 2012, to strike the appeal saying it was frivolous and a tactic to delay the trial. Pierantoni had a say in a two page order filed Aug. 9, 2012, stating he was confident of his legal opinions but had no authority to decide if the appeal was frivolous.

Prosecutors then requested the appellate court to consider expediting the appeal, which the Superior Court agreed resulting in deadlines for Hugo's lawyers to file their legal argument by Aug. 20, and prosecutors to file their response five days later. An attempt by Hugo's lawyers to strike down the expedited appeal was rejected by the appellate court.

The Pennsylvania Superior Court was true to their word with an expedited appeal as on Aug. 28, 2012, a three-member panel of the appellate court denied the appeal agreeing with the rulings of Pierantoni. The appellate court noted, "the procedure history and relevant facts of this case are extensive." On the topic of double jeopardy, the appellate court ruled the murders of Frank James and Adeiye Keiler were different from the murders of Michael Kerkowski and Tammy Fassett. Hugo's lawyers believed all the murders were the same as the skeletal remains and the buried bodies were recovered on the same Mount Olivet Road property, the witnesses and investigators were largely the same, a primary witness in all the murders was Weakley and all the murders were connected to drugs and money.

As the Superior Court struck down Hugo's appeal, Pierantoni immediately issued an order keeping the September 2012 trial. Only Hugo's lawyers had more tricks up their sleeves with deadlines to file additional appeals and they took full advantage.

When the three-member panel of the Superior Court rejected the appeal, Hugo's lawyers had 30 days to file what is called a "reconsideration," for the entire 15 member Superior Court to review, taking them to Sept. 27, 2012. The "reconsideration" request was filed Sept. 22, 2012. Less than a month later, the Superior Court on Oct. 18, 2012, refused to "reconsider" the appeal. Hugo's lawyers were then granted 30 days to request the Pennsylvania Supreme Court to review the Superior Court's three-member panel opinion, which they filed on Nov. 16, 2012. It took the Supreme Court 145 days when on April 10, 2013, the highest appellate court in Pennsylvania denied to review the struck-down appeal. The only other option Hugo's lawyers had was an appeal with the U.S. Supreme Court, which never materialized.

With Hugo's appeals working their way through the appellate courts, his lawyers continued their playbook with an aggressive offensive strategy placing prosecutors on their heels. In August and September 2012, prosecutors issued subpoenas for Hugo's psychiatric reports and secretly obtained them, knowing they were forbidden to have such reports. Centini learned about Hugo's psychiatric reports being in the possession of prosecutors on Dec. 3, 2012.

Centini fired off an angry letter to First Assistant District Attorney Samuel Sangeudolce on Dec. 5, 2012, stating Hugo's records are "privileged and confidential," obtaining the records was "prosecutorial misconduct," and an "egregious violation of Mr. Selenski's rights." Centini advised Sanguedolce she intended to address the issue with Pierantoni while demanding Hugo's original and any copies of Hugo's medical and psychiatric reports be delivered to her office immediately.

Prosecutors were not entitled to Hugo's medical and psychiatric reports as Hugo had never put his mental health at issue in his case. If he had, then prosecutors would be permitted to have those reports and have their own psychiatric evaluation performed on Hugo. When Centini did not receive Hugo's reports in possession of prosecutors within a week, she filed a motion for indirect contempt of court and sanctions against prosecutors for prosecutorial misconduct on Dec. 12, 2012. It was learned prosecutors obtained Hugo's psychiatric reports by issuing subpoenas to the Luzerne County Correctional Facility on Sept. 10, 2012, and to the

State Correctional Institution at Mahanoy City, where Hugo was housed

for a time, on Aug. 27, 2012.

Centini reminded Pierantoni that Judge Van Jura, when he presided

over Hugo's case, denied a request by prosecutors to have an independent

psychiatric evaluation of Hugo in September 2011.

Centini further argued prosecutors did not understand the enormity of

the situation it created or simply did not care as prosecutors never

surrendered Hugo's psychiatric records to her, demanding that the entire

case against Hugo be dismissed with prejudice as a sanction for

prosecutorial misconduct.

Pierantoni withheld his decision due to the appeal that was currently

pending at the time in Pennsylvania Supreme Court.

With the trial delayed, once again the location of Hugo's incarceration

spurred another legal fight. Prosecutors wanted Hugo transferred to a state

prison while his lawyers wanted him to remain for easier access at the

Luzerne County Correctional Facility. This time, prosecutors said Hugo

needed to be transferred citing concerns of overcrowding at the county

prison, specifically in the restrictive housing unit where he has been kept

due to the nature of the charges and his October 2003 escape. Another

burden on the county prison was Hugo's security classification as two corrections' officers needed to escort him and stand outside a room whenever he met with his lawyers.

During the hearing on the request to transfer Hugo back to a state prison on March 15, 2013, Centini argued prosecutors did not have any standing to make such a request and Pierantoni lacked jurisdiction to entertain the request.

Centini also dropped a bomb during the hearing alerting Pierantoni that she had not been paid since October 2012, and would refuse to travel to a state prison at her own expense. After Centini raised her compensation disputes, another issue was broached that prosecutors were keeping tabs on who visited Hugo in prison.

Assistant District Attorney Jarrett Ferentino said Centini had visited Hugo 144 times at the county correctional facility, co-defense lawyer Edward Rymsza met Hugo 17 times and James Sulima, a private investigator, met Hugo numerous times for a total of 300 hours.

In the end, Pierantoni ordered Hugo back to state prison due to the trial being delayed with no schedule in sight.

Centini would raise her compensation package to the point where she requested to withdraw as Hugo's lawyer. When Centini was appointed in January 2012, she was to earn an hourly rate of $85 without benefits with a cap of $40,000, equal to about 470 hours of work. The court order that hired Centini as a private contractor was subject to change.

234

Records from the Luzerne County Controller's Office showed Centini had been paid $90,869 from the time she was appointed until mid-March 2013. Sulima, the private investigator, had been paid $23,913 during the same time span. Nearly $200,000 had been paid for various work for the prosecution, including expert witnesses, airfare, lodging and meals from 2005 through 2012. Centini said the amount prosecutors have spent was more like $1 million.

With Hugo's funding seemingly being drained and not refurbished by Luzerne County, Centini and Rymsza wanted out by filing a 13 page motion seeking to withdraw on April 5, 2013. In the motion, Centini and Rymsza argued Hugo was already serving what is virtually a life sentence as he was sentenced to 37 to 65 years in state prison for being convicted by a Monroe County jury in the Samuel Goosay robbery and kidnapping. Despite the virtual life sentence, Centini and Rymsza argued prosecutors continued to seek the death penalty for Hugo at a huge and unnecessary expense.

As Hugo was classified indigent status, he relied upon Luzerne County and taxpayers to pay for his defense. Since Hugo's arrest in June 2003, his lawyers have been conflict attorneys who, at the time, were paid less than $40,000 per year. Funding for Hugo's attorneys changed when Centini and Rymsza were appointed in January 2012 due to being qualified to defend capital cases.

The initial cap of $40,000 for Centini was extended by the court in June and again in October 2012, when she was advised by the court there would be no more cap extensions. When Lampman left Hugo's defense team when he resigned as a conflict attorney, Lampman's tasks fell onto Centini and Rymsza taking up valuable time.

Simply, Centni and Rymsza wrote they were diligently working with the goal to give Hugo the best possible defense and not getting paid.

Faced with a situation of not being paid and the October 2012, decision by the court to issue a "final cap," Centini and Rymsza wanted out.

As the motion filed by Hugo's lawyers seeking sanctions for prosecutorial misconduct remained unresolved, District Attorney Stefanie Salavantis, First Assistant District Attorney Samuel Sanguedolce and assistant district attorneys Jarrett Ferentino and Micheal Melnick filed their response on May 6, 2013.

Prosecutors explained Dr. John S. O'Brien, their psychiatric expert, requested Hugo's psychiatric and psychological records to aid in his evaluation and ultimate assessment of Hugo in order to complete his report. Prosecutors claimed that Hugo was likely to introduce his psychiatric health if the case reached the penalty phase and prosecutors were given the green light by Judge Van Jura on Sept. 12, 2011, to secure an independent psychiatric evaluation of Hugo. Prosecutors further pledged that no assistant district attorney reviewed or read Hugo's psychiatric medical reports.

Pierantoni on May 23, 2013, imposed sanctions against the district attorney's office forbidding them to call Dr. O'Brien as a witness or use any report generated by Dr. O'Brien, and ordered the destruction of Hugo's psychiatric medical reports in possession of prosecutors. Pierantoni scrutinized the district attorney's office saying they misapplied Van Jura's order allowing a "supplemental examination," but not a full blown psychiatric evaluation.

Sanctions imposed by Pierantoni were not what Centini and Rymsza wanted as they sought to have the case entirely dismissed, prohibit prosecutors from seeking the death penalty and a $1,000 a day fine for each day prosecutors had in their possession Hugo's psychiatric medical records.

Shortly after the Pennsylvania Supreme Court on April 10, 2013, denied to review Hugo's appeal, Pierantoni scheduled the trial to begin June 24, 2013. All signs indicated the trial was to start with filings by Hugo's lawyers and prosecutors of their trial briefs, questions to be asked during the selection of the jury and proposed verdict slips. Any hope that the trial was to begin June 24 was shattered when Pierantoni on June 6, 2013, delayed the trial until Aug. 5, 2013.

In late spring 2013, rumors began circulating that a grand jury coordinated by the Pennsylvania Attorney General's Office was investigating Hugo's case. What the grand jury was investigating was unknown but the Luzerne County Courthouse has no secrets and a small circle of people in the district attorney's office including a few reporters would be aware of what was about to take place.

# GRAND JURY

Judge Pierantoni on July 19, 2013, held an off-the-record, closed door meeting in his chambers with prosecutors, Hugo and his attorneys, Centini and Rymsza, and Attorney Al Flora, who was not on Hugo's defense team. About 25 minutes into the private meeting, the court stenographer was called into the judge's chambers to record what they were saying. When they emerged into the courtroom two hours after the private meeting began, Centini was not among them.

Pierantoni asked Sanguedolce to go on the record and explain why discussions were held in private. Sanguedolce said the closed door meeting was held due to a grand jury that was convened by the Pennsylvania Attorney General's Office but did not explain what the grand jury was investigating. Prosecutors knew as did Hugo's lawyers including Flora, who sat next to Hugo. Rymsza said he was unable to proceed with the trial without Centini and asked for the trial to be continued, which Pierantoni agreed without objection from prosecutors. Rumors that began circulating within the courthouse in late spring in 2013, would be confirmed by sources that the grand jury was investigating Centini and Sulima, the private investigator for Hugo's defense team. With the trial delayed again, Hugo was sent back to state prison that had stricter rules and policies for when attorneys met with their clients.

In the subsequent days after the July 19, 2013, hearing, it was learned the easy access and face-to-face meetings Centini and Sulima had with Hugo when he was jailed at the Luzerne County Correctional Facility spurred an exchange of letters Hugo wrote to witnesses, letters that were allegedly delivered by Centini and Sulima. When witnesses reported they met with Centini and Sulima and were given letters written by Hugo, prosecutors waited nearly a year before requesting the Pennsylvania Attorney General's Office to convene a grand jury.

Did Centini and Sulima commit an illegal act by meeting witnesses in a public place? Isn't a prosecution witness also a defense witness? Is it illegal for a defense lawyer to ask and meet a witness in a public place as law enforcement has an intimidating interrogation room?

And, why did prosecutors wait nearly a year before requesting an outside law enforcement agency to investigate?

For how long the trial would be delayed this time was anyone's guess. Rampant court filings in late spring by prosecutors and Hugo's lawyers that indicated a trial was about to happen came to a sudden stop with no signs of reigniting. Court filings in Hugo's case became non-existent in July, August, September and October 2013, except for a few orders by Pierantoni that were sealed from public view. The tidal wave of petitions and motions filed by Centini and Rymsza throughout 2012 and the first half of 2013 had suddenly come to an end.

Other indications the trial was far from beginning was the transfer of Hugo back to state prison and Paul Weakley, who was kept at the State Correctional Institution at Retreat, about 10 miles from the courthouse, was sent across the country back to the U.S. Penitentiary in Tucson, Ariz., in August 2013.

As prosecutors waited for the grand jury and the Attorney General's Office to make a move, Paul Weakley threw a grenade threatening the case prosecutors had generated against Hugo.

Weakley in late November and early December 2013, sent letters to the local print media, including The Times Leader, indicating he had no intention of cooperating with prosecutors and had no plans to testify during Hugo's trial. Weakley was the key witness for the prosecution and had pledged in his federal plea agreement when he pled guilty to a racketeer charge incorporating the murders of Kerkowski and Fassett that he would cooperate. Weakley had already been sentenced to life in a federal prison so there was nothing to gain with him testifying for prosecutors besides a feeling of self-righteousness.

"My name is Paul Weakley. I am a federal prisoner in Tucson, Arizona. According to local media accounts I am going to be testifying at (sic) Hugo Selenski trial, should it ever take place. This is not true. I am not testifying," Weakley wrote in his letter to local print media, adding he had notified the Luzerne County District Attorney's Office and his attorney, Paul Galante.

Shortly after the publication of stories in the local print media about Weakley's intentions, prosecutors and Galante held a teleconference phone call with Weakley at the U.S. Penitentiary in Tucson, Ariz. During the phone call, Weakley assured he would testify telling those he only sent the letter to the newspapers because other federal inmates were depicting him as a "snitch." Not feeling satisfied, several members of the prosecution team flew to Arizona to personally meet with Weakley. All seemed to be in order for Weakley to testify.

But Weakley was not done playing games as a year later, he would threaten again not to testify.

# HUGO'S LEAD DEFENSE ATTORNEY INDICTED

Since the appointment of Attorney Shelley L. Centini in January 2012, to defend Hugo, she had filed a mountain of petitions and motions in her legal attempt to dismiss the criminal homicide case in its entirely, to prohibit prosecutors from seeking the death penalty, limit or exclude evidence and expert testimony and was successful, to a degree, in seeking sanctions against the district attorney's office for improperly obtaining Hugo's psychiatric medical reports. To say she was vigorously defending Hugo along with Attorney Edward Rymsza would be an understatement. Centini was a different type of a defense attorney who was not coasting through a case but an attorney who went beyond the normal effort in defending their client that, perhaps, caught prosecutors by surprise.

Remember, the Luzerne County district attorney's office lost the first trial against Hugo for the killings of Adeiye Keiler and Frank James. As Hugo was a very high profile case given the amount of media attention, prosecutors did not like the aggressive offensive defense style by Centini and Rymsza, especially after Pierantoni imposed sanctions upon prosecutors for obtaining Hugo's psychiatric reports.

With confidence of securing first-degree murder convictions in the strangulation deaths of Michael Jason Kerkowski and Tammy Fassett being somewhat wavered, there was no doubt prosecutors were heading into a courtroom battle with Centini and Rymsza on the other side.

Centini's aggressive and offensive style was her own worst enemy and used against her when evidence and testimony were presented before the state grand jury seated in Dauphin County, Pa. During the third week in January 2014, a reporter was told by a source not to call in sick, take any days-off or go on vacation in the coming weeks, an indication that an announcement was coming spurred by the grand jury.

Pennsylvania Attorney General Kathleen G. Kane dropped a bomb that exploded Hugo's defense team on Jan. 27, 2014, when she announced the grand jury recommended Hugo, Centini and Sulima be criminally charged with intimidating witnesses and each lied while testifying before the grand jury.

Hugo, Centini and Sulima were each charged with various counts of intimidation of witness, perjury and criminal solicitation to commit perjury, obstruction of justice and tampering with evidence to name a few. Bail was set at $1.5 million for Hugo and $50,000 unsecured for Centini and Sulima.

A 13-page presentment by the grand jury alleged Hugo hand-wrote letters that were then delivered to four witnesses by Centini and Sulima at a tavern in Larksville in Luzerne County. Each letter was addressed to each witness and discussed their families and how they should testify at his upcoming trial, according to the grand jury presentment. While the names of the four witnesses were not listed in the presentment, they were later identified as Michael Shutlock, Joseph Pilcavage, Jason McEvoy and Joseph Jay Phillips, and Carey Bartoo. Bartoo was a girlfriend of Hugo years earlier and a relative of Kimberly Kerkowski. The family relationship between Bartoo and Kimberly Kerkowski was how Hugo became acquainted with Michael Jason Kerkowski.

A common theme by many attorneys in Luzerne County and those closest to Centini called the language in the 13 page presentment, "extremely vague," described it as "fiction," and Hugo's case continues to have "many twists and turns, it's a new chapter for this story."

Luzerne County Detective Lieutenant Gary Capitano, one of the two lead investigators on Hugo, first learned of Hugo's handwritten letters from Shutlock in July 2012. Following the disclosure, Capitano alerted District Attorney Stefanie Salavantis and First Assistant District Attorney Samuel Sanguedolce. Nearly a year passed before Salavantis and Sanguedolce requested the Pennsylvania Attorney General to conduct an investigation.

The presentment briefly highlights the history of Hugo's case and the various attorneys who represented him through the years. "Selenski's criminal exploits have given him considerable infamy and notoriety, resulting in a cult-like following of supporters willing to go to great lengths on his behalf," while describing Centini's actions as, "an absolute disregard for the rule of law and reflect a win-at-any-cost mentality." The grand jury rejected the assertion by Centini, Sulima and Hugo that the passing of letters was justified as "zealous defense work."

When Hugo testified before the grand jury, he blamed the media despite Hugo "frequently appearing on television broadcasts on local networks making comments as he was transported into or out of the Luzerne County Courthouse. Selenski sent a clear message to those watching, stating that he would walk out the front door of the Luzerne County Courthouse and be free once again." Although the presentment did not mention her name, Janna DeSanto, a one time self paralegal for Hugo, was identified as "Follower 1," in describing Hugo's cult-like following of admirers, devotees and the curious.

A day after the Attorney General's Office charged Centini and Sulima, prosecutors in Luzerne County moved to remove Centini and Sulima from Hugo's defense citing a conflict of interest. Pierantoni held a hearing on the request on Feb. 10, 2014.

Sulima had already left Hugo's defense team on Jan. 27, 2014. So the only issue to discuss was the removal of Centini.

Hugo strongly objected to the removal of Centini from his defense. Sanguedolce only said a few words and had not even broached his argument when Attorney Al Flora, representing Centini, interjected, saying Sanguedolce should not offer arguments on the motion to remove Centini as Sanguedolce had testified before the grand jury. As Sanguedolce testified before the grand jury, Flora said Sanguedolce was a witness in the criminal witness intimidation case against Centini.

Sanguedolce disagreed with Flora but nonetheless, Assistant District Attorney Jarrett Ferentino argued the motion to remove Centini. In releasing limited information about the prosecution's plan on what they will present against Hugo when his capital murder trial begins, Ferentino said the grand jury presentment would surely be used. Ferentino further noted Centini and Sulima became witnesses for the prosecution by having Hugo's hand written letters. Only the hand written letters never surfaced. No one ever saw or read them besides Michael Shutlock, Joseph Pilcavage, Jason McEvoy, Joseph Jay Phillips and Carey Bartoo. When Centini was instructed to bring the handwritten letters to be presented to the grand jury, she said they got "lost." In making his strongest argument, Ferentino said Centini had "concerns of her own," referring to the criminal charges against her, and should not continue to defend Hugo in the capital murder trial. "I can't imagine calling Attorney Centini to the stand and then asking her at the same time to act as an advocate on behalf of Mr. Selenski and protect herself at the same time. It just can't be done," Ferentino said.

Ferentino was quick to point out that Attorney Flora was representing Centini, a point he illustrated that Centini was in need of an attorney. "This one, it defies the books. You won't find a situation like this in the books where an attorney is charged as a co-defendant of their client. The fact that Mr. Flora is here suggests the difficulty we're going to have proceeding forward. That's the concern we're raising," Ferentino said, adding, "We have been working diligently to bring this case to trial. We're going to find ourselves again lagging behind because of the roadblocks and the pitfalls that are going to be presented with this representation."

Attorney Flora representing Centini at the disqualification hearing argued she has been Hugo's lead defense attorney for two years and prosecutors did nothing to remove her when prosecutors first learned a year earlier of the allegations she passed Hugo's handwritten letters to witnesses. Flora noted prosecutors waited until "the eve of the trial" to remove Centini.

Flora's arguments had no leeway on Pierantoni who found a conflict existed with Centini continuing to defend Hugo. "Attorney Centini is certainly cloaked with the presumption of innocence. That goes without saying. From a review of the affidavits and complaints, it is clear to this court that counsel's alleged criminal actions related directly to this homicide trial as per the filed charges," Pierantoni stated, adding, "Counsel is placed in the role of a witness in this case as notified by the

District Attorney in their motion, while serving as an advocate for the defendant (Hugo) in this homicide case. Counsel's alleged criminal acts arose from her actions in relation to this case."

One more person needed to be heard about his opinion and that was Hugo.

Hugo blurted out several times he was willing to waive the conflict of interest and wanted to express his thoughts on the record. Before Hugo did, Ferentino argued Hugo's opinion was simply not enough to have Centini to continue defending him.

"Judge, I'll only note in response to whether or not Mr. Selenski wants to waive a potential conflict, this conflict is a bear trap; it's inescapable. It's unwaiveable, Judge. This cannot be waived. The fact that Ms. Centini is a co defendant of Mr. Selenski's cannot be waived. The fact that her representation is compromised cannot be waived. It's just….there are conflicts of interest that are so bad that they are unwaiveable. This, I submit, is one of those circumstances. I don't doubt for a minute Mr. Selenski is going to get up, and he's going to give you a knowing waiver, knowing full well he is waiving the conflict of interest with regards to Attorney Centini. That being said, it's not enough," Ferentino said.

Hugo took the witness stand with Attorney Rymsza by his side.

Following Judge Pierantoni advisement to Hugo about his rights and the issue at hand related to the removal of Centini, Hugo said he was waiving any conflict that existed as a result of the witness intimidation and perjury charges filed by the Pennsylvania Attorney General's Office against himself, Centini and Sulima.

After several routine questions, Pierantoni simply asked: "Do you understand that the Commonwealth is indicating that they may call Attorney Centini as a witness in this (homicide) proceeding?" "I hope they do," Hugo quickly responded. "I absolutely waive any conflict issue."

"All right. Let me say that I am very concerned for the sanctity of the proceedings, and I want to protect the rights of all parties involved. I refuse to accept the waiver of conflict. Attorney Centini will be removed from this case. The court acknowledges that you are presumed innocent of the charges which have been filed against you," Pierantoni said, directing the last sentence to Centini.

"Mr. Rymsza, with that being said, you will be appointed as lead counsel in this matter for Mr. Selenski" the judge said. Rymsza quickly replied, "I won't accept lead counsel, Judge."

"I will continue as counsel for Mr. Selenski, but I, very candidly, won't accept an appointment as first chair," Rymsza said, meaning he was refusing the post as Hugo's lead defense lawyer.

And with the removal of Centini, Rymsza was not going to defend Hugo alone as the trial was scheduled to begin March 3, 2014. "It would be impossible for me to proceed in three weeks' time in this case," Rymsza said, adding Hugo was once again interested in defending himself.

"Mr. Selenski has indicated, and I think what he may be indicating to the court, is for the court to, in light of that, entertain his own motion to proceed pro se," Rymsza advised the judge.

Pierantoni said he would entertain Hugo's interest in defending himself at another time while granting a continuance delaying the trial once again until May 19, 2014, a date that was required to be set to protect Hugo's rights to a speedy trial.

"Judge, I realize you have to set that date. I know it's somewhat of a hollow date. But we all know, everybody in this courtroom realizes that's not going to happen," Rymsza said.

"I don't know why you say that, Mr. Rymsza," Pierantoni rhetorically asked. "I've been ready to go forward on this case for two years. And I acknowledge that there were very meritorious appeals taken. And the Grand Jury investigation has also surfaced, and as a result, it's led to a delay."

"Judge, if this case gets scheduled for a May trial date, you mark my words, they're going to prosecute this case a second time because we will be ineffective. And at this point in time, I am the only attorney in the case. I don't know how long it's going to take to find somebody to become first chair in this case and get up to speed on this case. So that's fine. You could list it for that day but…," Rymsza argued.

"I have listed it for that day. Thank you for your argument," Pierantoni said.

At the conclusion of the proceeding, Flora, who was mostly silent and was there to represent Centini, asked for a private meeting with Pierantoni. After the media and other non-court personnel left the courtroom, Flora advised the judge he could be called as a witness by the Pennsylvania Attorney General in the witness intimidation case as Centini was charged with theft, having been paid to defend Hugo with taxpayer dollars. Pierantoni listened but did not seem concerned. At the end, Hugo was sent back to the State Correctional Institution at Mahanoy City. Two months after Centini was removed, Attorney Bernard J. Brown, of Carbondale in the neighboring county of Lackawanna, was appointed to be Hugo's lead defense lawyer. Brown, who was qualified to defend capital cases, was compensated $85 per hour to be paid monthly with a cap of $40,000, with the potential to earn more "with good cause."

The preliminary hearing for Hugo, Attorney Shelley Centini and private investigator James Sulima on the witness intimidation and perjury charges was held April 24, 2014, before District Judge David H. Judy in Royalton, Dauphin County, just outside Pennsylvania's capital of Harrisburg, about a two hour drive from Luzerne County. A heavy police presence with two officers armed with shotguns stood outside as two more officers used hand-held wands to search everyone entering the courtroom.

Centini was represented by Attorney Al Flora and Sulima represented by Attorney William Ruzzo. Hugo represented himself and he appeared to have enjoyed it for several hours.

Since Hugo at the time was in the custody of the Pennsylvania Department of Corrections, he wore state inmate clothing with DOC on the back. Hugo was also shackled at the ankles and his wrists fastened to a restraint belt.

At the start of the hearing, Hugo asked and was granted to be uncuffed to take notes. Two guards stood over Hugo during the entire three hour hearing.

Luzerne County Detective Lieutenant Gary Capitano was the first witness to testify, explaining how Michael Shutlock contacted him in July 2012, regarding a meeting he attended, a meeting set up by Centini and Sulima held at a tavern in Larksville. After interviewing Shutlock about the meeting, Capitano said the decision was made within the Luzerne County District Attorney's Office to request the Pennsylvania Attorney General's Office to conduct an investigation as many believed witnesses in Hugo's homicide case were intimidated.

Flora, Ruzzo and Hugo asked Capitano if the district attorney's office requested copies of the alleged letters. "No," Capitano replied.

Michael Shutlock was the second witness to testify, detailing how he was asked to attend a meeting at the tavern on July 24, 2012. Shutlock testified he was called by Joseph Pilcavage to meet with Hugo's lawyer, Centini. "They said they have a letter for me," Shutlock testified.

Shutlock explained he remained standing when he read the letter, detailing the first paragraph asked how he was doing and how were his children, and the second paragraph suggested Shutlock should change his testimony. "She (Centini) said Hugo likes to write letters and he's written one for you," Shutlock said. Shutlock said after he read the second paragraph about changing his testimony, he put the letter down and began to walk away returning to the bar area where he stayed for five to six minutes before exiting the tavern.

Flora, Ruzzo and Hugo had no questions for Shutlock.

Jason McEvoy's testimony was similar about the meeting at the tavern and was given a handwritten letter from Hugo. McEvoy said his letter told him, "I should have kept my mouth shut years ago."

McEvoy asked if he could keep the letter but was told no, and the letter was taken back.

Answering questions from Flora, Ruzzo and Hugo, McEvoy said the meeting felt "awkward." McEvoy said he was never intimidated by Centini and Sulima nor was he threatened.

In answering Hugo's questions, McEvoy said he remembered driving to the Mount Olivet Road property to help Hugo clean the in-ground pool and was talking to Hugo on his cellular phone when state police converged onto the property on June 5, 2003.

Joseph Jay Phillips testified after McEvoy, detailing how he was asked to attend a meeting with Centini and Sulima. Phillips said he was handed a handwritten letter he was told was from Hugo referencing a party they both attended. When Phillips was on the witness stand, both he and Hugo smiled at each other. Phillips said his letter was about a party he attended with Hugo but denied knowing about any party. When Phillips said he placed the letter back onto the table, it was taken away. Phillips said he got to the meeting one hour later as he considered not going at all. The only reason Phillips decided to go, he testified, was he felt he would receive a subpoena if he did not attend.

If Phillips said he testified how Hugo's letter wanted him to testify, he would have lied and committed perjury.

After Phillips, Joseph Pilcavage was the fourth witness to testify. When he took the witness stand, he asked Hugo how he was doing. Hugo simply smiled.

Pilcavage stated Centini asked him to get in touch with some people, a few old friends of Hugo, and called Michael Shutlock, Jason McEvoy and

Joseph Jay Phillips. Pilcavage said Centini gave them letters written by Hugo to read. Pilcavage said his letter began, "Hey what's up, how are the kids?" Pilcavage asked if he could keep the letter but was told no and the letter was taken away.

Pilcavage said he was good friends with Hugo and stated he wished he was riding all-terrain vehicles with Hugo once again. Pilcavage further stated, "I miss my friend Hugo," and did not feel his letter was intimidating.

When Pilcavage left the witness stand, he wished Hugo, "Good luck," and nodded his head toward Hugo.

The last witness was Carey Ann Bartoo, the ex-girlfriend of Hugo. Hugo's body language changed drastically when Bartoo took the stand. He slumped into his chair compared to when he leaned forward with his elbows on the table when Michael Shutlock, Joseph Pilcavage, Jason Mcevoy and Joseph Jay Phillips testified.

Bartoo testified Centini arrived at her apartment in Plains Township with Hugo's letter but was told she wasn't allowed to keep it. Bartoo said it seemed Hugo was angry with her on how she could not remember picking him up at the Kerkowski home in Hunlock Township. Bartoo said Centini gave her $15 to $20 to buy cigarettes and milk, furthering the mystery that Hugo somehow managed to pay her rent.

Bartoo believed Centini was stopping by her apartment to give her a subpoena but instead was surprised she was handed a letter from Hugo. When Bartoo reviewed the contents of the letter with Centini, she said Centini told her to tell the truth. Bartoo said she was never intimidated by Centini.

The last witness was an agent with the Pennsylvania Attorney General's Office acknowledging the testimony before the grand jury by Centini, Hugo and Sulima.

District Judge David Judy advised those on April 24, 2014, that he wanted to read the grand jury presentment and instructed everyone to return to his courtroom on June 4, 2014, for closing arguments before rendering his decision to dismiss or forward the charges against Centini, Hugo and Sulima to Dauphin County Court.

As it appeared on April 24, a heavy police presence once again was outside Judy's courtroom when the preliminary hearing resumed. No witnesses were presented as closing arguments got immediately underway.

Attorney William Ruzzo, representing Sulima, went first, arguing Centini and Sulima did absolutely nothing wrong. Ruzzo reminded Judge Judy that Centini and Sulima met with Michael Shutlock, Joseph Pilcavage, Jason McEvoy and Joseph Jay Phillips at a public place and they were free to leave at any time. There were no threats or deals made as the letters, Ruzzo explained, were mostly Hugo asking how they and their families were doing. Ruzzo continued that none of the four men stormed out of the tavern and there were no fights or any other type of violence.

Ruzzo noted defense lawyers have a right to confront and meet with witnesses, and that the four men did not testify they felt intimidated. Touching on why the four men were not permitted to take the letters with them, Ruzzo said the letters, perhaps, contained defense strategies. If the letters were taken by the four men, "They would be in the hands of the prosecutors the next day or sooner," Ruzzo said.

Flora matched Ruzzo's argument that Centini and Sulima "don't have badges and don't have guns," referring to meeting the four men in a public place as compared to law enforcement interviewing witnesses while armed and in a secluded, interrogation room.

One can reason when Detective Lieutenant Gary Capitano first learned of the tavern meeting and Hugo's handwritten letters in July 2012, prosecutors in Luzerne County were not sure how Centini would handle Hugo's case having been appointed just seven months earlier and getting up to speed with the voluminous discovery materials. In the months after July 2012 and after numerous court filings by Centini including being successful in seeking sanctions against the district attorney's office for obtaining Hugo's psychiatric medical records against a judge's order, prosecutors knew they had an aggressive opponent on the other side of the aisle. Nearly year after Capitano learned of the tavern meeting, the district attorney's office referred the investigation to the Pennsylvania Attorney General's Office, resulting in criminal charges being filed and the preliminary hearing before Judge Daniel Judy.

Hugo went after Ruzzo in closing arguments saying the presentment itself "reads like a horror story." Hugo said the four men described the meeting as "weird, awkward and strange," that did not rise to the level of criminal intent. Hugo said the letters mostly asked how his friends and their families were doing and be prepared in their testimony if called to testify at his homicide trial.

Flora said the criminal charges against Ceninti were a "grave threat" to lawyers throughout Pennsylvania as defense lawyers have a right to interview witnesses. On the issue of what happened to the letters, Flora said none of the four men believed the content of the letters were intimidating or threatening, nor did Centini commit perjury because no witness testified that they saw the letters or had knowledge that the letters were destroyed.

Flora said the district attorney's office was made aware of the letters in July 2012 but never obtained a search warrant or subpoena for the letters from Centini. It was only after Centini received a subpoena to testify before the grand jury in August 2013, which she was instructed to bring the letters with her.

When Centini and Sulima met with the four men at the tavern, she was in her seventh month preparing to defend Hugo from capital punishment having received in excess of 20,000 pages of discovery up until July 2012. Naturally, Flora said some documents will get lost when an attorney receives that many documents in a short period of time. "Not a single witness testified that they were intimidated by Attorney Centini," Flora said.

"I have never seen anything so outrageous in my life," Flora said, "Because she challenged the death penalty. As lawyers, we have to think outside the box, anything that is a disservice to justice."

Flora attacked the grand jury's presentment referring to Centini wanting to be known as a super lawyer.

"They attacked her nomination as a super lawyer only to smear her," Flora said, raising his voice. "This has gone way too far."

Ironically, Centini was designated as a super lawyer years later.

Ruzzo went as far as blaming Pennsylvania Deputy Attorney General Daniel Jacob Dye as asking leading questions directed to the witnesses who testified.

In his closing arguments, Dye asked that all the charges against Centini, Hugo and Sulima be sent to Dauphin County Court for a jury to decide. Dye argued 23 people who sat on the grand jury had authority to accept or reject the presentment. And as the grand jury accepted the presentment, Dye said let a jury of 12 people decide the fate of Centini, Hugo and Sulima.

Without actually seeing the letters and only going on the statements of four men, Dye said the letters and the delivery amounted to a conspiracy as the letters asked the four men to "reconsider" their testimony. Dye further said the four men had not seen Hugo in 10 years and out of the blue, Hugo drafted letters that he had delivered by Centini and Sulima.

After closing arguments ended, it was Judge Judy's turn to render a decision.

The words were not even out of the judge's mouth when Centini suddenly began weeping and hugged Sulima, Flora and her family when all the charges against her were dismissed. The judge also dismissed all the charges against Sulima. As for Hugo, Judge Judy forwarded eight counts of intimidation of a witness/victim, and one count each of obstruction of justice and tampering with evidence to Dauphin County Court. Many other charges were dismissed against Hugo.

Following the hearing, Hugo said he was considering going "pro se" once again at his double homicide trial, meaning acting as his own attorney, since Centini was disqualified from representing him.

Outside the courtroom, Flora and Ruzzo provided statements and answered a few questions from reporters.

"Had this case been sent up, it would have been a death mill for defense lawyers and it would have jeopardized the freedom we all hold so dear," Flora stated, while criticizing the entire process. "I'm surprised that the Attorney General of our state would have even allowed this prosecution to commence. And I think she (Attorney General Kathleen Kane) has an obligation to look at this personally and to see the impact it had on this lawyer (Centini) and to see the impact it had on the Selenski homicide case overall. This prosecution should not have been brought under any circumstance.

"We had serious problems with the language of the grand jury presentment, the freedom that was taken by the prosecutor in this case and the language that was developed in this presentment that read like a fiction rather than a piece of law. This should never have happened," Flora said.

"Shelley is not responsible for a crime and neither is Jim (Sulima). I love Shelley. I've known her since she came into the public defender's office as a very ambitious law student. I told our boss at the time, Basil Russin, Shelley is going to be a smart, fantastic lawyer, and she is. These charges are so outrageous about the drama and innuendo in the charging documents as the grand jury was led down the path. The questions that were asked to the witnesses were leading. And some of the questions to the grand jury by the prosecutor had no basis in fact were unreasonable," Ruzzo said.

Flora and Ruzzo praised Judge Judy for taking his time to decide and not rubber stamping the case to higher court. Being criminally charged had a definitive impact on Centini and Sulima both personally and professionally, Flora and Ruzzo said.

"I can tell you as for Attorney Centini, it has taken a real toll on her. It has taken a toll on her family. What we saw here play out in the last few months was unjustified," Flora said while getting noticeably angrier. "I can also tell you I am shocked that the district attorney of Luzerne County would have referred this matter to the Attorney General's Office. To me it shows the complete lack of experience in that office in dealing with matters like this. I have seen many situations like this over the years in Luzerne County where there have been allegations of minor overreaching by police, assistant district attorneys, and defense lawyers and it has never gone this far. Usually, the matter is addressed informally with the presiding judge and things are worked out. But for that office (Luzerne County District Attorney) to refer this to the Attorney General is outrageous and it shows just how inexperienced that office really is."

"I'm just thrilled for my client, James Sulima, who is a great investigator. He was a police officer for years without a blemish on his record. Maybe now some of the comments I've seen in the media….the citizens calling Shelley all kinds of names, and sleazy and everything else. She is anything but that. And for Jim, as I said, his record is unblemished except for these charges which were outrageous and unsupported by the evidence not only in my view but in the judge's view they are unsupported. You know the standard is very low, they have to overcome and they didn't even overcome that," Ruzzo added.

A reporter asked a question if the referral from the Luzerne County District Attorney's Office to the Pennsylvania Attorney General's Office over the handwritten letters was in retaliation for Centini being an aggressive attorney and for successfully seeking sanctions against the district attorney's office?

"In my view, I think there is strong evidence to suggest that. I think that the district attorney's office has clearly placed the Selenski homicide case in serious jeopardy. I don't know how they will recover. Because I think if I was Selenski's counsel, I would be raising all kinds of retaliation at this point. Just to remove counsel who zealously advocated on his behalf. This had really gone on too far," Flora responded.

As some of Hugo's charges were forwarded to Dauphin County Court, the Attorney General's Office opted to withdraw the entire case against Hugo after his trial on the killings of Kerkowski and Fassett was held in Luzerne County Court.

# NEW LEAD ATTORNEY

After the preliminary hearing in Dauphin County concluded with the dismissal of all charges against Attorney Shelley Centini and private investigator James Sulima, the task now was for Attorney Bernard J. Brown to get up to speed.

Hugo's co-defense counsel Edward Rymsza adamantly advised Judge Pierantoni he would not be Hugo's lead defense attorney. Another defense lawyer with qualifications to defend capital cases was hard to find in Luzerne County as many of the qualified attorneys had previously defended Hugo. Going across county lines into neighboring Lackawanna County, Attorney Brown was appointed by Pierantoni on April 17, 2014, as Hugo's lead defense attorney. Attorney Hugh C. Taylor III would also be assigned to assist Brown and Rymsza. Brown was to earn $85 per hour to be paid monthly with a fee cap of $40,000 while his earnings could be higher with good cause, according to the judge's order. Taylor, as a conflict attorney in Luzerne County, was to earn his $28,000 salary.

When Brown and Taylor were appointed to Hugo's defense team, the trial was scheduled to begin May 19, 2014. With a little more than a month to prepare, naturally Pierantoni continued the trial until Nov. 12, 2014.

During a pre-trial proceeding to settle outstanding issues May 7, 2014, Pierantoni prohibited prosecutors from introducing Hugo's conviction in Monroe County in the Samuel Goosay kidnapping and robbery, but allowed prosecutors to use evidence recovered from the Monroe County case. Prosecutors were also prohibited from introducing Hugo's 1994 bank robbery conviction and eight year federal prison sentence during the case-in-chief homicide trial.

A few days after the pre-trial proceeding, Brown filed a motion seeking to delay the Nov. 12, 2014, trial. Pierantoni held a hearing on the request June 6, 2014, when Brown said he needed at least 10 months to prepare, estimating the trial could be held in March or April 2015. Pierantoni stood firm denying the request, maintaining the trial will begin Nov. 12, 2014.

The preliminary hearing in Dauphin County was revisited in an attempt to disqualify the Luzerne County District Attorney's Office from prosecuting Hugo's case. Attorneys Brown, Rymsza and Taylor filed a motion Sept. 18, 2014, claiming the district attorney's office had a conflict, especially First Assistant District Attorney Samuel Sanguedolce, in prosecuting Hugo. Hugo's lawyers in the motion argued the district attorney's office became aware that handwritten letters from Hugo were passed to four witnesses, including Michael Shutlock, in July 2012, and failed to alert the presiding judge, Pierantoni. Instead, the district attorney's office referred the alleged intimidation related investigation to the Pennsylvania Attorney General's Office. Prosecutors had said the referral to the attorney general was to avoid a conflict with the pending homicide trial.

When the attorney general presented evidence to the grand jury, Sanguedolce and county Detective Lieutenant Gary Capitano testified before the grand jury. When the attorney general's office filed witness intimidation and perjury charges against Attorney Shelley Centini and private investigator James Sulima, prosecutors successfully had Centini and Sulima removed from Hugo's defense team stating on the record they were going to use the evidence presented to the grand jury during Hugo's homicide trial.

Brown and Rymsza cited the Feb. 10, 2014, hearing when Pierantoni removed Centini. Sanguedolce was told to step aside from making any arguments during the Feb. 10, 2014, hearing in response to Centini's attorney, Al Flora, who argued Sanguedolce had a conflict of interest because he testified before the grand jury. Brown and Rymsza were hoping to have the same luck as Flora had at the Feb. 10, 2014, hearing by filing the motion to disqualify the district attorney's office from prosecuting Hugo. "By virtue of his testimony before the grand jury, Mr. Sanguedolce has injected himself as a potential witness in the present homicide prosecution," Brown, Rymsza and Taylor wrote in their motion, noting it would be highly inappropriate to permit Sanguedolce to testify, take the witness stand and then resume the role as lead prosecutor.

When Sanguedolce at the Feb. 10, 2014, hearing was told he could not make any arguments, he sat silent as Assistant District Attorney Jarrett Ferentino presented arguments, saying Centini would be called as a witness but could not advocate for Hugo at the same time.

Now, Hugo's attorneys were using the same argumentative logic in their attempt to disqualify the district attorney's office. "The jury cannot be expected to provide an impartial judgment as to a prosecutor's credibility as a witness when he serves the dual role of the prosecutor on the same case. In its own submission justifying the removal of prior counsel (Centini), the District Attorney's office has conceded that the dual capacity appearance by counsel as an advocate and witness in the same case is precluded….This is a classic example of what is good for the goose is good for the gander," Hugo's attorneys argued in their motion.

While Hugo's attorneys were asking to disqualify Sanguedolce, they were also using a law clerk who formerly worked in Pierantoni's chambers was now employed by the district attorney's office. Lawyers for Hugo argued the law clerk was privy to private communications, sealed defense filings and defense strategy while employed as Pierantoni's law clerk. "...the entire Luzerne County District Attorney's Office should be

Hugo Selenski in 1990

Michael Jason Kerkowski - Luzerne County District Attorney's Office

Tammy Lynn Fassett - Luzerne County District Attorney's Office

Hugo Marcus Selenski mugshot June 2003

Overview picture of the Mount Olivet Road property where the bodies of Michael Jason Kerkowski and Tammy Lynn Fassett were found buried and a burn pit (upper left) contained the human remains of three people. - Luzerne County District Attorney's Office

Driveway leading up to the home where Hugo Marcus Selenski resided in June 2003. Detached garage is on the right - Luzerne County District Attorney's Office

The bodies of Michael Jason Kerkowski and Tammy Lynn Fassett were found in this grave behind the Mount Olivet Road residence where Hugo Marcus Selenski resided in June 2003 - Luzerne County District Attorney's Office

Troopers with the Pennsylvania State Police, Troop P, Forensic Services Unit and a K-9 handler search over the property at Mount Olivet Road on June 11, 2003 - Times Leader

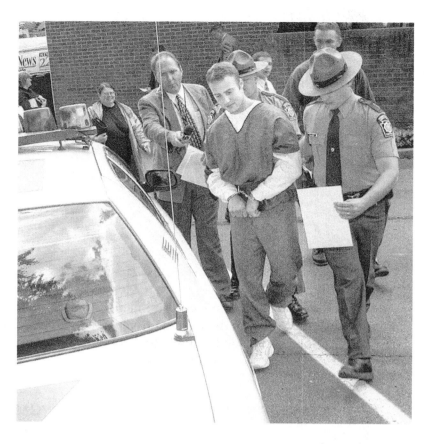

Hugo Marcus Selenski shown after he was charged on Oct. 6, 2003, for the shotgun slayings of Adeiye Keiler and Frank James and burning their bodies at his Mount Olivet Road residence - Times Leader

Adeiye Keiler - Luzerne County District Attorney's Office

The Luzerne County Correctional Facility with the bedsheet rope on the night Hugo Selenski and Scott Bolton escaped from the maximum security level on the top floor on Oct. 10, 2003 - Times Leader

Cell 9 where Hugo Selenski and Scott Bolton escaped from the Luzerne County Correctional Facility on Oct. 10, 2003. Notice the metal screen mesh on top bunk - Times Leader

Hugo Selenski in custody on Oct. 13, 2003, three days after he escaped from the Luzerne County Correctional Facility - Times Leader

Attorney Demetrius "Tim" Fannick - Times Leader

Luzerne County Assistant District Attorney
James L. McMonagle Jr. - Times Leader

A sketch by Marijo DePaola for the Times Leader showing Hugo Selenski (blue shirt) with his trial lawyers, from left: Demetrius Fannick, Stephen Menn and John B. Pike during a court proceeding on Feb. 21, 2006.

A sketch by Marijo DePaola for The Times Leader showing Luzerne County Judge Peter Paul Olszewski Jr. at a sidebar conference with Attorney Demetrius Fannick (left) and Luzerne County Assistant District Attorney James L. McMonagle during the 2006 trial of Hugo Selenski.

Luzerne County Judge Peter Paul Olszewski Jr. - Times Leader

Hugo Selenski leaving the Luzerne County Courthouse during his March 2006 trial - Times Leader

Lead investigators on the Hugo Selenski case, Luzerne County Detective
Lieutenant R. Gary Capitano (top) and Pennsylvania State Police
Corporal Gerard Sachney - Times Leader

District Judge James Tupper presided over all of Hugo Selenski's preliminary arraignments and preliminary hearings - Times Leader

Luzerne County District Attorney David W. Lupus (right), First Assistant District Attorney Jacqueline Musto Carroll (center) and Assistant District Attorney David Pedri at a news conference May 19, 2006, announcing Hugo Selenski and Paul Weakley were charged with the flex-tie strangulation deaths of Michael Jason Kerkowski and Tammy Lynn Fassett - Times Leader

Luzerne County District Attorney David W. Lupus (forefront), with Assistant District Attorney Jarrett Ferentino (left), Assistant District Attorney David Pedri and Pennsylvania State Police Lieutenant Frank Hacken after a preliminary hearing in Kingston Township on June 14, 2006 - Times Leader

Supporters of Hugo Selenski displayed T-shirts depicting Lupas vs Hugo Round #2 at a preliminary hearing on June 14, 2006 - Times Leader

Jacqueline Musto Carroll
became Luzerne County
District Attorney in 2007
- Times Leader

Geraldine Kerkowski with her husband, Michael Stanely Kerkowski, at
the Luzerne County Courthouse on June 16, 2006 - Times Leader

Lisa Sands, the sister of Tammy Lynn Fassett, during an interview at her residence in 2016 - Times Leader

Luzerne County First Assistant District Attorney Samuel Sanguedolce (left), and Assistant District Attorney Jarrett Ferentino. In rear is Luzerne County Sergeant Detective Sergeant Charles Balogh - Times Leader

Attorney Shelley L. Centini

Attorney Bernard Brown shown during Hugo Selenski's trial at the Luzerne County Courthouse on Feb. 5, 2015 - Times Leader

Attorney Edward Rymsza shown during jury selection for Hugo Selenski's trial at the Luzerne County Courthouse on Jan. 8, 2015 - Times Leader

Hugo Selenski on the final day of jury selection at the Luzerne County Courthouse on Jan. 14, 2015 - Times Leader

Patrick Russin is shown being escorted by Luzerne Detective Lieutenant Daniel Yurhsa after he testified against Hugo Selenski on Feb. 16, 2015 - Times Leader

Luzerne County Judge Fred A.
Pierantoni III - Times Leader

Luzerne County Lieutenant Detective Daniel Yursha escorts Paul Raymond Weakley inside the Luzerne County Courthouse on Jan. 5, 2015 - Times Leader

Ernest Culp, who died Sept. 13, 2014, testified during Hugo Selenski's first trial in March 2006. His preliminary hearing testimony from June 2006, was read during Selenski's 2015 trial - Times Leader

Forensic pathologist Dr. Michael Baden shown before his testimony on
Feb. 3, 2015, during the Hugo Selenski trial. Front, Luzerne County
District Attorney Stefanie Salavantis and rear, Pennsylvania State Police
Trooper Stephen Polishan and Luzerne County Detective Sergeant Charles
Balogh. - Times Leader

Jail cell artwork by Hugo Selenski

Samuel Goosay - Times Leader

Luzerne County Assistant
District Attorney
Mamie Phillips - Times Leader

Luzerne County Detective Lieutenant Gary Capitano with Michael Serbo who was charged in a murder plot to kill Paul Weakley - Times Leader

Geraldine Kerkowski (second from left) holds hands with Luzerne County Assistant District Attorney Jarrett Ferentino after a jury on Feb. 11, 2015, convicted Hugo Selenski of murdering her son, Michael Jason Kerkowski, and Tammy Lynn Fassett. At left, District Attorney Stefanie Salavantis and (far right) First Assistant District Attorney Samuel Sanguedolce. In rear is Lisa Sands, sister of Tammy Fassett, walking next to Luzerne County Lieutenant Detective Gary Capitano - Times Leader

Hugo Selenski, shown after a jury on Feb. 12, 2015, convicted him with murdering Michael Jason Kerkowski and Tammy Lynn Fassett - Times Leader

Hugo Selenski often responded to media questions when escorted inside the Luzerne County Courthouse - Times Leader

Hugo Selenski leaves the Luzerne County Courthouse after Judge Fred A. Pierantoni III sentenced him to two consecutive life terms in state prison with no parole on March 27, 2015 - Times Leader

disqualified from prosecuting this case," Hugo's lawyers wrote.

Hugo's lawyers further filed, yet again, a motion to continue the Nov. 12, 2014, trial until the first half of 2015. Brown in the motion seeking another delay claimed he received on June 10, 2014, nearly 23,000 pages of materials from the district attorney's office and more discovery from Centini. Brown wrote he spent five to six hours each day reviewing the materials in addition to handling two homicide trials unrelated to Hugo's case. Brown also requested to have a four-day trial week expecting the trial to last up to five weeks.

And as he once did previously, Pierantoni on Oct. 3, 2014, denied both requests, allowing the Luzerne County District Attorney's Office to prosecute Hugo and maintaining the Nov. 12, 2014, trial start date.

Then on Oct. 27, 2014, prosecutors found themselves in the same hole as they did when Judge Van Jura presided over Hugo's case in 2011. In a joint motion filed by prosecutors and Hugo's lawyers on Oct. 27, 2014, both sides raised concerns about the upcoming Thanksgiving Day holiday and their best estimates for a five week trial had the potential of proceedings going into Christmas and New Years. Assistant District Attorney Jarrett Ferentino suggested the days off for the holidays would create difficulty for jurors attempting to recall evidence and testimony, and family and friends seeking information about the case at holiday gatherings. Pierantoni said he found their arguments "speculative though notable" and granted the request to continue the trial while adding the delay would absolutely be the last continuance. While prosecutors and Hugo's lawyers wanted the trial to begin in March or April, Pierantoni ordered the trial to commence with jury selection on Jan. 5, 2015. "Everybody have your houses in order. We're starting jury selection that morning," the judge boldly said, noting there would be no more trial delays.

An indication the trial would actually take place came from court filings from prosecutors and Hugo's lawyers throughout December. Prosecutors moved to submit the preliminary hearing testimony of Ernest Culp, who died of cancer on Sept. 13, 2014, which was contested by Hugo's lawyers as they would not be able to cross-examine Culp's previous testimony. Culp, a landscaper who lived in a house trailer on the Mount Olivet Road property, stumbled upon Hugo and Weakley digging a hole with shovels on May 5, 2002, the same hole where the bodies of Kerkowski and Fassett were recovered June 5, 2003. Hugo and Weakley told Culp they were digging a hole to place a gasoline tank for their all-terrain vehicles.

A pre-trial conference was held Dec. 11, 2014, to finalize housekeeping issues, including 200 jury notices sent out with 150 potential jurors in the first wave with 50 people in reserve. Jurors would first be asked questions as a whole with individual questioning of each juror to follow. Attorney Rymsza renewed the request to have a four-day trial week instead of five days, which was objected by First Assistant District Attorney Samuel Sanguedolce. Pierantoni said he found the request to be "odd," noting the last time he had a four-day work week occurred when he attended Temple Law School.

As he did a year earlier when Paul Weakley sent a letter to local media threatening not to testify during Hugo's trial, he directly informed the district attorney's office on Dec. 17, 2014, that he would not testify. Prosecutors went into panic mode reopening up the lines of communications with Weakley, his lawyer Paul A. Galante, and filing a motion to submit Weakley's previous testimony at the preliminary hearing held eight years and six months earlier on June 24, 2006. Prosecutors wanted their motion sealed citing Weakley had been assaulted by other inmates for his cooperation but Pierantoni denied the request.

Arrangements were made to immediately transport Weakley from the federal prison in Tucson, Ariz., to Luzerne County. Under his federal plea agreement on Jan. 25, 2008, when he pled guilty to the federal Racketeer Influenced and Corrupt Organizations charge that incorporated the killings of Kerkowski and Fassett and the Samuel Goosay kidnapping and robbery, Weakley pledged to cooperate and testify against Hugo. Weakley had nothing to lose and his reputation restored in federal prison by not being known among inmates as a "snitch."

Weakley provided detectives and investigators many misleading versions of how Kerkowski and Fassett were killed. Only after detectives and investigators were unable to verify his statements did Weakly finally confess to his role in killing Kerkowski and Fassett and burying their bodies.

Pierantoni scheduled a pre-trial hearing for Jan. 2, 2015, on the motion by prosecutors to admit Weakley's prior statements and preliminary hearing testimony. Another request by prosecutors sought to include the witness intimidation case filed in Dauphin County during Hugo's trial.

Within minutes of the start of the Jan. 2, 2015, pre-trial hearing, prosecutors filed additional legal papers to support their argument to include Weakley's statements and testimony, which annoyed Pierantoni. Prosecutors maintained Weakley had been stabbed at least 50 times during his prison incarceration for cooperating and agreeing to testify against Hugo. To illustrate their point, Michael Scerbo was transferred from a state prison to the Luzerne County Courthouse. Scerbo was an inmate at the State Correctional Institution at Retreat where he met Hugo and Weakley. It was Scerbo who solicited other inmates to find him a hitman with intentions to kill Weakley for being a snitch and cooperating with law enforcement and prosecutors.

When Scerbo was charged and eventually sentenced to 15 to 30 years in prison for soliciting to kill Weakley, investigators and prosecutors were careful not to release who orchestrated and directed Scerbo to solicit Weakley's death. In court records filed on Dec. 29, 2014, prosecutors finally stated Hugo solicited Scerbo to kill Weakley. Scerbo was brought to the courthouse to testify during the Jan. 2, 2015, pre-trial hearing but was never called into the courtroom as Pierantoni ended the hearing only to resume the following Monday, Jan. 5, 2015.

Decisions needed to be made by Pierantoni as time was running out. When the pre-trial hearing resumed Jan. 5, 2015, 150 people who received jury notices to report for jury duty would be walking into the courthouse in preparation of selecting a panel of 12 people and four alternates for Hugo's trial. Pierantoni would permit prosecutors to submit the preliminary hearing testimony of Ernest Culp over the objections by Hugo's lawyers.

First Assistant District Attorney Samuel Sanguedolce withdrew the motion to admit Weakley's prior statements and testimony. Weakley and once again, Scerbo, were inside the courthouse on Jan. 5, 2015. A day earlier, Sunday, Jan. 4, 2015, county Detective Danuel Yursha went to Pierantoni's home to have the judge sign a transport order to have Weakley transferred from prison to the courthouse on Monday.

Sanguedolce told Pierantoni on Jan. 5, 2015, that prosecutors had a conversation with Weakley, who ultimately decided to testify against

Hugo, resulting in the motion to admit Weakley's prior statements and testimony to be withdrawn.

Those 150 people who reported for jury duty were sent home early on Jan. 5, 2015, and were instructed to return Thursday, Jan. 8, 2015, when the selection of the jury panel would begin. Another 50 people summoned for the jury pool would be held in reserve in case a jury of 12 plus four alternates could not be seated from the 150 people who initially reported.

After more than a decade involving the carousel changes of judges, attorneys, prosecutors, a prison escape, a murder for-hire plot, a grand jury investigation, witnesses allegedly being intimidated, numerous appeals and delays, jury selection for the trial of Hugo Marcus Selenski was finally going to happen. It was not a dream. "Going to trial," Hugo bellowed to reporters in the courthouse basement when he was taken back to the county prison on Jan. 5, 2015.

By the numbers since Hugo was charged in May 2006, for the killings of Kerkowski and Fassett, the trial had been scheduled 16 times, 11 attorneys had been appointed to defend Hugo and the case had been assigned eight times among six judges.

# TRIAL FINALLY BEGINS

Luzerne County Court Administrator Michael Shuchosky directed 200 jury notices be sent out specifically for Hugo's trial. Shuchosky noted 150 people would be individually questioned by Hugo's lawyers and prosecutors with the other 50 people placed on standby if efforts to seat a jury of 12 plus four alternates became exhausted from the larger group. Hugo will be displayed wearing a dress shirt, a tie, dress pants and unshackled.

With 150 people jammed into a courtroom in every possible seat in addition to folding chairs brought in, the jury pool was addressed by Pierantoni and introduced to Hugo and his lawyers, Bernard Brown, Edward Rymsza and Hugh Taylor, and the prosecutors, First Assistant District Attorney Samuel Sanguedolce and assistant district attorneys Jarrett Ferentino and Mamie Phillips. After the standard jury questionnaire was filled out by each potential juror, the jury pool was asked 24 questions whether they heard about Hugo, read about Hugo, had a fixed opinion about Hugo and whether anyone had moral or religious concerns about imposing the death penalty. If a potential juror said they were against or opposed the death penalty based on religious or personal beliefs, they were excused.

Selecting a jury was a slow and tedious process for Hugo's lawyers and prosecutors. Four jurors had been picked over the first two days.

When juror number 26 was being questioned for about 30 minutes on the second day of jury selection, politely answering a firestorm of questions directed at him by Hugo's lawyers and prosecutors, Judge Pierantoni asked both sides if they wanted juror number 26 on the jury. The potential juror then raised his hand saying he knew Kerkowski, explaining no one asked him if he knew Kerkowski or Fassett because they were not on the witness list. The jury pool was given a list of witnesses' names to determine if they knew the witnesses or were somehow related. The names of Michael Jason Kerkowski and Tammy Lynn Fassett were not on the list shown to jurors during the pre-selection phase.

As it turned out, juror 26 delivered supplies to Kerkowski's pharmacy near Tunkhannock, Wyoming County, Pa, and had delivered supplies to Kerkowski's Hunlock Township, Luzerne County, home. Juror 26 was at the crime scene and was promptly dismissed.

It took six full days from Jan. 8 to Jan. 15 to select 12 people to sit on the jury plus four alternates.

"Ladies and gentlemen, we have a jury," was the first paragraph of The Times Leader story, Jan. 16, 2015, in reporting the jury and four alternates were seated. Pierantoni scheduled the trial to begin Jan. 21, 2015.

Nearly 12 years after it all began, the long-awaited capital murder trial of Hugo Marcus Selenski finally got underway at 9:42 a.m. on Jan. 21, 2015, when the jury walked through the large oak doors into the courtroom, down the center aisle, past the judge's bench and witness chair and took their place in the jury box along the right side wall in old, wooden swivel seats.

"I'd like to welcome everyone to Courtroom No. 4 this morning. My name is Fred Pierantoni and I am the judge assigned to this case," Pierantoni began while introducing Hugo, his lawyers and prosecutors. Pierantoni gave a quick educational session advising the jury what to expect during the estimated four to five week trial. The jury was told and told again not to read any newspapers, watch television news, listen to news radio reports and not to conduct their own investigation and searches on the internet about the case. Jurors were also instructed not to discuss the case amongst themselves or with any family members.

Pierantoni made the decision not to sequester the jury during the trial allowing each juror to go home for the night.

Pierantoni's instructions lasted 20 minutes and gave the jury a 15 minute break before the actual case-in-chief began. As it is Pennsylvania trial procedure, prosecutors go first with opening statements followed by the defense if they choose.

Assistant District Attorney Jarrett Ferentino, a 2003 graduate of Dickinson School of Law, Penn State University, who had successfully prosecuted at least five homicide trials since 2006 at the time of Hugo's trial, gave the opening statement, telling the jury they were "about to go on a little journey together." It was anything but a little journey but a horrific sequence of events.

Ferentino advised the jury what they will be told and what they will see will shock them to their core describing the brutality how Kerkowski and Fassett were strangled to death with plastic flex ties and buried in a shallow grave outside the Mount Olivet Road home where Hugo lived with his then girlfriend, Christina Strom. Ferentino told the jury about Paul Raymond Weakley, how Hugo met him when both were inmates at the U.S. Penitentiary at Lewisburg, and how Hugo persuaded Weakley to come live with him when he got released from the federal prison.

Ferentino explained how Kerkowski and Fassett met when Fassett was a waitress at a bagel shop frequented by Kerkowski that soon blossomed into a romantic relationship. Just as quickly as Ferentino told the jury how Kerkowski and Fassett met, the prosecutor moved to the beginning of the relationship between Hugo and Kerkowski.

Referencing Kerkowski's legal troubles for selling prescription medications without prescriptions, Hugo's relationship to Kerkowski was through Carey Bartoo, who is the cousin of Kerkowski's estranged wife,

Kimberly Kerkowski. While Kerkowski faced a trial in Wyoming County for his dope selling without prescriptions, Hugo offered his services.

"You will hear that Hugo Selenski was this know-it-all guy who knew the system. You'll hear that Michael trusted Hugo. You will hear Michael said to his parents, Michael is a man on trial. He's facing the losing of his license, the loss of his freedom. He has attorneys, he's on trial. And he said, 'Mom and dad, I trust someone even more than my lawyers, I trust Mr. Selenski, this guy, this Hugo, who's my best friend,'" Ferentino told the jury in his opening statement.

Ferentino said Hugo was attracted to Kerkowski only for the money the pharmacist made by illegally selling prescription medications. Kerkowski was scheduled to be sentenced on May 14, 2002, in Wyoming County Court. When Kerkowski failed to appear as he was free on bail, Wyoming County District Attorney George Skumanick believed he fled the country. It would be another 13 months when the truth became known.

Ferentino then explained Weakley to the jury, describing how Weakley when he was released from federal prison ended up moving in with Hugo and Christina Strom at Strom's grandmother's house on Miller Street in Luzerne Borough. "Immediately, immediately upon his release, Mr. Selenski starts to tell (Weakley) about Michael. He says, you'll hear, he says, 'Hey, we got a mark, this guy, Kerkowski. He's got a lot of cash up at the house, he's got a lot of cash up there, let's rob him, let's kill him,'"

Ferentino told the jury.

Then Ferentino got into the actual motive of Kerkowski's murder.

At the real estate closing making Strom's purchase of the Mount Olivet Road property official, she issued a check in the amount of $10,079 knowing she had approximately $699.71 in her checking account. Strom knew the check would bounce and the anxiety kicked in as she expressed her dire concerns with Hugo.

With Kerkowski scheduled to be sentenced in Wyoming County Court on May 14, 2002, Hugo had a short amount of time to act on his plan to get Kerkowski's cash to cover the check.

"Hugo goes back to Paul Weakley and says, 'Paul, we got to take this Kerkowski out; I need the money to cover this check....We'll make it look like he fled, he fled his criminal troubles, that Michael took off and wasn't murdered," Ferentino said during his opening statement.

Ferentino described to the jury how Kerkowski and Fassett were brutally killed and Hugo depositing money into Strom's bank account to cover the check she had issued days earlier.

Ferentino's opening statement was 72 minutes.

Jurors were given a 15 minute break before the opening statement by Hugo's lawyers. When everyone returned to the courtroom, the trial almost came to an abrupt end when Hugo's co-defense lawyer, Edward Rymsza, requested a mistrial.

Rymsza made the request during the first of multiple side-bar conferences with Pierantoni, arguing a statement by Ferentino during his opening statement.

In describing Weakley and all of the lies he initially told investigators, Ferentino explained to the jury that Weakley admitted to the murders of Kerkowski and Fassett under the federal plea agreement and subsequent sentence in 2008. Telling the jury Weakley's lies would be highlighted by Hugo's lawyers, Ferentino described Weakley as a close associate of Hugo who brought him to Luzerne County. In needing help to kill Kerkowski and then Fassett, Hugo knew he could rely upon Weakley for his assistance. "Birds of a feather…they what, folks. They flock together," Ferentino told the jury during his opening statement.

During the side-bar conference, Rymsza objected to the statement and requested a mistrial. "I'm going to lodge an objection and ask for a mistrial regarding a comment that Mr. Ferentino made regarding, I believe it was raised in the context of birds of a feather flock together, and it was said in the context of Mr. Weakley entering a plea. Umm, I think that smacks of guilt by association and I think it, it, in that context. And so, I'm going to make an objection and move for a mistrial," Rymsza asked.

"What I said, Judge, was, birds of a feather flock together regarding their association. It had nothing, nothing to do with a plea or his entry of a plea. The bottom line is I'm simply making a point that these two individuals had a relationship, a friendship and association. That's what that expression was for. I think any time it's ever been used in, in literature or, in media, that's what it's said to mean. I'm in no way, I don't understand what that would mean with regard to, I don't understand the objection," Ferentino replied.

Pierantoni denied Rymza's request for a mistrial.

Hugo's lead defense lawyer Bernard Brown began his opening statement at 12:02 p.m.

A common tactic by any defense lawyer during opening statements is to describe what one believes is the definition of reasonable doubt and Brown did just that. To understand reasonable doubt, Brown asked the jury to think of driving away from your home and thinking 'did you lock the front door.' Simply by asking yourself if you locked the front door is reasonable doubt, Brown told the jury.

"This is the defense's opening statement, as I said, and I'm going to show you the areas of doubt. And the first area of doubt is regarding who killed Michael Kerkowski and Tammy Fassett: Paul Raymond Weakley," Brown said.

Brown informed the jury that Weakley is a liar and gave investigators several versions of how Kerkowski and Fassett were killed and the events leading up to and after the murders. Brown further explained the money used to purchase the Mount Olivet Road property, telling the jury Christina Strom earned $55,000 a year by working as a vehicle adjuster for a car insurance carrier and had substantial savings. Strom further received an inheritance from her grandmother, Brown said.

"Why would Hugo have to kill Michael Kerkowski and Tammy Fassett if Tina Strom was planning on purchasing this property, if she had a job, if she had money available to her," Brown rhetorically asked the jury.

Once again, Brown diverted his opening statement to blaming Weakley. After the Mount Olivet Road property purchase, Brown said Weakley rented a moving van and transported most of his belongings to the detached garage at the property. Being close to Hugo, Weakley became in awe of Hugo's lifestyle by having a girlfriend, always seemed to have lots of cash and a family who cared for him.

"(Weakley) wanted the life Hugo had. He wanted the girlfriend who was able to provide for him, Tina Strom. He wanted the family who was sticking by him. He wanted that, and he had the access to the property, and that's what happened," Brown said, adding that Weakley thought about killing Hugo by either pushing him off a cliff while they were riding their all-terrain vehicles or blowing him up with fireworks to make it appear as an accident on July 4, 2002. "He thought about killing Hugo Selenski, even though Hugo had taken him into his life," Brown told the jury.

"Paul Raymond Weakley was interviewed some 15 times during this investigation, maybe more. He always had a different version of events," Brown said, getting into the many lies and misstatements Weakley told investigators. After briefly describing some of the misstatements and lies, Brown told the jury it was not until December 2007, four years and six months after Hugo was arrested June 3, 2003, when Weakley admitted to his role in the murders and burying the bodies.

"You're going to hear Paul Raymond Weakley come here and testify. You're going to have to judge his credibility and weigh his evidence," Brown advised the jury.

Brown's opening statement was approximately 45 minutes.

After a 90 minute lunch, court resumed with Hugo's lawyers and prosecutors meeting at side-bar with Judge Pierantoni to discuss sequestration of all witnesses and the weather as snow was in the forecast. Anyone on the witness list, including a Times Leader reporter, were required to leave the courtroom.

Prosecutors began their case-in-chief at promptly 1:27 p.m. with Pennsylvania State Police Lieutenant Richard Krawetz, crime section commander at Troop P, Wyoming, being the first witness being asked questions by First Assistant District Attorney Samuel Sanguedolce.

Krawetz explained that Paul Weakley on June 3, 2003, wanted to speak with the state police about bodies being buried at the Mount Olivet Road property. Krawetz met with Weakley along with state police Trooper Gerard Sachney and Luzerne County Detective Lieutenant Gary Capitano. Weakley was represented at the meeting by Attorney Thomas Cometa from the Luzerne County Public Defender's Office.

After Weakley disclosed the bodies of Kerkowski and Fassett were buried at the Mount Olivet Road property, Krawetz said Weakley was driven past the property to show the investigators the home on June 4, 2003. The investigators took Weakley in a state police van that had no markings on the vehicle, passing the property twice before returning to the state police barracks.

The following day, June 5, 2003, Krawetz told the jury a team of investigators comprised of the Pennsylvania State Police, Luzerne County District Attorney's Office, Kingston Township police and federal agents assembled at a staging area at Francis Slocum State Park, a short distance from the Mount Olivet Road property. Krawetz further assigned troopers with the state police Vice and Narcotics Unit to conduct visual surveillance of the property. The staging area was set up as investigators at the state park were awaiting the signing of a search warrant by Luzerne County Senior Judge Patrick Toole.

The plan was nearly shattered when dogs on the property began to bark when they detected the vice and narcotic troopers. Having concerns for the troopers' safety, Kravetz said he made the decision to converge onto the property. Krawetz was in the lead car that turned onto the long, gravel driveway that led to the house and detached garage at about 11:45 a.m. As Krawetz parked the cruiser, Hugo approached asking what was going on. "I informed him that we had information that bodies were possibly buried on the property and that we were in the process of getting a search warrant. However, we were not going to attempt any type of search until such time that the search warrant was properly signed," Krawetz told the jury.

When told about bodies being possibly buried, Krawetz said Hugo's response was, "This is ridiculous, there's no bodies here, I'll even help you dig."

Krawetz waited 10 minutes until he received word at 11:55 a.m. that Judge Toole had authorized the search warrant. Detective Capitano and Trooper Sachney took the search warrant to a county judge who has the authority to seal search warrants. If the search warrant had been taken to a magisterial district judge, the search warrant could have been immediately released to the media and public, or shortly thereafter. Krawatz said the decision was made to have a county judge seal the search warrant due to concerns for the safety of witnesses who had been interviewed.

Krawetz explained Hugo was very nervous, paced back and forth and constantly gazed toward the right rear corner of the residence where the bodies of Kerkowski and Fassett were unearthed. Once Krawetz received information at 11:55 a.m. that the search warrant had been signed, a cadaver dog began a cursory search of the property.

As the canine began its search, Hugo saw the dog and ultimately agreed to be questioned, given a ride to the Wyoming barracks by state police Corporal Gary Vogue in an unmarked cruiser. When the canine was not able to give a strong indicator of human remains being buried on the property, Krawetz said Weakley was transported to the scene to show investigators exactly where the bodies were buried.

After Weakley described the area where the bodies were buried more than a year earlier, the cadaver dog was brought to the area and made a hit. Krawetz described the location next to a well, the source of water for the house and the house trailer where Ernest Culp lived on the property. Krawetz said the area had a mound of dirt that looked different from the surrounding dirt. As the digging commenced, Krawetz described the characteristics of the soil as different, noting the first lawyer was indigenous to the area, followed by a layer of coal and underneath the coal was potting soil.

Weakley, when he was interviewed by investigators on June 4, 2003, explained that there would be different layers of soil as he drove to Back Mountain Feed to buy bags of potting soil. The potting soil was poured onto the bodies, followed by coal and the natural soil of the area on top. Krawetz said the digging continued and suddenly stopped when the first evidence of a body was uncovered, a wrist with a flex tie around it.

Coroners from Lehigh County and Northampton County were called in to remove the bodies arriving at the Mount Olivet Road property on June 6, 2003. Fassett's body was on top of Kerkowski as both bodies still had flex ties around their wrists, necks and ankles. Kerkowski's hands were also bound by duct tape when his body was removed.

Sanguedolce ended his direct examination of Krawetz, setting up the cross examination by Attorney Rymsza.

Rymsza would attack Krawetz about going onto the property without a search warrant along with 15 to 20 law enforcement officers who were armed and most wearing uniforms. Rymsza would also ask Krawetz about his report of Hugo gazing or being fixated on the area where the bodies were eventually unearthed, a report Krawetz amended a year later in June 2004.

Krawetz on June 18, 2003, issued a report about the events of June 5, 2003, indicating his decision to go onto the Mount Olivet Road property when troopers with the Vice and Narcotics Unit were chased by several dogs through the woods. Concerned for their safety, Krawetz wrote those at the staging area at Frances Slocum State Park left and arrived at Mount Olivet at 11:45 a.m. There is no mention in Krawetz's report of June 18, 2003, of Hugo being fixated or gazed in the area where the bodies were unearthed.

A year later, June 24, 2004, Krawetz filed an amended report of the events of June 5, 2003, indicating "Selenski became fixated on the area in question, constantly observing the digging process."

Rymsza noticed discrepancies in the two reports trying to mix up Krawetz's memory of 13 years earlier. Hugo had agreed to answer questions at the Wyoming barracks and left with State Police Corporal Gary Vogue around 12 p.m. on June 5, 2003, but Krawetz said the actual digging did not begin until 1:20 p.m. after Weakley pointed to the area and where the cadaver dog had made a hit. Certainly Rymsza displayed to the jury the discrepancy in the initial report and amended report about whether Hugo remained at the property when digging began or he had already been taken away.

"And again, when you prepared your initial police report, you mentioned nothing about him being fixated or gazing in that area, right?" Rymsza asked. "That is correct," Krawetz answered.

Rymsza was not done about the discrepancy in the reports. Rymsza pulled out Krawetz's amended report of June 24, 2004, indicating in the last paragraph that Krawetz wrote "Mr. Selenski became fixated in that area, constantly observing the digging process."

"Didn't you just testify a moment ago that he wasn't even there when the digging began?" Rymsza asked. "To the best of my recollection, I can't recall him being there when we were doing the exhumation," Krawetz replied.

Krawetz was on the witness stand for more than 90 minutes before prosecutors and Hugo's lawyers ended their questions.

Sanguedolce asked and was given a recess after Krawetz's testimony. During the break, Brown and Rymsza complained prosecutors were going out of order calling witnesses, interfering with their defense preparation. Pierantoni advised prosecutors it was common courtesy to exchange the day before the names of witnesses they plan to call to testify in order for the defense to be prepared with their files on the witnesses.

Back inside the courtroom, Rodney Samson was the next witness, telling the jury he hung out with Hugo in 2001 and 2002 and often attended parties where they smoked crack cocaine and consumed alcohol. At a house party in April 2002, Samson said he was talking about his personal financial hardships due to being in debt on child support obligations for three children. Samson said he was also expecting a fourth child at the time.

During the party, Samson said Hugo motioned him into another room where he offered $20,000 to help his child support debt about taking care of the pharmacist in Tunkhannock.

"And when you say take care of, did you understand or have an idea of what Mr. Selenski meant?' Ferentino asked. Samson replied, "Yeah, I mean what else could it be, you know? Umm, murder."

After several hours, Samson said Hugo got up to leave the party and tossed a rock of cocaine at him while saying, "Think about what we talked about."

About a month after the party, Samson learned Kerkowski had gone missing but he knew what actually happened. Samson said he was afraid to report his suspicions to law enforcement as he was a drug addict and did illegal things.

When Samson learned Kerkowski's body was found, he did not call state police. It was only after Samson was jailed for being in child support debt, in late December 2003, is when he reported his suspicions.

On cross examination by Brown, Samson said the offer by Hugo to take care of "the pharmacist in Tunkhannock" and later learning Kerkowski's body had been found weighed on his conscience.

"Isn't it true that Hugo never said Mike Kerkowski's name?" Brown asked as Samson replied, "Yes."

"Okay. And he never said, 'I wanted to kill, he never said he wanted to kill Mike Kerkowski,' did he?" Brown asked. "Well, 'Take care of, and $20,000, I mean, I pretty much know," Samson said.

After Samson left the witness stand, Judge Pierantoni advised the jury that Hugo was not charged with any drug related offenses in regards to Samson's testimony about using crack cocaine and Hugo throwing a bag of crack cocaine at him.

The first day of testimony ended at 4:21 p.m. as the jury was instructed the second day of trial would begin at 9:30 a.m.

Only the second day began more than 30 minutes late due to a juror having vehicle mechanical issues on their drive to the courthouse.

The jury entered the courtroom at 10:07 a.m. and was greeted by Pierantoni. The first witness on the second day was Robert Melnick, an agent with the Pennsylvania Attorney General's Office Bureau of Criminal Investigations, who investigated and charged Kerkowski for selling prescription medications without prescriptions.

Upon questions by Assistant District Attorney Mamie Phillips, Melnick said he initiated an investigation of Kerkowski's pharmacy on a request by Wyoming County District Attorney George Skumanick in 1999. Melnick explained he served a search warrant at Kerkowski's pharmacy on April 20, 2001, based on information he received that Kerkowski was illegally dispensing controlled substances.

Trained in accounting, tax and business law and financial crimes in addition to Medicaid fraud and drug trafficking investigations, Melnick sought records from the pharmacy dating back to Nov. 1, 1999, when Kerkowski opened the pharmacy, through the date when the search warrant was served, focusing on the disbursements of hydrocodone and oxycontin medications.

Based on the search warrants and audit, Melnick determined there were 333,881 hydrocodone tablets and 5,012 oxycontin tablets of various milligrams unaccounted for from Kerkowski's pharmacy between Nov. 1, 1999 to April 20, 2001.

Melnick determined based on his expert opinion that Kerkowski made $839,721, if not much more in the illegal sales of the prescription medications in the one year and five months his pharmacy had been open. Melnick said Kerkowski was criminally charged with multiple offenses, including fraud, forgery, failure to keep proper records by a practitioner and conspiracy to distribute controlled substances.

Melnick was not asked about the outcome of Kerkowski's charges.

After Melnick was cross-examined by Hugo's lawyers about his training, teaching police officers about how to act, dress and testify during court proceedings and his investigation, prosecutors next called Wyoming County Senior Judge Brandon Vanston.

Vanston was the judge who presided over Kerkowski's trial.

Attorney Rymsza objected to Vanston being called in his capacity as a judge but Pierantoni allowed Vanston to testify.

Following a break and as the jury returned to the jury box, Sanguedolce named his next witness but in a way the jury took notice.

"Call Judge Vanston, your honor," Sanguedolce said.

After providing his background, Vanston testified to presiding over Kerkowski's trial and subsequent guilty plea hearing at the Wyoming County Courthouse in Tunkhannock.

Vanston's courtroom was large but the gallery where people sit is inclined as those in the gallery have higher elevated seats in the back and lower seats in the front.

Vanston said he did not know Hugo but came in contact with him during Kerkowski's guilty plea hearing on April 25, 2002.

Besides the prosecutor, Kerkowski's attorney and the necessary court workers, Vanston said there only was one other person in the courtroom and that was Hugo.

"Recalling back to 2002, was there anything particular about that day that caused you to remember it?" Sanguedolce asked.

"First of all, it started with the guilty plea. The gentleman seated at that bench, and it was a fairly lengthy proceeding, probably lasted a half-hour, stared at me the whole time in what I would call a glare. And that caused me some concern that subsequently took some of their actions about, but that's the first unusual thing that happened that day," Vanston said.

Vanston said Kerkowski's guilty plea hearing and Hugo's glare stood out in his mind and especially what he saw next.

Kerkowski was instructed by Vanston to go to the adult probation department on the third floor of the Wyoming County Courthouse to update the presentence investigation report, a report that covers a defendant's family, upbringing, lifestyle, education, employment and criminal history. A presentence investigation report, commonly called a PSI, on Kerkowski had already been initiated having been found guilty two months earlier of selling prescription medications without prescriptions. Since Kerkowski pled guilty to additional crimes, the PSI had to be updated.

Five minutes after the conclusion of the hearing held April 25, 2002, Vanston said he walked to his chambers and sat behind his desk and as he looked out a window, he said he saw Kerkowski and Hugo patting each other on the back and giving each other high-fives.

As Kerkowski and Hugo kept walking, Vanston moved to another window, continuing to watch them pat each other on the backs, and then went to another room to look out another window until Kerkowski and Hugo went out of view.

"In your career as a judge, as a judge, have you ever followed the activity of people outside in such a way?" Sanguedolce asked.

"I think that's the only time I've ever done something like that," Vanston replied.

Still concerned about what he saw out the window, Vanston said he went to the first floor of the courthouse and briefly spoke with a sheriff, ultimately learning the identity of the man with Kerkowski as Hugo Selenski.

Eight days after Vanston witnessed Kerkowski and Hugo patting each other and giving each other high-fives, Kerkowski was killed.

Vanston would issue a bench warrant on May 14, 2002, when Kerkowski failed to appear to be sentenced.

With Sanguedolce ending his questions, Vanston was cross-examined by Attorney Rymsza.

The jury learned prosecutors had issued a subpoena for Vanston to appear in court to testify as Vanston said he "did not volunteer to come to court." Vanston had been residing in Florida as travel arrangements were made to have him flown to Pennsylvania to appear in court.

Rymsza reviewed Kerkowski's cases that were before Vanston including a jury trial that ended in convictions on three felony counts of delivery or dispensing of a controlled substance by a practitioner, and the April 25, 2002, guilty plea proceeding when Kerkowski pled guilty to another count of delivery or dispensing of a controlled substance by a practitioner, insurance fraud, false or fraudulent medical assistance and recklessly endangering another person.

Vanston said he did not notice if Hugo attended Kerkowski's trial that ended Feb. 28, 2002, but he did notice Hugo being the only one seated in the courtroom gallery when Kerkowski pled guilty on April 25, 2002. "The gentleman seated there just stared and stared and stared at me, which, since he was the only spectator in the room, it was quite noticeable," Vanston testified.

When Rymsza asked if Vanston could have had Hugo removed from the courtroom, the senior judge replied, "No, I didn't feel intimidated."

Vanston said he did not report Hugo's "glare" until a year or two later when a Luzerne County assistant district attorney who also practiced law privately was before him on an unrelated child custody case. "I was chatting with him, and he told me he was going to be a prosecutor in this case, he's not now, and I said, 'When are you going to interview me?' and he said, 'About what?' So I told him," Vanston said.

Nearing the end of his testimony, Vanston said he was interviewed several times by state police and Luzerne County detectives.

Following a one hour lunch that had a 30 minute extension, Kerkowski's mother, Geraldine Kerkowski, was the next witness called to testify. She took the witness stand at 1:31 p.m. and was questioned by Assistant District Attorney Jarrett Ferentino.

After several questions about her family, Geraldine Kerkowski said she was married for 46 years before her husband, Michael Stanley Kerkowski, passed away in September 2006. They had two sons, Michael and Scott, and three grandchildren. To distinguish between the two, Gerladine Kerkowski said her husband was "Mike" and her son was "Michael."

Geraldine Kerkowski told the jury her son, Michael, graduated with honors from Lake Lehman High School and earned a pharmacy degree from Temple University in Philadelphia, Pa. Michael Kerkowski owned The Medicine Shoppe near Tunkhannock and was married to Kimberly Kerkowski.

Michael Kerkowski eventually separated from his wife and moved in with his parents on Vine Street in Lehman Township, not far from Harveys Lake. After a short time staying with his parents, Michael Kerkowski returned to his home on Pritchards Road in Hunlock Township.

Ferentino was moving fast with his questions as Geraldine Kerkowski acknowledged her son's legal troubles from the pharmacy. She also noted her son began dating Tammy Fassett as she worked in a bagel shop near the pharmacy.

"Tammy was a very, very nice girl and I liked her a lot," Geraldine Kerkowski said.

"Did your son introduce you to anyone around the time during his trial?" Ferentino asked.

"Yes, he did. Hugo Selenski," Geraldine Kerkowski responded.

After Ferentino asked Geraldine Kerkowski if Hugo Selenski was in the courtroom, she pointed to him seated next to his lawyers. While Ferentino was asking Judge Pierantoni to acknowledge Geraldine Kerkowski's identification, Hugo had a smirk on his face.

"Take that smile off your face," Geraldine Kerkowski said, resulting in Pierantoni admonishing her.

"Miss, please just answer the questions that are going to be asked of you, please. Now, regain your composure. Mr. Sanguedolce and Mr. Ferentino will ask you questions. Just answer them as they're posed to you," Pierantoni said.

Ferentino then examined how Geraldine Kerkowski met Hugo during her son's trial and was happy that her son had a friend. She felt so appreciative of Hugo helping her son that she invited Hugo for coffee.

"Did (Michael Kerkowski) talk to you about whether or not to trust Mr. Selenski?" Ferentino asked.

"He said, 'I trust him, whatever he asks for, give him, because he's trying to help me,'" Geraldine Kerkowski said.

Geraldine Kerkowski recalled the last time that she and her husband saw their son was having dinner at his Hunlock Township home with Tammy Fassett on May 2, 2002. She described after cleaning up the dishes and bathing his two young sons, Michael Kerkowski would always end their visits by hugging his mother and saying, "Thanks for everything, Mom,"

She said they had plans to meet up again on May 3, 2002, either before Michael Kerkowski picked up his two sons at daycare or afterwards. Their plans were for Michael Kerkowski and Fassett to stop at his parents house to see a television they had just purchased.

Geraldine Kerkowski called her son's house and spoke with Fassett to determine when they were planning to stop by, before or after picking up the children at daycare. She remembered speaking with Fassett sometime between 2:30 p.m. and 4 p.m.

"It wasn't a long conversation. It was only about 15 minutes and I said, 'Well, do you think you'll come down soon?' And she says, 'Well, we can't come down right now because we have company.'" Geraldine Kerkowski said.

Ferentino continued to examine the telephone conversation and the events that unfolded in the hours afterwards into the next day.

When Michael Kerkowski and Fassett failed to show up at his parents house, Geraldine Kerkowski said they called their son but got no answer.

"...so we figured either they went out to eat with the children and, like, it was no big deal. I mean, they are only coming to see a TV, so we figured we'll see them another time," Geraldine Kerkowski said.

Geraldine Kerkowski said she and her husband went out to dinner and took a drive ending up at the Lycoming Mall in Lycoming County. When they returned to their Vine Street, Lehman Township, home, at about 11 p.m. on May 3, 2002, two messages were waiting for them on their answering machine.

"The first message was from the people from the Little People Daycare Center, and they said that nobody came to pick the children up, and it was already 6 p.m. and they close at 6 p.m., and they were wondering who's going to pick them up," Geraldine Kerkowski explained from the witness stand.

Geraldine Kerkowski said she immediately became alarmed because her son always picked up the children if he could not, Geraldine and her husband would pick up the boys as they were on the list to pick up their grandchildren.

"The second message was from Kim Kerkowski, very, very, very furious, saying, 'I hope that you are in a ditch dead for not picking up the children,'" Geraldine Kerkowski recalled.

Concerned and alarmed, Geraldine Kerkowski said they called their son before driving to his home. Having keys to their son's house,

Geraldine Kerkowski and her husband entered the garage and immediately noticed the screen door entering the house was held open by a chair and the door itself was left partially opened. Another characteristic that was out of place was Michael Kerkowski's Toyota 4Runner was parked forward instead of backed-up facing out in the garage as their son always parked his vehicle that way. Tammy Fassett's Dodge Dynasty was parked in the driveway.

Upon entering the house, Geraldine Kerkowski immediately noticed a decorative baker's rolling pin that hung on the kitchen wall and five tapes used for recording from surveillance cameras were missing. The home's surveillance system was in the kitchen.

"Were you concerned at that point?" Ferentino asked and got a reply from Geraldine Kerkowski, "Absolutely."

The first person Geraldine Kerkowski and her husband called was Hugo Selenski.

"Well, we asked him, 'Do you know where Michael might be?' He isn't home, and we don't know where he is. He said, 'No, I don't know anything at all.' He said, 'I don't know anything about that,'" Geraldine Kerkowski said.

Believing they had to wait 48 hours before reporting their son missing, Geraldine Kerkowski and her husband called the Pennsylvania State

Police at Shickshinny to file a missing person's report on Sunday, May 5, 2002.

After weeks of not knowing about their son's whereabouts, Geraldine Kerkowski said Hugo requested a meeting with her and her husband at a donut shop.

"Well, we just had some talk, and I, I cannot remember what the talk was about, but I, I got a napkin, and I wrote on the napkin, Is he alive? And I pushed it over to Hugo. And all he did was put on that crazy smirk on his face and just went, like not giving us any definite yes or no," Geraldine Kerkowski testified.

In a strange twist, Geraldine Kerkowski said they were contacted by a man who identified himself as Eric Sullivan who had information about their son. She said Sullivan wanted to meet at the same donut shop.

When Geraldine Kerkowski and her husband arrived, they sat in Sullivan's vehicle.

"The nature of the meeting was, he asked my husband for $10,000. And he said he needed the $10,000 to buy a part for his computer to be in touch with my son," Geraldine Kerkowski said, adding, "Well, I didn't go for it because I didn't know who he was."

Sullivan was identified as Paul Weakley.

Geraldine Kerkowski and her husband got out of Weakley's car and called Hugo.

"He said, 'Don't ever give any money to anybody except me,'" she said about the phone call with Hugo.

In another twist of Hugo playing on the emotions of Geraldine Kerkowski and her husband, Hugo met with them in early June 2002. During the meeting, Geraldine Kerkowski claimed Hugo told them he spoke with state police Trooper Michael Appleman who was investigating the disappearance of Michael Kerkowski.

"(Hugo) told us that, this trooper that he spoke to, Appleman, Trooper Appleman, that he was going to nail our ass to a cross," Geraldine Kerkowski explained from the witness stand about Hugo's persistence. She became angry about what Hugo had told her of Appleman's alleged statements to the point they contacted their attorney, Basil Russin.

"When you say, 'Nail our asses to the cross,' who is "our" that Mr. Selenski is talking about?" Ferentino asked in a follow up question to clarify. "My husband and myself," Geraldine Kerkowski replied.

The alleged statement supported a widely growing notion that Michael Kerkowski was not dead but fled the area to avoid being sentenced in Wyoming County Court.

After contacting their attorney, Basil Russin, the lawyer sent a letter to Trooper Appleman.

The letter stated, "Dear Trooper Appleman, please be advised that I represent Michael and Geraldine Kerkowski. On June 6, 2002, Hugo

Selenski came to the Kerkowski residence and informed them about the disappearance of Kerkowski's son. Mr. Selenski indicated that you told him that 'I will nail their asses to a cross.' The Kerkowskis are very concerned about their son's disappearance. They are well aware that should any contact be made from their son or with their son, it will be reported to the authorities immediately so they can follow any leads and apprehend their son. I am requesting that you immediately cease and desist slandering and defaming the Kerkowskis to other persons. Yours truly, Basil Russin."

Only Trooper Appleman never said such a statement. Hugo made it up to feel out the Kerkowskis for his next scheme.

Geradline Kerkowski then told the jury Hugo came to her home several times during the summer and into the fall of 2002 saying their son was alive and needed cash as their son was getting new attorneys.

When Kerkowski was separated from his wife, Kimberly, he gave his parents $60,000 to hide in their Lehman Township home. Only Geraldine Kerkowski, her husband and Kerkowski himself knew about the cash that her husband hid in an unused air vent in the basement.

Hugo found out about the hidden money while Michael Jason Kerkowski was being tortured and strangled. And, Hugo wanted that cash.

Hugo made three visits, meeting each time with Kerkowski's father, Michael Stanley Kerkowski, telling him that his son was alive and needed money. As Kerkowski had told his parents to trust Hugo, Michael Stanley Kerkowski surrendered $30,000 during the first visit sometime in July 2002.

Hugo returned a second time in August 2002, telling Michael Stanley Kerkowski his son needed more money. Michael Stankey Kerkowski asked if he could speak with his son. In response, Hugo paced in the backyard with a cellular phone in his hand telling the elder Kerkowski he was having trouble reaching him. Hugo left with another $30,000.

Sometime in September or October 2002, Hugo returned to the Kerkowski's home a third time saying he would allow Michael Stanley Kerkowski to speak with his son. While sitting in the basement, Michael Stanley Kerkowski demanded to speak with his son or he would refuse to surrender any more cash. Hugo brandished a handgun and discharged a round that passed just above the elder Kerkowski's head.

Michael Stanley Kerkowski gave Hugo $40,000, who left the home with empty beer bottles he consumed. When the elder Kerkowski reported the incident, state police recovered the spent round in the basement wall.

Hugo was arrested for the robbery the same day when investigators converged onto the Mount Olivet Road property on June 5, 2003.

Geraldine Kerkowski was testifying about the visits by Hugo, saying he was present when her husband gave Hugo money during the first two visits, but her husband told her to leave the house for the third visit.

As Assistant District Attorney Ferentino asked Geraldine Kerkowski another question, Hugo's co-defense attorney Rymsza objected. Ferentino ignored the objection and began asking the question.

"Mr. Selenski on those visits…" Ferentino started to ask when Rymsza chimed in a second time. "Excuse me."

"We're going to approach because we're not going to have these fights in front of everybody," Ferentino snapped at Rymsza.

"Listen, I'm going to say this one time. If someone has something to say at sidebar, you come up and say it at sidebar, all right? Come up, please come up. There will be no outbursts in this courtroom by counsel," Judge Pierantoni warned.

During the sidebar meet, Rymsza raised his objection to Geraldine Kerkowski testifying that her husband surrendered a total of $100,000 to Hugo during the three visits without actually witnessing the transactions. Rymsza argued her testimony was hearsay.

First Assistant District Attorney Sanguedolce said her testimony was foreshadowing the testimony of Michael Stanley Kerkowski from the June 2006, preliminary hearing that was going to be presented to the jury. The admittance of the preliminary hearing testimony of the elder Kerkowski was twice appealed to the Pennsylvania Superior Court that resulted in long delays of Hugo's trial. As Michael Stanley Kerkowski passed away in

September 2006, prosecutors were successful in presenting his preliminary hearing testimony to the jury.

Geraldine Kerkowski was asked by Ferentino to explain the last visit with Hugo in September or October 2002. She said Hugo arrived at the home and they initially sat on the back porch. As it became darker and cooler, they went to the basement to continue their discussion.

With a cellular phone in his hand, Hugo went to another room in the basement and paced back and forth, telling Michael Stanley Kerkowski and Geraldine Kerkowski he was having trouble getting through. While Hugo was at the house, he consumed a six pack of cold beer and several bottles of warm beer.

Michael Stanley Kerkowski got a feeling to get his wife out of the house telling her to go grocery shopping. "He says, do you need groceries? And I said, 'No.' He said, 'Go shopping, get some groceries.' So I thought he was trying to tell me something, I didn't know what, so I got in the car and I went for groceries," Geraldine Kerkowski testified.

Geraldine Kerkowski said she returned home after one hour and encountered her husband and Hugo walking up the stairs from the basement. Hugo was carrying a bag filled with the empty beer bottles.

Despite firing a shot above the head of Michael Stanley Kerkowski, Hugo continued to prey upon their emotions. Hugo sent Patrick Russin to the home of Kerkowski's parents to pick up a money package as Hugo waited down the street.

Russin said he was there to "pick up a package for Hugo," Geraldine Kerkowski said. Instead, Geraldine Kerkowski gave Russin a list of five questions that only her son would know the answers to as proof he was alive. Those questions were: "Where were you during the Agnes flood of 1972? What is your maternal grandfather's name? Who did you take to your first prom? Who took you to Philadelphia to a hair show competition? What was the nickname that you called your son?"

Hugo kept making excuses delaying the response to Geraldine Kerkowski's questions, including the answers would be mailed to Geraldine Kerkowski's mother's house in Swoyersville.

In another attempt to siphon more money from the Kerkowskis, Hugo contacted them in December 2002, requesting a meeting. Michael Stanley Kerkowski did not want Hugo at his home so he agreed to meet at a fast food restaurant in Pringle Borough. Michael Stanley Kerkowski dropped off his wife at her mother's house in Swoyersville and drove to the restaurant to meet Hugo.

After the restaurant meeting, Geraldine Kerkowski testified her husband was "very upset, very nervous," and demanded she get into the vehicle without going inside to greet her mother. She said her husband always hugged and kissed her mother but not on this day.

At the restaurant meeting, Hugo threatened Michael Stanley Kerkowski telling him what happened to his son would happen to his family and his house would be set ablaze.

Michael Stanley Kerkowski and Geraldine Kerkowski reported Hugo's extortion and robbery scheme to the Pennsylvania State Police in mid-December 2002. Geraldine Kerkowski said she did not hear from Hugo for several months until he left two messages on their answering machine on May 3, 2003, the anniversary of her son's disappearance. The Kerkowskis had ceased any contact with Hugo.

Upon returning home from a bus trip with her mother on June 5, 2003, Geraldine Kerkowski said her husband was not inside their house, which she described as being unusual as her husband never went out. About 30 minutes after being home, Michael Stanley Kerkowski entered telling his wife the body of their son was found in Hugo Selenski's backyard with Tammy Fassett's body.

Assistant District Attorney Ferentino ended his examination of Geraldine Kerkowski at 2:58 p.m.

After a 20 minute break, Geraldine Kerkowski was cross-examined by Attorney Rymsza.

Right away, Rymsza quizzed her about the timing of her phone call with Fassett. Geraldine Kerkowski earlier said she remembered the call taking place between 2:30 and 4 p.m. but could not narrow it down to a closer time. Rymsza asked if the call was closer to 4 p.m. rather than 2:30 p.m?

"I really can't say. I just, I don't remember. All I know, it was the afternoon and it was right before it was time for them to go for the boys," Geraldine Kerkowski said.

Neither the prosecution or Hugo's defense team inquired if Geraldine Kerkowski was aware what time Michael Jason Kerkowski normally picked up his sons at the daycare center. Nor did anyone from the daycare center was called to testify to pinpoint the time when Kerkowski picked up his sons on a daily basis.

Geraldine Kerkowski upon questions from Rymsza said she never spoke to her son on the phone call as he was cutting grass and Fassett seemed relaxed. She said Fassett stated they "had company" but did not say who and Geraldine Kerkowski did not ask who the company was.

As Rymsza maintained his strategy, he switched his questions about what was found in her son's house. Geraldine Kerkowski said a gold ring and a diamond tennis bracelet were on a nightstand and she found $40,000 cash in the bottom drawer of an armoire.

Geraldine Kerkowski gave the cash to her husband and did not report the cash to state police until after their son's body was found 13 months later. During the missing persons investigation by state police, Geraldine

Kerkowski said she was aware investigators believed her son was on the run and the parents were somehow involved.

Switching questions again, Rymsza asked about their meeting with Hugo at the donut shop and the note she wrote on a napkin.

"Well, I slid it over to him, and he just looked at me and smirked at me, and he didn't give me any satisfaction," Geraldine Kerkowski said on the witness stand. She testified on direct examination she wrote a note on the napkin and passed it to Hugo asking if her son was alive.

Replying to questions from Rymsza, Geraldine Kerkowski admitted she never witnessed her husband giving Hugo any cash nor did they report giving cash to Hugo to the state police until after the December 2002, confrontation when Hugo claimed to have threatened them.

Rymsza ended his cross-examination of Geraldine Kerkowski taking less than one hour.

Pierantoni ended the second day of trial when he was advised that the next commonwealth's witness would be on the witness stand for a considerable amount of time. Pierantoni discharged the jury for the night at 4:14 p.m., earlier than planned.

# HUGO'S SCHEME OUTED

The third day of trial began with Pennsylvania State Police Trooper Thomas Appleman, who investigated the missing persons report filed by Michael Stanley Kerkowski and his wife, Geraldine, about the disappearance of their son, Michael Jason Kerkowski. Before the jury and Appleman entered the courtroom, First Assistant District Attorney Samuel Sanguedolce and assistant district attorneys Jarrett Ferentino and Mamie Phillips along with Hugo's attorneys, Bernard Brown, Edward Rymsza and Hugh Taylor, held a sidebar conference with Judge Pierantoni.

The sidebar was held for an offer of proof about what Appleman was going to say from the witness stand. During the private meeting, Pierantoni warned prosecutors not to have Appleman mention Lewisburg, a reference to the U.S. Penitentiary at Lewisburg where Hugo and Weakley met as inmates at the federal prison. Years earlier, Aug. 3, 2012, to be exact, Pierantoni issued an order prohibiting prosecutors from mentioning Hugo had been jailed at the Lewisburg federal prison.

Michael Stanley Kerkowski and his wife reported their son missing on May 5, 2002, and Appleman said he was assigned the following day to conduct an investigation.

Sanguedolce conducted the direct examination of Appleman who took the witness stand at 9:55 a.m.

Appleman explained he interviewed Michael Stanley Kerkowski and his wife, and met them at their son's home where he noticed vacuum cleaner lines on the carpet in the basement, a bed missing a bedspread and VHS tapes missing from the home's security camera system. As Sanguedolce continued to ask questions, he got to the letter Appelman received from Attorney Basil Russin.

Attorney Russin drafted a letter to Appelman in reference to what Hugo had told Michael Stanley Kerkowski and his wife that Appelman claimed to have said, "When this is all over, I will nail their asses to the cross."

There was a belief Michael Stanley Kerkowski disappeared with Fassett to avoid his sentencing hearing in Wyoming County. Neither Kerkowski's parents nor Fassett's sister, Lisa Sands, believed their loved ones fled the area.

"The letter even indicates why they're under that impression, correct?" Sanguedolce asked. "Yes," Appleman responded.

"And why is that?" asked Sanguedolce. "Umm, they were told by Mr. Hugo Selenski that I said that," Appleman replied.

"Did you ever say that?" Sanguedolce asked. "I did not," Appleman quickly said, adding, "That's not verbiage that I use. I would not say that."

Appleman said he interviewed Hugo as part of the missing persons investigation on June 5, 2002. Exactly one year later, June 5, 2003, the bodies of Kerkowski and Fassett were found buried at the Mount Olivet Road property where Hugo was residing.

During his interview with Hugo, Appleman said Hugo claimed he was friends with Michael Jason Kerkowski and explained a $5,000 check written from Kerkowski's pharmacy that paid Hugo $2,500 for his assistance and the other half to purchase a computer.

Hugo claimed he used the LexisNexis network to research case law and he personally had experience because he served time in prison, Appleman told the jury.

Sanguedolce explained to the jury LexisNexis provides online legal research services often utilized by lawyers and legal professionals, pointing out Hugo did not have an account with the online legal research firm.

Appleman said Hugo claimed he last spoke with Kerkowski in April 2002.

Sanguedolce took less than 30 minutes questioning Appleman, who was then cross-examined by Rymsza.

Rymsza's questions were long with Appleman giving mostly one or two word answers, "yes and okay."

Rymsza asked Appleman if he was aware of Michael Jason Kerkowski's legal issues in Wyoming County.

Appleman said he was familiar with Kerkowski's legal troubles in Wyoming County having spoken to his parents.

Rymsza asked Appleman if he spoke to any neighbors, specifically the closest neighbor Louise Besancon, and if any neighbors had a clear view of Kerkowski's home through trees. Appleman acknowledged he interviewed Besancon on May 10, 2002, and did not make the effort if there was a clear line of sight between her property and Kerkowski's house.

Besancon told Appleman she heard a vehicle estimating it was about 5 p.m. on May 3, 2002, leaving Kerkowski's property but did not actually see the car. She would later add to her story.

"She couldn't give you any description of what the vehicle looked like, right?" Rymsza asked. Appleman replied, "She didn't."

Rymsza pulled out Appleman's supplemental report about his interview with Besancon conducted June 12, 2003, more than 13 months after he first interviewed her.

"You interviewed her on June 12th, and she indicated that she can't see the Kerkowski residence very well from her residence due to the trees between the residences. Did I read that correctly?" Rymsza asked. "That's exactly what I wrote," Appleman responded.

Rymsza backtracked his questions about the letter Attorney Russin sent to Appleman.

"Now, you said that you, you testified regarding a letter you received from, umm, Attorney Russin, umm, isn't it true, Trooper, that you believe this was, you had some reason to believe or you, at the time, you thought the parents may have had some information or may know something about Mr. Kerkowski's whereabouts?" Rymsza asked. "I thought so," Appleman said.

"And, in fact, would you agree with me that, umm, you thought that they somehow may be responsible for Mr. Kerkowski being missing?" asked Rymsza. "Being responsible or assisting, I don't know," replied Appleman.

"But you were suspicious, were you not?" Rymsza asked. "I was suspicious," Appleman acknowledged.

Then Rymsza began asking about Appleman's arrival at the Kerkowski home where the father, Michael Stanley Kerkowski, insisted that Appleman go inside. Appleman noted he did not wear protective gloves as he walked through the house but quickly explained he did not handle any items. Michael Stanley Kerkowski told Appleman he found and ripped up a $100,000 cashier's check written out to cash under a pot on the kitchen counter inside his son's home.

Questions by Rymsza about the ripped up cashier's check resulted in a strong objection by Sanguedolce as Michael Stanley Kerkowski was deceased and could not explain why he ripped up the cashier's check.

Judge Pierantoni gave the jury a recess and took prosecutors and Hugo's lawyers into his chambers. Once again, Hugo's lawyers argued the unfairness of having the preliminary hearing testimony of Michael Stanley Kerkowski being read to the jury since he died in September 2006.

"...this is the danger in admitting his testimony of a preliminary hearing that has never been able to cross-examined. Whether past counsel didn't do it is, is their problem and I don't, and, again, it's not even really an issue at a preliminary hearing, impeachment. Credibility is not an issue (at a preliminary hearing.) So, I've never had a full and fair opportunity to cross-examine (Michael Stanley Kerkowski) on it. And it's, it's not being offered for the truth of the matter. And it's totally fair game," Rymsza argued in chambers.

"If that were the ruling, the statement wouldn't come in. It must be a full and fair opportunity for the statement to be admissible and that, you are offering it for its truth. You're offering it for what's in here to be true over what he (Michael Stanley Kerkowski) testified to under oath," Sanguedolce replied.

"It's impeachment, Judge. It's classic impeachment. And I can't, I can't cross-examine a dead man and the fact that he was, the fact that he was given a truncated, that Mr. Selenski was given a truncated hearing at a preliminary hearing…where credibility is not at issue to begin with, this is my only opportunity to do it," Rymsza said.

Ferentino then chimed in, "At the preliminary hearing, Judge, that statement was in their possession. They had the missing persons report, they had Mr. Kerkowski's statement that day they were given the full and fair opportunity as declared by this court to cross."

"Okay, then we'll come back for the (Post Conviction Relief Act hearing) 10 years down the road," Rymsza shot back.

"You don't get to cross-examine a different witness with some other witness's prior inconsistent statement," Sanguedolce said.

"Judge, I have no other way, I have no other way to get this in," Rymsza said.

Judge Pierantoni overruled Sanguedolce's objection allowing Rymsza to continue testing Appleman's investigation and about the ripped up cashier's check while raising issues with the credibility of Michael Stanley Kerkowski.

Pierantoni advised prosecutors and Hugo's lawyers they were free to make any objections in open court to protect the record before returning to the courtroom at 11:10 a.m.

Rymsza switched his line of questioning asking about the written statement Michael Stanley Kerkowski gave May 7, 2002, regarding what he found at his son's home four days earlier.

As good defense lawyers do, Rymsza dissected Michael Stanley Kerkowski's written statement highlighting that nothing was mentioned about vehicles being unusually parked, a vacuum cleaner being left out in the open, failed to state $40,000 was found in the bottom drawer of an armoire and no mention of the $100,000 cashiers check under a pot. Dead for nearly six years, Michael Stanley Kerkowski's credibility was being challenged by Rymsza through Appleman.

Ending his questions, Rymsza got Appleman to admit that testing for fingerprints and photographs were not performed inside Kerkowski's house.

When Rymsza rested, Sanguedolce asked several follow up questions and got Appleman to say a newspaper dated May 3, 2002, was found inside Kerkowski's Toyota 4Runner.

Appleman left the witness stand at 11:40 a.m.

Prosecutors immediately called their next witness, Robert J. Steiner, who was the owner of the Mount Olivet Road property he sold to Christina Strom.

Steiner took the witness stand at 11:42 a.m. and was directly examined by Assistant District Attorney Ferentino.

Leading up to the sale, Steiner said he was 78 and moved to Port St. Lucie in Florida to be closer to his children and grandchildren and lived at the Mount Olivet Road property for 30 years until he sold it to Strom in 2002.

"Who approached you about purchasing the property at 479 Mt. Olivet Road?" Ferentino asked. "Hugo Selenski," Steiner said, explaining he had known Hugo since he was riding a tricycle.

Steiner said he was at a tavern playing pool when Hugo came up to him to inquire about purchasing the property in March 2002. Steiner had the property listed for $180,000, receiving $10,000 in cash from Hugo as a down payment. Shortly after giving him the $10,000, Hugo gave Steiner another $5,000 in cash.

In addition to purchasing the house, Hugo gave Steiner $6,000 cash for living room and bedroom furniture, a tanning bed, a hot tub and an air compressor. Hugo also purchased an old four-wheel drive Chevrolet S10 pickup truck from Steiner paying $2,000 in cash.

Steiner said he initially believed Hugo was buying the property and did not know Christina Strom was the actual buyer until the real estate purchase agreement held in the office of Attorney Joseph Blazosek on March 29, 2002. At the meeting, Strom gave Blazosek $9,000 cash and was given a receipt as a down payment and an agreement of sale for the Mount Olivet Road property.

The sales agreement only reflected the $9,000 Strom had given to Steiner and not the $15,000 given to him by Hugo "under the table." The real estate closing was held April 30, 2002, at Blazosek's office when

Steiner was given a check for $149,225 as the property was officially granted to Strom.

Under an occupancy agreement, Steiner was permitted to stay on the property until May 15, 2002. In the following days after the April 30, 2002, closing, Steiner said Hugo approached him on the property asking him what he would be doing the next day, estimating it was a Friday or Saturday. Steiner said despite selling the house and plans to move to Florida, he continued to work as a truck driver leaving at 7 a.m. and arriving home at 5:30 to 6 p.m.

As Steiner was at work, Hugo was on the Mount Olivet Road property. When he returned, he noticed Hugo and Paul Weakley along with a pick, a shovel and a spade all covered with mud and dirt. Steiner said the two men were sweaty and had mud on their shoes standing in an area about 30 feet from the well, the source of water for the property.

Ferentino ended his direct examination of Steiner at 12:20 p.m. Steiner was cross-examined by Attorney Brown asking about the cash payments totaling $15,000 given to him "under the table" and Strom's $9,000 check issued at the sale agreement meeting at Attorney Blazosek's office March 30, 2002, when Steiner first learned Strom was purchasing the property, not Hugo. Steiner said he knew Strom as Hugo's girlfriend and met her when Hugo brought her and his father and brother to look at the Mount

Olivet Road property sometime in March 2002.

Brown then asked Steiner about his encounter with Hugo and Weakley when he returned to the property and encountered the two men with mud covered shoes and working with tools. Steiner said he advised Hugo he needed to install heat tape and insulation around pipes leading from the well to a reservoir as the pipes would often freeze during the winter. After wrapping the pipes, Steiner said he advised Hugo to cover the pipes with dirt.

Steiner further said Hugo was clearing the woods for trails to ride his all-terrain vehicles.

Brown's questions were specifically addressed to explain why Hugo and Weakley were muddy and using tools when Steiner encountered them. Brown ended his cross-examination of Steiner at 12:37 p.m.

During the afternoon session, Sanguedolce announced that Hugo's lawyers stipulated to the prosecution's next witness, which would have been Hugo's brother, Ronald Selenski. With the stipulation that Hugo's lawyers agreed to, Sanguedolce read to the jury that Hugo gave $500 to Ronald Selenski as a downpayment for a 2002 Chevrolet Trailblazer, a $100 check as an additional down payment and Hugo provided $9,436 in cash for the remainder of the down payment.

Clearly, prosecutors were showing the jury Hugo gave away a large amount of cash without having a job. A juror could wonder, "Where did Hugo get all this money?"

As their next witness was going to take an entire day, Judge Pierantoni ended the third day of trial at 3:20 p.m. for the weekend. Jurors were escorted to their vehicles behind the courthouse as it was snowing.

# HUGO'S FORMER GIRLFRIEND TESTIFIES

Light snow fell during the morning hours of Monday, Jan. 26, 2015, just as jurors were staggering into the Luzerne County Courthouse. Friday's snowstorm left 5.5 inches while the forecast called for additional snow Monday as a Nor'Easter moved up the Atlantic coastline.

Judge Pierantoni had advised the jury to keep alert of inclement weather and to check in with the jury room by telephone if proceedings would be delayed or postponed for the day.

As the jury returned to the jury box at 9:41 a.m. and were greeted by Judge Pierantoni, First Assistant District Attorney Sanguedolce called the next witness: Christina Strom.

Sanguedolce had Strom outline her relationship with Hugo, having known Hugo for most of her life as he played Little League baseball with her brother when they were children. Strom said she began dating Hugo in September 2001.

Sanguedolce then got right into Strom's own legal troubles she faced.

Strom was indicted by a federal grand jury on Oct. 21, 2004, on nine counts including criminal conspiracy to commit money laundering, money laundering, structure transactions to evade reporting requirements, obstructing an official proceeding and false declaration before a grand jury. The United States Attorney's Office for the Middle District of

Pennsylvania also filed a forfeiture petition to seize the Mount Olivet Road property.

The indictment filed against Strom did not mention Hugo by name but referred to him as an "unindicted coconspirator." The federal charges alleged Strom was aware Hugo was unemployed and had no legitimate source of income.

While residing with Strom, Hugo committed multiple criminal offenses including murders and robberies listing the murders of Kerkowski and Fassett, and Frank James and Adeiye Keiler, the indictment stated.

"On multiple occasions during the life of the conspiracy, the unindicted coconspirator provided CHRISTINA M. STROM with thousands of dollars in United States currency....most, if not all, of the currency provided by the unindicted coconspirator to CHRISTINA M. STROM was the proceeds of murder, robbery, and/or drug dealing," according to Strom's indictment.

A pregnant Strom entered a negotiated plea agreement with federal prosecutors on Jan. 18, 2006, when she pled guilty to conspiracy to commit money laundering and obstructing an official proceeding. The other federal charges were withdrawn against Strom.

Under the terms of the plea agreement, Strom agreed to cooperate with prosecutors in Luzerne County and testify against Hugo. She also agreed not to challenge the forfeiture petition against the Mount Olivet Road property, where she remained living until the end of January 2006. She was due to give birth to her first child in late July 2006, and had been working as a bartender at a tavern in Larksville.

Federal prosecutors would recommend 70 to 87 months in prison for Strom, depending on her cooperation in other cases, notably against Hugo.

When Strom took the witness stand against Hugo on Jan. 26, 2015, she had not been sentenced in U.S. District Court. Eventually, after Hugo's trial, Strom would be sentenced June 5, 2015.

"Can you tell the jury what you got charged for?" Sanguedolce asked Strom.

"I was charged with perjury, uh, for lying at a grand jury hearing and also for money laundering," Strom replied.

"Can you tell the jury what was the subject of the perjury?" Sanguedolce asked.

"Umm, I lied about where money came from. Umm, I told them that I had money saved away in a(n) urn in my house, and, umm, I did not," Strom responded.

"Can you tell the jury why you said that in front of the Grand Jury?" asked Sanguedolce.

"I said that because Hugo told me to," Strom answered before Hugo's lead defense attorney, Bernard Brown, objected on the basis of hearsay.

Sanguedolce responded to the objection that Strom's response was an admission "by a party opponent," meaning Strom. Judge Pierantoni overruled Brown's objection and allowed Sanguedolce to continue his line of questions.

Strom said she did not have any money saved and did not have any money stashed away in an urn or wine jug.

Sanguedolce then asked about the money laundering charge, with Strom saying she deposited cash given to her by Hugo and purchased money orders at a federal post office to pay credit card bills.

"Your guilty plea agreement with the Federal Government requires your truthful testimony in this proceeding, does it now?" Sanguedolce asked. "Yes," Strom said in reply.

Strom explained she lived at her grandmother's house on Miller Street, Luzerne, while her grandmother was in a nursing home suffering from Alzheimer's, and Hugo moved in with her. Strom said she was familiar with Michael Jason Kerkowski and knew he drove a Toyota 4Runner and had been at the Miller Street house to meet with Hugo.

During one such meeting, Strom said Michael Jason Kerkowski pulled up in front of the Miller Street house and Hugo ran out the back door sometime in January 2002. A reason why Hugo ran out the back door was never made known.

Strom then described meeting Paul Weakley through Hugo as Hugo claimed Weakley was his best friend. Strom explained Hugo asked if Weakley could stay with them as Weakley had no place to go when he was released from federal prison for making explosive devices in Michigan.

Strom said she helped Weakley buy clothes, a vehicle and find an apartment. When she returned home from work one day in March 2002, Strom said Hugo and Weakley were in a bedroom with cash spread out on a bed, estimating the amount to be $60,000.

"He told me that he got money from Michael Kerkowski, Michael Kerkowski; he was helping him out with his case," Strom said, noting Kerkowski's legal troubles in Wyoming County Court.

Sanguedolce displayed Hugo's W-2 for 2002 that listed his income as $187, and the $5,000 check given to Hugo from Kerkowski's business account at the pharmacy. The jury had heard about the $5,000 check but Strom went into further detail telling the jury the handwriting on the check was Hugo's.

Sanguedolce began to focus on Strom's purchase of the Mount Olivet Road property. She said she purchased the property from Robert Steiner for $160,000 and took a $149,000 mortgage from First Union Bank. The mortgage was only in Strom's name as Hugo did not have a job and did not have any credit. Strom explained she initially gave Steiner $9,000 during the sales agreement meeting held at the office of Attorney Joseph

Blazosek on March 29, 2002, and told the jury she got the cash from Hugo. At the closing to officially purchase the property held April 30, 2002, Strom said she wrote a check in the amount of $10,079.50, from her account at the UFCW Credit Union.

But there was a problem. Strom did not have sufficient funds to cover the check having only $669.71 in her checking account.

"Did that cause you any anxiety?" Sanguedolce asked.

"I was a nervous wreck about writing off a check and not having that amount in the bank," Strom said.

"Why did you write a check without having that amount in the bank?" asked Sanguedolce.

"Because Hugo told me he was going to have the money for me," replied Strom.

April 30th was a Tuesday when Strom wrote the $10,079.50 check at the closing. In the following days, Sanguedolce displayed Strom's statement of her credit union checking account showing a $9,900 deposit on Monday, May 6, 2002, which was actually deposited on Saturday, May 4, 2002. There was a second deposit of $458.83 on May 6, and a $313.02 deposit on May 8, into Strom's checking account.

Strom said Hugo made all three deposits.

"Did he discuss with you why he was going to get $10,000 from Michael Kerkowski? What was the reason he thought he would get this money?" Sanguedolce asked.

"Because he told me he was helping him with his case," Strom answered.

"When the money wasn't appearing, what did you do?" Sanguedolce asked.

"Umm, I was in a panic that I was not going to have the money. I wrote out that check for that large amount, and it, it was just, it was a terrible feeling knowing, I didn't think I was ever going to have that money. I didn't have the money….and I was just, I was just a nervous wreck that I wasn't going to get this money for the down payment," Strom replied.

Strom said Hugo pledged he would get the money to cover the $10,079.50 check she wrote on April 30, 2002. For the next three days, Strom explained she was frightened about what would happen with the check being returned for insufficient funds.

Strom said she could not find Hugo for several days and he was not answering her phone calls while she repeatedly made several inquiries to see if Hugo had deposited money into her checking account as he promised.

Hugo deposited the cash into Strom's account on Saturday, May 4, 2002. Since it was the weekend, the transaction was dated for the next business day, Monday, May 6, 2002, on Strom's checking account statement.

Strom said she learned Michael Jason Kerkowski was missing when Michael Stanley Kerkowski called the Miller Street house for Hugo on May 4, 2002.

A month later, June 5, 2002, Strom described driving Hugo to the Pennsylvania State Police barracks in Shickshinny where he was questioned about the disappearance of Kerkowski.

When Hugo emerged from the barracks, he told Strom, "Oh, he's probably down in South America somewhere."

At this time during Strom's testimony, Sanguedolce requested a sidebar conference with Judge Pierantoni advising his next line of questioning for Strom involves Hugo's cocaine use.

"...I'm going to ask her about an incident in January of 2003 where she observed the defendant doing cocaine and then, for some reason, wants to go speak with police. She tells him she thinks that's a crazy idea, and he wants to go and talk about a robbery. He's acting high and very nervous. It's being offered in line with her previous testimony to show his behavior after he had done it and how it's erratic," Sanguedolce said.

Naturally, Hugo's lawyers objected to any reference of Hugo using cocaine and argued the incident in January 2003, was more leaning toward the Samuel Goosay robbery and kidnapping.

Assistant District Attorney Ferentino said Hugo was under the influence of cocaine when he met with the Pennsylvania State Police on June 5, 2002. "What he tells her why he's going there is one thing, what he does when he goes there is another," Ferentino said, noting Hugo told state police Kerkowski is in Belize, South America.

Judge Pierantoni sustained the objection prohibiting prosecutors from introducing any information about Hugo meeting with police in January 2003. But only prosecutors thought they could not bring up Hugo's cocaine use as he was not facing any drug possession charges.

At the conclusion of the sidebar conference, Judge Pierantoni gave the jury a 10 minute break.

Like most breaks during trials, there is always an extra 10 to 20 minutes added on. The jury returned to the jury box at 10:54 a.m. with Strom still on the witness stand.

"Okay, I'd like to skip ahead to January 2003 briefly. There was an occasion where you went with the defendant to the Dallas Police Department, do you recall that?" Sanguedolce asked.

"Yes," Strom said.

"Okay, and how did it come about that the defendant wanted to go to the Dallas Police Department?" asked Sanguedolce.

"Umm, he just said, you want to go with me? I want to go to the Dallas Police Department and talk to the police…I asked him why, and he said he had information about a robbery," Strom said.

Sanguedolce began asking his next question until Hugo's lawyers and Hugo himself chimed in.

"What is he talking about?," Hugo said while Attorney Brown said, "I thought we agreed," with Attorney Rymsza asking for a sidebar conference.

"I thought we talked about this, anything that resulted about going down there regarding a robbery was…is a different incident that was talked about. How is that relevant?" Brown argued and asked.

"This was the incident where she has alleged he went to the state police barracks on or about January of '03; am I correct. And I sustained your objection…" Judge Pierantoni said.

"As to the drug use," Sanguedolce explained his interpretation of Pierantoni's ruling earlier.

"No, the drug use and her going there, and him going there, him going there under the premise that he may have been under drugs at the time," Pierantoni said.

"Right, we're not going to talk about drugs," Sanguedolce explained.

"What are you trying to introduce?" Pierantoni asked.

"She, she, he initially makes a statement to her that he wants to talk about a robbery. He actually goes there and then testifies, well, so then he makes a statement that Michael Kerkowski is in Belize," Sanguedolce said, noting Hugo has made statements that he knows the whereabouts of Kerkowski.

"It is six or seven months after this incident is alleged to have occurred, he is not charged with any drug offense and I find it prejudicial. Just move to another area," Pierantoni advised prosecutors.

The sidebar conference continued with Sanguedolce, Ferentino and Assistant District Attorney Mamie Phillips making one last push to get the reference of what Hugo told Strom about Kerkowski being in Belize, South America, told in open court.

"This defendant is charged with killing and making the victim look like he fled. He's furthering that conspiracy by making a statement that he fled…" Ferentino argued.

Prosecutors and Hugo's lawyers went back and forth making their respective arguments during the sidebar conference. At one point, Judge Pierantino appeared to have understood from Ferentino the direction prosecutors were headed with their line of questions for Strom. Pierantoni then resumed the argument in chambers giving the jury another break.

Behind closed doors in the judge's chambers, Ferentino explained in greater detail Hugo had told Strom he wanted to go to the state police barracks with information about a robbery, but then tells Strom that Kerkowski is probably in South America.

"...It's a statement about Michael Kerkowski having fled. That's the motive for this crime. It's a statement of the defendant. We have curbed our presentation of this portion to remove any reference that he was blasted on cocaine when he did this...my understanding of the nature of the objection was the drug use..." Ferentino argued, noting Hugo had told many people that Kerkowski fled.

Hugo's lead defense attorney, Bernard Brown, argued any reference to a robbery Hugo did not partake was highly prejudicial toward Hugo and would confuse the jury. Brown referenced a Dallas Township robbery that involved Weakley, Pat Russin, Greg Pockevich and Carey Bartoo, and also the Samuel Goosay robbery and kidnapping.

"It's about a crime that (Hugo) was not involved in and any reference of him going there for a robbery created a prejudicial impact in the minds of the jury because he's charged in this case with robbing Michael Kerkowski. It creates the presentation that he was going there to speak about the Michael Kerkowski incident," Brown argued.

Rymsza had a slightly different approach arguing the jury may mistakenly believe Hugo wanted to talk to state police about the robbery of Kerkowski.

"If you leave this amorphous concept out there that he was going to talk about robbery, it very well could have been perceived and could be perceived by the jury that, he's talking about this robbery, that he got some epiphany that he wanted to come and speak to police, I think it's highly prejudicial and I think it's going to leave the jury with that impression," Rymsza argued.

Ferentino also had a different argumentative path explaining a timeline of events, recalling the "shakedown" of Michael Stalney Kerkowski at a fast food restaurant in December 2002.

"In December of 2002 was the Luzerne McDonald's meeting with Michael Kerkowski Sr. Michael Kerkowski Sr. testifies that he told Selenski he's going to the police, leaves in December 2002, in fact, goes to the police. January of '03, just weeks later, Selenski goes to the police and creates this impression that Kerkowski fled, knowing damn well Michael Kerkowski, Michael S. Kerkowski's going there to say he's being shaken down. All Selenski's doing is trying to beat him to the chase to create, to fester that impression, Judge," Ferentino said.

Judge Pierantoni opined that any reference to the context of a robbery would be prejudicial, asking the parties to move onto the next issue, noting prosecutors will have their opportunity about Hugo claiming Kerkowski is in South America will be revisited when Trooper Gerald Sachney testifies.

The argument behind closed doors grew more heated when Rymsza said he never received Sachney's report about Hugo claiming Kerkowski is on another continent, resulting in Ferentino giving him a look.

"I'm not...why do you look at me like in disbelief?" Rymsza said, looking at Ferentino.

"Because that's the third time we've given you the discovery. It's there. It's there," Ferentino responded.

Assistant District Attorney Mamie Phillips said the statement by Hugo claiming Kerkowski was in South America is in Trooper Sachney's report turned over to Hugo's lawyers through discovery, the exchange of evidence.

Some clarity came about clearing up confusion where Hugo told Trooper Sachney that Kerkowski was in South America. The interview between Sachney and Hugo took place inside the Dallas Township Police Department, not the state police barracks or the Dallas Borough Police Department.

Judge Pierantoni finally made a ruling prohibiting prosecutors from soliciting Strom from testifying about Hugo wanting to speak with police about a robbery and prohibiting any drug use by Hugo. The judge allowed prosecutors to solicit testimony about what Hugo told Strom regarding

Kerkowski having fled to South America when he emerged from the Dallas Township Police Department.

"Let's go back out," the judge said as all parties returned to the courtroom at 11:14 a.m.

Once everyone was back in their respective seats including the jury, Judge Pierantoni instructed the jury to disregard Strom's last response about a robbery. "That last response is stricken," the judge said before returning the floor back to Sanguedolce to continue his direct examination of Strom.

"When the defendant exited the police department, you guys, you had a discussion with him; correct?" Sanguedolce asked if the discussion involved Kerkowski.

"He said that Paul did it," Strom said.

"Did he tell you where Michael Kerkowski was, where he believed he was?" Sanguedolce asked, resulting in a strong objection from Brown.

Only a minute later when Sanguedolce resumed his direct examination of Strom following a 14 minute break, Rymsza asked to meet the judge at sidebar.

"Judge, one of my concerns is the fact that now what the offer, apparently, is that, umm, Mr. Selenski said that Paul Weakley did something. The only thing is, the only thing I thought you were ruling on, that you were permitting them to talk about, was that, that Mr. Selenski said to Miss Strom that Mr. Kerkowski's in Belize; that was the extent.

Now, all of the sudden, we're hearing information that, that is coming out

of thin air and that is, again, it's information now that's highly prejudicial

that shows that, apparently, Mr. Selenski had information now on the

whereabouts of Mr. Kerkowski and, when he did it, when she said that

Paul Weakley did it, did what? The only thing that it could, the only thing

that it could suggest is that he committed a crime and he's responsible for

the, for the, for the whereabouts of Mr. Kerkowski," Rymsza argued at

sidebar.

"When we were in chambers, the ruling was clear that she was going

to be asked if he said anything, Mr. Selenski that is, allegedly said

anything to her when he came out of the State Police Barracks as to the

whereabouts or location of Mr. Kerkowski," Judge Pierantoni said.

"Yes, your Honor, and that's what I expected her to say, so I think she

must be confused about what time we're talking about after all these

recesses," Sanguedolce said.

Ferentino said Strom was confused about the robbery when she meant

Paul Weakley committed a robbery. The jury perceived Strom's testimony

that Hugo told her, "Paul did it," was in reference to the murders of

Kerkowski and Fassett.

"But the problem is the bell's been rung. And now she's now what

she's hearing is what could be construed as some, maybe not an admission but at least something that suggests that Mr. Selenski is privy to information that Mr. Weakley did it, that he knows it," Rymsza said.

Assistant District Attorney Phillips explained in a way to make it more understandable, indicating Strom accompanied Hugo to the Dallas Township Police Department to tell police Paul Weakley committed a robbery. When Hugo emerged from the police department, he told Strom "Paul did it," referring to the Hadle burglary in Dallas Township where firearms were stolen.

In less than five minutes, Judge Pierantoni issued his second instruction to the jury to disregard the testimony of Strom referring to Paul Weakley.

"We will take another 10 minute recess, and we'll have you back. I apologize, but another recess is required," Judge Pierantoni said.

When the jury returned to the courtroom, Sanguedolce resumed his direct examination of Strom for the third time at 11:32 a.m., changing the subject asking if she saw flex ties around the Mount Olivet Road property and inside her Honda Accord that Hugo normally drove. Strom said she had seen flex ties.

For the next hour, Sanguedolce had Strom review financial transactions of deposits and debits from March through the end of August 2002. Strom earlier testified she saw Hugo and Weakley in a bedroom when they lived at Strom's grandmother's house on Miller Street, Luzerne, with $60,000 spread out on a bed.

Hugo's spending habits certainly exceeded $60,000.

From buying diamond jewelry, furniture, electronics, a sport utility vehicle, a motorcycle, an all-terrain vehicle and at least two trips to a casino in Atlantic City, Sanguedolce had Strom tell the jury a total of $128,852.57 had been deposited into her bank accounts from April through the end of August 2002, with most of the money lavishly spent. Strom said all the cash came from Hugo.

By the end of October 2002, Strom said $150,678.57 had been deposited and most of the money spent.

Sanguedolce ended his direct examination of Strom after he displayed the check she wrote on April 30, 2002.

Attorney Brown cross-examined Strom quizzing her about her employment with Geico Insurance where she was paid $55,000 a year in salary and was given a company vehicle, a Dodge Stratus, and a company issued cellular phone and a laptop computer. She also did not have to pay for gasoline for the Dodge. Strom said she lived "rent free" at her grandmother's house but had "everyday expenses," such as payments for her personal vehicle, a Honda Accord, insurance for the vehicle and utilities for the Miller Street house.

Strom said she also took an Alaskan vacation.

In securing a mortgage from First Union Bank, Strom said she drafted a letter indicating she saved money while living rent-free for three years and had the letter notarized. When she testified before the federal grand jury on Feb. 24, 2004, Strom said she lied about stashing away money while she lived at the Miller Street house. She had no money saved.

Attacking Strom's credibility before the jury, Brown reviewed her testimony before the grand jury and the lie she told claiming she saved $15,000 while living rent-free. Brown then directed questions to have Strom admit she paid off a brother's gambling debt but the amount was never disclosed. Strom further testified Hugo took off for another Atlantic City trip without her and withdrew thousands of dollars in cash advances on her credit cards.

Judge Pierantoni gave the jury a lunch recess at 12:50 p.m., advising everyone to return at 2 p.m. Brown resumed his cross-examination of Strom at 2:04 p.m., going over the $10,079 check she issued at the real estate closing for the Mount Olivet Road property knowing she only had $699.71 in her checking account. Brown had Strom confirm she had three credit cards and each card had a line of credit where she could take cash advances totaling $17,000.

"And we can agree that if you wanted to, you could draw upon those accounts to pay for the check?" Brown asked as Strom replied, "Yes."

"Okay. So you didn't need Hugo to go kill Michael Kerkowski and Tammy Fassett to get the money, did you?" Brown asked. "Say that again," Strom said.

"Because you had the money available, you didn't need Hugo to go kill Michael Kerkowski and Tammy Fassett to cover the check; correct?" Brown asked. "Correct," Strom replied.

"You just testified that you wrote a bad check, a check that you knew couldn't be covered, on April 30th (2002)?" Brown asked.

"Sir, I wrote the check out because Hugo told me that the money would be in the account for that amount," Strom said.

Brown then advised he was going to display a series of photographs of Hugo until Sanguedolce raised an objection resulting in a sidebar conference with Judge Pierantoni.

"Judge, I don't understand the relevance. These are pictures of the defendant playing with puppies? We've admitted photographs to show what he looks like. We have pictures of the victim playing with his kids. Are we allowed to introduce those, too?" Sanguedolce argued.

"Well, your Honor, it's not offered, it's not offered for any sympathy or any purpose. He's not arrested until June of 2003. These pictures are offered to show what he looked like in 2002," Brown said.

"Playing with puppies, Judge, come on," Sanguedolce said.

"Listen, I don't need people chiming in. And I've been very patient with everybody so far, but if you push me, you're going to face the wrath. The objection is sustained. I don't see the relevance," Pierantoni said.

Brown never showed the jury the picture of Hugo playing with puppies. Instead, Brown reviewed Strom's perjury and money laundering offenses and her agreement to cooperate and testify against Hugo. Strom said she had no idea what sentence would be given to her as she initially faced up to 40 years in a federal prison but also could face no prison time.

When Brown began asking questions of letters Strom wrote to Hugo when he was jailed in 2003 and 2004, Sanguedolce objected. Judge Pierantoni gave the jury a 10 minute recess and spoke with prosecutors and Hugo's lawyers.

"...what I would be doing is introducing letters from, umm, 2003, 2004, 2005, the main relevant guilt letter, guilt phase letters have to do with 2003 and 2004..." Brown explained.

"Your Honor, he wasn't charged with this until 2006, and so, these letters are actually about the first trial, which I don't think we really want to get into," Sanguedolce said.

"It specifically references a case, Judge. And the only case that was pending in '03 was the Rudy/Redmond homicide. The Kerkowski/Fassett wasn't charged until March of '06," Ferentino said.

"The problem is, the problem is I do not have a date, but it was the final letter that she wrote in which she says, I am the one to lose everything; I saved all that money for all those years to buy the house that I always dreamed of only to have people question me about it; the cars, everything was mine. I worked for it, not you; how dare you put me through this. So that would be about this case," Brown argued.

"Yeah, you're trying to show bias or motive on her part, basically," Judge Pierantoni said in recognizing Brown's efforts at attacking Strom's credibility, allowing the letter to be presented to the jury.

The break lasted until 3:25 p.m. when the jury returned to the jury box.

Brown just touched upon the letter Strom wrote about her finances and the Mount Olivet Road property belonged to her and she stood to lose everything. Surprisingly, Brown did not display the letter to the jury.

Brown ended his cross-examination of Strom.

Sanguedolce took the opportunity to ask Strom follow-up questions on redirect examination, specifically about her not needing Hugo to kill Kerkowski and Fassett.

"You were asked a question on cross-examination that Hugo did not need, that you did not need Hugo to kill Michael Kerkowski and Tammy Fassett to cover check, the check; do you recall that question?" Sanguedolce asked.

When Strom said she remembered, Sanguedolce asked, "He never told you that was his plan, did he?" "No," Strom answered.

Sanguedolce reviewed Strom's finances once again and got Strom to tell the jury she last lived at the Mount Olivet Road property in January 2005.

"They took it from me on January 30ths, of the year 2005," Strom said.

Strom's time on the witness stand came to an end at 3:47 p.m.

Questions that were not asked of Strom by prosecutors and Hugo's lawyers: Did she notice any recent digging near the well? Did she notice her dogs digging in the area where the bodies were unearthed?

Judge Pierantoni ended the fourth day of trial advising the jury a winter storm was in the forecast and to report back to the courthouse by 10:30 a.m. for the fifth day of trial, Jan. 27, 2015.

# CONTESTED IN-CHAMBERS MEETING

The winter storm that was in the forecast never materialized as it was considered a nuisance snow, less than one inch of snow had fallen Monday, Jan. 26 through the next morning of Tuesday, Jan. 27, 2015.

Jurors began gathering in the back of the courthouse around 10 a.m. for the fifth day of trial and were escorted through the basement hallway to the elevator, walking past the county detectives' conference room where the next witness, Paul Raymond Weakley, waited. Upstairs on the second floor, First Assistant District Attorney Samuel Sanguedolce, first assistant district attorneys Jarrett Ferentino and Mamie Phillips and Hugo's lawyers, Bernard Brown, Edward Rymsza and Hugh Taylor were meeting with Judge Fred Pierantoni in the judge's chambers for a private meeting. Pierantoni's chambers were on the second floor while the trial was being held in a larger third-floor courtroom.

Ferentino announced Weakley would be their next witness, giving a brief outline about what he would say on the witness stand.

Weakley had previously threatened twice not to testify as he was regarded as a "snitch" in federal prison where he was attacked by other inmates. Weakley's reputation behind prison walls as a snitch was talked about in the private meeting as Ferentino wanted to introduce the assaults to the jury.

But there was a problem.

Prosecutors did not have a corroborating witness to say Weakley was assaulted and repeatedly stabbed because he was a snitch and agreed to testify against Hugo. All prosecutors had was Weakley's word describing how the attacking inmates were shanking him saying he was a snitch.

Prosecutors did not suggest Hugo had anything to do with Weakley being assaulted but Hugo was certainly aware as investigators obtained a recorded jailhouse telephone call with Hugo laughing about Weakley being shanked.

As Brown was going to cross examine Weakley, Rymsza demanded to know if prosecutors gave Weakley any promises to receive preferable treatment in prison or seek to modify his sentence of life in prison for his testimony.

"...I think, in light of that, we're entitled to know what changed his mind. I mean, I'm, if there's any, been any sort of benefit or any additional promises that have been made, I think we need to know it," Rymsza said.

Judge Pierantoni ruled if Hugo's lawyers ask Weakley about preferential treatment for his testimony, prosecutors on redirect examination could inquire about Weakley being attacked. Pierantoni also renewed his earlier ruling about the Goosay robbery and kidnapping, following the Pennsylvania Superior Court's opinion that only the evidence - flex ties, duct tape - used in the Goosay crime could be introduced to the jury, not Hugo's conviction for the Goosay robbery and kidnapping.

Sanguedolce made the argument about Weakley being "an expert" of knowing Hugo, having been together for nine years inside and outside federal prison and Weakley had seen Hugo sober and under the influence of a controlled substance and intoxicated. Hugo's drug use was not relevant, his lawyers argued, because Hugo was not facing any drug related offenses.

Sanguedolce and Ferentino argued Hugo being under the influence of cocaine was the reason why the bodies of Kerkowski and Fassett were left in Weakley's vehicle for three days before being buried at the Mount Olivet Road property.

Pierantoni wanted some time to think about his ruling regarding Hugo being under the influence of cocaine, ending the private meeting at 10:55 a.m. And the judge took little time as prosecutors and Hugo's lawyers returned to Pierantoni's chambers at 11:16 a.m.

Only Pierantoni did not immediately issue his ruling as Sanguedolce and Ferentino raised another issue that needed to be addressed secretly.

Ferentino brought up Hugo's legal services to Michael Jason Kerkowski when Kerkowski was facing trial for selling prescription drugs without prescriptions from his pharmacy near Tunkhannock in Wyoming County. Ferentino explained the services involved Hugo's intention to intimidate jurors during the Kerkowski trial but there was no allegation of jury tampering. According to Weakley, he joined Hugo in an attempt to follow a juror when leaving the Wyoming County Courthouse.

Ferentino said there were no charges filed about intimidating a juror or the jury in Wyoming County but wanted to bring up the issue as it related to the relationship between Hugo and Weakley and Hugo's services paid for by Michael Jason Kerkowski.

Rymsza quickly argued against any information of jury tampering as the judge who presided over Kerkowski's trial, Bernard Vanston, had testified about Hugo "glaring" at him.

Judge Pierantoni prohibited prosecutors from introducing any information about the attempt to intimidate the jury during Michael Jason Kerkowski's trial but this issue was not over. As for Hugo's behavior after the murders, Pierantoni allowed prosecutors to solicit such information from Weakley with a stipulation.

"As to the statements regarding the alleged cocaine use between the May 2nd and May 5th, after the death and before the burial, I'll allow Mr. Weakley to testify to any statements, behavior, conduct that he observed from or of Mr. Selenski without referencing the word cocaine," the judge ruled.

When it seemed the private meeting in the judge's chambers was ending, Sanguedolce requested a clarification on Hugo's legal services he provided to Michael Jason Kerkowski. The argument at one point became heated.

Sanguedolce explained Hugo was getting tens of thousands of dollars from Kerkowski by offering him legal services while Hugo has no legal training.

"Sam, if you intend to elicit from Mr. Weakley that Mr. Selenski was helping Michael Kerkowski with his legal services…that is fine," Pierantoni said.

"By his conduct, though," Sanguedolce stated.

"But by intimidating, allegedly intimidating a juror, no. It's too prejudicial. He was never charged. Selenski was never charged. From the record, it doesn't seem like there was ever an investigation," Pierantoni noted.

Ferentino said Hugo never intimidated a juror but only followed the juror describing Hugo as Kerkowski's "muscle."

"But he wasn't charged," Pierantoni said, quickly followed by Ferentino saying, "But that doesn't matter."

"If he was charged, we might not be sitting here," the judge said.

The judge and Ferentino went back and forth for a minute before Sanguedolce explained further.

"The defense is asking the jury to believe that these were legitimate legal services that, by the way, (Hugo) got paid more than any lawyer I ever heard of for providing legal services and the truth is, that's not what was being paid for. (Hugo) had no legal training," Sanguedolce explained.

"Well, did you bring that out? Did you bring out that he's not a lawyer, he was not a member of the Bar? Do you plan to do that with another witness?" Pierantoni asked.

Sanguedolce made the effort to introduce Hugo's intimidation of a juror but was forbidden.

"It's prejudicial. I already ruled. Anything else?" the judge said.

With that, the private meeting inside the judge's chambers ended at 11:22 a.m. and all gathered in the courtroom at 11:32 a.m. to begin the fifth day of trial.

# WEAKLEY TESTIFIES

After a lengthy and tense private meeting, the trial resumed with Assistant District Attorney Jarrett Ferentino calling Paul Raymond Weakley to the witness stand.

Weakley was Hugo's side-kick and partner-in-crime. Hugo's girlfriend, Christina Strom, once testified her relationship with Hugo was perfect until Weakley moved in with them.

Ferentino got right into the fire with Weakley, who said he was born in Albion, Michigan, and resides in Tuscan, Arizona, at the United States Federal Penitentiary where he is serving a life sentence plus 10 years.

"And the sentence you're serving, Mr. Weakley, is it a sentence for the murders of Michael Kerkowski and Tammy Fassett?" Ferentino asked.

"Yes, it is," Weakley replied, who also acknowledged the sentence involved the robbery of Monroe County jewelry store owner Samuel Goosay.

As Ferentino asked the next four questions - three questions asking Weakley about being charged with conspiracy and who his co-conspirator was, and the fourth question related to his federal plea agreement and what sentence was imposed upon him - Attorney Brown objected to each question. Clearly, Hugo's lawyers were worried about Weakley, who was considered the prosecution's best witness despite telling investigators multiple lies and who was involved in the murders of Kerkowski and Fassett.

After Brown's fourth objection, Ferentino asked for a sidebar conference.

"It's in anticipation of the plea agreement and the contents of the plea agreement that he would testify truthfully. It would be witness vouchering. Witness vouchering, vouching for the witness and the credibility of the witness," Brown argued.

"Okay. If I was allowed to finish my question, it would have been, Have you agreed to testify in this case? So, the objection is premature. It's an attempt to break my flow. It's the fourth objection on four questions. I'm allowed to ask that question," Ferentino shot back.

Pierantoni overruled Brown's objection and cautioned Ferentino not to respond or repeat Weakley's answers.

Ferentino carefully reviewed with Weakley his federal plea agreement and life sentence. Weakley said he was promised "absolutely nothing" for testifying against Hugo with the stipulation that the criminal case he faced in Luzerne County related to the robbery and murders of Kerkowski and Fassett would be dropped.

"Mr. Weakley, did you originally bring the homicides of Michael Kerkowski and Tammy Fassett to the attention of law enforcement?" Ferentino asked.

"Yes, I did," Weakley said.

Weakley acknowledged when he reported the murders of Kerkowski and Fassett, he was not truthful. In fact, Weakley distanced himself, originally implicating Patrick Russin conspired with Hugo to kill Kerkowski and Fassett.

"I was trying to protect myself. I was trying to isolate myself from, umm, criminal charges," Weakley explained.

Weakley testified Russin had absolutely nothing to do with the murders.

Once Weakley's untruthfulness was out of the way, Ferentino dived deeper into Weakley's cooperation.

Weakley said he was charged several times in the spring of 2003 with several burglaries of homes and churches including possession of child sexual abuse materials on a computer. In exchange for his participation, those burglaries and child pornography offenses were not prosecuted.

Ferentino had Weakley acknowledge that he was interviewed by investigators more than a dozen times and provided false information during each interview.

"Why should the men and women of this jury believe you today?" Ferentino asked.

"Well, the, uh, the truth is all I had left to give. All the other things were crumbling, and the only thing that the evidence supported was the truth," Weakley replied.

"And, Mr. Weakley, as the evidence and the investigation of Detective Gary Capitano and the State Police began to unfold, did they bring the evidence to you and show you the case they were building?" Ferentino asked.

"They did," Weakley said, noting the evidence pointed at him and Hugo.

Weakley said he met Hugo while they were in prison but was not permitted to say they met at the United States Penitentiary at Lewisburg.

Weakley said that he and Hugo were friends and Hugo was released from federal prison 14 months before he was released on March 12, 2002. Their plan was for Weakley to live in the Dallas/Wilkes-Barre area of Northeastern Pennsylvania where Hugo was raised.

Weakley said Hugo was in his debt owing him $16,000 but the reason that Hugo owed Weakley money was not pursued.

Weakley said he met Michael Jason Kerkowski through Hugo with the understanding that Hugo's relationship with Kerkowski was financial as Hugo was performing certain legal services.

"...Mr. Weakley, there's been testimony that Kerkowski and Selenski were friends. Is that the impression that you got of the relationship?" Ferentino asked.

"Absolutely not. Mr. Selenski hated Mr. Kerkowski. It wasn't a friendship at all, it was a..a financial relationship," Weakley replied.

Weakley told the jury despite Hugo being paid by Kerkowski to perform legal services, he never saw Hugo perform any work on Kerkowski's behalf in the four months Weakley lived with Hugo and Strom at the Miller Street residence in Luzerne.

When Kerkowski came to the Miller Street house, Weakley said Hugo often ran out the back door to avoid Kerkowski.

"It was a situation where Mr. Selenski was telling Mr. Kerkowski that he was going to perform certain duties or tasks for him and just never did. He was avoiding Mr. Kerkowski," Weakley explained.

In answering Ferentino's questions, Weakley said Hugo discussed other intentions notably to rob and murder Kerkowski. Weakley said he was released from federal prison and moved into the Miller Street home on March 12, 2002, and two days later, March 14, Hugo began talking about killing Kerkowski and stealing his money.

With Michael Jason Kerkowski going to prison upon his jury conviction and guilty plea to separate cases involving the sale of prescription drugs without prescriptions, Hugo wanted to rob and kill him before he was sentenced in Wyoming County Court, Weakley said.

Weakley said Hugo's motivation was strictly money.

When Hugo proposed to Weakley about robbing and killing Kerkowski, Weakley said he considered it and conducted research of Kerkowski learning about his legal troubles in Wyoming County. Weakley decided Kerkowski and Hugo were too close, which would bring the investigation "too close," despite Hugo telling Weakley that Kerkowski had $1 million in cash stashed away inside the Hunlock Township home.

Explaining the source of the $60,000 Strom had seen on the bed inside the Miller Street house in early March 2002, Weakley said Hugo showed up with the cash in a shoebox claiming the money came from Kerkowski. Weakley said they "burnt" through the cash really fast with about $5,000 used to buy Weakley a used Dodge Avenger, part of the $16,000 Hugo owed Weakley, and under the table payments to Steiner to buy the Mount Olivet Road property.

One would wonder how fast Hugo and Weakley spent the $60,000 as by April 30, 2002, Strom did not have enough funds in her checking account to cover the $10,079 check she issued at the real estate closing for the property.

Weakley said he knew this as Strom confided with him about not having sufficient funds in her checking account.

"Ms. Strom had asked me about, without Hugo being present at this point, about the $10,000 check that she wrote. She did not have anywhere near that kind of money in her checking account or access to that kind of money at all to cover that check, but she was assured by Hugo that the money would be there in time to cover this check," Weakley testified.

Weakley said Hugo was worried and asked again to participate in the robbery and murder of Kerkowski.

Hugo's original plan, Weakley explained, was to rob, interrogate and assault Kerkowski for the hidden cash inside Kerkowski's house. Once the cash was in hand, Hugo intended to kill Kerkowski and leave the body inside his Hunlock Township home.

"But now the plan had changed to something that was a bit more acceptable in that we would, first, rob, then murder Mr. Kerkowski and then take his body with us," Weakley said.

Weakley said Hugo's intentions by taking Kerkowski's body was to make it appear he fled to avoid being sent to prison.

"I thought it was a pretty good idea," Weakley said.

Weakley said he changed his mind and decided to go along with Hugo to rob and kill Kerkowski to help Strom cover the $10,079 check.

"That was a crucial element in my agreeing to this crime," Weakley said, quickly adding that Strom had absolutely no knowledge of Hugo's intentions.

It was Wednesday, May 1, 2002, the day after Strom issued the check and expressed her concerns to Weakley about not having enough funds, when Weakley decided to assist Hugo in the robbery and murder of Michael Jason Kerkowski.

Materials such as gloves, a 9mm handgun, duct tape, flex ties and wire cutters were gathered and ready to go for the evening of Friday, May 3, 2002, to carry out their plan.

While Weakley disclosed the use of duct tape and flex ties, Ferentino wearing protective gloves displayed duct tape and flex ties to the jury.

The protective gloves worn by Ferentino showing demonstrative duct tape and flex ties he passed to Weakley, who was not wearing gloves, resulted in an objection by Hugo's lawyers.

"Judge, I'm sorry. If it's a demonstrative exhibit, he can take off the rubber gloves….he can do away with the bravado and get rid of the rubber gloves," Rymsza argued.

Judge Pierantoni instructed Ferentino to remove the gloves since the duct tape and flex ties were demonstrative exhibits.

Weakley said he pre-looped several flex ties prior to traveling to Kerkowski's home in Hunlock Township.

Their plan to kill Kerkowski Friday night changed to Friday afternoon when Weakley informed Hugo he had the day off.

Earlier on Friday, May 3, 2002, Weakley went grocery shopping and withdrew $200 from an automated teller machine just in case something went wrong with the robbery. Weakley returned to the Miller Street home, ate lunch with Hugo, and packed up their materials for the drive to Kerkowski's home.

Weakley said he drove his Dodge Avenger with Hugo in the passenger seat giving him directions arriving at about 2 p.m.

"When we first pulled in the driveway, we saw Michael Kerkowski and Tammy Fassett doing yard work. Mr. Kerkowski was on a riding lawnmower and Tammy Fassett was using a weed wacker around the perimeter of the house," Weakley testified.

Weakley said he had the looped flex ties in the back of his pants, unlooped flex ties, gloves and wire cutters in the pockets of his cargo pants while Hugo was armed with the handgun.

Weakley almost backed out when he saw Fassett and asked Hugo what he wanted to do.

"Well, after I saw Ms. Fassett, I had a, I had a conversation with Hugo. We didn't plan on Ms. Fassett being there at all. This was supposed to be Hugo and I robbing and then murdering and then taking Mr. Kerkowski's body with us. Ms. Fassett, we had no intentions of, we had, we had no knowledge that she was going to be there. This was a curveball," Weakley testified.

Weakley said he wanted to call it off but was faced with a time constraint due to the check issued by Strom.

"We could have done this the next day or something, but it took Hugo a long time to convince me to get to this point. You know, we were there, we were ready to go, we were in the driveway, Kerkowski is right there," Weakley said.

Kerkowski and Fassett were wearing safety glasses when they stopped what they were doing and began to approach Weakley and Hugo, still seated inside the Dodge Avenger.

"...And there was a comment made concerning them wearing the safety glasses. Hugo said, 'I wonder if they're wearing bulletproof vests, too,' in, in a comment relating to us getting ready to rob and kill them," Weakley said.

Kerkowski and Fassett asked Hugo what he was doing there and Hugo told them he was there to shoot the shit.

Hugo and Weakley were invited inside the house and all four sat around a kitchen table. Kerkowski only had warm beer that Hugo accepted bringing in a six pack of Corona beer from the garage. Weakley said Hugo consumed the entire six pack but was not feeling its effects as he described Hugo as having a high tolerance to beer.

Weakley said the original plan involved Hugo pulling the gun on Kerkowski and Weakley fastening the flex ties around his hands and wrists behind his back and ankles as soon as they entered the house.

While sitting at the table, Weakley said Hugo was engaged in awkward conversations with Kerkowski and Fassett. During the one hour of awkward conversations, Weakley was giving Hugo "looks" to get moving with their plan and they also learned Kerkowski had to pick up his two sons at daycare, needing to leave the home by 3:30 p.m. for the long drive to the daycare facility in Kingston.

Knowing Kerkowski needed to leave, Weakley said he became concerned.

"Mr. Selenski holds out the handgun, stands up, reaches in his back, pulls out the handgun, points it at Mr. Kerkowski..." Weakley testified.

Weakley said Kerkowski looked at Hugo as if it was a joke and did not immediately take it seriously.

"Mr. Selenski told him again, Get the fuck on the floor. And then, at that point, both Mr. Kerkowski and Ms. Fassett got down on the kitchenette floor," Weakley said.

With Kerkowski and Fassett on the floor, Weakley removed the flex ties from his pants and fastened them around the wrists of Kerkowski and Fassett behind their backs while also placing flex ties around Fassett's ankles. Kerkowski was led to the basement where he was placed on a wooden stool and his ankles fastened with flex ties. Hugo stayed with Kerkowski in the basement and Weakley returned to the kitchen where he used the wire cutters to cut the flex ties from Fassett's ankles, took her to a bedroom on the second floor and replaced the flex ties around her ankles all the while Fassett was crying and pleading, "Why are you doing this?" Weakley said.

Weakley said he told Fassett what they were doing had nothing to do with her and were there to rob Kerkowski. As Weakley returned to the basement, he noticed and grabbed a baker's rolling pin that was hanging on the wall.

"I was thinking that I could, perhaps, use it as a, as a tool of interrogation. I could use it to maybe work Michael over with it," Weakley said.

As Fassett was left alone bound at her wrists and ankles in a second floor bedroom, Weakley was in the basement with Hugo and Kerkowski and realized he needed more flex ties and duct tape that were in his Dodge Avenger parked in the driveway. Weakley said he sent Hugo to retrieve the items and to park Kerkwoski's Toyota 4Runner in the driveway and to move the Dodge into the garage.

Weakley said while Hugo was gathering the flex ties, duct tape and repositioning the vehicles, he was holding the baker's rolling pin. "I knew

I was going to work Mr. Kerkowski over with it, you know, beat him, torture him for information."

Weakley's use of the word "torture" brought upon another objection from Hugo's lawyers and another sidebar conference.

Brown and Rymsza said "torture" was used as an aggravating factor to seek the death penalty if Hugo is convicted of first-degree murder. They argued the word torture should not be presented during the guilt phase of the trial.

Pierantoni agreed, instructed Ferentino to advise Weakley not to repeat "torture," and told the jury to disregard hearing "torture." Only Ferentino could not just go up to Weakley and tell him not to say "torture" in front of the jury. Pierantoni took a 10 minute recess and during that time, Ferentino advised Weakley not to say "torture."

The jury was brought back into the courtroom and Weakley's testimony continued.

Ferentino asked what happened in the basement.

Weakley explained Hugo returned with the flex ties and duct tape and it was their intention to interrogate Kerkowski to find out where money was hidden inside the house.

"So, when you say interrogate, Mr. Weakley, what do you mean?" Ferentino asked. Weakley replied, "To inflict pain."

To enhance the fear factor, Weakley said he wrapped duct tape at least 10 times around Kerkowski's head covering his eyes and wrapped another 10 times around his wrists. Picking up the rolling pin, Weakley said he asked Kerkowski the combination to the safe that was in the basement.

"His response was that it took two people to get into the safe. It required both him and his father to get into the safe. I wasn't satisfied with that answer. I knew it to not be true and, using the rolling pin, I hit him in his knee really hard," Weakley said.

Hugo was a spectator while Weakley began beating Kerkowski with the rolling pin. Each time Weakley asked for the safe's combination, Kerkowski gave the same answer and was struck in the knees with the rolling pin.

Weakley knew he was not going to get the combination to the safe. So he moved to his next tactic by locking a flex tie around Kerkowsk's neck.

At first, Weakley tighten the flex tie to cause just enough stress resulting in Kerkowski lightly choking. "I was trying to scare him. He's blindfolded at this point. He's got, his hands are taped. He's zip tied. I mean, he's helpless, and now, he's got this thing around his neck. After a brief period of time with this around his neck, I cut it off and then again asked him, you know, 'Where's the money at? Where's the combination, what's the combination to the safe.'"

Weakley said he was screaming at Kerkowski because they were up against time and needed to get out of there. Kerkowski gave the location of an envelope with $20,000 hidden above the safe and above a ceiling tile behind insulation.

After carefully moving the ceiling tile and pushing aside the insulation, Hugo and Weakley found the hidden cash envelope. Placing the ceiling tile back in its place, Weakley went back to Kerkowski saying they know there is more money hidden in the house, hitting Kerkowski several more times with the rolling pin.

"He still wasn't giving me the information that I wanted. Then I took another flex tie and told him to nod his head when he was ready to tell me where more money was. And then I put the flex tie around his neck and tightened it," Weakley said.

Unable to breath, Kerkowski nodded his head as Weakley used wire cutters to cut the flex tie from his neck. Kerkowski gave up another location where an envelope was hidden in the drop ceiling.

Hugo and Weakley removed the ceiling tile and found the envelope with $40,000.

When they returned to Kerkowski, Hugo and Weakley were becoming more frantic having just acquired $60,000. They wanted more.

Hugo took over the beatings of Kerkowski with the rolling pin but Weakley felt the best way to inflict pain was the use of flex ties.

"...Mr. Seleneki put a zip tie around Mr. Kerkowski's neck. This, this had proved already an effective way of getting money out of Mr. Kerkowski, these flex ties. You know, I've used two flex ties, and I got two money bags. Hugo puts another, puts a zip tie around Mr. Kerkowski's neck for the first time, puts it on really tight," Weakley testified.

`    Weakley said Hugo began beating Kerkowski with the rolling pin resulting in Kerkowski rolling around on the floor to escape the blows but suffered a hit to his forehead that split open.

"Now, Mr. Kerkowski, this whole time, he's bound at his ankles, bound at his wrists, he's blindfolded. There's really nothing he can do, but he's like, rolling around on the floor, trying to avoid being beat by this," Weakley said.

During the violent assault upon Kerkowski, Weakley said Kerkowski confessed to having $40,000 hidden at his father's house. Weakley said he took this as "misdirection."

A fourth flex tie was tightened around Kerkowski's neck applied by Hugo as Weakley described its tightness as Kerkowski's skin was coming through the locking mechanism on the zip tie. "It couldn't have been put on any tighter," Weakley said.

The flex tie was left on and Kerkowski's face turned purple and he stopped breathing. After several minutes, the flex tie was cut from Kerkowski's neck.

To make sure Kerkowski was dead, Weakley said he placed a fifth flex tie around his neck, tightened it, and left it on.

Hugo and Weakley discussed what they needed to do next. Hugo instructed Weakley to clean up the house and Hugo would take care of Fassett.

Hugo left the basement and Weakley began picking up the cut flex ties and to account for all the items they brought into the house, including the duct tape and rubber gloves.

While Weakley was working in the basement and cleaning up Kerkowski's blood from the carpet, Hugo returned to the basement.

"I said, you know, 'Did you take care of it?' He's like, "Yeah, she's taken care of," Weakley said.

When Hugo returned to the basement after killing Fassett, he was carrying a comforter taken from a bed. They used the comforter to wrap Kerkowski's body and then duct tape it to hold the body in place before carrying out the body to Weakley's Dodge parked in the garage.

Weakley said he had to cut the flex tie from Kerkowski's ankles to carry the body.

Kerkowski's body was placed in a hallway and then Hugo and Weakley went upstairs to get Fassett's body, the first time Weakley saw her dead.

Weakley said a flex tie was placed around her neck as her body was carried and placed next to Kerkowski.

Hugo and Weakley then went through the house gathering the beer bottles Hugo had emptied and removed several firearms from the house in an attempt to conceal their crimes.

When it came time to remove the bodies from the house, Weakley said the door to the garage was propped open and they opened the trunk to Weakley's Dodge where Kerkowski's body was placed. Fassett's body was put in the back seat.

Once the bodies were inside the Dodge, Weakley went back inside the house and took the surveillance tapes from the VCR and Fassett's purse.

Weakley had the bodies, the money, VCR surveillance tapes, Fassett's purse and the cut flex ties in his vehicle. Worried about time, Weakley said they still needed to place Kerkowski's Toyota back into the garage and put away the lawn tractor and weed wacker.

Hugo told Weakley not to worry about the rest and to just take off as Hugo wanted to stay. Weakley said he was worried because Hugo did not have a vehicle and was out in the middle of nowhere.

Weakley left Kerkowski's house leaving Hugo behind as he wished.

Judge Pierantoni ended Weakley's testimony for lunch at 1:50 p.m., instructing the jury to return at 2:30 p.m.

When court resumed, Weakley testified he drove to the Miller Street house in Luzerne keeping the bodies inside his Dodge parked on the street. After he entered the house, Strom arrived.

Weakley said Hugo showed up several hours later not knowing how he got there since Hugo did not have a vehicle.

"What happened when he came back in?" Ferentino asked.

"Well, he was, he was erratic. He was, you know, his eyes were all bugged out. He looks to be out of his mind a little bit," Weakley replied, telling the jury Hugo was repeatedly sniffing and had a runny nose.

Weakley said he had a million questions for Hugo, such as how did he get to the Miller Street house and what were they planning to do with the bodies but the conversation did not produce results as Hugo was not acting rational.

Hugo suddenly took off in Strom's Honda Accord leaving Weakley to ponder what was happening. A few minutes after Hugo sped away, he called Weakley telling him about having a bad feeling and advised Weakley to get out of the Miller Street house.

"...I had been through this with him before. This was this irrational paranoia thing he had going on, and at this point, I felt it might not be a bad idea just for me to get the hell away from there," Weakley said.

Weakley drove away in his Dodge with the bodies inside and went to the Wyoming Valley Mall in Wilkes-Barre Township where he purchased toiletries and a change of clothes as he was going to stay at a hotel. Concerned about someone seeing Fassett's body wrapped in a comforter in the back seat, Weakley parked next to a police cruiser outside the police department's substation at the mall.

"Yeah, yeah, yeah, I figured that was the safest place for my car to be; nobody would break into it next to a police car," Weakley told the jury.

After buying items inside the mall, Weakley said he drove north on Interstate 81 and saw a billboard for a hotel near the Wilkes-Barre/Scranton International Airport where he checked in on May 3, 2002. Weakley ended up staying a second night checking out on May 5, 2002.

Weakley parked his Dodge near the entrance doors of the hotel as a deterrent from someone breaking into the car.

Weakley sat in the hotel room for several minutes and realized he needed to communicate with Hugo because he did not want to take the chance of using the hotel room phone. So, Weakley got back into his Dodge where the bodies were and returned to the Wyoming Valley Mall to purchase a mobile phone at a kiosk.

Ferentino displayed phone records of the cellular phone Weakley purchased listing the numerous outgoing phone calls to Hugo. Weakley said Hugo was still not acting rational in the few times they spoke about what to do with the bodies.

Weakley began to feel more stressed and walked to a restaurant to get something to eat. After his late night dinner, Weakley said he managed to contact Hugo two or three times on the cellular phone.

"I left him a message, giving him an ultimatum that if he didn't get back to me in a certain period of time...I was going to take care of the situation myself," Weakley said.

When Hugo did not respond on Saturday, May 4, 2002, Weakley got into his vehicle and began pulling out of the hotel's parking lot intending to discard the bodies in another state. As Weakley was headed for Interstate-81, he spotted Hugo driving toward him driving the Honda Accord.

Weakley and Hugo parked in the hotel's parking lot and Weakley got into the Honda. Weakley described Hugo's behavior as the same with a runny nose, jumpy and paranoia.

"A lot of it was him asking me for ideas on where we could get rid of this instead of him telling, you know, this is his neck of the woods, you know. Umm, he had finally come up with several ideas on where we could dispose of them," Weakley said.

Several ideas Hugo came up with, Weakley said, was burying the bodies under power lines or weighing the bodies and disposing them in a pond. Weakley discarded dumping the bodies in a pond as Hugo mentioned it was at his friend's house and was a decorative pond.

So, it was burying the bodies under power lines by the cover of darkness.

Hugo and Weakley drove in the Honda as the bodies were left in the Dodge in the hotel's parking lot as the two men traveled to the Arena Hub Plaza near the Wyoming Valley Mall where they purchased two short handled spades at a home improvement store. They were also going to patronize another store to buy dark colored clothing but Hugo went inside the store alone.

"...On my part, a poor idea to send Mr. Selenski into, to purchase those clothing. He was still, the sniffling, the rationality, the complete inability to interact in a social situation," Weakley said.

Hugo was inside the store for 20 minutes and emerged with a jacket.

Weakley was getting fed up with Hugo's antics and bluntly told him to drive away. Instead of driving away, Hugo drove to another area of the large parking lot in Arena Hub Plaza and told Weakley of his plan to bury the bodies.

Hugo told Weakley they could bury the bodies at the Mount Olivet Road property. Weakley thought it was a good idea as he was familiar with the property and could have access to the bodies in case they decided to burn the corpses in the future. Hugo dropped Weakley off at the hotel and the two men went their separate ways for the night. The bodies remained in Weakley's Dodge parked outside the hotel.

Hugo returned to the hotel the next morning, Sunday, May 5, 2002, to pick up Weakley. After several minutes, Weakley followed Hugo to the Mount Olivet Road property. Weakley waited inside his Dodge with Fassett's body in the back seat and Kerkowski's body in the trunk as Hugo got out of his Honda and knocked on the door, having a quick conversation with Steiner, who was allowed to stay at the house until May 15, 2002.

After Steiner drove away in his vehicle, Weakley and Hugo walked around the property and decided to bury the bodies in an area that had a depression in the ground. As they began digging, Weakley said the ground was extremely rocky and realized there was not enough dirt and natural materials to bury the bodies. Hugo suggested buying bags of top soil from a nearby feed and seed store on the Dallas Memorial Highway.

Weakley made several trips to the feed and seed store completely loading up the Honda Accord with numerous 40 pound bags of topsoil. On his first trip, Weakley loaded the trunk with the topsoil bags to test the durability of the passenger vehicle. When he made the first trip without any problems, Weakley loaded the backseat and trunk with bags of topsoil.

While they were digging, Weakley said Ernest Culp walked up from the house trailer to see what they were doing near the water source for his house trailer and the home. It was the first time Weakley met Culp he described as a hippie, friendly type of guy.

Fearing Culp would see the bodies in the Dodge, Hugo and Weakley had Culp face away from the Dodge as they reluctantly talked to him. Culp asked what they were doing and Hugo told him they were digging a hole to install an underground gasoline storage tank for all-terrain vehicles.

Not wanting to get into a conversation with Culp, Weakley said they mostly ignored Culp who eventually left the two men to their task of digging.

Once they had a suitable hole and multiple bags of topsoil, Hugo and Weakley removed the bodies and placed them next to the hole. Duct tape that wrapped comforters around the bodies was cut, placing Kerkowski's body first in the hole with Fassett on top, leaving zip ties around their necks and wrists.

Burying the bodies continued to be difficult. Hugo and Weakley first used the dirt they removed digging the hole, then used the bags of topsoil. They still needed more dirt and managed to scrape more indigenous soil in the area followed by dead vegetation to cover up the freshly filled hole. At a later time, Weakley said coal was thrown on top of the hole in addition to dog feces. Coal was placed to prevent Strom's dogs from digging in the grave.

When Hugo and Weakley finished burying the bodies, Weakley picked up the many empty topsoil bags, comforters and duct tape he placed inside his Dodge and then drove to a car wash on Wyoming Avenue in Kingston, Pa., to discard the items.

After leaving the car wash, Weakley drove to the Miller Street house where he burned the surveillance tapes and Fassett's purse.

Money taken from Kerkowski's home was not evenly split as Weakley kept $40,000 and Hugo got $20,000.

Spending the money went fast. Weakley spent nearly $4,000 to purchase a Ford Aerostar van and paid approximately $4,000 to cover an entire year to lease a half-double house on Pulaski Street in Kingston on May 11, 2002. Hugo's pilfering of Kerkowski's money was addressed to the jury when Strom testified.

Having been told by torturing Kerkowski about money hidden in the home of Michael Stanley Kerkowski, Weakley told the jury of Hugo's scheme to scam the elder Kerkowski to get the money. Weakley said Hugo's plan was to have Weakley identify himself as Eric Sullivan and meet the elder Kerkowski and his wife, Geraldine, outside a donut shop on Dallas Memorial Highway in Dallas Township. During this meeting, Weakley - pretending to be Sullivan - told the Kerkwoskis their son was alive and needed $10,000 for a computer and a communications system.

Ferentino then directed questions about the Samuel Goosay robbery in Monroe County having Weakley explain the same modus operandi that he and Hugo used targeting a small jewelry store business owner that dealt in cash and items that could easily be converted to cash.

While Hugo and Weakley were successful in getting $60,000 by torturing Kerkowski with flex ties, the two used the same tools, flex ties, duct tape, and a firearm upon Goosay.

As Ferentino was just getting into the Goosay robbery, he asked Weakley to identify a picture depicting Goosay with a bruised nose. Hugo's lawyers immediately objected, resulting in a 17 minute sidebar conference with Pierantoni where they, once again, debated about evidence being introduced during Hugo's trial from the Goosay robbery.

This issue was appealed twice to the Pennsylvania Superior Court resulting in an approximate three year delay of Hugo's trial.

Hugo's lawyers, Brown and Rymsza, believed the picture of Goosay with a bruised nose would be prejudicial and argued against any use of a firearm. The Goosay picture with the bruised nose was not one of the many pictures Pierantoni had previously viewed in making a decision on what pictures could be introduced during the trial. Pierantoni did leave the door open for the picture to be produced when Goosay testified.

Related to the mention of a firearm being used in the Goosay robbery, Sanguedolce, Ferentino and Phillips argued the Superior Court's opinion allowed them to inform the jury that a firearm was used during the Goosay robbery while Brown and Rymsza claimed prosecutors were conducting a trial within a trial saying the appellate court gave specific "perimeters" of what evidence in the Goosay robbery could be introduced during Hugo's trial.

Pierantoni had both sides reread the Superior Court's opinion.

After 17 minutes arguing once again about the admissibility of the Goosay robbery, Pierantoni overruled Hugo's lawyers and allowed prosecutors to introduce the firearm while questioning Weakley.

Ferentino did not wait and had Weakley explain after he and Hugo kicked in Goosay's back door, Hugo pulled out a handgun and ordered Goosay to the floor where Weakley secured his wrists behind his back with flex ties.

"Mr. Goosay immediately got down. He was terrified. He was…kicked in his backdoor. As soon as he got down on the ground, I used the same flex ties that we used at the Kerkowski robbery to, the same type of flex ties to bind Mr. Goosay," Weakley testified.

Weakley said Goosay was taken to a bedroom where duct tape was placed over his eyes and his ankles were bound together by a flex tie.

Once they had Goosay, Weakley said they began interrogating him wanting to know the combination to the safes at his business and security codes for alarms. While Goosay was being interrogated by Hugo, Weakley was grabbing jewelry from a dresser when a drop of blood from his forehead dripped onto the bedroom carpet.

Weakley said he was involved in an altercation and suffered a laceration on his forehead prior to committing the Goosay robbery. He removed a bandage from his forehead, placed it in a plastic sandwich size bag and put it in his pocket, placing a new bandage on his forehead.

After Goosay gave up the combination and security codes for his jewelry store, Weakley said the plan was for him to steal Goosay's vehicle so as not to bring attention when parked outside the jewelry store after hours.

"I opened up the front door to the jewelry store with Mr. Goosay's keys, went inside, attempted to disarm the alarm system, but almost as soon as I had gone into the…business, police lights were flashing outside," Weakley said.

Ferentino did not ask what Weakley did when he saw the flashing lights but as it became known, Weakley fled out another door and managed to elude capture only to be picked up later by Hugo.

Weakley said he sold the jewelry stolen from Goosay's home at a jewelry store in Dewitt, N.Y.

Ferentino was finished asking Weakley questions.

Now it was Hugo's lawyers' turn to question Weakley, the witness they have been waiting for to discredit and destroy in front of the jury.

"Mr. Weakley, it all just fits together nice and perfect, doesn't it?" Brown asked without getting a response.

"Do you agree that you're an important witness; correct?"

"I guess, yes, I would," Weakley said.

"...who got you the suit?" Brown asked as Weakley said his defense lawyer.

Brown asked Weakley why state police and Luzerne County investigators met with him 17 times between June 2, 2003 through December 10, 2007, highlighting to the jury that Weakley told many lies and provided misinformation.

"My stories had a lot of holes in it," Weakley said.

"And that's because you are an admitted liar; correct?" Brown asked. "Yes," Weakley replied.

From June 2003 through December 2007, Weakley said he told investigators he was not involved in the murders of Kerkowski and Fassett and only assisted in reburying the bodies.

Brown went through each and every lie and misinformation Weakley told investigators in an attempt to challenge his credibility before the jury.

"I told numerous lies to the investigators at that point," Weakley said.

Brown was able to tell the jury the search warrant that was served on the Mount Olivet Road property on June 5, 2003, was based on Weakley's lies and misinformation. But Brown could not get around the fact that the bodies of Kerkowski and Fassett were discovered on the property after the search warrant was served.

Weakley acknowledged it was hard to keep track of all the lies he told.

As the time hit 5 p.m., Pierantoni adjourned for the day sending the jury home for the night, instructing them the next day, Wednesday, Jan. 28, 2015, will begin at 9:30 a.m. Brown was not close to being finished with Weakley as he would return for another round the next day.

The next day did not begin in the courtroom but inside Pierantoni's chambers with an alternate juror just after 9:30 a.m.

The alternate juror advised Pierantoni's secretary that his father was in dire ill health with cancer and had been rushed to the hospital the weekend prior. After the alternate juror was questioned, Pierantoni released the juror without objection from Sanguedolce, Ferentino, Brown and Rymsza, leaving three alternate jurors.

At 9:49 a.m., Weakley returned to the witness stand to continue the barrage of questions from Brown.

Brown blasted Weakley with rapid fire questions about his lies, getting Weakley to admit he had no trouble pointing the finger at Patrick Russin who, along with Hugo, killed Kerkowski and Fassett. Weakley also admitted he lied when he told investigators Joseph Pilcavage and Kerkowski's estranged wife, Kimberly, were involved in the murders.

Weakley said he was amending his lies each time to fit his narrative when confronted with his misinformation by Capitano, Sachney and Luzerne County Detective Daniel Yursha.

"I was evolving my story in hopes of making it more believable," Weakley said.

"To save and protect yourself?" Brown asked. "Absolutely," Weakley replied.

Brown then directed questions relating to Weakley's meetings with investigators on Dec. 4, 2007, and again Dec. 10, 2007, when Weakley claimed he began telling the truth about the murders of Kerkowski and Fassett.

"Uh, the December 4th (2007) is the truth. That's where I completely implicate myself and Mr. Selenski," Weakley said.

"Right, but as you said, you're here testifying today to save and protect yourself; correct?" Brown asked. "Today? No, I'm here to do what's right today. I've already received my punishment," Weakley said.

Surely, the jury got the picture that Weakley was a career criminal and the jury heard from Weakley himself he was given special treatment for testifying against Hugo as prosecutors opted not to prosecute him for possessing child sexual abuse materials and committing numerous burglaries.

Referencing Weakley's plea agreement with the U.S. Attorney's Office, Brown had Weakley confirm that prosecutors in Luzerne County could, at a later point, request Weakley's life sentence be modified.

"...at this point, I'm here just to do what's right. I've already received my sentence. I realize I'm going to do the rest of my life in prison," Weakley said after an onslaught of questions from Brown.

Brown's rapid pace questioning of Weakley came to a halt when Ferenitno objected to a letter Weakley wrote to Janna Desanto, a self-proclaimed Hugo paralegal whose residence was searched by investigators on July 7, 2010. Brown was seeking to admit Weakley's letter to Desanto when Ferentino objected, resulting in the first of two sidebar conferences within five minutes.

At the first sidebar at 10:47 a.m., Ferentino advised Pierantoni that Weakley's letter involved other crimes and murders Hugo took part in and feared any reference to other crimes could be prejudicial toward Hugo. Ferentino further said Desanto interfered with Hugo's case and had the entire investigative file when her house was searched by investigators on July 7, 2010.

"...I just think we're opening up Pandora's box by admitting that in a vacuum and I will close the box if it gets opened, and it's not going to be good," Ferentino said, knowing if Weakley testifies about other crimes, it permits Ferentino to question Weakley on redirect examination.

"...We're going to come back and talk about all the crimes that involve this defendant (Hugo). That's why this is dangerous," Sanguedolce noted.

Weakley's letter to Desanto involved telling the truth on a multitude of murders and Sanguedolce and Ferentino raised their concerns that Hugo is only on trial for the murders of Kerkowski and Fassett.

Pierantoni said he will make a ruling if Brown elects to admit the letter Weakley wrote to Desanto, advising prosecutors and Hugo's lawyers that he was giving Hugo's lawyers "great latitude" since Brown was cross-examining Weakley.

The first sidebar conference ended at 10:52 a.m.

Brown provided Weakley his letter he wrote to Desanto that discussed "the truth not existing."

"Yes, I wrote that," Weakley said.

"Okay. And what you say is that you don't think the truth exists but rather a melding of different versions to a version that the jury will believe; correct?" Brown asked. "I wrote that," Weakley replied.

Ferentino quickly raised another objection resulting in Pierantoni giving the jury a 15 minute break at 10:54 a.m., calling prosecutors and Hugo's lawyers into chambers for a private discussion.

In chambers, a lengthy argument took place over an objection by Sanguedolce and Ferentino about a picture of Weakley dressed in an orange prison jumpsuit walking with Luzerne County Detective Daniel Yursha in 2005. Sanguedolce and Ferentino argued Hugo's lawyers were successful in getting a previous judge to ban any pictures of Hugo being shackled and wearing prison inmate clothing be shown to the jury. Brown countered that prosecutors had no problem dressing Weakley up in a suit and instructing him to shave prior to testifying.

The argument continued with Ferentino and Rymsza taking shots at each other about the presentation of witnesses and how they are treated by both sides on the witness stand.

Pierantoni quizzed prosecutors and Hugo's lawyers about the picture depicting Weakley in shackles and wearing the orange prison jumpsuit. When told the picture was taken in 2006 about the same time Weakley was charged with the murders of Kerkowski and Fassett, Pierantoni allowed the picture to be shown to the jury.

The in-chambers conference concluded at 11:19 a.m. and by the time the jury returned to the jury box, Brown's questioning of Weakley resumed at 11:23 a.m.

Brown's first question upon returning to the courtroom: "Mr. Weakley, umm, during one of the interviews, do you recall saying that you wanted to kill Hugo?" "I did," Weakley said.

"And when you said that, you said that you wanted to blow him up one time on 4th of July; correct?" Brown asked. "Yes," Weakley said, quickly noting he also thought about pushing Hugo off a cliff.

Brown then changed tactics and asked Weakley about his decision not wanting to testify against Hugo?

"What is it that the DA said to change your mind?" Brown asked.

"The DA really didn't say anything, it was me coming around. I'm, I was, there's nothing in this for me. I'm not up here to get anything for testifying. And the repercussions I was receiving in prison for my role in testifying at, in this case were severe. I had been attacked and stabbed over 30 times," Weakley said, which brought an objection from Brown as being non-responsive to his question.

"He asked the question, your Honor," Ferentino said.

"Overruled," the judge responded.

"He opened the door," Ferentino replied as Pierantoni told Brown to move on to the next question.

Ferentino asked for another sidebar conference.

"Here we, here we stand. Umm, the question was asked as to why he wasn't coming forward. He was answering and you objected to your own question. We raised this issue in chambers, as the court directed us to, that..that would open the door for the attacks, and it just opened it. And I intend to pursue that very line of questioning as the motivation for why he was hesitant to testify. That door is open and it's not limited to the scope of that letter….the door is wide-open at this point…" Ferentino said.

With the quick pace of Brown's questions, Sanguedolce and Ferentino missed Pierantoni overruling Brown's own objection to Weakley's answer about being attacked and stabbed more than 30 times in prison.

"I allowed the answer and I said move onto the next question. I don't know why we're at sidebar," Pierantoni said, sending the parties back to their tables.

Brown concluded his cross-examination of Weakley, giving Ferentino another shot at re-direct examination.

As Ferentino pledged during the lengthy sidebar conference about Brown opening the door to Weakley's treatment by fellow prisoners for testifying against Hugo, the assistant district attorney got right to the point.

"How's life been as somebody who's an informant for the Commonwealth in prison?"

"It's extremely difficult," Weakley said over an objection by Brown. "Extremely difficult."

Piereantoni overruled Brown's objection allowing Ferentino to open the door much wider.

"How so, Mr. Weakley?"

"You're considered one of the lowest members of prison society, and you're often victimized physically for…for being labeled as an informant," Weakley said.

"And have you been victimized?"

"Several, on numerous occasions. I've been stabbed and beaten numerous times for my role in the testimony," Weakley replied.

Weakley said not only was he stabbed more than 30 times, he was also physically beaten numerous times by other prisoners.

"I'm here today to do what's right for the families of the victims, the Kerkowskis, the Sands, and it's what I believe is the right thing to do," Weakley said as Ferentino ended his re-direct examination.

Weakley's time on the witness stand ended at 12:03 p.m. on the sixth day of trial, Wednesday, Jan. 28, 2015.

As soon as Weakley left the courtroom, Judge Pierantoni gave an instruction to the jury about how they should consider his testimony, advising the jury that despite Weakley explaining the Goosay robbery, Hugo was not facing charges related to the Goosay robbery in Luzerne County.

Pierantoni gave the jury a lunch recess instructing jurors to return at 1:10 p.m.

With Pierantoni back on the bench and prosecutors and Hugo's lawyers at their respective tables, the jury was brought back into the courtroom following a 90 minute lunch at 1:42 p.m.

Kimberly Benscoter, the employee at Agway Back Mountain Feed and Seed, testified about a man she identified as Paul Weakley buying many 40 pound bags of topsoil and loading the bags into a Honda Accord. The sale stood out in Benscoter's mind because the bags were heavy and were loaded into a passenger vehicle that bottomed out when leaving the parking lot. Benscoter's time on the witness stand was just shy of 15 minutes.

Next up was Louise Bensacon, Kerkowski's neighbor in Hunlock Township, who told the jury she last saw Michael Kerkowski mowing his grass on a Cub Cadet tractor. Several hours after seeing him cut grass, Bensacon said Michael Stanley Kerkowski called her the night of May 3, 2002, asking if she had seen his son.

Sanguedolce had Bensacon tell the jury when she was questioned by State Police Trooper Thomas Appleman, who investigated the missing person's report filed by Kerkowski's parents, she initially said she "heard" a vehicle accelerate from Kerkowski's home. It was several years later, May 23, 2006, when Bensacon added she saw an older boxy brown colored vehicle occupied by two people drive past her house a few hours after she saw Kerkowski mowing grass. More than four years after seeing the brown car drive past her house, Bensacon was able to remember what the passenger looked like, a white man with cropped or no hair and a tattoo on his arm that hung out the car window.

Bensacon, when asked questions by Rymsza, narrowed down the time when she saw the tattoo armed man drive past her house as late afternoon, estimating it to be around 5 p.m. on May 3, 2002. Bensacon's time on the witness stand lasted 70 minutes.

Pierantoni gave the jury a 15 minute recess and held a private meeting in chambers with Hugo's lawyers and prosecutors to go over the testimony of the next witness: Carey Bartoo.

Ferentino pushed for the admittance of a hand gesture made by Hugo directed at Bartoo where he slid his finger across his throat. Ferentino explained after Hugo was detained at the state police barracks on June 5, 2003, he somehow found out Bartoo was questioned by investigators. While both were jailed at the Luzerne County Correctional Facility, Bartoo claimed she came in visual contact with Hugo who mouthed the words, "What did you tell them?" while sliding his index finger across his throat. Bartoo took it as a threat and Ferentino wanted the jury to hear it.

Hugo's lawyers objected, arguing Hugo was never charged with threatening Bartoo.

Pierantoni allowed Ferentino to bring up what Bartoo perceived as a threat by Hugo by mouthing the words and sliding his finger across his throat, telling Hugo's lawyers they will have the opportunity to address the alleged threat during their cross examination of Bartoo.

However, Pierantoni reversed his decision disallowing any mention of the mouthed words and Hugo's hand gesture finding it prejudicial.

With the jury back in the jury box, Bartoo was called as the next witness at 3:53 p.m.

Bartoo was the person who introduced Hugo to Michael Jason Kerkowski as she is related to Kerkowski's estranged wife, Kimberly. Bartoo also shared a daughter with Hugo.

The introduction between Hugo and Michael Stanley Kerkowski happened in April 2001, when Bartoo needed a ride to Kerkowski's home in Hunlock Township where Kerkowski was loaning her money to pay her car insurance premium. Hugo drove Bartoo in the Honda Accord.

Ferentino was moving fast with questions as after Bartoo explained how Hugo and Kerkowski met, he had Bartoo tell the jury she saw Hugo on May 3, 2002, when Hugo gave her $700 and another $300 for Bartoo to give to Kimberly Kerkowski. Only Kimberly Kerkowski refused to accept the $300, Bartoo said, because Hugo claimed the cash came from her estranged husband, Michael Jason Kerkowski.

Bartoo said she used the money to buy heroin.

The jury heard from Bartoo that she owned a four-door brown Oldsmobile in 2002.

"Did you pick up Mr. Selenski on May 3rd, 2002, at Michael Kerkowski's house in the late afternoon?" Ferentino asked.

"Umm, I...I can't say yes, that I did. It...it's a possibility that I did," Bartoo said.

Ferentino quickly ended his direct examination of Bartoo.

Bartoo again upon being asked by Brown said it was possible she picked up Hugo from Kerkowski's house on May 3, 2002, as she also noted her memory was clouded due to her drug use. Bartoo was on the witness stand for 20 minutes.

The next witness, Cheryl Breen, a teller at the UFCW Credit Union in May 2002, testified Hugo entered the credit union on May 4, 2002, to deposit $9,900 into Strom's checking account. Breen said she remembered Hugo because of his sparkling eyes. Hugo's lawyers had no questions for Breen, who spent 8 minutes on the witness stand.

After Breen, Pierantoni ended the sixth day of trial, sending the jury home for the night at 4:25 p.m. instructing them to return to begin the seventh day of trial at 9:30 a.m., Thursday, Jan. 28, 2015.

# PRELIMINARY HEARING TESTIMONY

Day seven of the trial began once again in chambers where Judge Pierantoni met with assistant district attorneys Jarrett Ferenino and Mamie Phillips and Hugo's lawyers, Bernard Brown and Edward Rymsza. First Assistant District Attorney Sam Sanguedolce was not in the room when the meeting began and his absence was noticed by Pierantoni.

The in chambers meeting began at 9:23 a.m. where prosecutors and Hugo's lawyers strategized the testimony of the next two witnesses: Michael Stanley Kerkowski and Ernest Culp, who were both deceased. Both men testified at the June 14, 2006, preliminary hearing with the testimony of Michael Stanley Kerkowski twice being challenged in the Pennsylvania Superior Court resulting in lengthy delays of Hugo's trial. Ultimately, the appellate court permitted prosecutors to introduce the preliminary hearing testimony of Michael Stanley Kerkowski, who died of a heart attack at his Lehman Township home on Sept. 19, 2006.

Soon after Culp died of cancer on Sept. 13, 2014, prosecutors moved to submit Culp's preliminary hearing testimony during Hugo's trial, which was granted by Pierantoni on Jan. 5, 2015, citing the state's Superior Court's legal analysis related to the submittal of the preliminary hearing testimony of Michael Stanley Kerkowski.

Placing it on the record, Rymsza objected to the introduction of the preliminary hearing testimony of Michael Stanley Kerkowski and Culp knowing he would be overruled by Pierantoni.

The in chambers meeting concluded at 10:47 a.m.

The jury marched into the courtroom at 11 a.m. as Pierantoni apologized for the lateness of getting started for the day as legal issues needed to be addressed.

Sanguedolce called the next witness, "Ernest Culp," resulting in Pierantoni instructing the jury that Culp's preliminary hearing testimony would be read during Hugo's trial by James Balavage, a retired police chief in Kingston Township. Culp testified during the June 2006, preliminary hearing of encountering Hugo and Weakley with shovels digging near the well, the source of water for the property.

Culp, in his preliminary hearing testimony, said state police held onto the Mount Olivet Road property for six to seven weeks. When the property was released back to Christina Strom, Culp said Strom asked him to fill the hole where the bodies were found and removed.

The next witness was retired state police Trooper Gerald Sachney who, along with Luzerne County Detective Lieutenant Gary Capitano, were the primary investigators on Hugo.

Sachney testified he received a phone call from Dallas Township Police Officer Fred Rosencrans on Jan. 17, 2003, about an individual who showed up at the Dallas Township Police Department with information about the disappearance of Michael Jason Kerkowski.

Sachney said he immediately drove to the Dallas Township Police Department where he met Hugo.

"He said that he had been in contact with some unidentified individuals from New York, he was awaiting the transfer of a large amount of money, approximately $500,000 from these individuals, which he was to deliver to Mr. Kerkowski in the Country of Belize," Sachney said of his meeting with Hugo on Jan. 17, 2003.

Hugo further told Sachney he was going to deliver the $500,000 to Kerkowski in Belize, also suggesting the state police could find Kerkowski if they follow the subscription of a financial newspaper.

Sachney said he followed up with the information Hugo provided and reached out to Hugo to ask him more questions.

"(Hugo) indicated that he had not received any…any information or money from these individuals," Sachney said.

Sachney said he never heard anything more from Hugo nor could he substantiate any of the information Hugo had told him.

Rymsza asked Sachney if he conducted an investigation to prove or disprove Hugo's information and if Hugo had access to $500,000. The line of questions related to Hugo independently going to the Dallas Township

Police Department and what he told Sachney seemed odd, even for Hugo's lawyers.

"...did Mr. Selenski also tell you that he knew who killed President Kennedy?" Rymsza asked before he was shut down by Pierantoni.

"He didn't tell you he knew who killed President Kennedy, but he told you he had information regarding the whereabouts of Michael Kerkowski, didn't he?" Ferentino asked.

"That is correct," Sachney said, who earlier noted the bodies of Kerkowski and Fassett were found at the home where Hugo was living with his girlfriend.

The next witness would be the preliminary hearing testimony of Michael Stanley Kerkowski, read by Charles Prula, only the jury was not told Prula was a retired state police trooper.

As Michael Stanley Kerkowski recalled his son had told him to trust Hugo, the elder Kerkowski gave Hugo $60,000 and another $40,000 in October 2002, when Hugo fired a round from a handgun above the head of the elder Kerkowski. The $40,000 came from the armoire inside Kerkowski's Hunlock Township home found by Gerladine Kerkowski in the days after their son disappeared.

After Michael Stanley Kerkowski completed his testimony read by Prula, Judge Pierantoni instructed the jury why it was being offered. "This testimony, again, if you choose to believe it, is before you concerning

(Hugo's) motive, intent and knowledge involving the alleged crimes against Michael Sr. Kerkowski and Tammy Fassett that may or may…shed light on the alleged criminal transaction you are considering," the judge instructed the jury.

Hugo's lawyers, Brown, Rymsza and Taylor were helpless as they were unable to cross-examine Culp and Michael Stanley Kerkowski in front of the jury.

Following the elder Kerkowski's testimony, Pierantoni gave the jury a lunch recess instructing them to return at 1:30 p.m., giving them 45 minutes outside the courtroom.

After lunch, Pennsylvania State Police Corporal Leo D. Hannon Jr. was called to the witness stand at 2 p.m.

Hannon told the jury he investigated the extortion of Michael Stanley Kerkowski by Hugo when he received the report on Dec. 17, 2002.

During his interview with Michael Stanley Kerkowski, Hannon said the elder Kerkowski reported he was visited by Hugo who asked for $30,000 in July 2002, another visit for another $30,000 in August 2002, and another visit in September 2002 when Hugo demanded $40,000 and fired the shot above the head of the elder Kerkowski.

Hannon said he had Trooper Edward Urban from the State Police Troop P Forensic Services Unit process the basement of the elder Kerkowski's home, taking measurements and estimating the trajectory of the bullet. Finding a hole in the wall behind the chair where Michael Stanley Kerkowski was seated when Hugo fired the shot, Hannon and Urban found the bullet in a storage room.

Hannon said as Michael Stanley Kerkowski was seated in the chair with Hugo across and directly facing him, the bullet passed 12 to 16 inches above the head of the elder Kerkowski.

After the shooting in the basement, Michael Stanley Kerkowski and his wife were contacted by Patrick Russin in October 2002. Russin knocked on their door saying he was a friend of Hugo's and was there to pick up a package. Russin left without a package but did leave with a list of questions written by Gerladine Kerkowski to which only her son would know the answers.

Two or three days later, Hugo and Russin showed up at the home of Michael Stanley Kerkowski and told him the answers would be sent to Gerladine Kerkowski's mother's house in Swoyersville in a week. No answers were ever received, Hannon said.

At their last encounter with Hugo, Hannon said Michael Stanley Kerkowski reported Hugo called him on Dec. 11, 2002, claiming today was the day he would talk to his son and asked to meet at a fast food restaurant in Luzerne Borough. Michael Stanley Kerkowski traveled alone leaving his wife behind.

When the elder Kerkowski and Hugo met, Hugo attempted to extort him out of another $40,000. As the elder Kerkowski refused to surrender any more cash, Hugo then demanded $55,000 and threatened to harm his family and burn their home on Vine Street in Lehman Township.

On Dec. 17, 2002, Michael Stanley Kerkowski reported the extortion by Hugo to the Pennsylvania State Police resulting in Hannon conducting the investigation.

Michael Stanley Kerkowski would also report on Jan. 22, 2003, of finding an unsigned note stuck in the rear storm door of his home that read, "Mr. K., it is very important that you call this number from a pay phone ASAP, 639-9958."

Hannon said the phone number came up again when a search warrant was served on Hugo's Ford F150 pickup truck several months later. The phone number was written by hand on a UFCW Federal Credit Union bank envelope recovered from the Ford truck.

However, the phone number was not linked to anyone as prosecutors and Hugo's lawyers never asked if investigators called the number or if the number was a cellular phone number or a house phone.

On cross-examination of Hannon, Rymsza was moving fast with his questions as Hannon methodically responded. Rymsza asked and Hannon confirmed Hugo was charged with robbery related charges for extorting and threatening the elder Kerkowski.

"Those charges were subsequently withdrawn?" Rymsza asked but before Hannon was able to respond, Ferentino pounced.

"Objection, you know what, if he wants to ask this question, go ahead," Ferentino said.

"The question was, were charges withdrawn?" Rymsza asked.

"Yes, they were," Hannon replied.

Confused, Rymsza asked for a sidebar conference.

"Judge, there...I may have taken the bait by Mr. Ferentino. Umm, it was..it was my understanding that these charges were withdrawn once, refiled and withdrawn a second time," Rymsza said.

Ferentino explained the robbery case against Hugo for extorting the elder Kerkowski was withdrawn due to Pennsylvania's Rule 600, commonly known as the speedy trial rule. Ferentino said the robbery case against Hugo was filed to hold him in jail until Hugo was charged with criminal homicide charges relating to the shotgun murders of Adeiye Keiler and Frank James. Ferentino said the robbery case was not withdrawn due to the merits of the investigation.

Ferentino and Phillips said Rymsza "opened the door" to allow them to ask Hannon questions about the robbery of the elder Kerkowski on re-direct examination but Pierantoni did not want to venture into that issue.

Getting annoyed by two prosecutors "chiming in" at the same time, Pierantoni said he was not going to recognize any further arguments from them.

"And I'll tell you, the last time, when you come up, one person, okay, not three people chiming," the judge said.

"Judge, three people didn't chime," Sanguedolce noted.

"Two did. Two did," Pierantoni said.

"But you're letting the defense do it," Sanguedolce responded with Phillips adding, "Yeah, they…." before Sanguedolce chimed in, "You're letting the defense do it."

"Thank you. Well, I'll tell you what, who's in charge of the prosecution?" Pierantoni asked.

"We all are," Sanguedolce said.

The discussion about chiming resulted in an 18 minute off-the record conversation at sidebar.

Rymsza resumed his questioning of Hannon who responded in the affirmative that the robbery charges he filed against Hugo were withdrawn. Rymsza ended his questioning of Hannon who spent 126 minutes on the witness stand.

Pierantoni sent the jury home for the night ending the seventh day of trial at 4:09 p.m., instructing them to return the next day to begin at 9 a.m.

## 'BIG PROBLEMS'

The eighth day of trial, Friday, Jan. 30, 2015, began as usual, later than previously scheduled with Judge Pierantoni meeting with prosecutors and Hugo's lawyers in chambers to review the testimony of witnesses for the day.

After the 35 minute private meeting, Pierantoni had the jury brought into the courtroom at 10:24 a.m.

Timothy Reese was the first witness for the day, telling the jury he met Hugo in a bar some time ago. In December 2002, Reese said he was hanging out with Hugo driving around in Hugo's Ford F150 pick up truck when Hugo said he needed to meet with someone at a fast food restaurant in Luzerne Borough to collect $40,000. This was the meeting with Michael Stanley Kerkowski when Hugo threatened to burn the Vine Street house in Lehman Township.

Reese said he believed his role was to "intimidate the guy and stuff." When they arrived, Reese said he went into the restaurant to eat while Michael Stanley Kerkowski sat in Hugo's truck.

After eating, Reese said he stood outside the truck as the elder Kerkowski got out in an agitated state telling Hugo he was not giving him any more money and did not know if his son was alive or dead.

Reese said Hugo explained the meeting was about a pharmacist being out of the country.

On cross examination, Rymsza had Reese admit he pleaded guilty to three separate criminal cases for providing false information to law enforcement. The question and response had the jury questioning Reese's credibility.

But on re-direct examination, Ferentino had Reese say the false information to law enforcement had nothing to do with his interviews with investigators or Hugo's criminal case.

The next witness was Robert Gober, a licensed electrician who was working on the house and detached garage at the Mount Olivet Road property in the summer and into the fall of 2002. Gober said he met Hugo through friends and stopped work because he was owed $1,600 from Hugo.

While inside a men's restroom at a restaurant, Gober said Hugo stuffed three bundles of cash totaling $3,000 into his back pocket for money he owed him and to continue to work at the property. Gober knew Hugo did not have a job as Hugo told him he had a patent pending on a weight lifting glove, did day trading on the stock market, and was involved in real estate. All lies as Gober knew. During dinner with Hugo, Strom and Gober's friend, Gober said he kept asking Hugo about his jobs knowing

Hugo was unemployed. Finally, Gober testified, Hugo said he killed people for a living.

"...he laughed it off when he, when he said it and we were pressing him for it, what he did," Gober said.

Sanguedolce verified for the jury that the United States Patent and Trademark Office never granted a patent to Hugo nor did Hugo have a patent pending.

Hugo's cousin, Brian Higdon, was the next witness.

Higdon said he injured his back so he asked Hugo if he could obtain painkillers. Hugo replied he once knew a pharmacist but had a falling out.

Not knowing what Hugo meant, Higdon said he begged Hugo to call his friend the pharmacist but Hugo kept repeating they had a falling out and Hugo took care of him. Still not knowing what Hugo meant, Higdon asked if the pharmacist was dead and Hugo replied "yes."

Higdon told the jury he briefly resided with Hugo at the Mount Olivet Road property and was there when state police served the search warrant on June 5, 2003.

"Can you tell us, did (Hugo) say anything to you at that time?" Ferentino asked. "After we were served the search warrant, he read it. Then, he handed it to me and I read it. And then he was going crazy because the police were everywhere, all over his property," Higdon said.

Higdon said Hugo was flipping out as he asked Hugo, "...what the fuck was going on?"

"And he said that he had big problems," Higdon said.

Brown cross-examined Higdon who noted Hugo, when state police converged onto the property, offered to provide shovels and help dig up the property. Higdon also said while living at the house, he saw Paul Weakley nearly every day on the property.

Ferentino took a second shot at Higdon on re-direct examination, having Higdon explain further about Hugo's reaction when state police converged onto the property.

"He..he was flipping out; screaming and hollering, didn't want police in the backyard or anywhere on his property. It was crazy," Higdon said.

Ferentino was on a roll to the point Brown requested a mistrial.

"Mr. Higdon, you did learn that a pharmacist was found on his property; correct?" Ferentino asked. Higdon replied, "yes."

"And that's who he said he had a fallout with; correct?" asked Ferentino. "Yes," Higdon said.

During a brief sidebar conference, Brown asked for a mistrial because he believed Ferentino mentioned Kerkowski as the pharmacist being found on the property.

Ferentino said he never said the name Kerkowski as Pierantoni agreed, denying the mistrial request.

Higdon finished testifying and walked out of the courtroom at 12:06 p.m.

The next four witnesses were Pennsylvania State Police troopers Joseph Plant, Joseph Cocco, Edward Urban and James Shubzda, members of the Troop P Forensic Services Unit. Plant, Cocco and Urban testified about their meticulous search and seizure of evidence from the Mount Olivet Road Property, including carefully digging to remove the bodies after they were found with the assistance of Weakley to point out the area of the burial site. Fassett's body was found about two-to-three feet below the surface with Kerkowski under her.

Shubzda's role was to attend the autopsies conducted by the forensic pathologist Dr. Michael Baden collecting the flex ties from the necks and hands of Kerkowski and Fassett and from the ankles of Fassett. Duct tape from around Kerkowski's hands and eyes were removed using liquid nitrogen to freeze it in an attempt to preserve latent fingerprints.

During Shubzda's testimony, the jury learned a tab on the flex tie removed from Kerkowski's neck was damaged by a previous member of Hugo's defense team during an evidence view.

After Phillips ended her direct examination, Rymsza followed up having Shubzda say a wrist watch was removed from Kerkowski and several pieces of jewelry removed from Fassett.

Shubzda would be the last witness to testify on the eighth day of trial exiting the courtroom at 3:41 p.m., Friday, Jan. 30, 2015.

That weekend was Super Bowl weekend between the New England Patriots and the Seattle Seahawks. The weekend also called for a winter storm Sunday into Monday as Pierantoni directed the jury to arrive at the courthouse at 11 a.m., Monday, Feb. 2, 2015, to start the third week of Hugo's trial. In the event the forecast changed, Pierantoni said court administration will notify the jury early Sunday evening whether Monday's court session will be postponed.

Jurors received notification early Sunday night not to report Monday due to the winter storm. A total of 4.2 inches of snow blanketed the Wilkes-Barre area with high temperatures in the low 30s with even colder wind chills due to gusty winds. Thanks to Mother Nature, the jury got an extra day off while prosecutors and Hugo's lawyers caught up on rest and trial work.

# RUSSIN TESTIFIES

After a snow day Monday, Hugo's trial resumed Tuesday, Feb. 3, 2015, with the jury arriving at the courthouse at 9:30 a.m.

As what was becoming routine, the expected start time of 10 a.m. was delayed as prosecutors and Hugo's lawyers met with Judge Pierantoni in chambers to review the witnesses for the day, which were Patrick Russin and forensic pathologist Dr. Michael Baden.

Attorneys Brown and Rymsza had an issue with Russin related to their strategy as they were severely limited to the type of questions they could ask on cross examination. Their issue began years earlier when the district attorney's office decided to sever Hugo's trials into two: One trial for the murders of Frank James and Adeiye Keiler and the other trial for the murders of Michael Jason Kerkowski and Tammy Lynn Fassett.

Russin's involvement in the two homicides differed but his testimony for prosecutors was critical.

Since the jury was prohibited from hearing Russin's involvement with Hugo in the murders of James and Keiler and subsequent plea agreement to third-degree murder for his role, Brown and Rymsza had difficulty in creating a strategy to attack Russin's credibility.

Russin pled guilty to two counts of third-degree murder, two counts of abuse of corpse, two counts of robbery, and one count of criminal conspiracy to commit robbery on Nov. 6, 2003, related to the murders of James and Keiler. As part of the plea agreement, prosecutors recommended a sentence of 20 to 40 years in state prison with the condition Russin had to testify against Hugo, as he did during the trial in 2006.

Then District Attorney Jacqueline Musto Carroll on Nov. 9, 2011, along with assistant district attorneys C. David Pedri, Michael S. Melnick and Ferentino modified Russin's plea agreement that excluded the 20 to 40 years in prison leaving Russin's sentence at the sole discretion of Judge Chester B. Muroski. Brown and Rymsza were not defending Hugo when prosecutors modified Russin's plea agreement.

Judge Muroski on Dec. 22, 2011, sentenced Russin to 10 to 20 years in prison for all the charges he pleaded guilty. Russin was given a reduction in his sentence in May 2012, when his lawyer, William Ruzzo, filed a motion to award him an additional four months, 25 days time served since Russin was arrested June 6, 2003. Eventually, Russin's minimum sentence of 10 years was shortened by five months.

When Russin came up for parole with the Pennsylvania Department of Parole in 2015, Ferentino in 2014 wrote a letter to the parole board on Russin's behalf, which Brown and Rymsza had in their possession.

Certainly, Brown and Rymsza wanted to attack Russin's credibility as a bad person, who was a drug addict and committed multiple robberies and burglaries, not only with Hugo but with Weakley, Carey Bartoo and others.

Brown and Rymsza had trouble addressing the modified plea agreement for Russin because it involved the murders of James and Keiler, not Kerkowski and Fassett. Russin's plea agreement had nothing to do with the murders of Kerkowski and Fasset and the danger of Brown and Rymsza asking Russin questions about his modified plea agreement could elicit discussion about the murders of James and Keiler, which would be prejudicial for Hugo.

After discussing the expected testimony of Dr. Baden, the in chambers meeting concluded at 10:14 a.m. as Pierantoni advised everyone to be in the courtroom to start at 10:30 a.m.

Only, another in chambers meeting took place at 10:52 a.m. with Attorney William Ruzzo, who was representing Russin.

Ruzzo wanted the judge to know Russin was going to testify without concern of being prosecuted unless he committed perjury and requested some sort of protection for Russin in state prison as he was going to testify against Hugo. Pierantoni instructed county detectives who would return Russin to state prison at the conclusion of his testimony to notify officials at the state prison that Russin cooperated with prosecutors.

Pierantoni brought the jury into the courtroom at 11 a.m. to begin the ninth day of trial with Russin being called for the first witness of the day.

Answering questions from Sanguedolce, Russin said he had known Hugo for nearly 30 years and helped Hugo at the Mount Olivet Road property. Sanguedolce then got right into Russin's plea agreement for third-degree murder but pointed out the plea agreement had nothing to do with Hugo's trial for the murders of Kerkowski and Fassett.

Russin discussed Hugo's plan to have Russin pick up a package of $40,000 from Michael Stanley Kerkowski as Hugo claimed he was owed the money for helping Michael Jason Kerkowski flee the country. Hugo drove Russin to Vine Street in Lehman Township and let Russin out of the vehicle before driving off as Hugo said he was under intense police investigation and could not stay in the neighborhood. Russin said he went to the wrong house and was told Michael Stanley Kerkowski lived next door. With an open cellular phone in his pocket, Russin said Hugo wanted to listen to the conversation Russin had with the elder Kerkowski.

As Russin believed the package would be given to him as Hugo claimed it was a prearranged deal, the elder Kerkowski told Russin to go to the back yard.

"Mr. Kerkowski tells me he's not giving me any package because he hasn't heard from his son and he believed he's dead," Russin testified.

Russin told the elder Kerkowski that Hugo assured him Kerkowski was alive.

Walking away empty handed, Russin said he was picked up by Hugo down the road away from the elder Kerkowski's home.

Believing Hugo that Kerkowski was alive, Russin said he pleaded with Hugo to get in touch with Kerkowski to have him talk to his father.

With the failed first attempt, Hugo devised another plan to hit up the elder Kerkowski.

Russin explained Hugo grabbed a gun to scare the "bejesus" out of the elder Kerkowski as their plan was for Russin to knock on the front door while Hugo waited in the backyard.

Russin said the elder Kerkowski answered the door and immediately refused to turn over any money. Instead, the elder Kerkowski gave Russin a list of five questions that their son would know the answers to. If the answers were correct, the elder Kerkowski would relinquish the $40,000 to Hugo.

After a week, Russin said he asked Hugo if he got the money and if he received the answers to the questions. Russin testified Hugo told him he was not able to get in touch with Kerkowski because he went "underground."

Russin said Hugo "flip-flopped" many times telling him Kerkowski was dead and alive.

It was now Brown's turn to cross examine Russin and right away, problems arose.

In recalling the number of times Russin said he was questioned and interviewed by investigators, Russin said, "not just solely Michael and Tammy."

Brown put the brakes on but Sanguedolce requested a sidebar conference.

"Just...the other reason for the objection is he's making it look like this is the only thing they discussed in all those interviews. He's been instructed not to talk about other murders, but there were a lot of things, robberies, burglaries," Sanguedolce said.

"All right. But just remember, at this particular juncture, the questioning from both sides, if any, should be designed specifically only to this particular prosecution to avoid opening any type of gate," Judge Pierantoni advised.

Brown said he was specifically developing his questions to begin with "With regards to Michael Kerkowski and Tammy Fassett."

Brown highlighted several dates when Russin was interviewed by Detective Capitano. Then Brown got into Russin's heavy drug use in the early 2000s and the 2002 party where Hugo reportedly solicited Rodney Samson for assistance to kill a pharmacist in Tunkhannock. Russin said he did not witness Hugo and Samson go off together to talk privately.

Russin said he moved into the Mount Olivet Road house in late summer or early fall 2002 as he helped Hugo around the property. Russin said Weakley would sometimes show up, recalling a conversation he had with Weakley after Thanksgiving 2002. It was Weakley, Russin said, who told him Kerkowski and Fassett were dead and Weakley claimed he could put Hugo away for the rest of his life.

Hugo was preparing to host a party for his sister who graduated nursing school when state police converged onto the property June 5, 2003. Russin said he was present and told the jury he was standing next to Hugo.

As Weakley testified he initially pointed to Russin and Hugo as the two men responsible for the murders of Kerkowski and Fassett, investigators thought they had both their suspects.

"Hugo…now, I'm going to tell you my best recollection and it's pretty good. I was standing right next to Hugo when the cops came up the driveway, and when I say…I imagine it was the whole State Barracks, it looked like, coming up that driveway. I'll never forget…it's something you don't forget. I was standing next to Hugo Selenski and if you want me to go into the…" Russin said before Brown objected to his answer as being nonresponsive.

Russin said Hugo turned to him and asked, "'Did I go to the police?' and I said I didn't."

A month prior to state police arriving at the property, Russin and Hugo, according to prosecutors, killed James and Keiler and burned their bodies. But the jury was not going to hear any information about those murders.

Brown then directed questions about Russin's plea agreement doing his best not to mention or link the plea agreement to the James and Keiler murders. In doing so, the jury heard Russin initially was going to be sentenced to 20 to 40 years in state prison but his agreement to testify against Hugo, the Luzerne County District Attorney's Office modified the plea agreement giving Russin's punishment at the discretion of the sentencing judge, resulting in Russin being sentenced to 10 to 20 years. Brown finished questioning Russin by asking him if he met with prosecutors and Detective Capitano prior to the start of Hugo's trial, which he did. When Brown asked why Russin denied to meet with Hugo's lawyers, he responded, "No, that's because I don't help people that are in the business of hurting people."

Brown ended his cross examination of Russin.

Sanguedolce followed up with several questions getting Russin to say the only two people to tell him that Kerkowski and Fassett were dead were Weakley and Hugo, although Hugo would sometimes say Kerkowski was stowed away.

Russin left the witness stand at 12:03 p.m., the perfect time for Judge Pierantoni to end the morning's session to give the jury their lunch recess.

At 1:30 p.m., when the afternoon session was to start, Pierantoni met with prosecutors and Hugo's lawyers in chambers to go over the testimony of the next witness, forensic pathologist Dr. Michael Baden.

Sanguedolce, Ferentino and Phillips were instructed to avoid Baden having to explain his medical opinion that Kerkowski was tortured.

Kerkowski was surely tortured when he was struck in the knees and shins with the baker's rolling pin and flex ties engaged around his neck, fracturing the hyoid bone and Adam's apple, all while he was blindfolded and unable to defend himself being bound to a chair.

# AUTOPSIES DISCLOSED

After a near two hour lunch, the jury returned to the courtroom after 2 p.m. to hear the testimony of forensic pathologist Dr. Michael Baden, a former New York City chief medical officer.

Baden conducted the autopsies of Kerkowski and Fassett at Wilkes-Barre General Hospital on June 8, 2003.

Fassett was removed from the body bag and placed on the autopsy table. Her body was discolored from decomposition having been underground for 13 months. Before Baden began his autopsy, a Temple University sweatshirt, a turtleneck sweater, pants, underwear and sneakers had to be carefully removed.

Baden said Fassett's hands were behind her and her ankles bound together with flex ties, including a flex tie tightly around her neck. Baden further told the jury Fassett sustained an injury to the right side of her face near her right ear possibly by the butt end of a handgun.

Weakley previously testified he remained in the basement with Kerkowski while Hugo went alone to the bedroom where Fassett was thrown on a bed after being bound by flex ties.

Baden said his examination of Fassett revealed a fracture of the right side of her hyoid bone caused by compression of the neck as a result of the flex tie. As he conducted the autopsy, Baden listed Fassett's cause of death as strangulation.

Next for the jury to hear were autopsy results of Kerkowski. Prosecutors were warned not to have Baden say Kerkowski was "tortured" despite his findings.

Baden explained Kerkowski's hands were bound behind his back with flex ties and duct tape, when uncurled, was about 10 feet in length. Pieces of the duct tape were shown to the jury.

During Kerkowski's autopsy, Baden said the duct tape was wrapped around Kerkowski's head covering his eyes and neck with a flex tie fastened around the neck. Baden explained the tightness of the flex tie around Kerkowski's neck would not permit the passage of a finger and was up against the spine bone, noting for the jury the right hyoid bone and the thyroid cartilage, or Adam's apple, were each fractured.

As Baden discovered the separate bone fractures, he opined there must have been another flex tie at one point tightened around Kerkowski's neck. Using a model demonstration of the neck, Baden pointed out a flex tie, once fastened, could not be unfastened and moved.

The flex tie removed during Kerkowski's autopsy fractured the hyoid bone and due to the fracture of the thyroid cartilage about one inch below the hyoid bone, another flex tie had to be placed around the neck, Baden told the jury.

Baden said while reviewing the statements by Paul Weakley to investigators, the placement of flex ties and the removal of flex ties while he was being tortured was consistent with his autopsy findings relative to the two bone fractures in the neck.

With Baden discussing multiple fractures to Kerkowski's neck, Rymsza objected resulting in a lengthy sidebar with Judge Pierantoni.

Rymsza complained Ferentino's questions directed at Baden resulting in multiple fractures involved torture and bolstered Weakley's testimony that Kerkowski's face turned blue when a flex tie was fastened around the neck. If the jury recalled Weakley's testimony, Weakley said he placed several flex ties around Kerkowski's neck, cut one off and then placed another while they continued to interrogate him about hidden money.

Ferentino had asked Baden which flex tie around Kerkowski's neck would have caused death. Baden said either one would have restricted the ability to breath and blood flow to the brain.

Pierantoni warned Ferentino to stop reciting Weakley's testimony while asking questions directed at Baden, but allowed Baden to answer for the sake of clarifying for the jury whether one or both flex ties could have caused death.

Baden again said either flex tie, the one placed that fractured the thyroid cartilage or the one that fractured the hyoid bone would have caused Kerkowsk's death.

After extensively going over the injuries to Kerkowski's neck, Ferentino directed his questions to other areas of Kerkowski's body that showed signs of trauma.

Baden said he found a bruise on the right side of Kerkowski's right knee, a bruise on the forehead and a skull hemorrhage all caused by being struck by a blunt object.

Ferentino showed Baden the baker's rolling pin and asked if the rolling pin could have caused the trauma to Kerkowski's knee, forehead and skull. Baden confirmed, repeating himself that the injuries were suffered before death.

Kerkowski died from strangulation and the manner of death was homicide, Baden said.

Throughout Baden's testimony, he was guided by pictures that were taken during the autopsies of Fassett and Kerkowski and displayed to the jury.

Baden said due to the decomposition of the bodies of Fassett and Kerkowski, he estimated they were killed and buried together about 13 months prior to conducting the autopsies.

When Ferentino completed his direct examination of Baden, Rymsza asked the pathologist how he became involved in conducting the autopsies.

Baden explained he had assisted the Luzerne County Coroner's Office in prior years and had experience with bodies being buried. He also noted he was paid approximately $20,000 as a consultant while working on the Hugo case.

Baden also gave the jury an education as Rymsza noted the date of death for Fassett was June 5, 2003, and the date of death for Kerkowski was June 6, 2003, despite investigators saying they were killed on May 3, 2002.

Baden said the time of death is listed when the body is found, highlighting the word "found" to the jury.

Rymsza got Baden to say in front of the jury he did not list any bruises to the bodies of Fassett and Kerkowski after conducting the autopsies. It was not until Weakley finally proclaimed the truth about what happened inside Kerkowski's home did Luzerne County Assistant District Attorney Michael Melnick and Det. Daniel Yursha visit Baden in New York City, N.Y., and asked to review his autopsy findings to corroborate what Weakley had claimed.

After the meeting in New York City and reviewing Weakley's statement, Baden submitted another autopsy report indicating the bruises on the bodies of Kerkowski and Fassett.

While the jury never heard Kerkowski was tortured, Rymsza's questions about bruises was an attempt to redirect Kerkowski was beaten prior to being strangled to death. He asked Baden if bruises can occur after death as the forensic pathologist said "yes," but the bruise would have to be inflicted immediately after death.

Baden completed his testimony at 5:14 p.m., spending more than three hours answering tough questions from Ferentino and Rymsza as the jury were shown horrific autopsy pictures.

The 10th day of trial on Wednesday, Feb. 4, 2015, could be considered "a case within a case within a case" as it related to the next witness for prosecutors, Samuel Goosay.

Goosay was the owner of Finishing Touches Fine Jewelry in Monroe County who was attacked inside his own home in Chestnuthill Township by Hugo and Weakley on Jan. 27, 2003. A Monroe County jury convicted Hugo on 14 felony and misdemeanor counts, notably kidnapping, robbery and burglary following a two day trial in July 2009, and subsequently sentenced to 32 years, six months to 65 years in state prison. Weakley's federal plea agreement to the Racketeer Influenced and Corrupt Organization included the murders of Kerkowski and Fassett and the Goosay kidnapping and robbery.

The Goosay evidence consisting of flex ties, duct tape and a firearm was appealed to the Pennsylvania Superior Court that caused a long delay in Hugo's trial in Luzerne County. Ultimately, the Goosay evidence was allowed to be used by prosecutors in Luzerne County but with conditions.

During an in chambers meeting with Judge Pierantoni to start the 10th day of Hugo's trial to review Goosay's testimony, prosecutors had to be careful not to have Goosay say Hugo was convicted by a Monroe County jury as such a statement would be prejudicial in his homicide trial. There was also a debate in chambers as Hugo's lawyers believed the Superior Court's ruling that allowed the Goosay evidence only involved flex ties and duct tape and not the firearm. Attorney Brown also believed a picture of Goosay with a tiny abrasion on the bridge of his nose he sustained during a physical fight with Hugo inside the home should be kept from being shown to the jury.

Ferentino said he did not want to retry the Goosay Monroe County case in front of the Luzerne County jury who were tasked with deciding Hugo's fate on the murders of Kerkowski and Fassett. The Goosay case was relevant to the murder trial, Ferentino believed, as it showed the modus operandi, or pattern of crime, used by Hugo and Weakley in searching out a small business owner to rob using the same tools of the trade, flex ties, duct tape and a firearm.

Pierantoni prohibited the Goosay photo showing the nose abrasion but allowed, as he ruled previously, the firearm to be introduced to the jury.

At 10:45 a.m., the jury was brought into the courtroom as Goosay was called to the witness stand to testify again to what happened to him inside his home on Jan. 27, 2003.

Goosay testified about being attacked while eating hot dogs and beans inside his home by two men, who handcuffed him with flex ties and blinded him with duct tape. Goosay told the jury he was threatened to give up the pass codes to his jewelry store.

One man left to burglarize the jewelry store while the other man stayed behind and ransacked Goosay's house stealing items placed in a pillow case. When the store's alarm company called Goosay's house, Goosay said he was struck in the head with the firearm and the man fled.

Brown's cross-examination of Goosay focused on two photo arrays shown to Goosay months and years after the kidnapping and robbery at his home. During the first review of photographs of possible suspects, which included Hugo in November 2003, Goosay said he was not able to identify the person who stayed behind while the other drove to the jewelry store.

Then on Jan. 5, 2005, nearly two years after the incident, Goosay said state police had him review more photographs of possible suspects that involved an updated picture of Hugo. In the second photo array, Goosay said he picked the third picture on the top row that was Hugo.

Goosay finished testifying at 12:32 p.m. During his testimony, the jury did not hear anything about Hugo's conviction in Monroe County and decades long sentence.

Sanguedolce submitted to the jury Hugo's 2002 W-2 wage and tax statement showing he earned a total of $187 for 2002.

And with that, Sanguedolce, Ferentino and Phillips rested their case in chief against Hugo taking 10 days and 30 witnesses.

Next up was Hugo's defense but the jury would have to wait as Judge Pierantoni released them for the day, instructing them to return at 10 a.m. on Thursday, Feb. 6, 2015.

# DEFENSE OPENS

Jurors made their way inside the courthouse a little after 9:30 a.m. and were escorted to the jury waiting room on the second floor of the courthouse. Just around the corner and down the hallway was Pierantoni's chambers where the judge met with Sanguedolce, Ferentino and Phillips and Hugo's lawyers, Brown and Rymsza.

The purpose of the in chambers meeting, as usual, was to proffer or review what witnesses would say on the witness stand.

Hugo's lawyers had several witnesses they were going to present, including a police officer with the Scranton Police Department's Bomb Squad who searched the apartment of Paul Weakley in February 2003.

Brown and Rymsza wanted the officer to testify he searched Weakley's apartment on Pulaski Street in Kingston as there was a concern Weakley was in possession of an explosive device.

Weakley met Hugo in federal prison where he was serving a sentence for manufacturing explosive devices in Michigan. So, there was a concern by investigators in Luzerne County that Weakley had his apartment wired with explosives.

In early February 2003, Weakley was under investigation for several robberies and burglarizing his place of employment, a water filtration business.

A federal judge denied a search warrant for Weakley's apartment as he was at that time under federal probation but then District Attorney David W. Lupus ordered the search of the apartment without a search warrant out of an abundance of caution to neighbors and adjacent structures. No explosives were found.

Brown and Rymsza wanted the Scranton police bomb squad officer to testify to illustrate Weakley's testimony that he considered pushing Hugo off a cliff or blow him up with a firework on the July 4th holiday.

Sanguedolce and Ferentino objected to having the bomb squad officer testify calling the February 2003 search of Weakley's apartment was outside the time frame when Kerkowski and Fassett were killed and it would be highly prejudicial. Sanguedolce and Ferentino said the only purpose to have the bomb squad officer testify was to slander Weakley as no explosive devices were found.

Pierantoni agreed, prohibiting the bomb squad officer from testifying on behalf of Hugo.

Other defense witnesses were reviewed as Brown and Rymsza said they would testify they visited the Mount Olivet Road property and saw no criminal or suspicious activity.

The in chambers meeting concluded at 10:29 a.m. and the jury was brought into the courtroom at 10:59 a.m. to begin hearing Hugo's defense.

Several neighbors on Mount Olivet Road and Hugo's younger sister, called by Hugo's lawyers, testified they had free reign of the property to ride all-terrain vehicles and explore the woods. None of them said Hugo prohibited them from concentrating their time in the area where the bodies were buried.

Another witness called to the witness stand by Hugo's lawyers was Kerkowski's neighbor on Pritchards Road in Hunlock Township. She told the jury she believed she saw a carpet cleaning van in Kerkowski's driveway at about 1 p.m. on either May 2 or May 3, 2002.

One particular witness, Mary Ann Selenski, who is Hugo's younger sister, testified she was at the Mount Olivet Road home studying while her brother was preparing for her graduation party from nursing school. Mary Ann Selenski said when the state police converged onto the property, she came out onto the porch and noticed Patrick Russin near her, estimating Russin was at least 30 yards away from Hugo.

Hugo's lawyers wanted to highlight Russin's location through Mary Ann Selenski's testimony as Russin previously testified he was standing next to Hugo when state police drove onto the property.

The first day of Hugo's defense involved seven witnesses, all saying they did not see any suspicious activity at the Mount Olivet Road property.

After the jury was excused for the night, Judge Pierantoni met in chambers with prosecutors and Hugo's lawyers to review the next several defense witnesses and what they would say from the witness stand.

Lengthy arguments took place involving Pennsylvania State Police

Trooper Christopher O'Brien, one of several troopers assigned to conduct

surveillance of the Mount Olivet Road home prior to Lieutenant Richard

Krawetz leading the caravan of state police investigators onto the property

on June 5, 2003. O'Brien was hidden in the woods and observed Patrick

Russin digging with a shovel in the area of the burn pit where the charred

remains of Frank James and Adeiye Keiler were recovered.

Rymsza wanted O'Brien to testify about what he overheard Russin say

to another person about "joining them," referencing the burn pit while

Ferentino argued the burn pit was nowhere near the grave sites of

Kerkowski and Fassett. Russin's overheard comment was made three

weeks after James and Keiler were killed and burned and was still fresh in

Russin's mind.

Hugo's lawyers resumed presenting witnesses on Feb. 6, 2015, the

12th day of trial. A landscaper who excavated the earth for a retaining wall

at the Mount Olivet Road property testified he did not have any

restrictions on the property, while another defense witness, the owner of

the water filtration business where Weakley was employed, described

Weakley as dishonest.

Trooper Christopher O'Brien was called to testify telling the jury his

assignment was to conduct surveillance of the Mount Olivet Road property and got close enough to overhear Patrick Russin say to another person they were going to be "joining them" while using a shovel to dig. The location was near the burn pit where the charred remains of Frank James and Adeiye Keiler were recovered and far away from the gravesites of Kerkowski and Fassett.

O'Brien did say he did not see Russin standing next to Hugo when state police converged onto the property, contrasting to what Russin told the jury he stood next to Hugo. O'Brien was on the witness stand for seven minutes.

After O'Brien, Kingston Police Sergeant Sam Blaski testified he was conducting surveillance on Feb. 2, 2003, searching for Paul Weakley who was wanted at the time by the U.S. Marshals Service. Blaski said after apprehending Weakley, a search of Weakley's van resulted in the discovery of hand tools, including a pickaxe, a shovel and a handcuff key hidden in Weakley's buttocks.

Luzerne County Detective Lieutenant Gary G. Capitano was called by Hugo's lawyers to the witness stand. Capitano joined Pennsylvania State Police Trooper Gerard Sachney in leading the investigation that began June 3, 2003, unraveling the mystery of what happened to Kerkowski and Fassett and uncovering the murders of Frank James, Adeiye Keiler and a third unidentified person whose remains were burned in a pit at the Mount Olivet Road property.

Capitano was questioned by Attorney Rymsza who did his best to exploit the many falsehoods and lies told by Paul Weakley. Capitano acknowledged Weakley provided misleading information in an attempt to insulate himself from the murders of Kerkowski and Fassett, but eventually when confronted with those falsehoods, Weakley decided to tell the truth.

Rymsza also quizzed Capitano about any preferential treatment Weakley received but the seasoned detective said no promises were made to Weakley. Capitano's time on the witness chair lasted less than 40 minutes.

# HUGO OPTS NOT TO TESTIFY

As the jury was on a lengthy lunch break, Judge Pierantoni, prosecutors and Hugo's lawyers met in chambers where it was made known Hugo would not testify in his own defense. When a defendant in any case opts not to testify, they are questioned by the judge in open court but outside the presence of the jury.

In Hugo's case, prosecutors and his lawyers wanted Hugo to be colloquial in chambers and out of public view for a number of reasons as stated by Sanguedolce.

"We've discussed this at length with defense counsel. Due to, you know, the extensive media coverage, the fact that we've come so far along and, for various safety concerns, we completely agree that the colloquy should be done in chambers so that there isn't any fanfare at the time that he's announced his decision. I note that the gallery is filled and largely filled with a number of members of the media…" Sanguedolce stated.

Pierantoni agreed and had Hugo brought into chambers to go over his constitutional rights. In front of Hugo, Attorney Brown echoed what Sanguedolce had previously stated.

"Well, your honor, in…in an effort to…to have Mr. Selenski be colloquied as to whether or not he's going to testify, umm, and for the reasons already stated on the record, such as exposure not only to the jury but also to other members of the media and/or gallery, we would like to do this in chambers in order to address the issue of whether Mr. Selenski would testify on his own behalf," Brown said, making it known Hugo would not testify.

With that, Pierantoni advised Hugo he had the absolute right to remain silent, had an absolute right not to testify if he choses, and inquired if anyone had threatened him not to testify. Hugo gave his appropriate responses saying he understood.

Rymsza asked several questions including, "You're making this decision, knowingly, intelligently and voluntarily?

"I don't know about how intelligently, but I'm making it, yes," Hugo stated.

Hugo's remark caused a brief silence only to note, "I'm…that was sarcasm. I'm sorry, Judge, I shouldn't have said that. I apologize. I couldn't help it." With the jury about to hear closing arguments in the next few days, Hugo showed he had a sense of humor despite the seriousness of the death penalty trial.

"To indemnify the attorneys, they've clearly talked to me about it since day one, I mean, all way through every visit. So, I mean, to make it clear, I've spoken to them at least a couple times every time I've seen them, so…." Hugo said.

"Mr. Selenski, as I stated to you when I began," Pierantoni began asking before Hugo interrupted, "Ultimately, I…I understand that it's clearly mine and mine alone. And as I said, to indemnify all parties, I understand that fully…I don't know how much clearer I can make it."

After Pierantoni said he found Hugo's decision not to testify was made voluntarily and intelligently, he sent Hugo back into the courtroom and allowed prosecutors and Hugo's lawyers a 10 minute break. Before they left the judge's chambers, Pierantoni reminded those about the court imposed gag order, prohibiting prosecutors and Hugo's lawyers from publicly speaking about the case, specifically, what just occurred in chambers.

"Everybody, take 10…now remember the gag order. Just a gag order. I know in 10 minutes, they're going to know the rest but remember the gag order," the judge said.

"I'm not saying anything," Sanguedolce stated.

"I believe once people see everybody coming in here, including the defendant, they start wondering what's up, you know what I mean," Pierantoni said.

The jury returned to the courtroom at 2:20 p.m. and shortly after, Hugo's lawyers rested their defense. There was no mention in open court that Hugo would not testify.

Pierantoni sent the jury home telling them to get good rest for the weekend and return to the courthouse at 10 a.m., Monday, Feb. 9, 2015.

Prosecutors presented 30 witnesses over 10 days and Hugo's lawyers presented 13 witnesses in two days.

# CLOSING ARGUMENTS

The jury had an extra day to their weekend thanks to a winter storm that brought snow, sleet and freezing rain upon Luzerne County on Sunday, Feb. 8 and Monday, Feb. 9, postponing closing arguments until Tuesday, Feb. 10.

At 9:30 a.m., Judge Pierantoni met with prosecutors and Hugo's lawyers in chambers to review the charging documents that require detailed language relating to each criminal charge. Known in Luzerne County simply as "the charge," the judge gives a crash education on criminal law to the jury explaining how they should weigh the testimony of witnesses, definitions of crimes, conspiracy, guilt by association, malice and being an accomplice or a principle. Issues such as a flex tie being considered a deadly weapon was also discussed. To assist Sanguedolce, Ferentino and Phillips with the undaunting and laboring task of finding the language from the standpoint of the district attorney's office, Assistant District Attorney William T. Finnegan, a veteran of many homicide and felony trials, was brought in to help.

The hour-long meeting ended and the jury was brought into the courtroom at 10:32 a.m. to hear closing arguments.

In Pennsylvania criminal courts, prosecutors give opening statements first followed by the defense if they chose. For closing arguments, the order is reversed as prosecutors give their closing arguments after the defense.

Attorney Brown reminded the jury of the core principle in the American system of justice that each defendant has the presumption of innocence. Brown instructed the jury of reasonable doubt and immediately challenged the credibility of Paul Weakley.

Brown went over all the false statements, lies and misleading information Weakley gave to investigators. It was Weakley, Brown said, who admitted to taking the flex ties and duct tape to Kerkowski's home. It was Weakley, Brown added, who admitted to fastening the flex ties around Kerkowski's neck and beating him with the baker's rolling pin.

Brown continued his attack on Weakley's credibility that it was Weakley who wrapped up the body of Kerkowski and placed the body along with Fassett's body in his vehicle, driving around the Wyoming Valley for days looking for a place to bury them.

And it was Weakley, Brown said, who benefited by cooperating with prosecutors in hopes of better conditions in prison and possibly an amended sentence.

After 12 years with multiple law enforcement agencies, scientific laboratories and mountains of alleged evidence, Brown said there was absolutely no forensic evidence connecting Hugo to the murders of Kerkowski and Fassett.

As for the bodies being found 15 feet behind the back porch of the Mount Olivet Road house where Hugo lived with his girlfriend at the time, Christina Strom, Brown described it as "circumstantial evidence."

Brown reminded the jury that they heard Hugo enjoyed riding all-terrain vehicles and would often go to other areas and ride ATVs in woods and forests.

"Does that make sense that he would bury those bodies 15 feet out his back porch in his backyard or does that cause you to say, wait a second, that's more reasonable for somebody trying to set him up, somebody that wants a quick job, somebody that's driving all around the area, who's not from the area, looking to put…for a place to dump bodies, and that person was Paul Weakley," Brown said.

Brown reviewed the testimony of several prosecution witnesses who benefited by testifying against Hugo in exchange for leniency or the dismissal of criminal cases against them. But, Brown always found a way to return to Weakley.

"I apologize, when I think that Hugo has the potential of being convicted on the word of Paul Weakley, it gets my blood boiling and my Irish up…" Brown said.

Brown ended his closing by saying, "...the fact is Hugo Selenski did not rob and murder Michael Kerkowski and Tammy Fassett and that's why you should find him not guilty of these charges. Thank you for your time and attention."

As Ferentino gave the opening statement on behalf of the district attorney's office, Sanguedolce gave the closing argument.

Acknowledging Paul Weakley gave testimony that heightened their direct evidence during trial, Sanguedolce said they could have prosecuted Hugo without him.

"Now, ladies and gentlemen, I submit to you that we made this case without Paul Weakley and we've corroborated each and every thing he said," Sanguedolce said, noting Detective Lieutenant Gary Capitano checked and verified all of Weakley's falsehoods until there was nothing left but to tell the truth.

Sanguedolce described Hugo as one of the two farmers in the story "The Goose that laid the Golden Eggs," as the goose laid a golden egg daily. Kerkowski was the goose with the source of illegitimate money earned through illegal sales of prescriptions and Hugo wanted the money. Even after Kerkowski was killed, Hugo continued to obtain his golden eggs in cash by scamming Kerkowski's parents telling them their son was alive and in hiding, Sanguedolce said.

As most prosecutors do during closing arguments, Sanguedolce reviewed the testimony of each witness who testified against Hugo, specifically Rodney Samson who claimed Hugo solicited him to kill a pharmacist. It was Hugo who wanted Robert Steiner off the property on May 3, 2002, and later the same day, it was Ernest Culp who encountered Hugo and Weakley digging in the same area where the bodies were found, Sanguedolce said.

"I submit to you also, all the evidence that I've referenced so far has nothing to do with Paul Weakley. All of it was found independently by Detective Lieutenant Capitano and Trooper Sachney and everyone that worked with them.

"The reason to believe the testimony of Paul Weakley is not Paul Weakley, himself. The corroborating evidence is the reason to believe Paul Weakley. Detective Capitano and Trooper Sachney were the investigators who dedicated years of their lives. They didn't jump to conclusions. They're not just discussers of data, they went out and chased down leads. When push came to shove, they stepped up and called Weakley out on his lies," Sanguedolce said.

Sanguedolce continued, saying, "The victims may never know it in this case but these detectives worked day after day proving and disproving statements by Paul Weakley and other witnesses until, as Paul Weakley said, all that was left was the truth. It didn't come easy, and it only got done because they did it."

In seeking a first degree murder conviction, Sanguedolce told the jury the case was a textbook example of premeditated murder as Hugo and

Weakley planned the execution of Kerkowski the night before by gathering up the duct tape, flex ties, gloves and the handgun.

"...They get in the car together, they drive to Hunlock's Creek. They actually…the defendant actually makes a statement, when they're wearing safety glasses, 'I wonder if they're wearing bulletproof vests.' Could the intent be any clearer?" Sanguedolce said before reminding the jury of what actually occurred inside Kerkowski's home.

Picking up the baker's rolling pin, Sanguedolce banged it three times on the oak railing in front of the jury to illustrate Kerkowski was beaten. Using a flex tie he locked as a demonstration, Sanguedolce said it was Hugo who put the last flex tie around Kerkowski's neck as Weakley said Kerkowski turned blue and stopped breathing. With the use of a flex tie, Sanguedolce asked the jury to consider it a deadly weapon.

Coming to the end of his closing argument, Sanguedolce said, "...in our opening statement, we promised you a look into this defendant's world. We've proven that these two victims, that Michael and Tammy, became nothing more than flotsam and jetsam in the swift current in the life of Hugo Selenski. These two victims were murdered with exceptional brutality. In exchange for paper (money), their lives were taken away. Two lives forever altered, if you don't count their parents, their siblings, their children, their friends.

"All these people thought monsters didn't exist until Hugo Selenski befriended Michael Kerkowski. And I stand here before you as the last person that gets to speak on behalf of Michael and Tammy, until you do. There won't be any fancy words or clever lines for you to define for us what happened on May 3rd, 2002. We'll get only your verdict, not more and not less," Sanguedolce ended.

As Pierantoni began addressing the jury after Sanguedolce ended his closing argument, Attorney Rymsza interrupted saying Hugo needed to use the restroom as he suddenly became ill. Hugo was taken by deputy sheriffs through a side door leading to a hallway that had a restroom.

# VERDICT

Judge Pierantoni began the long task of charging the jury at 1:55 p.m. and ended at 3:38 p.m. as he ordered 12 jurors to courtroom 6, a small room behind the third floor court administration office used for jury deliberations, keeping the three alternate jurors in the courtroom. After the 12 member panel left, Pierantoni advised the alternate jurors they were to remain in another room in case one of them needed to replace a main juror for reason, such as an illness or death in the family.

"We will just stand in recess, awaiting the jury. Thank you all," Judge Pierantoni said, excusing prosecutors and Hugo's lawyers at 3:41 p.m. Hugo remained under guard inside the courtroom.

The jury returned to the courtroom at 7:22 p.m. when the jury foreperson asked to recess for the night due to exhaustion. The jury had been at the courthouse since well before 10 a.m. With no objection from prosecutors and Hugo's lawyers, Pierantoni sent them home for the night, directing them to return at 9:30 a.m. on Wednesday, Feb. 11, 2015. Jurors left the courthouse and were escorted to their vehicles by deputy sheriffs.

The Luzerne County Courthouse has its own clock as those who regularly attend proceedings practice the "hurry up and wait" method. A 9 a.m. hearing is more likely to begin much later.

Such was the case for Hugo.

As jurors filed into the courthouse just before 9:30 a.m. on Wednesday, Feb. 11, 2015, they were kept in the large jury commissioner room on the second floor on purpose as Judge Pierantoni, prosecutors and Hugo's lawyers dealt with not one, but two issues that could have jeopardized the last four weeks.

Hours earlier, about 6:30 a.m., Sheriff Deputy Eric Aigeldinger and another sheriff deputy while performing their morning security sweep of the courtroom and jury deliberation room found two comic strips on a chair used by judges when the deliberation room is utilized as an auxiliary courtroom.

Aigeldinger placed the comic strips in an envelope and contacted Judge Pierantoni.

Meeting in chambers just after 10:30 a.m., Aigeldinger explained the discovery of the comic strips during the security sweep.

Sanguedolce reviewed the comic strips noting both were named Tundra, with one strip depicting a picture of a courtroom with a lawyer talking to Goldilocks and the jury full of bears, and it says, "Sorry Goldilocks, it's not looking good." The second strip showed a picture of a reindeer migrating on a frozen tundra with the words "jury duty."

The prior night, sheriff deputies were not able to sweep the deliberation room as cleaning staff were in there. The last person to leave the deliberation room the previous night was a court employee, assigned to assist the jury with gathering and escorting them to the courtroom, reported seeing nothing out of place.

Sanguedolce and Hugo's lawyers felt the comic strips did not rise to the level of a possible mistrial but wanted Pierantoni to provide a cautionary instruction to jurors not to read, listen or communicate with anyone about the case.

Before leaving the judge's chambers at 10:45 a.m., Pierantoni reminded prosecutors and Hugo's lawyers about the gag order. The discovery of the comic strips would not become public.

Soon after leaving Pierantoni's chambers, Attorney Rymsza was walking up the stairs to the third floor when he received a text message from Attorney Hugh Taylor, the third attorney for Hugo. Taylor had forwarded a message he received from Janna Desanto related to a talk radio program on WILK-AM Radio where a caller identified himself as a brother to a juror on Hugo's jury and the jury believed Hugo was guilty from day one.

Prosecutors and Hugo's lawyers met again in Pierantoni's chambers at 11:14 a.m. to discuss the text message.

"...I think it opens the door to potentially, umm, if...if indeed, it's true, I think it potentially opens the door to a number of different problems," Rymsza said in chambers.

One of the many concerns, Rymsza felt, was jurors disobeying the judge's instructions not to talk about the case amongst themselves and not to talk about the case with anyone else. Rymsza feared if the radio station caller was true, it would appear the jury or several jurors had already made up their minds.

Desanto had interjected herself in Hugo's case by working as his unpaid paralegal and keeping documents of the case at her residence, which was searched by investigators on July 7, 2010. Desanto was on the witness list during Hugo's trial but was not called to testify.

"Judge, I think, I feel compelled to state for the record, number one, this Janna Desanto is the girlfriend or supposed…." Sanguedolce began as Pierantoni interrupted, "Wait a minute, Where does she come in from, though?"

"…you may also recall from prior hearings, she's a person that has taken great steps to inject herself into this case and had proclaimed on the stand under oath that she's in love with the defendant. She was the subject of a search warrant, because she was keeping his files, umm, she continuously visits him in prison, and to…to the extent of her attempting to inject her into this case, she has gone so far as to, in my opinion, nearly interfere with this case," Sanguedolce said.

"The other thing about Miss Desanto, judge, she actually did interfere with the case in writing a letter to Judge Muroski regarding pieces of evidence in supplied discovery. So, that's…that was preempted by the warrant. I just…in addition, I mean, as we're…we're heading into…now half of the day is gone. We…you know, there's going to be things commented on in newspapers, and there's going to be things in the media. The bottom line is, we…our jurors remain under oath, and they could be cautioned as they've always been cautioned. We have no control over what…I mean, this is a case that's received a lot of media attention," Ferentino added.

As the discussion about the radio caller neared the end, Judge Pierantoni said he would give his admonition instructions to the jury and have the jury deliberation room swept by the sheriff's office at the end of the night.

More than two hours after the jury believed they would begin their second day of deliberation, the jury was brought into the courtroom at 11:46 a.m. where Pierantoni read them their cautionary instructions once again.

"I previously instructed you, and you have repeatedly represented you have not discussed this case with anyone, including family, friends or acquaintances. You, obviously, are during the course of deliberations, discussing the case amongst yourselves. I have additionally instructed you to avoid media accounts and any information from any source, other than what has transpired in the courtroom," Judge Pierantoni said before polling each juror if they had followed his cautions and instructions.

As each of the 12 jurors and the three alternates acknowledged their oath, they returned to the deliberation room at 11:49 a.m. as the three alternates went to the jury commissioner room.

Later that day while in chambers at 1:35 p.m. reviewing a note passed by the jury foreperson seeking clarifications on the definitions of conspiracy, murder and does a verdict on each of the counts need to be unanimous, Attorney Rymsza said he learned the caller to the radio talk show was a relative to one of Hugo's sisters' boyfriends.

Rymsza said in light of what he learned about the call, he felt confident the jury had obeyed the judge's instructions.

The jury foreperson sent a second question seeking the definitions of first- and- second degree murder at 4:18 p.m. After the jury was brought into the courtroom and Pierantoni reread the definitions of the different degrees of murder and malice, the jury returned to deliberate at 4:40 p.m.

A third note was passed by the jury foreperson at 6:25 p.m. asking to provide a definition and an example of a principal and an accomplice in first degree murder and how it applies to the definition of first-degree murder that had been read to them during the 4 p.m. hour.

Pierantoni had the jury return to the courtroom and reread the part of his charge relating to principal and accomplice.

"Jurors, a principal, is a person who is the actor or perpetrator of the crime. A crime can be completed by one or more principals….When two or more people are charged with a crime of first degree murder and one or more of them did not actually commit the murder, they may still be guilty of first degree murder if they are found to have been an accomplice of the one who did," Pierantoni advised the jury.

The jury returned to the deliberation room at 6:47 p.m.

At 8:16 p.m., the jury returned to the courtroom as they reached a unanimous verdict on all 11 counts after a combined 12 hours of deliberating.

More deputy sheriffs were brought into the courtroom as the tension was thick with a large contingent of Hugo's family and the families of Kerkowski and Fassett sitting just feet away from each other.

Before Pierantoni had the jury foreperson read the verdicts, he warned those in the gallery to keep their composure and remain in their seats.

Lisa Sands, the sister of Fassett, and Gerladine Kerkowski sat together holding hands in anticipation of the verdict being announced.

Hugo was convicted on two counts of first-degree murder as an accomplice, and found guilty on two counts of criminal conspiracy to commit criminal homicide, two counts of robbery, one count of criminal conspiracy to commit robbery and one count of theft by unlawful taking. The jury acquitted Hugo on charges of criminal conspiracy to commit robbery and criminal solicitation to commit criminal homicide, related to asking Rodney Samson for his help in killing Kerkowski.

As customary in court, each juror was polled to acknowledge their independent decision.

After the verdicts were announced, Pierantoni advised the jury the next step would be the sentencing phase and instructed jurors to return to the courthouse at 9:30 a.m., Tuesday, Feb. 17. The delay in beginning the sentencing phase was required to allow Hugo's lawyers to prepare and for out-of-state witnesses time to travel.

When the jury foreperson read the verdict for the first charge, first-degree murder related to Kerkowski, Hugo did not flinch and maintained his stillness as the other verdicts were announced. Gone was the smirk Hugo normally had on his face. Hugo said little as he was escorted by deputy sheriffs from the courthouse to the Luzerne County Correctional Facility.

Geraldine Kerkowski held the hand of Ferentino, who were joined by Sanguedolce, Detective Lieutenant Gary Capitano, Detective Daniel Yursha, District Attorney Stefanie Salavantis and Lisa Sands as they emerged from the elevator in the courthouse basement and walked into the detectives' office conference room. Seconds earlier before the prosecution team with Geraldine Kerkowski descended the third floor with the elevator door open, an agitated Ronald Selenski Jr. appeared before them yelling threats.

While making a hand gesture in the form of a gun, Ronald Selenski Jr. reportedly yelled, "You, I'm going to get you," directing his comment toward Ferentino.

Sheriff deputies immediately grabbed Ronald Selenski Jr., handcuffed him, and was taken away by a sheriff deputy and Chief Detective Michael Dessoye.

Ronald Selenski Jr. was charged with four counts of terroristic threats by the sheriff's department. At his preliminary hearing, Ronald Selenski Jr. pled guilty to a summary count of disorderly conduct and received a $25 fine. The terroristic threat charges were withdrawn by prosecutors.

The work by prosecutors and Hugo's lawyers was not finished. Judge Pierantoni gave them three days to prepare for the sentencing phase, time well deserved to catch up on sleep.

# HUGO LIMITS EVIDENCE

First Assistant District Attorney Sam Sanguedolce and assistant district attorneys Jarrett Ferentino and Mamie Phillips were joined by assistant district attorneys William T. Finnegan and Luke Moran for the penalty phase, while Hugo had his trial attorneys, Bernard J. Brown and Edward J. Rymsza. It was four against two.

All parties joined Judge Pierantoni in the judge's chambers just after 9:30 a.m. on Tuesday, Feb. 17, 2015, to discuss issues that were to remain private from the jury and public.

A juror reported she observed someone taking pictures of her while she walked into a pharmacy in Hanover Township while another juror requested a court official to hold his phone as he expected a phone call from a family member about his dog dying and wanted to leave. And, Hugo fought with his attorneys about a mitigation issue he did not want to pursue.

Another issue discussed were victim impact statements from Geraldine Kerkowski, Lisa Sands, Ashley Owens, who is Sands' daughter and niece of Fassett, and two letters from Kerkowski's sons, Connor and Tyler, who were young boys when their father was killed. Pierantoni ruled the impact statements of Geraldine Kerkowski, Sands and Owens would be permitted during the penalty phase but precluded the letters from Kerkowski's sons as those letters were turned over to Hugo's lawyers too late. The letters from Kerkowski's sons were given to Hugo's lawyers on Jan. 28, 2015, during the guilt phase of the trial as the impact statements from Geraldine Kerkowski, Sands and Owens were turned over in 2012. Pierantoni did allow prosecutors to call Kerkowski's sons to make a statement during Hugo's sentencing hearing.

As prosecutors and their witnesses were warned not to mention "torture" during the trial, prosecutors wanted to use torture as an aggravating factor, one of 18 aggravating factors to seek the death penalty in Pennsylvania.

Finnegan, an experienced prosecutor with many homicide trials under his belt, addressed the use of torture against Kerkowski, not Fassett, as Kerkowski was blinded by duct tape, bound to a chair by flex ties, and beaten with a baker's rolling pin while he was being interrogated by Hugo and Weakley about money hidden inside his Hunlock Township home. The other three aggravating factors were Hugo had a significant history of felony convictions involving the use of threat of violence, convicted of federal or state offenses that carried a sentence of life imprisonment or death, and being convicted of murder at the time of committing another felony offense.

Earlier in the morning, Rymsza filed a motion to preclude the death penalty and to stay the penalty phase as, at the time of Hugo's trial,

Pennsylvania Governor Tom Wolf had imposed a moratorium on the death penalty.

Sanguedolce countered saying the governor did not have the authority to ban prosecutors in any county to seek the death penalty, as the governor only indicated he may not sign death warrants and has stayed the signing of any death warrant.

Pierantoni immediately said the penalty phase will proceed, denying Rymsza's motion to preclude the death penalty against Hugo.

With the judge issuing his ruling, he wanted to address the issue involving the juror who had her picture taken but was stopped when Attorney Brown wanted to bring up another topic.

Brown said over the weekend, a family member of Hugo sent him an email claiming that an alternate juror ate dinner at a restaurant where the alternate juror was exposed to media reports. Brown further claimed another juror on the 12 member panel was a 2009 graduate of Lake Lehman High School where Kerkowski's brother, Scott Kerkowski, was a teacher.

Pierantoni said during the jury selection process weeks earlier, the juror who graduated from Lake Lehman High School indicated he resided in the Back Mountain area and did not have any relationship with Scott Kerkowski while he attended school.

Pierantoni then moved to address the juror who reported someone took her picture when she walked into a pharmacy.

The juror was brought into the judge's chambers, took the oath, and was asked several questions by Pierantoni with Sanguedolce and Rymsza declining to ask questions.

The juror said on Friday, Feb. 13, 2015, an off day for the jury, as she walked into a pharmacy, she noticed a heavyset man in a dark-colored vehicle took a picture of her from the driver's side window. She reported the picture to the jury commissioner's room, who alerted police in Hanover Township. The juror was interviewed by Hanover Township police on Sunday, Feb. 15, 2015.

The juror said she did not tell other jurors and was not planning to tell any of them. Pierantoni thanked her and allowed her to continue with her jury service. She left the judge's chambers with instructions, if asked by other jurors, that she was sequestered for several minutes. She did not have to go into detail with her fellow jurors about why the judge needed her to be sequestered for a brief time.

The next issue to address in chambers would be a lengthy one to digest.

Hugo was adamantly against using a mitigating circumstance as the verdict, as announced related to being an accomplice and not as principal, found him guilty of first-degree murder but at the level of participation of a homicidal act as a minor participant. Basically, the jury found Hugo guilty as being the lesser participant in the murder of Kerkowski.

Rymsza advised Judge Pierantoni that Hugo did not want to present a substantial amount of mitigation during the penalty phase and asked that Hugo be colloquied by the judge to get Hugo's side of his beliefs.

"He expressed, in no uncertain terms, that there's a variety of mitigation that he will not allow us to present," Rymsza stated.

Louise Luck, a mitigation expert and owner of a company called Court Consultation Services, conducted approximately 70 interviews with Hugo's family and friends over the years and Hugo did not want any of the information she reported to be brought up during the penalty phase. Simply, Hugo did not want his upbringing to be mentioned in open court in an attempt to protect his family from any embarrassment.

Luck and Hugo were brought into chambers and were questioned separately.

Luck went first, responding to questions from Rymsza that as a mitigation specialist, her work is needed during the penalty phase of death penalty cases and has worked on more than 300 cases. For Hugo, Luck said she has worked on Hugo's mitigation since his trial for the murders of Frank James and Adeiye Keiler, which was a death penalty case, and completed a "comprehensive" report.

After Hugo was convicted in the murders of Kerkowski and Fassett, Luck said she discussed the importance of presenting the mitigation evidence. In response, Luck said Hugo did not want to pursue most of the mitigation involving his family.

When Luck was asked questions by Ferentino, she appeared to side-step her answers as she claimed her mitigation report was a "confidential attorney work product."

Luck was asked if she had shown Hugo any of her mitigation reports and skirted with her answer, saying she verbally told Hugo who she interviewed.

"Did you talk to him about the subject matter in which you interviewed those individuals?" Ferentino asked. Luck replied, "Probably apart, yes."

Hugo jumped in saying, "You're trying to skew the issue and protect me. Let me do this."

"I'm not trying to protect you at all," Luck replied.

"Ms. Luck, throughout your many years on this case, I've been on it for many years too, has Mr. Selenski ever waivered on his desire to not present mitigation evidence of his family? Ferentino asked.

"Did he ever waiver on his desire?" was Luck's response.

"Yes," Ferentino said.

"We would be talking about…it was difficult for him to go through some of these issues," Luck said before Hugo jumped in again.

"Answer the question. Just answer the question. I have never waivered, not once. Let's be straight about this. I have multiple times put it on prison record phones for you to have it. Bring it. I mean, I never waivered. Let's not hedge the issue. I'm getting aggravated," Hugo stated.

Next up was the colloque of Hugo, first by Judge Pierantoni.

The judge asked basic questions to get Hugo's understanding of what he faced, life in prison or the death penalty. Hugo said he understood. Hugo said he also understood the jury would weigh aggravating factors and mitigating circumstances when reaching their verdict of punishment.

"…I understand your attorneys plan to present the following mitigating evidence….first, that your participation in the homicidal act was relatively minor; second, any evidence of mitigation concerning the character, background and record of the defendant and the circumstances…" Pierantoni was asking before he was abruptly cut off.

"Judge, can I stop you there?" Hugo chimed, only to add, "I have an issue with the first one…I have a big issue."

Pierantoni cleared his chambers and allowed Hugo to privately talk with Rymsza and Brown.

When their private discussion ended, Rymsza informed the judge that Hugo did not want to proceed with the mitigation circumstance that

Hugo's participation in the homicidal act against Kerkowski was relatively minor, as the jury convicted him of being an accomplice to first-degree murder.

"I totally…I object to that. I object to that," Hugo bolstered.

"…And do you not want any presentation to the jury or argument…" Pierantoni was asking before Hugo interrupted again.

"Of minor role of any sort, no," Hugo stated.

Pierantoni asked Hugo why he did not want his attorneys to argue before the jury that Hugo was found guilty of being an accomplice in the murder of Kerkowski.

Hugo went into a long explanation.

"In caution of the way I coach my things I'm about to say, I want to clearly enunciate for the record that I stand by my innocence and I want nothing given to that jury that would dignify or lend some sort of credence to the verdict that they came back with. That just takes me right into the whole mitigation with my family. I seek to protect my family.

"I believe that the system is somewhat skewed in the way that we spent a month here fighting innocence and then when you take that mitigation and present it in a manner that, well, look, this is what he went through; this is what happened; there might have been some sort of disfunction, possibly alcoholism and all of this could lead up to some, sort of, type of behavior that lends a credibility to the verdict. To me, it's absolutely asinine. It's totally contradictory to everything we fought for the last five weeks. I want no part of that.

"I have been…I've seen psychologists. They have done their testing of me. There is nothing wrong with me, Judge. This is nothing new. We have gone through this in the first trial with Olszewski and Attorney Fannick. I stood by this since day one. I just will not lend any credibility to any verdict at all by saying, oh, there was some sort of minor role. To me, that's like acknowledging some sort of guilt that I want no part of," Hugo said.

Hugo continued, "I will do anything I can to indemnify the record, even as far as phone records in the prison, tapes, that I have been saying this since day one, incorporate it if you would like, incorporate any mental health things that I have tested and passed fine. There is nothing wrong with the judgment and the way I am thinking about this. I mean, I'm asking the court not to postpone this to have, you know, a competency hearing because it's clearly been stated that I'm competent. I would just like to incorporate everything that we need to in the past," Hugo said.

Pierantoni responded that he found Hugo to be competent. Rymsza said there were funds allocated for a psychiatric evaluation of Hugo but did not recall any competence evaluation while Rymsza was representing Hugo.

Pierantoni was quick to point out during Hugo's colloquy that Hugo's lawyers never raised Hugo's mental health or competency as a defense strategy. Rymsza's concern, at this time in chambers, was Hugo's competency to prohibit most of the mitigating circumstances.

"Let me state, I have observed Mr. Selenski. I've interacted with him during the pretrial and trial. I observed his assistance of counsel during the trial and cooperation, no reason to conclude Mr. Selenski is not competent to proceed," the judge said.

Rymsza said Hugo was not precluding all mitigation evidence but Hugo's persistence not to use his minor role as an accomplice in the murder of Kerkowski and his family upbringing made it, "extremely, extremely, extremely limited on what he is permitting us to produce or to bring up in court."

Rymsza said the area Hugo is demanding to keep private involved his family, issues with his family and his family history.

Hugo said he understood the issues his lawyers wanted to address during the penalty phase were important but was not persuaded to let those issues be raised in open court.

"I'm aware of the ramifications of my decision. I mean, I don't know how much clearer for the record to make it. There will not be any type of retraction or some sort of appellate issue if there was ever a condemned sentence. I mean, I don't know how much clearer to make it for the record that my family preservation is of the utmost importance to me. Period. I mean, I just…they have gone through enough and I've always said that I would never do it. I'm standing by that," Hugo said.

As Judge Pierantoni was ending his colloquy of Hugo, Ferentino wanted to quiz Hugo on the mitigating circumstance of being found guilty of being a participant in Kerkowski's murder.

"Go ahead. Absolutely. I think it's fair that they should be able to, Judge," Hugo said.

"This is a new development," Ferentino, perhaps sarcastically, said.

Ferentino asked Hugo if he understood that being found guilty of being an accomplice in a murder he can still maintain his innocence?

"I understand it but I feel it's just contrary to what I believe. It's a personal belief that I'm not just going to…I'm not going against," Hugo said.

Hugo said he could "set off really quick if somebody does something to my family."

With Hugo's refusal to allow most of the mitigating circumstances gathered by Luck to be used during the penalty phase, Rymsza said he was left with "not much," leaving him to present to the jury Hugo's acts of kindness to his family and his artistic talent.

"That just right there, narrowing the scope. That should…nothing is of any surprise," Hugo said.

Pierantoni gave his final ruling on the issue, finding Hugo voluntarily and intelligently waived his right to offer mitigating circumstances to the jury.

Hugo was playing Russian roulette with five bullets in a six cylinder revolver.

With all the issues that needed to be addressed, Pierantoni gathered everyone in the courtroom to begin the penalty phase just after 12 p.m.

Before prosecutors presented their evidence of aggravating factors, the judge once again gave his cautionary instructions and this time, asked jurors individually if they refrained from reading, watching and listening to any media reports. After each juror confirmed they had obeyed the judge's orders, prosecutors began their case to persuade the jury to put Hugo to death.

Assistant District Attorney Jarrett Ferentino gave the opening statement in the penalty phase telling the jury that people make choices in their lives and Hugo made a choice by killing Michael Jason Kerkowski and Tammy Lynn Fassett. As prosecutors and their witnesses were prohibited to say the word "torture" during the guilt phase, the penalty phase was a different proceeding.

"...ladies and gentleman, the torture factor. Let's talk about that area. It is our position that Michael Kerkowski was tortured. Michael Kerkowski was not the victim of a clumsy improvisation as these events fell out," Ferentino said, reminding the jury that Paul Weakley testified flex ties were used to strangle Kerkowski who was blinded by duct tape wrapped around his head, and then beaten by the baker's rolling pin.

"The rolling pin, ladies and gentlemen, is not a murder weapon. It's a torture weapon. It was a weapon used to do nothing more than inflict pain upon Michael Kerkowski," Ferentino said.

Ferentino then went over the three other aggravating factors as Hugo robbed Kerkowski during the commission of a felony, Hugo led a life committing violent crime and Hugo committed multiple murders in a single act by killing Kerkowski and Fassett.

Attorney Edward Rymsza gave the statement on behalf of Hugo telling the jury despite being disappointed by their guilty verdicts, they had to accept their findings.

"Remember this, by your verdict last week, Mr. Selenski will die in prison. He will die in prison. The question before you is whether that death will occur by natural causes or whether that death will occur of him being removed from his cell and taken to an execution chamber and put to death. Those are really the only two decisions you have to make," Rymsza said.

After Rymsza completed his statement, Pierantoni gave the jury a lunch recess.

Meanwhile, in light of Hugo's decision earlier in the morning not to present most mitigating circumstances, a sister who lived in South Carolina wanted to testify on his behalf. Rymsza said his sister did not have any funds to travel as Pierantoni granted a request to pay for airfare not to exceed $600.

With the jury back in the courtroom, Assistant District Attorney Mamie Phillips began calling witnesses with Vincent McGraw, a retired FBI special agent, the first one.

McGraw said he investigated the bank robbery of Mellon Bank in Plains Township on June 10, 1994, which he charged Hugo and his roommate at the time, Earl Nagle. McGraw said approximately $4,100 was stolen during the armed robbery as a dye pack exploded while Hugo and Nagle made their get-away in a stolen vehicle.

McGraw said Hugo was taken into custody when he returned to Northeastern Pennsylvania after visiting his biological father in the Las Vegas, Nevada, area.

Phillips then read into the record Hugo's federal conviction of bank robbery and federal prison sentence to the jury, including the conviction in Monroe County for the robbery and kidnapping of Samuel Goosay.

Prosecutors then concluded presenting their aggravating factors to the jury.

Pierantoni sent the jury home as Hugo's defense team required an additional day for their witnesses to travel to Luzerne County.

The jury returned to the courtroom just before 10 a.m. Wednesday, Feb. 18, 2015, to hear Hugo's lawyers make their pitch at saving his life.

Hugo's sisters and daughters were called to testify, telling the jury how Hugo helped each one of them, giving them advice, and never forgetting a birthday despite being in prison. Hugo also sent letters with words of encouragement to their children and often sent pictures of cartoon characters he drew or stenciled. Hugo was certainly talented with his artwork and some of his drawings were shown to the jury. Hugo would somehow use flavored drinks and coffee for colors in his artwork.

One sister described Hugo as being "very intelligent, very loyal and very protective," while another sister who earned a degree in criminal justice and thought about attending law school portrayed him as "very caring, outgoing and a fighter."

Several family pictures with Hugo were shown to the jury.

A teacher at Dallas School District was called to testify, telling the jury Hugo was one of her students in economics. The teacher said she had not seen or heard from Hugo in years and decided to send him a letter in 2005 while he was in prison because she enjoyed seeing his pictures in the Times Leader newspaper.

"I sent him a Bible because my main objective was to introduce him to Christ. I am a Christian," the teacher said before Sanguedolce objected to the religious reference, which was sustained by the judge.

The jury through the testimony of family and friends were told Hugo was a caring individual who protected his loved ones, never forgot birthdays and had an artistic talent.

But was it enough as Brown and Rymsza were severely limited with presenting mitigating circumstances due to Hugo's position prohibiting the use of his family upbringing.

One person who did not testify during the penalty phase was Hugo himself. Hugo opted not to testify as he advised Judge Pierantoni in chambers.

With testimony concluded, the stage now went to closing arguments where prosecutors and Hugo's lawyers go over the evidence presented during the trial in a manner they hope would be most favorable to their side.

Sanguedolce thanked each juror for their service and acknowledged the mental exhaustion that comes with a long trial. Again, the jurors were told they needed to weigh aggravating factors and mitigating circumstances noting emotions must be kept out of their decision. Simply parading witnesses who described Hugo as a caring and a loving man who protects his family involves emotion, Sanguedolce said.

Sanguedolce argued they proven that torture was used to kill Kerkowski as evidence by Dr. Baden's autopsy report and the testimony of Paul Weakley.

"If…that scale tips even slightly in favor of the Commonwealth, if you find that the aggravators even slightly outweigh the mitigating circumstances, the penalty must be death. There is no room for emotion and it is not a choice," Sanguedolce said.

A point Sanguedolce brought up that may have leaned toward emotion was Michael Stanley Kerkowski and his wife, Geraldine Kerkowski, never had the chance to ask Hugo for mercy when he was torturing and killing their son, and Lisa Sands never had the chance to ask for mercy when Hugo killed her sister, Tammy Fassett.

Sanguedolce ended his closing argument telling the jury Hugo earned his sentence, and if the jury would strictly apply the law, they would find the aggravating factors outweighed mitigating circumstances and their verdict should be death.

Rymsza began his closing argument saying it was a "solitary time," as the jury has the most difficult choice to make, sentence a man to death or sentence a man to life in prison with no possibility of parole.

"Mr. Selenski's life is in my hands right now, but very soon will be in yours," Rymsza said to the jury.

In seeking a life sentence, Rymsza said such a sentence does not mean Hugo can take a walk around a neighborhood or go to a beach. Hugo's life, Rymsza described, mirrored an Italian poet who talked about the gates of hell with an inscription, "All hope abandoned, ye who enter here."

"That's the life we talk about here when we talk about life without parole," the defense attorney said.

As Rymsza contrasted the aggravating factors and mitigating circumstances, he touched upon the one mitigating issue Hugo forbade him to use, which was the jury convicted Hugo of being an accomplice to Weakley in the torture killing of Kerkowski.

"I would submit to you that if you recall Mr. Weakley's testimony, Mr. Weakley said that throughout most of the duration of that, that he indicated Mr. Selenski was merely a spectator," Rymsza said.

Hugo immediately bellowed, "E.J., that's enough. I warned you about that. Stop."

It was the third time the jury heard Hugo's voice during the entire trial.

Rymsza reviewed how Hugo's family described him as a caring, loving and protective figure with an artistic talent.

"...You heard about his skills. You heard about Mr. Selenski mentoring other people. Again, these are special skills, and a special individual who can teach these things as well even in the institution," Rymsza said.

Rymsza was nearing the end of his closing statement telling the jury they need to determine if Hugo was beyond redemption and should be eliminated from the human community.

"In the end, every one of us in this room, all of you, the prosecutors, myself, the Judge, everyone of us shares a common humanity with Mr. Selenski and we all learned that, since our childhood, that through everything, there's a season and a time to every purpose under the heaven.

"Now, I would submit to you, is the time to punish, but it is not the time to kill," Rymsza said ending his argument.

Once again, Judge Pierantoni gave the jury instructions, or charge, educating jurors how to weigh aggravating factors and mitigating circumstances of their monumental task when deliberating a verdict of life in prison without parole or death. On the issue of torture, a word that was forbidden to be used during the guilt phase, was described to the jury by the judge.

"For a person to commit first degree murder by means of torture, the person must intend to do more than kill his or her victim. He or she must intend to inflict unnecessary pain or suffering; and, he or she must do so in a manner or by means that are heinous, atrocious or cruel and show exceptional depravity. There must be an indication that the killer was not satisfied with the killing alone," Judge Pierantoni said, advising jurors that they must also consider Paul Weakley's role in the torture and murder of Kerkowski. The jury had to consider if Hugo shared in the intent to torture Kerkowski.

Assistant District Attorney William Finnegan was brought in to assist for the penalty phase and was relied upon to deal with torture when prosecutors and Hugo's lawyers debated the language to be read to the jury during the judge's charge.

Following the lengthy charge from Pierantoni, the jury returned to the deliberation room at 3:52 p.m. Exactly two hours and 20 minutes later, at 6:11 p.m., the jury's verdict of life in prison or death was about to be announced.

"We, the jury, unanimously sentence the defendant to life imprisonment," announced the jury foreperson regarding the murder of Kerkowski.

"As to the death of Tammy L. Fassett, we, the jury, unanimously sentence the defendant to life imprisonment," the jury foreperson said.

Hugo played Russian roulette with five bullets in a six cylinder revolver and won his life and his lawyers, Brown and Rymsza, beat the odds.

Judge Pierantoni thanked the jury for their service and excused them at 6:18 p.m.

Hugo would formally be sentenced to life in prison without parole on March 27, 2015.

# PROSECUTORS EXPLAIN STRATEGY

With the trial and penalty phase concluded, the court imposed gag order prohibiting prosecutors and Hugo's lawyers from publicly speaking about the case ceased to exist.

Immediately after the jury announced their verdict giving Hugo life instead of death, District Attorney Stefanie Salavantis attempted to schedule a news conference but the television and print media reporters and photographers were in a frenzy, huddled in a rope off area in the corner of the basement near the inmate entrance/exit waiting for Hugo to be taken out of the courthouse while at the same time, chasing Hugo's family and jurors willing to be interviewed.

So, Salavantis scheduled a news conference the next day.

First question was about the identity of human remains recovered with the charred remains of Frank James and Adeiye Keiler from the burn pit. When the charred remains were recovered and analyzed, only James and Keiler were identified leaving a third person whose body was burned unidentified.

"At this point, that investigation is still ongoing. If anyone has information with regards to that investigation we ask that they come forward and call the state police or the district attorney's office," Salavantis said.

Sanguedolce added more: "As you guys know, we conducted extensive testing on the remains found at 479 Mount Olivet Road. Part of the problem that the fire burned the remains, the fire was so hot, we weren't able to extract DNA evidence. The DNA we did find on the property came from human tissue found on the garage door and not from any of the bones. The reason we know there were three different bodies in the burn pit was because our experts found three left mandibles. Obviously, the human body has one left mandible. But we were unable to obtain any information from any of our witnesses from all the things they told us in the first trial and the second trial, no one seemed to have any information about that fifth body."

Ferentino said the case was a "long journey," recalling the time when he was assigned to the Hugo prosecution team shortly after Hugo's first trial in the murders of Frank James and Adeiye Keiler.

On a personal note, Ferentino said he made a private pledge to Michael Stanley Kerkowski and his wife, Geraldine Kerkowski, to prosecute Hugo with all his might.

"This team has been inspired by their support, particularly by Mrs. Kerkowski. We lost Mr. Kerkowski along the way but this group became a family. We've been through a lot. We've been through every court in the state. We've been to the Supreme Court, we've been to the Superior Court. We fought because we believed there were pieces of evidence we believed the jury needed to hear. Sam Goosay for example, we fought at every level we needed to fight because we believed that evidence was important and we committed to these families that the truth will come out and the people will hear that the crimes of Paul Weakley and Hugo Selenski committed. We wanted to present this case the way we needed to present it. And we wanted to give the jury as much information as possible to make the best decision they could make and they did," Ferentino said.

On the jury's decision to impose a life sentence for Hugo and not death, Sanguedolce said the burden to get the death penalty is a "tremendous hurdle." It was the first time Sanguedolce had argued before a jury for death.

In the end, Sanguedolce said Hugo was "off the streets no matter what."

Ferentino answered a question about what Hugo's life would be like in prison.

"Mr. Selenski is a certain classification due to his escape charge so wherever he remains, wherever he is eventually housed, he remains in protective, a restrictive housing unit. His days will typically involve 23 and all likelihood 23 ½ hours a day in a cell. Anytime he is moved, he is moved with an extra guard due to the nature of his charges and due to the fact he is an escape risk. Basically, that is a sense of his current housing for the foreseeable future; it's worse than death row," Fernetino said.

Question: "Mr. Selenski maintains his innocence and he wanted to testify? Anything that the district attorney or detectives would want to say on that?"

"I have something to say on that. We understand Mr. Selenski is maintaining his innocence, we think that is preposterous based on the evidence that was put forth. Let's not forget there was evidence that we were not able to put forth and one of those things was his admission that we would find five bodies in his yard. His statement yesterday was he would want to know how they got there. He knew when we came to the scene exactly how many bodies would be found at a time when we didn't know yet. He has had a number of chances to take the stand. Obviously, he could have taken the stand in the first trial. He could have taken the stand in his robbery trial in Sam Goosay, he could have taken the stand in the guilt phase in this trial and again in the penalty phase. He declined each and every time. So as far as that is concerned, I don't think he wanted to take the stand as he wanted people to think he wanted to take the stand," Sanguedolce answered.

Sanguedolce believed Hugo opted not to testify in his own defense because there was an overwhelming amount of evidence against him and feared being cross-examined.

During the trial, one of the five people who allegedly received jailhouse letters from Hugo through his then lead defense attorney, Shelley

Centini, in 2012, testified. And that was Carey Bartoo. The witness intimidation allegations levied upon Hugo, Centini and private investigator James Sulima, was not brought up during the trial. Sanguedolce explained why.

"Let me begin by saying when we learned about the conduct that we felt was inappropriate, first of all, we weren't even sure we were going to act on it. We waited so long for this trial, and we were finally coming upon the eve of trial that we had some hesitation. In fact, we organized a meeting with seven or eight other district attorney offices. We held a meeting with them and basically threw stuff in the air and they fell out of their chairs when they heard about what was happening. They basically felt…we are probably too close to the case because we wanted to get to trial but they felt it was going to be a reversible thing had we not at least sent it to investigate. Based on what our witnesses told our investigators, we then referred it to the (Pennsylvania) attorney general's office. They made whatever decisions they made. We are not responsible or took part in, in fact we were completely screened to every part of that investigation.

"The decision not to call the witnesses in trial was a strategic one. As I said before, the case was going as well as we could hope it to go. We didn't feel a need to introduce another little trial. We didn't need to introduce another list of five to 10 witnesses, drag the trial out another few days, and there were other components to take another week or so. At some point, we wanted to get this case to the jury. We had I think approximately 60 witnesses that we planned on calling. When you organize your witness list, assuming not every witness is going to say what you need them to say, so you have backup people to do that. Our witnesses really went as planned. In the backup people, we started to cut off and that was a section of the case that we thought was some flaw that was going to be introduced that he was conscious of his guilt and he was trying to affect witnesses," Sanguedolce explained.

# FAMILIES SPEAK

They waited 13 years to speak directly to Hugo. And speak they did.

Geraldine Kerkowski and Fassett's sister, Lisa Sands, did not testify during Hugo's penalty phase. First Assistant District Attorney Sam Sanguedolce explained "emotion" had to be taken out of the penalty phase and to put two women on the witness stand and likely cry, it would have contrasted his argument to the jury of weighing aggravating factors and mitigating circumstances. It was a reason why victim impact statements written by Geraldine Kerkowski and Sands were not introduced during the penalty phase.

So, on March 27, 2015, Geraldine Kerkowski and Sands had their opportunity when Hugo appeared before Judge Pierantoni to be sentenced to life in prison with no chance at parole. Geraldine Kerkowski went first.

"...Hugo, no matter what I say to you or about you, the one you'll answer to knows everything that you have done and how you made my son and Tammy suffer without any remorse. Hugo, you are going straight to hell. I could stand here and scream and shout about what you did to my son, to my husband, to my grandsons, tearing my whole family apart and depriving me of 13 years of my life; but, with your narcissistic, sociopathic personality, you are not capable of feeling sorry, hurt, sympathetic or any empathy to what you did to our families.

"I know I can be satisfied knowing you will spend eternity suffering in hell because there is going to be an eye for an eye; that you will suffer remorse more than my son did. This will bring some satisfaction to me. But Hugo, you know, you will be right where you belong, in hell, with Satan; because you are the devil in every sense of the word. You will be where you should be, burning in the fires of hell."

"Hugo, you are a narcissistic sociopath, a murderer, a fraud and a liar. If you're not smart enough to understand those words, I'll tell you what they mean. You only have love for yourself, and you have no sympathy or feelings for anyone you hurt or destroy."

"Hugo, while I'm reading this, take that smirk off your face again. Just let the justice system put you out in the population at prison. Then you will know how much you're worth. The inmates will chew you up and spit you out."

"Hugo, while you're sitting there waiting for your sentencing, I'll give you something to think about. Remember, 13 years ago when my son thought you were his best friend. Just think about how brutally you tortured him, beat him, then strangled the life out of him. Just think about that. I know you have no remorse because killing is in your blood."

"Hugo, I want you to know that I wore this outfit to remind you where you will spend the rest of your life in prison," Geraldine Kerkowski said.

Geraldine Kerkowski wore a striped black and white shirt to illustrate what Hugo would wear as an inmate.

"On May 3rd of 2002, I found out my sister went missing. Then later on, on May 6th (2003), I found out she was murdered by Mr. Selenski and Mr. Weakley. You can't imagine what I have felt losing my best friend, not to mention my father losing a daughter and my sister and three brothers losing their best friend, too. I know you have no remorse for what you've done because I can tell by the look on your face right now," Sands began saying.

"What else I have to say is, I hope that some day you rot in hell because you will die before I will. I will make sure of that. I have been to every hearing that we have had over the last 13 years and all I've seen is a smirk, a smile, a bobbing head or whatever. You get to see your family. I have to go to a grave site to see my sister. Now, do you really think that is fair for our family, for what you have done? One other reason is, I want to know why you thought you had to murder her and Michael? Just for money and drugs and whatever you wanted. That is all I have to say," Sands said ending her statement.

Sands' daughter, Ashley Owens, said she was a senior in high school when her Aunt Tammy went missing.

"There's not a day that goes by that I don't think about my aunt. She was a wonderful person. She was a wonderful mother, daughter, sister, aunt and friend. She was taken from her two boys too soon. Her youngest son and I, all celebrated our birthdays together. She has seven nieces and three nephews that she doesn't know. My children and I talk about her all the time. Do you know how hard it is to explain to two little kids what happened to their aunt? We have her picture on the wall along with her heart and her butterflies. We use her angel on our Christmas tree. It's a continuous struggle to deal with this every day, to get up in the morning and not cry because she's no longer here. When we want to talk to her, we have to go to a head stone at the cemetery," Owens said.

As Geraldine Kerkowski, Lisa Sands and Ashley Owens read their statements, Hugo looked away.

First Assistant District Attorney Jarrett Ferentino began reading a victim impact statement written by Kerkowski's oldest son, Tyler Kerkowski, but was not able to finish as emotions got the better of him.

"My name is Tyler Kerkowski. I am the son of the late Michael Kerkowski. I would like to take a few minutes to tell you how I was affected by the loss of my father. How it was and how it felt growing up without a father. Without the loving, caring, companionship of my devoted father. I know my father…" Ferentino said before pausing saying, "Your honor, I'm going to ask Attorney Sanguedolce to read this." Ferentino, a father himself, became overwhelmed with Tyler Kerkowski's letter.

"I know my father and I would have been best friends. My love for the great outdoors would have been a common love that we would have shared. I was deprived from all the great memories that could have been created with him in the outdoors. I was never able to have father-son bonding time. He was never able to share his interests with me such as music or movies which I'm sure we would have shared a lot of things in common.

"He was also never able to see some of the biggest moments of my life, such as becoming Homecoming King or becoming a Dallas Mountaineer and will never be able to see events to come later in my life such as graduating school and so on. The loss of my father will forever be engraved into my life's story. I was never even able to talk to him. I never got to know all the great things that could have been because my father was taken away from me. He suffered things that no one in this world should ever suffer. My family and I have suffered a tragedy that no one should ever suffer."

"No one will ever know how empty it makes one feel. No one will ever be able to understand how I feel. I was denied of even knowing my father because he was robbed of his life. If I could have anything, all I want is justice," Tyler Kerkowski wrote in his victim impact statement.

A victim impact statement written by Connor Kerkowski was also read to Judge Pierantoni by Sanguedolce.

"My father, Michael Jason Kerkowski, was supposed to be at Little People to pick me and my brother up on the same day he was brutally and innocently murdered. He never showed up, which wasn't like him. Just one day he didn't. That one day was all it took. He was also supposed to be there for my third birthday a few days later. He wasn't. I noticed as I got older that something was wrong, and wondered why I never had what all the other kids had - a father. Pieces of my life were slowly torn away from the very beginning, starting off with growing up without a father. I cannot fathom the words I need to write or speak to describe how hard it is to grow up with a very broken life without the father that is supposed to watch me graduate from high school and college, and watch me accomplish great things in life. But what is unbelievably unbearable to accept is that he will never be there for any of it. Or any other significant event to come about in my future as a three-year-old infant who was never raised without a father," Connor Kerkowski wrote.

Connor Kerkowski continued to say it had been a long 13 years and his father did not deserve what happened to him.

"I deserved to be able to know what he looked like in person and to know how his voice sounded when he spoke. This deranged man, Hugo Selenski, took it all away without even thinking twice about how it would affect his family and the people that loved him dearly. I don't feel sorry for him (Hugo). I don't really think people can change. At the end of the day, you are who you are and it's probably who you have always been and if this man were given the opportunity to manipulate another father or mother or anyone in the world, he would do it again. He is the man who tore my family apart and made us live with a gaping wound never to be healed."

"Justice will be served, on Earth or in hell. Either way, I wish nothing but the worst for Hugo Selenski. I hope he will never live to see a day where happiness is granted. I hope he will carry the murders of my father and Tammy Fassett around with him forever. If there is a God, and if there is a place for people who have done such deceitful, horrendous things, I hope it becomes Hugo Selenski's home very soon. He is a waste of the air we breathe, and a waste of life that doesn't deserve to be lived. If this man were to be allowed the time of day to be sentenced to death, maybe justice will prevail after all. But either way, there is no winner. I will still never have a father for the rest of my existence, and my grandmother will never have her son back, and my brother will never get to experience hunting and outdoors with our father. Nothing will ever be okay. Why should the man who took two innocent lives be allowed to live when my father and Tammy Fassett will never live another day, and because of Hugo Selenski's planned actions of murder," Connor Kerkowski wrote.

Sanguedolce paused near the end of Conner Kerkowski's letter becoming overwhelmed with emotions as to the next paragraph. When Sanguedolce briefly stopped, Judge Pierantoni thanked him.

"There's more. One more line, Judge. Dad, if you're listening, know that I love you with all my heart. I'm sorry this had to happen," Sanguedolce read ending Conner Kerkowski's letter.

Prosecutors and Hugo's lawyers reviewed sentencing guidelines that are used when a defendant is sentenced. With an automatic two life sentences for being convicted of two counts of first degree murder, attorneys had to debate what the sentences would be related to the criminal conspiracy and robbery.

"With respect to the sentence, Your Honor, on behalf of the Commonwealth, I would state for the record that, in my career in the district attorney's office, this is among if not the most heinous crime that I have ever been a part of to prosecute," Sanguedolce said.

As expected, Hugo opted to stay silent.

"Mr. Selenski, the sentence of the court will be as follows," Judge Pierantoni said when he began imposing the sentence.

"On Court 1, murder of the first degree, victim Michael J. Kerkowski, I sentence you to life imprisonment without parole in state prison. At Count 2, murder of the first degree, victim Tammy L. Fassett, I sentence you to life imprisonment without parole in state prison, consecutive to the sentence imposed at Count 1," Pierantoni said, continuing to impose sentences on two counts of criminal conspiracy to commit criminal homicide and two counts of robbery.

In all, Hugo was sentenced to two consecutive life sentences without any chance of parole followed by 56 to 120 years in state prison.

"The wheels of justice often turn slowly, but the wheels of justice do not stop turning," Judge Pierantoni said.

Hugo's appearance before Judge Pierantoni was his second appearance before a judge that day. Hugo earlier on March 27, 2015, was before Senior Judge Chester B. Muroski to finish unfinished business.

Judge Muroski sentenced Hugo to 20 months and 15 days to 41 months and gave him credit for time served for his brazen escape from the Luzerne County Correctional Facility on Oct. 10, 2003.

# APPEALS

As with most criminal convictions, an appeal follows. Hugo was no different.

Exactly one week and three days after Hugo was sentenced, his lawyers filed a motion for post-conviction relief on April 6, 2015, challenging restitution he was mandated to pay.

Judge Pierantoni ordered Hugo to pay a total of $198,715.22 in court costs and restitution to the district attorney's office for the lengthy investigation when he was sentenced on March 27, 2015. Hugo believed the restitution was speculative and excessive.

At a hearing held April 29, it was agreed upon Hugo was to pay $140,000.

Hugo's real appeal challenging his conviction was filed with the Pennsylvania Superior Court on May 21, 2015, claiming he deserved a new trial as his right to counsel was violated when Judge Pierantoni, based on a request from prosecutors, disqualified Attorney Shelley Centini on Feb. 10, 2014. Hugo also claimed prosecutors failed to disclose impeachment evidence that they would advocate on behalf of Christina Strom at her federal sentencing hearing in an attempt to lessen her federal sentence and Judge Pierantoni failed to provide a cautionary instruction to the jury when the jury was told about Paul Weakley's federal guilty plea to

Racketeering Influenced and Corrupt Organizations that incorporated the murders of Michael Jason Kerkowski and Tammy Lynn Fassett, and the robbery and kidnapping of Samuel Goosay.

Other issues Hugo complained about in his appeal was the introduction of the firearm used in the Goosay robbery, the testimony of forensic pathologist Dr. Michael Baden regarding bruises on the bodies of Kerkowski and Fassett caused by blunt force trauma, and Judge Pierantoni's denial when Attorney Bernard Brown requested a mistrial when Strom testified about taking Hugo to the Dallas Township Police Department to "talk about a robbery." Hugo's last and seventh challenge in his appeal involved Judge Pierantoni erred in allowing retired Wyoming County Judge Bernard Vanston to testify during his trial.

Fifteen months after Hugo's lawyer, Edward Rymsza, filed the appeal, the Pennsylvania Superior Court on Aug. 11, 2016, denied each and every one of the seven issues Hugo challenged and included Judge Pierantoni's 77 page opinion as the reason why the state appellate court upheld Hugo's convictions and sentence.

The Pennsylvania Supreme Court refused to review Hugo's appeal in a one page order issued Feb. 22, 2017.

Hugo then filed a petition under the state's Post Conviction Relief Act (PCRA) claiming his trial attorneys, Bernard Brown and Edward Rymsza, were ineffective. A PCRA hearing is held before the trial judge and in his case, Judge Pierantoni, presided.

Judge Pierantoni held two PCRA hearings for Hugo, on Oct. 14, 2020, and March 12, 2021. In a 38 page order, Judge Pierantoni denied Hugo's PCRA petition on Aug. 26, 2021.

What follows after the presiding trial judge denies a PCRA petition is another appeal with the Pennsylvania Superior Court, which was filed on Sept. 23, 2021. Nearly two years later, Sept. 8, 2023, the Superior Court denied Hugo's appeal upholding Judge Pierantoni's denial of the PCRA petition.

As for Christina Strom, she faced a maximum sentence of 40 years in a federal prison and a $750,000 fine following her guilty plea to conspiracy to commit money laundering and obstruction of an official proceeding on Jan. 24, 2005. For her cooperation in testifying against Hugo and having no criminal history, Strom was hoping for a reduction of her sentence when she appeared before U.S. District Court Judge Thomas I. Vanaskie to be sentenced on June 5, 2015.

Strom's attorney, Joseph A. O'Brien asked for probation indicating Strom was a critical witness against Hugo during his homicide trial. To show Strom cooperated with prosecutors, First Assistant District Attorney Sam Sanguedolce and Assistant District Attorney Jarrett Ferentino, and Luzerne County Detective Lieutenant Gary Capitano testified on her behalf, telling Judge Vanaskie that Strom was a key witness in their prosecution of Hugo.

"I would have to say that Ms. Strom's testimony was extremely significant to our case because it tied exactly into our position on what motivated Mr. Selenski's crimes, particularly the murders. And we found Ms. Strom to be somebody that told a compelling...told a compelling tale of what had occurred here, and I think that the jury found her to be very credible," Ferentino testified on behalf of Strom.

During Strom's sentencing hearing, it was brought out that Strom actually feared Hugo and there were times of domestic violence. Hugo had smashed Strom's head against a mirror and another incident involved Hugo discharging a firearm next to her head.

Vanaskie noted Strom's cooperation and having to wait more than 10 years to be sentenced while caring for a child but could not nullify she provided false testimony before a federal grand jury and laundered money that Selenski obtained through crimes.

Strom's family and friends let out a loud gasp apparently in shock when Vanaskie sentenced her to one year plus one day in federal prison.

What was said during Strom's sentencing hearing was not picked up by reporters. Strom's attorney, O'Brien, asked Ferentino if he would classify Hugo as a dangerous person?

"Absolutely, probably the most dangerous person I ever encountered in my 37 years," Ferentino said of Hugo.

# ACKNOWLEDGEMENTS

Despite graduating college with criminal justice and political science degrees, I turned my career path to journalism, first working at a weekly newspaper, then as an assignment editor for a local television station, before being hired as a police reporter for a small newspaper in Wilkes-Barre, Pa, in 1999. Being ambitious and eager, I took many assignments and gradually learned the craft, becoming a faster writer and gained valuable sources within law enforcement and legal fields in Luzerne County.

I was in my fourth year of being a police reporter working second shift when the Pennsylvania State Police and the Luzerne County District Attorney's Office served a search warrant at the Mount Olivet Road property on June 5, 2003. For the next 12 years, I covered Hugo Selenski and got to know his life and the lives of the people he was convicted of killing, Michael Jason Kerkowski and Tammy Lynn Fassett, and their families. During my first interview with Fassett's sister, Lisa Sands, I remembered my eyes teared up when Lisa described Tammy as her best friend, Tammy's love for her family, her many attributes and how her favorite cartoon character was Piglet from the Winnie the Pooh series.

I sat at the kitchen table of Michael Stanley Kerkowski and his wife, Geraldine Kerkowski, several times interviewing them for stories and on a few occasions, they just wanted to talk with no purpose of a story. I took phone calls in the middle of the night from investigators whose purpose was to vent their frustrations as they believed the investigation was being impeded by higher ups. I was threatened to be held in contempt of court by two Luzerne County judges for refusing to name sources. I dealt with editors that had excellent critical thinking skills at the same time working with inept editors. I interviewed Hugo Selenski and, unbeknown to me at the time, would get me kicked out of covering his second trial as my name made it onto a witness list.

On Friday, Oct. 10, 2003, as I was just about to leave for the night, about 9:30 p.m., I heard on the police scanner, "we need flashlights up on the roof." It quickly dawned on me there was an escape at the Luzerne County Correctional Facility. As I told the assistant night editor there may be something happening at the county prison, she yelled because I bothered her. When I arrived at the county prison being the first reporter there, I quickly learned two inmates escaped and noticed the rope of tied-together bed sheets hanging from the top floor. I called back to the newsroom and the same editor yelled at me for bothering her again and she hung up. This actually happened.

State police troopers began to arrive along with Wilkes-Barre police officers, getting out of their cruisers and searching parked vehicles and the shore of the Susquehanna River. Not wanting to get pushed back outside the perimeter that had not been set up, I joined in searching parked vehicles and the river bank.

Robert Kadluboski, who owned City Wide Towing and had the towing contract at the time for Wilkes-Barre City, told me Hugo Selenski and Scott Bolton were the inmates who escaped. This was easily confirmed by a Wilkes-Barre police sergeant at the scene.

The weekend of Oct. 10 through Oct. 13, 2003, was one I will never forget.

There were hundreds of stories written about the case, and with the many twists and turns, the story was hard to follow. This is the reason why I wanted to write a book detailing the Hugo Marcus Selenski saga in one setting.

For this book, I relied on hundreds of recorded interviews, notes, recorded news conferences, thousands upon thousands of court filings, preliminary hearing and trial transcripts, plus my own experience, memories and observations of covering the story. Quotations in the book and the language by judges and lawyers are how they appear in the transcripts.

There are many people I need to thank for their assistance in covering the Hugo Selenski story from June 5, 2003, through the final chapter of this book. First, the late Luzerne County Detective Lieutenant Gary Capitano who steered me as a young reporter to "just write the facts." Sadly, Capitano died July 18, 2021, not long after he retired from the district attorney's office. David W. Lupus, who was the district attorney of Luzerne County from 2000 through 2008, Jaqueline Musto Carroll, who was first assistant district attorney and became district attorney in the 2007 election; former Assistant District Attorney Timothy Doherty; former Assistant District Attorney Joseph Giovannini; former Assistant District Attorney C. David Pedri; former Assistant District Attorney Michael Melnick; Assistant District Attorney James McMonagle; Attorney Demetrius (Tim) Fannick; Attorney John B. Pike; Attorney Stephen Menn; retired Pennsylvania State Police Lieutenant Richard Krawetz; retired State Police Trooper Gerard Sachney, retired Pennsylvania State Police Captain Frank Hacken, numerous state police troopers; the late Michael Stanley Kerkowski and his wife, the late Geraldine Kerkowski who passed away Oct. 7, 2019; clerks in the Luzerne County Clerk of Courts Office and Prothonotary Offices; clerks at the Wyoming County Courthouse; former Luzerne County Correctional Facility Warden Gene Fischi; former Luzerne County Commissioner Thomas Makowski; Attorney Shelley L. Centini; Attorney Basil Russin; Attorney Al Flora; the late Attorney Bill Ruzzo and the late Attorney Mark Singer; and most of all Michelle Giza, trial assistant/case manager for the Luzerne County District Attorney's Office, Luzerne County District Attorney Sam Sanguedolce and Assistant District Attorney Jarrett Ferentino. Many thanks to Times Leader publisher Kerry Miscavage, former newspaper editors Paul Krzywicki, Dan Burnett, Roger DuPuis and Joe Butkiewicz;

former newspaper reporters Fred Ney, Elizabeth Skrapits, Sheena Weiss, and James O'Malley. Peter Conway, co-author of *Cobra Killer*, for his advice about book publishing. Above all, heartfelt love for her support, Lisa Sands, who is one of the strongest women I have ever met and became a dear, close friend. Nobody should have endured the emotional pain and trauma Lisa Sands and Michael Stanley and Geraldine Kerkowski had to experience due to the many court delays.

Lastly, to my family, wife Lori, and children Zachary, Emily and Stephanie, the ZES crew. My wife spent many nights alone as she gave me time to conduct research, interviews and write and Emily encouraged me several times a year for many years to finish this book. Emily designed the book cover after reviewing hundreds of pictures. Without the support of Lisa Sands and my family, this book would not have been written.

Made in the USA
Middletown, DE
22 August 2024

59611282R00296